I0673020

I See No Angels

three novellas

second edition

Also by Michael-Patrick Harrington:

Deep Autumn

Saving Magdalene

www.michaelpatrickharrington.com

I See No Angels

Michael-Patrick Harrington

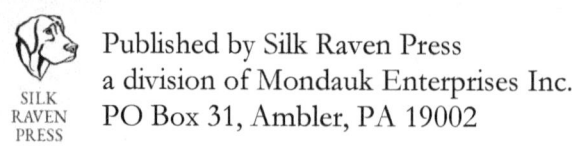

Published by Silk Raven Press
a division of Mondauk Enterprises Inc.
PO Box 31, Ambler, PA 19002

SILK
RAVEN
PRESS

(SRP-002)

I See No Angels © 2004, 2013 by Mondauk Enterprises Inc. &
Michael-Patrick Harrington
All rights reserved.
ISBN: 0615848664
ISBN-13: 978-0615848662

SECOND EDITION

Originally published in 2004 by Xlibris.
The text of this edition contains all corrections and revisions that
have been made since the original publication.

I See No Angels is a work of fiction. Names, characters, places, and
incidents are the product of the author's imagination or are used
fictitiously. Any resemblance to actual events, locales, or persons,
living or dead, is entirely coincidental.

Cover artwork by Margaux © 2004
All rights reserved.

Reissue design by Pepper Lillie
www.pepperlillie.com

Quotes from the following works appear in this novel. The author wishes to acknowledge the writers and publishers.

Donna Tartt's quote is from the *Book* magazine article, "The Adventure of the Vanishing Lady Writer" by Liz Seymour, November/December 2002 © Book Magazine

All the Names by José Saramago © José Saramago e Editorial Caminho SA; English translation © Margaret Jull Costa

The Wolf Man, directed by George Waggner, screenplay by Curt Siodomak © Universal Studios

The Power and the Glory by Graham Greene © Graham Green

"O, the Burning of the Leaves" composed by Jared Brey © Jared Brey

"24-Hour Store" composed by Brett Sparks & Rennie Sparks © Handsome Family Music (BMI)

"Rocket Man" composed by Elton John & Bernie Taupin © Universal Songs of PolyGram (BMI)

"Johnny, Are You Queer?" composed by Bobby Paine & Larson Paine © Warner-Tamerlane Publishing Co (BMI)

"The End" composed by John Lennon & Paul McCartney © Sony/ATV Tunes LLC/Beatles (PRS)

The Gospel of Thomas: The Hidden Sayings of Jesus by Marvin Meyer; English translation & critical edition of the Coptic text © Marvin W. Meyer; Interpretation by Harold Bloom © Harold Bloom

"992 Arguments" composed by Kenneth Gamble & Leon Huff © Warner-Tamerlane Publishing Corp. (BMI)

"Milk Cow Blues" composed by Kokomo Arnold © Universal MCA Publishing (ASCAP)

"That's Alright" composed by Arthur Crudup © Crudup Music & Unichappell Music Inc. (BMI)

"Blue Moon" composed by Lorenz Hart & Richard Rodgers © EMI Robbins Catalog Inc., EMI April Music Inc., & EMI Publishing (ASCAP)

"Trying To Get To You" composed by Rose Marie McCoy & Charles Singleton © Red Storming Heaven Music, Slow Dancing Music LLC, & You Look Good Music Publishing (BMI)

"When It Rains, It Really Pours" composed by William Emerson © Riverline Music (BMI)

"Baby, Let's Play House" composed by Arthur Gunter © Embassy Music Corporation & LPGV Music (BMI)

John Wesley by John Wesley © Oxford University Press

"Mercedes Benz" composed by Janis Joplin, Michael McClure, & Robert Neuwirth © Strong Arm Music (ASCAP), Ruminating Music (ASCAP), Wixen Music Pub. Inc. (ASCAP), & Sethward Songs (BMI)

"Verb: That's What's Happening" composed by Bob Dorough © American Broadcasting Music Inc. (ASCAP)

"Do Not Go Gentle Into That Good Night" by Dylan Thomas © Dylan Thomas, the Trustees for the Copyrights of Dylan Thomas, & New Directions Publishing Corp.

Dracula, directed by Tod Browning, screenplay by Garrett Fort © Universal Studios

The Last Temptation of the Christ by Nikos Kazantzakis © Simon & Schuster

"Just Out of Reach (Of My Two Empty Arms)" composed by Virgil F. Stewart © Sony/ATV Acuff Rose Music (BMI)

"Someone to Pull the Trigger" composed by Matthew Sweet ©
Charm Trap Music & EMI Blackwood Music Inc. (BMI)

"Two Vultures" composed by Margaux © Margaux & Lola and the
Shivers

"Jean" composed by Rod McKuen © Twentieth Century Fox Music,
WB Music Corp., & Warner Chappell Music Inc. (ASCAP)

"Spinning Wheel" composed by David Clayton-Thomas © EMI
Blackwood Music Inc. (BMI)

"All By Myself" composed by Eric Carmen © Eric Carmen Music &
Universal Songs of PolyGram (BMI)

"The Morning After" composed by Joel Hirschhorn & Al Kasha ©
Warner-Tamerlane Pub. (BMI), Twentieth Century Fox
Music (ASCAP), WB Music Corp. (ASCAP), & Warner
Chappell Music Inc. (ASCAP)

The Great Gatsby by F. Scott Fitzgerald © Charles Scribner's Sons

"Slip Slidin' Away" composed by Paul Simon © Paul Simon Music
(BMI)

"Born to Run" composed by Bruce Springsteen © Bruce Springsteen
(ASCAP)

"Invitation to the Blues" composed by Tom Waits © Fifth Floor
Music Inc. (ASCAP)

"Sister Golden Hair" composed by Gerald Beckley © WB Music
Corp. (ASCAP)

"Strange Fruit" composed by Allan Lewis © Music Sales Corp.
(ASCAP) & Allan Lewis (BMI)

"Tutti Frutti" composed by Dorothy LaBostrie, Joe Lubin, &
Richard Penniman © Sony/ATV Songs LLC/ATV Venice
(BMI)

"Bad" composed by Adam Clayton, David Evans, Paul Hewson, & Larry Mullen Jr. © Universal PolyGram International Publishing Inc. & Universal Music Publishing Group (ASCAP)

Wild at Heart by Barry Gifford © Barry Gifford

"Love Me" composed by Jerry Leiber & Mike Stoller © Sony/ATV Songs LLC

"Knock Three Times" composed by Russell Brown & Irwin Levine © EMI Sosaha Music Inc., Forty West Music Corp., & Irwin Levine Music (BMI)

"You're No Good" composed by Clint Ballard Jr. © Beardog Publishing Co. (ASCAP)

"Mr. Sandman" composed by Pat Ballard © Edwin H. Morris & Co. Inc. & MPL Communications Inc. (ASCAP)

"Pink Elephants" composed by Oliver G. Wallace & Ned Washington © Bourne Co. & Ms. Beebe Bourne (ASCAP)

"Yummy Yummy Yummy" composed by Joe Levine & Arthur Resnick © Alley Music Corp. & Trio Music Company (BMI)

"I Will Survive" composed by Dino Fekaris & Frederick J. Perren © Perren-Vibes Music Inc. & Universal PolyGram International Publishing Inc. (ASCAP)

"Chick-A-Boom" composed by Richard Delvy & Janis Lee Gwin © Magic Touch Music, RHI Television Music Co., WB Music Corp., & Warner Chappell Music Inc. (ASCAP)

"My Melody of Love" composed by George Buschor, Henry Mayer, & Bobby Vinton © Galahad Music Inc. (BMI), Songs of Universal Inc. (BMI), RMI Edition (GEMA), & Rolf Budde Musikverlag (GEMA)

"Hopelessly Devoted to You" composed by John Farrar © Ensign Music Corporation, John Farrar Music, & Unichappell Music Inc. (BMI)

"Take Me Home, Country Roads" composed by William T. Danoff, John Denver, & Taffy Nivert © Cherry Lane Music Publishing, DreamWorks Songs, & WB Music Corp. (ASCAP)

"O-o-h Child" composed by Stan Vincent © Frantino Music & Kama Sutra Music Inc. (BMI)

"Saturday Night" composed by Philip Coulter & William Martin © Colgems EMI Music Inc. (ASCAP)

"I Don't Know How to Love Him" composed by Andrew Lloyd-Webber & Tim Rice © Universal on Backstreet Music & Universal MCA Music Publishing (ASCAP)

"Mandy" composed by Scott David English & Richard Kerr © Morris Music Inc. & Screen Gems-EMI Music Inc. (BMI)

"The Bare Necessities" composed by Terry Gilkyson © Wonderland Music Company Inc. (BMI)

"Alone Again (Naturally)" composed by Raymond O'Sullivan © OSM Inc. (BMI)

"Top of the World" composed by John Bettis & Richard Carpenter © Almo Music Corp. & Hammer and Nails Music (ASCAP)

"I Wish I Were an Oscar Mayer Weiner" composed by Richard D. Trentlage © JWT Music Inc. (ASCAP)

"Dream Weaver" composed by Gary Wright © Universal MCA Music Publishing (ASCAP)

"Yesterday Once More" composed by John Bettis & Richard Carpenter © Almo Music Corp. & Hammer and Nails Music (ASCAP)

"When I Need You" composed by Albert Louis Hammond & Carole Sager © Albert Hammond Enterprises Inc. & Music of Windswept (ASCAP)

"The Trolley Song" composed by Ralph Blane & Hugh Martin ©
EMI Feist Catalog Inc., EMI April Music Inc., & EMI Music
Publishing (ASCAP)

"You Don't Know What Love Is" composed by Gene DePaul &
Don Raye © Universal MCA Music Publishing (ASCAP)

"Renegade" composed by Tommy Shaw © Almo Music Corp. &
Stygian Songs (ASCAP)

"Le Freak" composed by Bernard Edwards & Nile Rodgers ©
Bernard's Other Music & Sony/ATV Songs LLC (BMI)

"Band of Gold" composed by Donald Dunbar & Edythe Wayen ©
Gold Forever Music Inc. (BMI)

"I Can See Clearly Now" composed by Johnny Nash © Dovan
Music Inc. (ASCAP)

"Angel of the Morning" composed by Chip Taylor © EMI
Blackwood Music Inc. (BMI)

"Streets of Philadelphia" composed by Bruce Springsteen © Bruce
Springsteen (ASCAP)

Mrs. Dalloway by Virginia Woolf © Harcourt, Brace, & World Inc. &
Leonard Woolf

"Suspicious Minds" composed by Mark James © Sony/ATV Songs
LLC (BMI)

"Do-Re-Mi" composed Richard Rodgers & Oscar Hammerstein 2nd
© Williamson Music Co. (ASCAP)

Red Wine Moan by Jeri Cain Rossi © Jeri Cain Rossi

"Don't Be Cruel" composed by Otis Blackwell & Elvis Presley ©
Cherry River Music Co., Chrysalis Songs, & EMI Unart
Catalog (BMI)

"Gloria/In Excelsis Deo": "Gloria" (Van Morrison version) composed by Van Morrison © Unichappell Music Inc. (BMI); "In Excelsis Deo" composed by Patti Smith © Linda Music Corp. (ASCAP)

"Love Song For Someone" composed by Michael-Patrick Harrington © Lola and the Shivers, Mondauk Enterprises Inc., & Michael-Patrick Harrington

"I'm Left, You're Right, She's Gone" composed Stanley Kesler & William Eugene Taylor © Hi-Lo Music Inc. (BMI)

"Who Do You Love?" composed by Ellas McDaniel © Arc Music Corp. (BMI)

Illusions: The Adventures of a Reluctant Messiah by Richard Bach © Creature Enterprises Inc.

Every effort has been made to ensure proper credit was given. If there have been any inadvertent oversights, the author would be pleased to correct the situation at the first opportunity.

DEDICATIONS:

I was diagnosed with multiple sclerosis in May of 2002.

I See No Angels is dedicated to:

Dr. Rebecca S. Walker, who on May 13 diagnosed me
and helped set me on the right medical path. Without her diligence
and dedication, the road would be darker still.

This book is also dedicated to
all the doctors, nurses, and therapists who have
helped me along the way, especially
Dr. Gregory W. Cooper,
Dr. Maurice D. Gross,
Dr. Harold P. Koller,
and Vicky Lee McKelvey, physical therapist,
who became my friend.

IN MEMORIUM:

My grandmother, Ro-Ro Woods, died while I was finishing this
book. Aside from my mom, Ro-Ro was my First Friend,
and nothing is quite the same since she left.

In memory of my brothers:
Matt Harrington 1968-1987
Dennis Keith Miller 1966-1996

GRATITUDES:

Much gratefulness and appreciation to:

Beth Meier, my tireless copyeditor

and

Margaux, the cover artist, who helped me with everything else.

Thank you:
Mom and Vince and my sister Kathie
Mighty Mike & Karin Berson
Lorraine Heil
and
my boy, Helium Raven Teardrop

John Irving has been a huge influence on my writing. As a tribute, I mixed in tidbits from some of his novels in "The Gift Room."

I borrowed the phrase "red wine moan" for "The Gift Room" from the title of Jeri Cain Rossi's short story collection. If you can find it, return the favor and read it.

No religions were harmed
in the writing of this book.

TABLE OF CONTENTS

"The voice comes and you just listen and just do what it said."
Donna Tartt

"What words are as simple as 'fall'?"
Margaux

"Everything is different now;
October's over and you know
That's when everything goes down…"
Jared Brey, "O, the Burning of the Leaves"

"When we announce the beginning of something,
we always speak of the first day, when one should really speak of the
first night, the night is a condition of the day,
night would be eternal if there were no night."
José Saramago, *All the Names*

I See No Angels

Purgatory:

The Priest's Story
or
The Singing Bones

This is Purgatory.

"No, no one hears the singing bones,
And no one sees the crying ghosts,
And everyone thinks, 'I'm all alone, all alone.' "
The Handsome Family, "24-Hour Store"

"Now this man purchased a field with the wages of iniquity; and
falling headlong, he burst open in the middle and all his entrails
gushed out. And it became known to all those dwelling in Jerusalem;
so that field is called in their own language, Akel Dama,
that is, Field of Blood."
The Acts of the Apostles 1:18-19

"Death was not the end of pain—
to believe in peace was a kind of heresy."
Graham Greene, *The Power and the Glory*

Sir? He's here.

I KNOW.

Should I—should I let him in? Sir?

DON'T BE ABSURD.
ROLL THE TAPE, ARCHANGEL.

February 25, 6:47 a.m.

"Even a man who is pure in heart
and says his prayers by night,
may become a wolf when the wolf bane blooms
and the autumn moon is bright."
The Wolf Man

Exegesis:

I wake, those words dissolving on my tongue like the Holy Wafer.

I was remembering being little, staying up late, waiting for some movie to come on television after Johnny Carson, monster movie books spread out on the kitchen table. I had phoned the library right before they closed. Someone told me that if you called the library, they would answer any question you had; I believed it then. I was disturbed that I could not suss out the identity of the actor playing the werewolf in the 1935 film The Werewolf of London. *The librarian placed me on hold for a long time. When he returned, he read the cast list to me. The filmmakers were clever: the credits, as noted in a library horror movie compendium, did not list anyone as specifically portraying the werewolf. I told the librarian that in some of the old horror movies, the lucky actor who inhabited the makeup of the monster was usually listed dead last, after the hapless villagers and the humpbacked assistant. I had never seen* The Werewolf of London, *you see, and didn't know the name of the central character that transformed into the werewolf. I didn't know the actor's name was Henry Hull, nor do I remember where I eventually found the answer. I just remember the determination of the little kid on the hunt for a werewolf and the absolute faith that the library held all the answers to every question I ever had—even those about werewolves—except for one: can something that is spoiled be redeemed? The answer then, as now: faith and prayer. Faith and prayer.*

Not a day goes by that I don't miss that kid…

The Book of Winter 1

"I wish I was there now," the priest muttered to himself. The afternoon seemed to fulfill its promise of scorching the earth beneath his shiny black Florsheims. Block collection. There were only two words the priest despised more than "last call": "block collection"—knocking on the doors of the faithful (ha!) and making small talk with the husband while the wife scattered the pile of bills and junk mail collecting in hills on the underused dining room table to find the Church envelope, writing a check so quickly that the cursive blended into something resembling the graffiti growing on the west side of the convent. The grizzled dad would smell like cans of Pabst Blue Ribbon, his stomach sloping so his nipples met his navel ("How-do-you-fuckin'-do?")—the wife reappearing (a *poof* of hairpins and smeared eye shadow), harried and underfucked—children upstairs smoking pot or jerking off or killing themselves to Black Sabbath records. The priest hated block collections.

He looked down at his list and checked his street map. He had been ordained four years ago, and Our Lady of Chastity was his first and only parish. The boundaries of the parish, as determined by the archdiocese, stretched from the edge of the woods on the west side of Pennypack Park to the bus terminal that marked the official end of the Avenue. All the souls between these points were his to save and nurture in the word of the Lord. The priest spat on the sidewalk and peeked both ways to make sure no one witnessed his trajectory. His mouth felt like a cotton ball soaked in his mother's brine soup; when he burped, he could taste last night's final vodka and tonic.

Growing up, the future priest—Donald—embraced Baby Jesus in his heart while the Crowd was copping feels, cutting school, and sneaking out their bedroom windows. What saved him from getting beaten up was his record collection and his sense of humor—he was cool in a clutch, cool in an otherwise uncool Crowd that mixed the wayward jock with the class clown, ties based more on neighborhood affiliations than schoolyard tiers. If Big Mike and Ritchie were the twin totems that kept the engine chuffing (sensitive jock and the aforementioned class clown, respectively), then Donald and Ronnie—Ronnie, whose baby round face nevertheless appeared underfed, forever proclaimed points of interest gleaned from *People* and *Rolling Stone*, spittle escaping his perpetually wet lips—shared the caboose.

But the other kids in Rhawnhurst Grade School, and later in high school, respected Donald's religious space, and he was rarely, if ever, teased—Donald was quite demure in his beliefs, but he still wore a scapular around his neck on the outside of his shirt and sang along at top volume to the hymns in chapel. No, Donald only felt the need to hide his scapular or stuff his Bible in his book bag if the Crowd was around. He knew he needed the Crowd more than they needed him. Compared to the perpetually satisfied communion grins plastered across his parents' faces, the Crowd was unruly, more a rabble than a flock. The Crowd would circle him, ask for forgiveness, draw detailed genitalia on the holy cards he used for bookmarks. Donald could not imagine a life without their constant presence and opinions and bickering—the Crowd was *real* in a way his parents could only read about in newspapers—but his religious devotion made his friends uneasy—with the exception of what Donald called Saturday Night Confession.

The Crowd gathered every Saturday evening (Friday night was date night) in the bowl of Lincoln High School or in Big Mike's basement. (Hell, Big Mike's mom even bought their beer if they gave her the money and promised to sleep over, a license to drink until they passed out.) Sometimes at Big Mike's, the boys spun records and danced and played air guitar; other times, they told tall tales (usually involving previously reticent Catholic girls) or watched porn (which made some of the boys nervous, left them twitching in their seats; one time, they swore Ronnie did it right in his pants, but he later told Donald that he got so scared looking at the female star's unkempt pubic hair that he had peed himself). Most nights would end, however, with one or more of the boys pulling Donald outside through the cellar storm doors so they could smoke or else into the tiny basement bathroom, where the liquor eased their tongues and assisted in the unburdening of their souls.

"I think Humper's—"

"Deb?"

"Yeah, I think I knocked her up."

"Jesus, Mike. I thought you said she'd only give you a hand job."

"Yeah, well. Things might have happened. Things might have happened."

"Jesus, Mike. Things. Jesus."

Or:

"You know the Elton John song, Donnie? The one that goes: *'I'm not the man they think I am at all, no, no, no, I'm a Rocket Man?'* "

"Yeah, I could never figure out the next line either."

"No, I mean, do you know what he means when he sings *'I'm not the man they think I am at all?'* "

"I thought you were just into the Who."

"Ronnie, what the fuck are you chewing Donnie's ear off about?"

"Ritchie, man, Ronnie's trying to figure out an Elton John song."

And so on.

In grade school and high school, the Crowd was always there, omnipotent it seemed: Big Mike Sullivan, Ritchie Valetta, lover man Craig D'Angelis, Ronnie Kerr, Billy J. (so named because no one could spell his Ukrainian last name), Nicky Ruggerio—and former tomboy turned gun moll Deb Humper. They all lived no more than four blocks from one another and very little escaped the notice of the Crowd.

"Craig banged Lori in his dad's caddy last night."

"How do you know? Did he tell you?"

"No, not yet anyway. We were sitting on Whore Lenore's lawn. Saw the whole thing. Think he went three times, Donnie."

Or:

"Donnie, you think Ronnie's, you know, queer?"

"I know that song! They play it at the Lincoln dances sometimes. *'Johnny, are you queer, boy?'* "

"No, no, I mean—tell him, Ritchie."

"You think Ronnie's gay, Don? Don't tell Big Mike we asked, alright?"

And so on.

When Donald announced his intention to enter the seminary once he graduated high school, his friends threw a wanton party, celebrating the future priest's future descent into the bottle. "Happens to 'em all," Nicky said, "They can't fuck, so they drink. Makes sense to me."

Toward the end of the festivities, Ritchie, his face drawn into the seriousness afforded only the most inebriated, slid up behind Donald. "Is it true, Donnie? Is it? You're not allowed to pull the pud even? Just to clear the plumbing?" The priest-to-be had no answer, but he spent the better part of the weeks leading up to his self-interment choking, flogging, servicing the old euphemism until his foreskin was covered in little pinpricks of crimson. And then he would do it on more time, just to make sure.

Despite the Crowd's concerns about Ronnie, their questions gathering like a flock of birds after a storm, hovering on every telephone wire, they never questioned the priest-to-be on his own sexual preferences—until the Judas Moment. But even now, the priest didn't consider himself gay; he dreamed of women at times—but what did it matter: all God's children come unto me, right? When he awoke with an erection, whether the cause was male or female, the priest would scurry into the shower, unburden himself, then scrub his body until little droplets of blood tinted the water escaping down the drain. He wrote the gay overtones off to his feminine face—a collection of sharp angles hidden beneath a slight layer of booze flesh—he saw himself as a well satisfied angel on one of the church's stained glass windows. Only the faint black stubble on his cheek and chin gave his gender away—that, and his Adam's apple, appropriately named, the priest thought. It was just that his face sometimes intrigued homosexual men—women seemed to care less—and the priest would then again face the werewolf. Only now, he knew the werewolf's name.

The priest peered down his list: cross the street and down at the end of the block—Saul and Bridge Streets—he was to start there. At Mrs. Winter's house. Suddenly his throat was sucked dry, his tongue clicked and stuck to the roof of his mouth. Tomorrow. Too many ghosts on the wires today. Tomorrow he would start with Mrs. Winter and proceed from there.

February 26, 6:17 a.m.

"Nobody ever said the fallen angels were the ugly ones."
Graham Greene, *The Power and the Glory*

Exegesis:

In seminary, we called these Faith Journals; sometimes it was the only place to actually see *what you believed, they told us. But why would we need to see if we had faith?*

As a child, I had an imaginary friend, and his name was Johnny Galoshes. He was my one true friend outside of the Crowd as I grew up with Robert ("Just call me Rob!" and then the palm—WHAM—against your back) and Harriet "Happy Homemaker" Hoskins in a super-Catholic, Jesus as superhero, household. I could describe the zippers on Johnny's leather jacket (just like the Fonz!), I could detail his black leather cowboy boots, the insouciant way his hair fell into his eyes—but I still cannot tell you what he looked *like. I don't think he ever had a face. When I was younger, he was my friend when my love of Christ kept me away from the Crowd as they submerged themselves in what they described as nooky orgies in Big Mike's basement (not that I believed them). Johnny Galoshes was a walking contradiction: no galoshes, just his black leather cowboy boots and tight black jeans. Even as a pre-teen, Johnny and I would huddle beneath my blankets and talk of Christ and His sacrifice and what it meant for us sinners stranded on this planet of temptation, this globe of desire. Johnny and I played Risk, Monopoly, Othello. Then, as we fell asleep in the dim light of my Baby Jesus night-light, we would talk of girls we liked (girls I liked) and how we imagined they'd taste to us (to me) when finally we'd be allowed to kiss them on the last day of school.*

I was the last in the Crowd to kiss a girl—even Ronnie was forced to locks lips with Amanda Janney during a vigorous seventh grade bout of Seven Minutes in Heaven that ended with all but Big Mike and Craig slinking off under the cover of Quadrophenia *severely cranked—and for this transgression, I was tortured mercilessly. And it killed me. I couldn't get past my friends, and I couldn't comprehend that there were no connections there, just needs. I had to accept that I had fallen into the Crowd; I had not been chosen.*

I spent the better part of fourth grade being pummeled by the Crowd in a made-up game—Kamikaze Ball—that consisted of equal parts basketball, street hockey without the sticks, and the brain-numbing wallop of full contact dodge ball. Ronnie was spared somewhat in this onslaught due only to Big Mike's careless protection—that is to say, Big Mike didn't want to be seen as protecting his little buddy, but Ronnie was often sent on Slurpee runs or Nab and Grabs for Playboy *or* Hustler *at Lily's Newsstand. Yet, when the time came for the sacrament of Confirmation, the boys all huddled on my back stoop, trying to cop last minute knowledge in the fear that the bishop would point and ask one of them a question concerning, well, anything. My Crowd was diligently ignorant when it came to the whys and wheres of God, and when we left grade school for high school, their main concerns focused on which of the commandments they could bend or break without causing much trouble with either their parents or local law enforcement or both.*

So, in the fourth grade, enter Johnny Galoshes: he didn't care much for Kamikaze Ball or pretty girls who wore their mother's eye shadow or back stoop crib sessions. He just cared about me. That was my world in grade school: the Crowd on one side, noisy, enticing, but hopelessly scary, and Johnny Galoshes and my parents on the other: maybe not humble, but defiantly striving for piety.

Until the peach fuzz.

In the sixth grade, a caterpillar of silk appeared wriggling to life upon my upper lip. One day I had my mother's lips—the next, a trembling approximation of my father's moustache. If it wasn't enough to be deeply in love with Jesus in the sixth grade, I now found myself swiveling my head to and fro, furtively canvassing for others suffering the same malady. It didn't take long for the teasing to start, but I ignored it as best I could, for the struggling fuzz was indicative of some stirring in a much lower region, a region that itself would become coarse and wiry—as if what infected my upper lip was somehow contagious.

My father brought it up in his own subtle way, announcing at Easter dinner (attended by a collection of aunts and uncles and the wet medicinal kisses that inevitably accompanied them) that he had bought me a razor.

"He's in sixth grade," my mother said.

"A little peach fuzz never hurt no one," Uncle Bill said, winking to me as if he knew—just fucking knew—about the thin meadow of hair sprouting below sea level.

I excused myself and hummed a hymn in harmony with Johnny Galoshes to drown out the hushed comments and choked low-level chuckles streaming from the Easter table.

Then in seventh grade came Thursday Nights Out. My parents, separately, would ready themselves and then, separately, leave the house on announced destinations—bingo for mother, a card game with the boys for father, say— leaving me in the hands of Aunt Grady and Uncle Bill or, at times, the chubby high school girl Maria from down the street—that is until I started eighth grade and suddenly Maria's chubbiness transmogrified into something my mother referred to as "fleshiness." When my father, quick to the defense of the weak as all good Christians are, offered to "drive your old bones home, Maria; you must be tired after watching this werewolf all night," my mother fired the babysitter, and I spent another year of Thursday Nights Out eating Hungry Man frozen dinners with Aunt Grady and Uncle Bill, trying in vain to hear the television over Grady's slurping—she had very few teeth—as she inhaled the requisite Salisbury steak.

Thursday Nights Out, according to my mother, on the phone to someone, was her "one night to breathe, you know, really breathe."

Thursday Nights Out, according to my father, as he sipped a Budweiser with Mr. O'Brien, both of them resting their elbows on the fence that separated their backyards, was the only thing he looked forward to besides Sunday Mass.

Then something perceptibly changed, shifted. My father bought himself some new clothes—and not for church. He started wearing aftershave on Thursday Nights Out. He started whistling while he ran the water to catch a shave before going out.

I asked myself: why did my father need to shave again? He shaved every morning; he didn't need a smooth clean face for his poker buddies.

"Bastard."

That was my mother's take, slamming the fridge shut so hard, the little yellow smiley "God Loves You" magnets clattered to the floor.

And from that Thursday Night Out onward a pattern was etched: my mother stayed put in the kitchen, although I could never see anything simmering, no longer even going through the motions of actually preparing herself for an evening out; my father busied himself with what my mother called a whore's bath. Even Johnny Galoshes was nervous. I stopped flinching at the Crowd's finger flicks during recess. I stopped caring that Kamikaze Ball increasingly caused external bleeding—mostly on my part. I stopped pretending to be morally mortified when the Crowd copied their homework from mine.

Then I drew blood and everything went to hell.

Johnny Galoshes told me what to do; he told me to reach out and save my father.

My mother was facing the stove; I could see or smell nothing cooking. My father was in the bathroom whistling as the sink filled for his Thursday Night Out shave. I stood in my room, running my fingers over my peach fuzz, brushing the bristling sideburns that had sprouted early in eighth grade.

Werewolf, werewolf, werewolf, *the Crowd called me.*

Savior, Savior, Savior, *Johnny Galoshes swore to me.*

I didn't knock on the bathroom door; I just pushed it open with both hands and there was my father, stark naked, steam like a halo around his tapering hair, his thick penis dangling, semi-aroused, between his legs, disposable razor to his face, a song on his lips. The door hit the wall and the whistle fell flat, the razor catching his cheek, fat droplets of crimson staining the water in the sink, coloring the mountains of shaving cream that skimmed the surface.

"Teach me to shave," I demanded, and my mother was behind me, pulling me out of the steam, slamming the door on my father and his penis and the sink's red sea.

And that was it: I drew blood and everything went to hell and my father moved to New Jersey.

The night my father left, I stayed in bed with Johnny Galoshes. I craned my neck to stare out the window at the stars, but I couldn't see them. I thought my father was falling apart, piece by bloody piece. I thought nothing was stuck together, least of all me: I didn't belong anywhere. I was dislocated. All I could hear was the rattling of my bones as I shivered in bed, their internal clanging just enough to cover the skinny wave of my mother's sorrow, her sounds creeping down the hallway, past the Mother, Mary of God, night-light in the hallway.

And I prayed for something beyond faith. Faith I already had. I prayed for proof.

I stared at the ceiling and past it, into the stars that I knew encircled my house—thousands of bright little bones strewn in the wake of the darkness—stars that some nights I couldn't even see from my backyard for the pollution, that some nights seemed farther away than I could ever imagine. That was eternity to me: a forever jump to the stars—I could reach and reach and never bring them all together again. Their disparateness dappled my eyes.

I closed my lids and stared into my own stars. I wanted God to reveal Himself and bring it all together—my parents, the Crowd—I wanted to feel some physical manifestation of His glory; I wanted to feel His love in return; I wanted a love convincing enough to turn true faith into conviction, my childhood beliefs into action. My mother's agony traversed the hallways of a house suddenly too large for only two souls, and I knew her hugs would never be the same—either too needy or withheld altogether—and beneath her cries I sought to hear the angels singing. I told God: I know they are there though I cannot see them, such is my faith; now I want to bring the bones and the stars and the angels together. I wanted Him inside of me. This demand I made of God: I want to feel love.

And there it was: the final day of classes, eighth grade, and Winifred Waxman was on the corner with Betty and Veronica (really Megan and Kelly, but they dressed the Archie parts in my mind). I had lied to my mother that morning; I didn't have lunch with Craig, Ritchie, and Nicky. Instead I rode my silver bike (just lines of jet-chrome at top speed, I'd always imagined) across the Boulevard and bought the only pair of earrings I could afford in Gimbels. I believed I was in love with Winifred Waxman, see. The earrings had little purple stones that dangled from the posts; Winifred had a purple coat that made her look like a princess to me, real royalty. I jerked off ceaselessly to her image. I imagined her peeing behind my parents' garage while I sat appreciatively nearby.

Johnny Galoshes had stopped talking to me the night before. It was one thing to talk about girls, to dream about Winifred Waxman, but another to force a step in the real world. Oh, we had prayed for the physical, Johnny Galoshes and me—this was when real love was entangled in all things physical in our eggshell psyches: the gentle turn of an ankle encased in navy blue socks and saddle shoes, the swelling of a thigh beneath a Catholic girls' school uniform. But they forced us in school to pray incessantly for all the Pagan Babies and there seemed no end to that mess. Johnny and I didn't know how to pray for real love just like we didn't know how to pray for real friends—friends that looked at differences as signs of uniqueness. Leather-jacket-cool wasn't just a concept with me and Johnny. It was a way of life. Johnny thought I would get hurt in the real world. And guess what? Johnny was dead-on on the money. But it was oh-so easy to discard advice from an imaginary friend, especially when you're about to enter high school.

After the last bell rang, I ran past my friends, jumped on my silver flying machine (repeating the Lord's Prayer a record forty times), and sped down Loretta Avenue, hoping to have enough time to compose myself and catch my breath before Winifred and Betty and Veronica reached the intersection of Bradley Street and Loretta. When they appeared, fifteen agonizing minutes later, I presented Winifred, flanked by the Archies, with the earrings.

Dappled: the sun in my eyes and I hear Him whisper my name.

Then, like a movie—JUST LIKE A GODDAMN MOVIE—out of nowhere came the Goons—you know who I mean; every neighborhood has them; they're the older boys banging away at the love of your life while you're at home with a fistful of dick. Anyway, they picked me up (the Silver Flyer crashed to the ground, scraping the paint—I never rode it again, as if the bicycle had somehow betrayed me) and held me in the air, my legs spread. Winifred took one look at my nut sack encased in a pair of navy blue trousers and promptly kicked the loudest field goal in all of Rhawnhurst. I screamed so tremendously (and, if truth be told, a little dramatically, for Winifred's precision was distracted by the cheering of the Archies), the Goons dropped me on the pavement, next to my bike, and hopped into a car with Winifred and the Archies. I walked to Craig's house, where, without any explanation, his mother allowed me to use the bathroom to freshen up and clean the train tracks the tears had laid; I didn't want my mother to see me freaked out and distraught and, yes, horny. Later, I walked the Silver

Flyer home, limping, praying:
>Lord God of all that is holy, hear my prayers!
Lord God of all that is holy, hear my prayers!
Lord God of all that is holy, hear my prayers!
Lord God of all that is holy, hear my prayers!
WHY WON'T YOU GODDAMN ANSWER ME?
Lord God of all that is holy, hear my prayers!
Lord God of all that is holy, hear my prayers!
ARE YOU EVEN FUCKING LISTENING?
SHOW YOURSELF!
Lord God of all that is holy, hear my prayers!

That night in bed, Johnny Galoshes returned, lay on his back, and let me put my penis between his legs as I huddled on top of him, rubbing against his bottom, soiling the already dirty sheets of my bed...

The Book of Winter 2

Mrs. Winter's house looked like a bomb had hit it. The priest had been there a few times before—assisting Father Sailor during last year's block collection, picking up bags of old clothes, dropping off a forgotten coat—the Winters were not especially Catholic, but when any of the clan attended Mass, they tended to leave items behind as proof of their pilgrimage—and he knew that the inside wasn't much different from the outside. The front porch had been enclosed years ago, and it was a tottering castle of discarded toys, old magazines, pet paraphernalia (there always seemed to be at least a half dozen dogs or cats wandering in and out of the Winter doorway), stained clothes, old cups and dishes, all accumulating on cracked tile that hadn't been mopped since Moses was but a child among the reeds—all this before you even entered the house proper. It wasn't so much that the Winters were slobs, per se, but more like the experience each of those objects represented was significantly more important than the objects themselves; the toys and such were forsaken as the experience waned. And what with experiences taking up a large part of the day, who had time to properly dispose of old toys and dog playthings?

During the morning and most of the afternoon, Mrs. Winter held court with her granddaughter Jenny. Her other grandchild, Daniel, would be at school. Jenny and Daniel's mother, Gloria, would either still be asleep or out at the playground trying to score some dope—the '60s weren't quite over for Gloria. Once when the priest was dropping off collection envelopes, Mrs. Winter invited him in for coffee, and there was Gloria: spread out on the couch with the television blasting, folds of flesh drooping out of her pajama top. During the priest's visit, Gloria only spoke once—to announce to her mother, at the top of her lungs, that she was FUCKING STARVING. Mostly, she smoked with a grudge, glaring at the television between rapid hurricanes of gray exhalations. Gloria was thirty-five. In addition, Mrs. Winter's youngest son, Freddie Junior, still lived at home. During what Mrs. Winter referred to as "the good times," Freddie Junior would be working some menial job somewhere, but more often than not, he would be upstairs, sleeping off another bender following a night with his poker buddies, a job the least of his concerns. And, for good measure, Mrs. Winter's youngest daughter, Janie, shared Gloria's room when she was on break from dance school. Janie was a good girl; she attended Mass when she was home. Although a trifle skinny, Janie was strong; her bony face belied years of trying to swim upstream past the family's shared ability to stand still. Janie was her mother's daughter—a worker bee, as if there were no other way to exist. Although the priest hardly knew the girl, he felt sorry for her and was careful never to fantasize about her skinny legs and sharply drawn nose on those nights when the bottled poison led to a battle of the penis.

Mr. Winter—Fred Senior—was a mountain—a solid 300 pounds. Mr. Winter drove a truck; he was rarely home. The priest imagined his truck never spilled out on the highway—Mr. Winter's girth would easily cover much of the passenger side of the cab as well; Mr. Winter, on the road at least, was the perfect anchor. At home, his growling joined Gloria's and whomever else's—only Mr. Winter's shouts and demands hid a needy whining beneath his haze of volume. Who knew when this man surrendered his station and ceased to be a husband, a father? The priest met him only once: a violent, sweaty handshake. Mrs. Winter, on the other hand, was so obviously grounded in the strength her family avoided like the plague. Perhaps her family—save Janie—saw the sweat upon her brow and retreated behind it, terrified at the effort necessary to do more than just survive.

"It's all about the little girl," Father Sailor had said the night before. "She's not baptized even."

As the priest mounted the steps, nearly tripping over the overgrown ivy, Father Sailor's dramatic pronouncements fading away, he could hear a high-pitched screeching coming from within the house. The priest knocked on the unfinished wooden door even though Mrs. Winter had told him during a previous visit that it was never locked. The noise escalated, and he could hear Gloria shouting to her mother that SOMEONE'S AT THE FUCKING DOOR. Underneath Gloria's greeting, the thin line of screaming continued and increased in volume as Mrs. Winter pulled open the door, wiped her brow with the back of her thick, callous hand, and squinted into the priest's face.

"Oh, Father. Time again, is it? Where are my manners? Come in, why don't you? Coffee's on. I could butter some bread for you. Got sugar water if you need it."

"Mrs. Winter." The priest bowed his head quickly and then met her face: a railroad of dead-end passages and one-way tickets to anywhere but away from here. Her silk blouse was old and stained and opened at the throat, revealing wrinkled but full cleavage. The grandmother's 5'4" frame was sturdy and muscular; her fingers gripped the door as the screaming inside rattled the frame.

"Jenny." Mrs. Winter again mopped her forehead with the back of her hand. "She's not well today. She doesn't like her medicine." Mrs. Winter's mouth shifted into a brief smile line, shaky and sincere. Her voice was like a Tennessee Williams play—its notes descended down a grand spiraling plantation staircase, landing with an audible slip into yellow roses, dirt roads, and stain resistant remnants.

"I could come back another day, Mrs. Winter. Tomorrow perhaps."

"COULD YOU CLOSE THE FUCKING DOOR IF YOU'RE GONNA TALK? I CAN BARELY HEAR THE GODDAMN TELEVISION!"

"I think Jenny's crying has gotten to Miss Gloria, so, please, beg her pardon. Tomorrow sounds fine, Father. I'll have a fresh pot on and make something warm to eat in this cold."

"I was just making the rounds for the block collection. You don't have to—"

"Nonsense. Tomorrow. I love you."

The door closed upon a fresh outbreak of jungle cries. The priest found himself at a loss. He stood on the cracked concrete steps for another ten minutes or so before descending to the pavement and its cracked wads of old bubble gum and bird excrement. For reasons he determined he would rather not investigate, the priest decided to bag the rest of the day and, careful not to drag his cassock into the gum and poop, walked quickly to McCullough's for a brisk, short glass of fresh air.

He was in the bar, ensconced comfortably within the confines of a whiskey glass, the werewolf abated, his faith hung like his coat in a dark corner of the dark bar, when it occurred to him, the thought flashing through the cigarette smoke like a voice from a burning bush:

It *was* all about the little girl.

The priest closed his eyes and shook it off. He downed the contents of his glass and ordered another.

February 27, 6:02 a.m.

"Yea, dogs are round about me;
a company of evildoers encircle me;
they have pierced my hands and feet—
I can count my bones."
Psalms 22:16-17

Exegesis:

It's not that I no longer have faith —quite the opposite. I have faith to spare, but I no longer believe. *That is to say, I reject the idea of a common belief system. What does it matter? Look at the Judeo-Christian mythos. Somehow, along the way, the idea that a God, formerly (and formally) arrayed in "eye for an eye" rhetoric—imagined/personified by a band of loyal, yet savagely beaten tribesmen, armed with thunder-of-the-gods-type solutions to the problems of the day (what with the flood and the locusts and a seemingly impassable Red Sea)— suddenly changed His mind, created a Son, and sent Him here to be sacrificed so that all sinners could ascend to heaven, seemed to scale the heights of bad theater. The idea of a Christ seems ridiculous to me—not that we don't need a messiah-figure, a savior—but I thought God the Father was our savior! It's like in the middle of the story, Yahweh decided to dangle a Messiah. Indeed, His coming was believed to have been foretold in the Scriptures and was eagerly awaited. The True Believers knew the litany: born of a virgin descended from the House of David in the hovel of Bethlehem; betrayed for thirty pieces of silver; sacrificed only to rise from the dead. True Believers quoted Scripture passages like:* "For you will not leave my soul in Sheol, nor will you allow your Holy One to see corruption." *But to believe this stanza (Psalms 16:10) is a messianic prediction is like believing a blow job isn't adultery. And of course, the True Believers were far from ready for the Messiah to completely take a 180 on the tenets of God the Father's philosophy: turn the other cheek instead of poking out an eye or extracting a tooth. Good philosophy and a great way to approach living. A good fable, in other words.*

I'm not arguing that Jesus didn't exist historically, and yes, the early church, a breakaway Hebrew sect, took His pacifistic words and deeds and turned them into words that breathed fire even while preaching peace, words that, even as a young child, pierced my heart in five different places until I would cry myself to sleep imagining Christ's suffering at the hands of the Romans, delivered unto them by His own people.

Even the Muslims hold Jesus as the greatest prophet bar Mohammed and maybe they're right. But to me, it's like God went backwards. He started as the Fat Elvis: recipient of sacrifices, giver of the scarf, asking his desperate audience to follow along as his jowls bounced to an empty Las Vegas death rattle: "Um, yeah, here's the Promised Land, folks, and for my next number: the Messiah!" The Israelites accepted their suffering, their loss of the plot, as part of the cost on their way to redemption: if the Big E could just get one more hit, sneak one more Memphis-via-Bethlehem-session-type number past the Dark Colonel, then maybe, just maybe they could be redeemed. His audience, hoodwinked time and again, a loyal cadre, buying enough tickets to the tombs that passed as movies, fainting in the aisles in Vegas, held on to a promise Fat Elvis long ago swallowed like so many hot dogs and barbiturates.

Then: WHAM BAM THANK YOU MA'AM, here comes the rockabilly hellcat, all Shure 55, mother-love, royal hiccup, pompadour ascending to the heavens like the Holy Ghost—wisps of Vaseline caught in the early morning sun, hips swiveling, exploding the suffocating rules and strict script of the Fat Elvis ("Do as I say," the Fat Elvis seemed to intone, "follow these rules to the letter—no, never mind that feeling of abandonment—and while I down my twelfth Twinkie with a healthy shot of Demerol and Morphine, you can mop up my sweat to bottle and worship and wish away, for one brief moment, your terrible, painful existence—oh, and don't miss my new film Double Trouble!*"), defining freedom not as ten commandments, but rather as two: love me and love thy neighbor—"In these two commandments," Cool Elvis seemed to say, "the path to freedom is as clear as the sneer on my face." Cool Elvis never dared promise it would last here on earth, but if by following His swiveling twist on hundreds and hundreds of years of Hebrew teaching and tradition, it was as if He promised more than any version of Himself had ever dared—even more than immortality: life after death.*

To hell with Jerry Lee Lewis and his "Great Balls of Fire."

"And in the end, the love you make is equal to the love you take," *so, it matters little to me which Holy Action Figure you worship (hell, collect all twelve!—like the way I hoarded holy cards from funerals as a kid)—but rather the action that comes from the digestion and gestation of the base philosophy. Like I wrote earlier, I have plenty of faith, I have faith to spare. I just don't accept the belief system thrust upon me as a child. One doesn't need to join the Elvis Fan Club to be saved. Judgment must be determined on something far baser than blind acceptance. Isn't it about actions? Isn't it about living a good life?*

The faith that I scribble into these pages is a faith in myself—for God—

sometimes—works through me because—sometimes—inside of me there is God. Isn't that recognition enough? I know His flaws because they are mine. Isn't that the dilemma of the werewolf: a pernicious lack of self-awareness? To save yourself is to overcome the bane of human weakness, the curse of the werewolf.

And what is being saved compared to saving others—the true work of a priest? Why do I need a belief system when I recognize God inside of me? In the banned Gospel of Thomas, *Jesus said,* "Fortunate is the lion that the human will eat, so that the lion becomes human. And foul is the human that the lion eats, and the lion will become human."

I believe in good acts, I believe in being true, I hope that at the end of our suffering, we will find redemption, if only in overcoming the stink of the world with our insides intact, but I don't think a single bit of importance lies in the messenger.

That said, I know there is a Higher Power; I know God is there: hidden among my autumn stars when I was a child or gestating inside my stomach now, awash in copious amounts of sacrificial wine, but I don't pretend to understand His level of involvement. I fear that He is ambivalent, for if there is a divine omniscient power overseeing all, if there is a single entity, a thought made large in the utter emptiness of outer space, watching impassively the down dirty evil perpetrated every single fucking second, ignoring our prayers unless they particularly strike His/Her holy ears—yeah, save Keith Richards (God bless him!), but screw the little girl kidnapped by the mean ol' wolf—then He/She/It chose a fucked up way to inspire the masses...but like they're drawn to a bad summer movie, the congregation keeps coming back, going to mass on Sunday (or at least on Easter and Christmas Eve, especially Christmas Eve—why ruin Jesus' birthday by going to Mass?) and fingering their daughters on Monday.

Therein lies the problem in all organized religions: attempting to control our actions by promising the flickering flames of Hades for those that stray or blissful communion with all the holy action figures if we take the path less strewn with nipple and neon. But they're missing the point! You can't organize God! All the rewards and punishments in the universe can't SAVE. The faithful have to be ready to fulfill their part of the promise. To be evil, you must sacrifice good, but to be good is to sacrifice EVERYTHING.

Who cares what God looks like?

Look in the mirror.

Repeat after me:

My power comes from Him, and yet I am *almost* utterly powerless.

Maybe the Buddhists have it half-right: sit and you will discover the god in you; *or rather, if you're quiet enough, the essence of* you *will rise above the* earthly body. *Only those who throw away everything have everything to gain, or in Buddhist thought, they gain nothing, or at least comprehend what nothing really means; no god figure needed. The problem here (besides reincarnation, their pseudo-pragmatic resurrection myth) is that the most devout Buddhists make of this grand practice a* religion—*the Buddha and his lieges' words are taken as holy text, the rest of the world is ignorant to their own impermanence, rituals must be adhered to in order to ascend the ladder…blah blah blah. One handbook on meditation, after pages of sound advice on sitting and quieting your thoughts, actually informs the reader that they may see a bright sphere or a lotus flower after mastering the initial stages of mediation. How fucking ridiculous! It takes the air out of the exercise. Why do we need this magic? We're all supposed to see the same flower? Buddhism masquerades as an impersonal religion. "Without a method, you will suffer. Then you will suffer much," one meditation teacher I sought outside of seminary said to me, his voice ascending a minor scale as if he were speaking to a child. The seminary was going to give me the authority to act in the name of God—in the name of goodness; I would have a pulpit, but still, I was without a center. I had promised myself to God—to goodness after Emily died, but still I had to find a way to make up for What Happened Next, for my Judas Moment. Meditation seemed a way to quiet down the pillow-smothered voice of Johnny Galoshes, his long-dead moans echoing in my ears:* Emily—Ronnie— Emily—Ronnie. *I thought that Buddhism would allay my needs—sacred and otherwise—so that I could see the task at hand. But that was not to be.*

The sheer impersonal approach is the height of absurdity: everything is personal; you can't make it otherwise just by wishing it so. To make it through the lows, this teacher intoned, one has to level out everything. If you hear that Johnny Cash song on the radio, you know the one, the one you've been waiting to hear during an interminable hundred mile drive, you are supposed to temper your exhilaration at the bass in his voice so that your suffering during, say, an entire block of progressive '70s rock won't make you want to blow some red lights or smash up the family sedan.

But if the impersonal approach is so central to the Buddhist thought, explain the enlightened state to me: the teacher becomes infallible in wisdom, a little Pope, doling out dollops of gum drop riddles, so much so, that the following year this same teacher, this friend I'd sought out just before taking my vows, stopped speaking to me because I dared question his method. He was someone who at least tried *to make a difference to me with concrete advice before descending into the same mysticism being force-fed in the seminary. But I was in the seminary to set things right. I was fulfilling my covenant—my promise after Emily. And now I am preparing to atone for Ronnie. It's all personal.*

And again:

My power comes from Him, and yet I am *almost* utterly powerless.

So—if you see the Buddha on the road, hug him until he throws up. *Everything that Christianity and Buddhism teach is sound advice. Why the trappings?...why the infallibility?...where do we turn as devout people? Where do we seek succor in a wilderness of open legs and hung over Saturday mornings? The answer: in the little things, in people, in the seemingly random acts that connect us, if we dare listen, to every blade of grass*—"Under a rock, you will find me..."—*how true, all of it...my boner is not the sin here, rather it's what I'm going to do with it when I'm done writing in this notebook...it's the damage I do as I surrender to WANT rather than rejoice in WAIT...it's the act, stupid, not the philosophy...*

The Book of Winter 3

It was Mrs. Winter's habit of declaring her love whenever she bade farewell that had brought the priest back. He knew she said it to everyone, but to the priest, it was the first hangover cure that worked: her voice rang between the temple drum throbs like a shiver. Her words brought focus: the priest knew Jenny was the answer.

Mrs. Winter's kitchen table was made of oak and stretched across the room like an arm trying to bring together the scattered tendrils of the Winter family—not that many of them flew far from the roost. On the contrary, the priest thought, maybe the arm was Mrs. Winter's way of keeping them all in one place. Her family gave her purpose; it gave her a reason to wake up in the morning, the priest concluded as Mrs. Winter poured him a fresh cup of coffee.

Jenny sat facing the corner on a small blue chair with a seat made of meshed straw, her uncombed long brown hair sticking out like a scarecrow's arms. She wore a faded white (yellow, really) t-shirt, and diapers. The priest put her age at seven. The house smelled strongly of cat piss and musty, decaying books.

"That's what we're here for—to save souls, Donald. Surely, you can't disagree with that," Father Sailor had said a fortnight ago. "We need to save her soul. We *must* save her from eternal damnation. The grandmother is too afraid to bring her to us. We need to save the child's soul, Donald."

The priest sat on a long bench against the breakfront, which was piled high with old bills, books, torn pages from magazines, and empty cat food cans. To his left, under the high windows, was an overstuffed black bookcase, its inhabitants' spines peeling in the heat of the kitchen. Mrs. Winter sat across from him. A Merit smoldered in an ashtray. The priest wanted to ask Mrs. Winter if he could bum one but considered it impolite and tapped his shoes instead.

Mrs. Winter laughed, and her Texan accent found its way and mixed with her strong Philadelphia overtones. She brushed a few curls out of her eyes with a chubby hand.

"Yup, we had roses, climbing up the side of the house, just like my ivy now. Roses don't do that here, Father." A fresh cigarette appeared between the old woman's stained fingers like magic, and the priest was surprised a few seconds later when he looked down to find Mrs. Winter had smoked it to the filter. He never saw her put it to her mouth or exhale. "Here, roses are for looking at and giving and keeping inside 'til they die—then pressing a petal in a book. Can't live here the same as down there, Father."

The priest glanced over at Jenny in the corner. Something was in the girl's hair—a clump of something lumpy.

"So, you're here for the block collection, Father?"

The priest pulled his eyes back to the old woman's wiry, steel gray hair. Her glasses dangled above her partially exposed, full bosom, and the sun, glinting through the dirty, tall windows above the bookcase, glanced its rays over her lenses and into the priest's eyes.

"Yes, yes, Joyce. Yes. But I wanted to talk to you about the little one," the priest said, gesturing toward the corner. He stole another quick glimpse—what the fuck was growing in Jenny's hair?

"Father Sailor mentioned to me that she hasn't been baptized, and we thought—I thought—we could remedy that. Perhaps get her some, well, some—"

Mrs. Winter's voice was like the rough side of an old winter blanket: "Some what?"

The priest faltered, stopped, then breathed: "Assistance."

Mrs. Winter laughed. "Nonsense, Father. We teach her all about God right here in the home. Jenny doesn't need assistance. She's just a little hard of hearing, is all. Can't afford to send her to one of those special schools, so we teach her here."

"And you're certified to do that?" The priest didn't know if a caregiver needed to be certified to homeschool a child; it was just the first thought that popped into his preoccupied mind. He cringed a little and peeked into the corner as the little girl's fingers reached into her hair, tangling more strands into the brown chunk.

Mrs. Winter laughed again, and the priest exhaled.

"About as certified as you are, Father, no offense."

"I'm not sure what you mean," said the priest. As he sipped his coffee, he tasted something sweet on the tip of his tongue.

Don't look in the corner. Don't dare look in the corner.

"You go around to the houses and say Mass in the church, but you don't really *believe* in Jesus our savior, now do you, Father? One hundred percent?"

The priest blushed and willed his eyes away from the corner. Maybe Jenny was mentally disabled. *Something* was wrong with her.

"Mrs. Winter...Joyce...my faith is strong, and my life's work rests on that faith." The priest hoped his testimony didn't sound like a recitation.

"Good, then let me tell you a story they should put in the *next* King James. You know the Macy's Thanksgiving Parade in the city, right?"

The priest nodded; he hated parades and firmly believed that if there *was* a Christ, He surely didn't want His resurrection commemorated by the launching of a giant Underdog float into the sky.

"So I take Jenny down to the parade. This was three years ago, understand. Everyone around here had big plans, so I took her myself."

Mrs. Winter was holding another freshly lit cigarette—hadn't she just lit one a few seconds ago? Maybe it was just a trick to distract him from making any judgments about her family. Everyone was busy—right. He had passed a snoring Gloria, comatose on the couch on his way in, a very full ashtray balanced on her not inconsiderable belly.

"Crowded as all get-out, no kidding, Father. Never saw nothing like it myself. People were drinking and dancing and watching the balloons. Everyone seemed to be having a good time. Did you ever eat one of those funnel cakes, Father? The Pennsylvania Dutch funnel cakes with the powdered sugar on top?"

The priest doubted very much the Dutch connection, but nodded in assent anyway. Jesus Christ, what the hell was on his coffee cup?

"Well, Jenny's just cuckoo for them funnel cakes, and I stop at one of those trucks to get her one, but it was so windy, and the sugar's just blowing—that's Jenny's favorite part—and the paper plate is so darn hot, I let go of her hand to hold the thing with both mitts and kinda grab a napkin with my pinkie. I turn around, and Jenny's gone. In this whole big mash of people and huge balloon floats and God-knows-what-else, Jenny is gone. Poof. Scared the bejesus outta me, I can tell you."

It was peanut butter. There was peanut butter all along the rim of his coffee mug. How hadn't he noticed it before?

"I'm yelling, I'm screaming, I'm looking for a policeman. Suddenly, no police, no firemen. Just me and the guy who makes the Dutch funnel cakes—he's not helping, mind you. I go to the pay phone near the truck, but everyone at the house is busy and can't help me, and besides, they can barely hear me from the noise of the parade, see. Now, I'm beside myself. I'm crying, I'm grabbing people by the coat. Someone's got to help me, but I'm just a crazy old lady to them—in the city, I guess, losing a child isn't that big of a deal. And there He comes, just walking from around the other side of the funnel truck, just plain as day."

The priest resisted the urge to peer into the corner.

"I'm sorry. Who? Who was it?"

"Why, Jesus Christ himself! Just up and found my Jenny, walking through the thick crowd toward me, carrying her piggyback style. 'Course I wasn't *completely* sure it was Him, but I was pretty sure. He had those robes on, like in the Bible pictures, but a lot of people were dressed up, so I didn't want to assume."

Suddenly the room was too small, the coffee too hot—the priest could feel his balls crawl up into his belly, and his tongue lashed around for relief. Why don't they just take priests' balls when they enlist? Was Mrs. Winter for real? Where was all the peanut butter coming from?

"He walks up to me, Jenny riding behind, and I say to him, 'I know you,' and He smiles at me and says back, 'Everybody does.' Tells me Jenny crawled under the truck when she saw the sugar fly off the damn funnel cake. 'Wanted to save the sugar,' I say. He says, 'Your girl likes peanut butter. Why don't you take her home and make some peanut butter sandwiches with bananas. Better than funnel cake.' And He turns to Jenny and asks her, 'Doesn't that sound good, Jennifer?' And Jenny answers Him! 'Peanut butter is always good,' she says to Jesus." Mrs. Winter exhaled a long finger of smoke. "Don't that beat all, Father?"

The priest wiped the peanut butter from his sleeves onto his trousers.

"Joyce. I guess it does, Joyce. I guess you had a close encounter," the priest replied, managing a smile.

Mrs. Winter swallowed his grin in hers and released a series of giant smoke rings that encircled and chased one another across the dusty kitchen.

"He knew her name, Father."

"I'm sure you were screaming it."

"He knew her name." The cigarette was out and smoldering in the ashtray. Another one was sprouting between her stained fingers.

"In the end, Joyce, in the end all that matters is what *you* believe. If you believe Jesus found Jenny under a Pennsylvania Dutch funnel cake truck, then He did. What I believe matters little here."

Jenny's chair scraped against the floor, and the priest could see large chunks of peanut butter matting her dirty hair, creating tunnels and valleys and ripples on the back of her head.

"It matters a great deal, Father. Not to me necessarily, but to you. To you, it means everything. It's the dividing line."

The priest looked at Joyce, cigarette smoke twisting from her full chest to the wires in her hair, and then back to the corner. The chair was turned halfway around now, and the priest recognized the painted ears and the cloth tail drooping from the seat—a donkey. The priest had seen that kind of child's chair before. A donkey's muzzle had been painted on the back, and the legs of the chair ended in little black chips: hooves.

"Where did...? Jenny left the chair."

Mrs. Winter stood up and wiped peanut butter and ash off the table with a gray dishrag.

"Hell, she wasn't in dutch, Father. She wasn't in the corner 'cause of any kind of trouble. That wasn't why she was sitting. She was *listening.* My Jenny's *always* listening. She knows she's special to the Lord. That's why she don't talk much. It's not her not hearing. She's just listening to Jesus. It's a full time job, I think. Wouldn't you say, Father?"

The priest sipped from his coffee cup, and his teeth and lips were smothered with peanut butter. The kitchen was an inferno.

Mrs. Winter sucked in a deep drag and released a steady-stream tunnel of gray; the priest felt himself ensnared within its walls. Mrs. Winter pulled the cigarette from her mouth and stared at the filter, flicking her tongue over her lips. "Girl does like her peanut butter, don't she?" Mrs. Winter said. "I love you."

"Why do you say that?" *To everyone,* he wanted to add, *to everyone.*

"In case I don't ever see your face again, Father."

The priest pushed away from the table and let himself out into the sunshine, a quick vodka and tonic the only thought he could maintain to hold back the volley of vomit awaiting release. He no longer craved a cigarette.

March 3, 5:42 a.m.

"The image is one thing and the human being is another;
it's very hard to live up to an image."
Elvis Presley, 1972

Exegesis:

I killed a girl in a story once. This was in my junior year in high school: editor of the literary magazine, full time virgin, no longer a nerd in training—now a certified geek. My mother rarely left her bedroom. I would enter her room before I left for school each morning and pick up the dirty tissues littering the floor. The Crowd nuzzled me; they encouraged me with the opposite sex, taught me to drink, borrowed my records, and never returned them.

Emily was the name of my muse—only she didn't know it. Emily Who Smelled Like Flowers. A friend of one of my pal's girlfriends, Emily was always a puff of perfume, a half-smile, and a tangle of tossed mud-brown hair—but what intoxicating mud! We barely passed two words, except the Louis Armstrong Conversation, the one that led to Emily's death—fictionally, at least.

I was deejaying a party for the Crowd. I had no DJ equipment, just hundreds upon hundreds of records. I set up in the corner with two turntables plugged into the receiver and played records and drank, watching girls out of the corner of my eye, and there, in the middle of an O'Jays tune ("All this fussing and fighting we're doing / Don't you know it's got to stop?"*), stood Emily: a soon-to-be-vintage '70s t-shirt, nubby sweater tied around her inviting waistline, self-consciously holding a cup of beer, laughing a little too hard, and finishing the laughs a little too soon. All winter long, I had planned on asking Humper or Kim to help me out, pass along a kind word about the kid with the records, the near invisible kid whose nose would be frequently stained black from book ink; I wanted the ground to be prepared: I wanted to ask Emily to my junior prom.*

So, back to the party: I was downing beers with two fists, searching out the most obscure and cool tunes from the milk crates that doubled as my record bins, trying to bend the party to my will. Emily was slightly dancing in the corner—you know the dance—with Kim and two other girls. Deb Humper was beside me. Swaying, she said, "Forget it. She's out of your league. She's a senior." But what did Humper know? Humper ran her hand up my jeans. "Forget her," she said and stumbled away. Fuck this, I thought, chugged another beer, turned up Louis

Armstrong and the Hot Seven, and made a jagged beeline for Emily. She knew my name, and I thought that was a good start.

"What's the Louis Armstrong tune they use in that car commercial?" Emily asked me, and I blanked—completely. Emily laughed a little and said, "Oh great and wonderful Oz? Hello?" My cheeks were approaching code red levels when she laughed again. "Donnie, I'm sorry…just thought you closed down for the night." I stammered my way through a few sentences, a lamb lost in the deepest part of the wood, until the clearing, until the moment was ready. Emily was staring, her eyes growing curious, as if my words were strings and clumps rather than whole thoughts and passages, and truth be told, they probably were. I was praying, see. Inside my head, I was praying to God to help me ask this pretty girl to be my date to the junior prom. I was praying to the Lord Jesus to aid me in overcoming my embarrassment. Surely, the Lord knew of love, I thought. Not that He wouldn't be busy, saving starving Ethiopians or settling the differences in the Middle East. But I had been a pretty good kid—imaginary sodomy aside. Sure, I was sore about Winifred Waxman—my communication with the Lord had trickled down to rote recitation—but my love for Him was devout and absolute, a cold, clear stream of water flowing through my bloodstream.

And then, somewhere in those half sentences, somewhere amid the briar patch of syllables, I asked Emily to my prom. Emily Who Smelled Like Flowers. And just like a movie—JUST LIKE A GODDAMN MOVIE—the sound slowed down, Louis Armstrong's trumpet slurred and stuttered like some of my drunk friends, those same friends now frozen in acts of surprise, their eyes cartoon-wide, jutting from their skulls like jack rabbits escaping their holes in the wake of stomps from a hunter's boots. I had stepped out of my self-induced high school role. I WAS TALKING TO A GIRL. As Billy J. would say: I WAS MAKING TIME. I could smell the beer on my upper lip, and the last thing I consciously remember before the gates of Hades squeaked open on its well-oiled hinges was wishing for a stick of gum in case Emily Who Smelled Like Flowers wanted to commence the kissing right then and there.

Dappled: fluorescent lights in my eyes and I hear Him calling my name.

Emily blinked once or twice and asked, "With you?" The party swung a hard left and resumed without so much as a hitch or a hiccup. Except for Louis. Louis Armstrong skipped and repeated, skipped and repeated: the same trumpet phrase snagged, caught on Hades' hinge. "Yes, with me," I said, and then, for reasons still completely unknown to me—maybe I knew this ship had already run aground—I bowed deeply with a great exaggerated flourish of arms and fingers. I noticed her mouth drawn into that half circle before I actually heard the noise: it wasn't laughter as much as it was the sound of a rat trapped beneath a porch, mewling its death song yet aroused at the scent of its own demise.

And that was pretty much the end of the scene. I proceeded to become rip-roaring drunk, playing patently un-danceable numbers by unconventional voices like Townes Van Zandt, Leonard Cohen, Lou Reed—songs of betrayal, songs of utter fucking despair. I awoke in a corner in the same basement that just minutes before (okay, hours before) had been the life-pulse of the party. A drunk blonde (Tammy? Denise?) was sucking on my turgid penis. I didn't know her name, and I let myself finish before pushing my way to what I thought was the bathroom, throwing up into the open Maytag washer. I gathered my records, cursing the number of vinyl I found without sleeves under the couch. The Blow Job Blonde was gone too, just a phone number atop the turntable. I crumpled the little slip of paper and drowned it in a half cup of beer. That's when I began plotting the Death of Emily.

I was discreet—only Johnny Galoshes—oh, Johnny was back now, fucking Johnny Galoshes—was privy to my carnal intentions; I transfigured all the Little Pieces of Emily I had conjured when I masturbated into voodoo-like talismans, and then forged them into words, my typewriter's keys striking home like a blacksmith's hammer. I personified her scent into a Christ-like figure, a martyr for the cause of my continued, self-inflicted, hand-greased fulfillment. And then I killed her. In the sparse light of adverbs and incantations and dangling participles, right before the eyes of the high school lit magazine's advisory staff: I killed Emily dead, her own soon-to-be-vintage '70s t-shirt strangling the soft-scented vanilla of her neck, smothered by what I imagined was her own insatiable lust lurking just beneath the surface of her fucking prim and neatly tucked turtle necks and saddle shoes.

But it was only fiction, mind you.

And do you know we what prayed for that night—me and Johnny Galoshes, down on our knees—not an unfamiliar position for either of us—praying until our tongues cried out for a drop of moisture, sacrificing our sperm to the altar of all that is contrary and difficult? We prayed AGAINST the withholding, against those who withheld—we prayed for their eventual and all encompassing surrender. And, know what else? I never masturbated over her little frame again. I never again awoke in the middle of the night with her name creeping over my drool, past my lips, stealthily stalking my tumescence. That's when I started to slowly stop believing in a particular Holy Action Figure. If my literary liquidation of Emily was the manifestation of my own particular evil, I knew there was true goodness stranded upon the far shore, awaiting its recognition by my pissy, twisted heart…but I also knew deeper forces were at work, and one didn't need to bow to a statue to tap into it. I had faith in its existence because it worked: Emily was gone from my head.

Until she died for real.

But as the cliché goes: the seeds were sown, and if I did it once, I can do it again. Now I know the consequences of action; then I did not. But now my actions will lead to the freedom of another soul, not the satiation of my pulsing member. Mrs. Winter: superstition with a bosom, that poor little girl, Jenny, awash not only in strewn peanut butter finger paintings, but also damn near buried alive within Mrs. Winter's bizarre incarnation of Jesus Christ as random hippie savior. I suppose that's what the modern day Church sometimes presents Him as, but to attribute Jenny's recovery at the Easter parade to the little girl's conversation with a messianic street person bordered on the criminal. Something is wrong with Jenny, something that requires more than just blind assignment on the part of a broken old lady. And this is my real job as a Roman Catholic priest, not saying Mass or hearing confession (which turns my stomach at the accounting of pettiness and the smell of the real behind-the-fridge-gunk-type sins lurking just below their body odor and perfume: the smell of anal sex, the scent the abandonment of others creates, the burnt match and shit odor rising from the mark of Cain), but rescuing a soul from the clutches of the ignorant. I don't need a saint or a Mary statue to tell me this was the True Bible Truth, as my fastidiously faithful but blissfully clueless (and frequently absent) father would say when commenting on subjects no longer open to debate. I rose above his ignorance and beyond his mythical beliefs, and now I help others rise above the lack of awareness seeping into their lives as their personalities disappear with a Big Suck down the drain. This is why I am a priest. The dogma means little. I need to help. I need to save, not to raise myself above but to give others a boost up. I need to redeem myself through their redemption.

I remember thinking of all these things at Emily's funeral—redemption, covenants, the Big Suck. I had read about her death by strangulation in the paper: walking back from a night class to her dorm in her first semester of college. She wanted to be a nurse, the paper said. I sat in the back and struggled not to surrender myself to the priest during her service, but as the reading hit the part about Mary Magdalene ("For this reason I say to you, her sins, which are many, have been forgiven, for she loved much; but he who is forgiven little, loves little…"*), I knew: faith and prayer, redemption and retribution: all stemmed from the same mustard seed:* "be uprooted and be planted in the sea."

I also remember thinking about Ronnie at Emily's funeral. I remember getting hard.

The day of Emily's funeral was the day Johnny Galoshes stopped coming around, stopped sleeping over, stopped whispering in my ear, stopped allowing me between his legs. I had needed saving as a teenager. I even needed saving later in my early twenties. I knew of no one who did not. Fuck the saints and angels and Baby Jesus. As a priest I could save, *I thought then. But Emily wasn't my Judas Moment, just the prologue; my betrayal was yet to come and even a werewolf needs a silver bullet to shed his skin.*

And now, with Mrs. Winter, the opportunity for redemption once again presents itself, for I recognize the devil in disguise: ignorance. Ignorance led me to abandon God, ever so briefly, after the Winifred Waxman Incident. Ignorance made me believe Johnny Galoshes was the big bad wolf when the hair on my palms should have exposed the true werewolf. Ignorance led me to kill the fictional Emily without thought of the consequences. And now ignorance keeps Jenny away from proper education, not to mention medical and psychiatric attention.

And let's not forget:

Ignorance led some drifter or other to strangle the real Emily Who Smelled Like Flowers with her own scarf, immediately after ripping out her (according to her friends) fiercely held virginity.

That's the True Bible Truth why I chose the priesthood. I had to make up for Emily Who Smelled Like Flowers; I had to make up for what I did—a misuse of power. I promised God my life when high school was finished. And, if I ever get to it, you'll know why I have to rescue Jenny. If my vows erased at least the fictional death of Emily, then maybe saving Jenny will be my redemption for What Happened Next, for my Judas Moment. Emily is watching, Emily Who Smelled Like Flowers.

One shaking hand washes the blood off the other.

Perhaps if I just stuff Mrs. Winter's mouth with cigarettes until she begins to choke. Perhaps if I just start writing of her death, here, now, in the early morning light. Oh man, I am so fucking hard right now. Goodnight, Mrs. Winter, swallow hard. Faith and prayer: redemption and retribution…

The Book of Winter 4

Hold it fellas—that don't move me.
Let's get real, real gone for a change...

The priest stood outside of Mrs. Winter's house for two hours, chain-smoking cigarettes. He assumed the parish would have heard if Mrs. Winter had choked to death on a pack of Merits or chunks of peanut butter, but knocking for someone you tried to murder (if *only* fictionally) seemed the height of bad manners. Still—a Catholic priest lurking beneath a sycamore tree, staring intently at the dirty porch windows seemed a cause for alarm. The priest smiled—as if a Methodist or a Congregationalist lurking in the front yard were possibly acceptable—and said, "Fuck it," crossing himself as his Florsheims led him to the Winters' front door.

Mama, she done told me—Papa done told me too:
Son, that gal you're fooling with; she ain't no good for you...

The air was heavy with ammonia and it stung his eyes. It was stronger than his alcohol breath. The priest knocked on the unfinished wood and waited. After a few respectable minutes, the priest banged his fist upon the door. In a house constantly full of people, the priest found the silence beyond disturbing. Perhaps he had done it again: made the written word the truth—only this time in God's name instead of Lucifer's. Perhaps he *had* saved the little girl.

Blue moon, you saw me standing alone
Without a dream in my heart, without a love of my own...

The priest paused, uttering not prayers, but old Sun sides. Cool Elvis.

I just had to reach you, baby,
'spite of all that I been through.
I kept traveling night and day,
I kept running all the way,
Ba-by, trying to get to you...

The door wasn't locked, and as the priest pushed it open, waves of cat piss, gusts of shed skin assaulted his nostrils. He tried to open his mouth to announce his entrance, to breathe without inhaling; the air hitched in his throat as if he'd swallowed a lit match. The priest's hands tiptoed across his neck, and his trousers skipped with static electricity. Mute, the priest bent his constricted throat: the cats surrounded his legs, rubbing their bodies against his shins, screaming their mewls deep inside his skull. He shuffled his way toward the kitchen. Something tickled the back of his throat.

You know what it takes, you got it ba-by.
You are the only one I chose
That don't leave me with all these heartaches.
Only you and heaven know
About my troubles, troubles, troubles.
When it rains, it really pours...

Jenny was sitting on the donkey chair, facing the corner.

"Jenny." The priest whispered the little girl's name, a decidedly mushy taste migrating from his esophagus. He could smell the peanut butter just below the skull-dust and cat urine. "Jenny." Little puffs of stale air made their way into the priest's lungs, smaller and smaller until: "Jenny." His teeth mashed down upon the cigarette paper, and his tongue was crushed under the weight of what tasted like two full packs of Merits. Jenny turned her head toward his, a cigarette thick with peanut butter dangling from between her chapped lips. The little girl crossed herself, opened her mouth, letting the cigarette drop to the kitchen floor, stubbing out the embers with her bare, filthy toes. Jenny parted her chapped lips, and the priest could see her mouth, stuffed to the gums with cigarettes. She grinned and lifted her bottom from the donkey chair.

Listen to me baby,
Try to understand:
I'd rather see you dead, little girl,
Than to be with another man...

The priest turned and made for the door, tripped over what seemed like dozens of cats, their cries melding into a choral recording played at the wrong speed. The smell of peanut butter overwhelmed the taste of tobacco and filter paper infiltrating his mouth. He pushed himself off the floor and didn't stop running until he reached the bus depot near the end of Penn Street. There the priest dropped to his knees and clawed at his empty mouth. A group of people waiting for a trolley rushed to his aid, and one man pounded his back until the priest vomited on another man's shoes. From the corner of his eye, the priest watched Fat Elvis, his sequins winking in the bus lights, hop the 57, its destination sign flashing: TERMINAL, then MARGARET & ORTHODOX, then TERMINAL, then, BRIDGE & PRATT, then TERMINAL, TERMINAL, TERMINAL. The priest lifted himself off the ground and pushed his way toward the bus, not at all surprised that exact change laid waiting in his trouser pocket. The priest covered his eyes, curled up on the bubble gum bumps decorating the cold plastic seat, and waited for his stop, ignoring the throb emanating from his trousers.

March 7, 5:02 a.m.

"Now, I beseech you to consider calmly,
how is God good or loving to this man?
Is not this such love as makes your blood run cold, as
causes the ears of him that heareth to tingle?"
John Wesley, "Predestination Calmly Considered"

Exegesis:

The first time Ronnie sucked on my penis, he spit my sperm out behind a radiator, so surprised was he at the amount of liquid streaming into his mouth, and wouldn't suck on it again for a couple of weeks, although he allowed me complete access to his. He was two years younger than me; he played guitar too. Ronnie was a sophomore; I was a senior. As I've mentioned, after the Death of Emily Who Smelled Like Flowers, Johnny Galoshes was gone, regulating himself to a mental closet filled with stuffed animals and Baby Jesus night-lights. Ronnie was my catalyst. Ronnie had to happen for God to give me the power to try to vanquish ignorance and to rescue Jenny; I know that now. My Judas Moment started out innocent enough on the surface—healthy sexual curiosity—but just below the thin line separating what occurs from what is intended, my desperation lay barely still, stretching my skin until I believed I would burst from the pressure building up inside my bones.

This is What Happened.

This is the Beginning of What Happened Next.

Ronnie was picking his nose one day as we sat on his bed trading guitar riffs. Emily had been in the ground only a brief time. "That's just built-up dirt," I said. Ronnie looked at me, the fair skin around his eyes crinkling. "That's just what it is," I said. Ronnie laughed. "Guess I like to see what's rolling around inside," he replied. "Well, wait 'til you see this," I said, pulling my penis out of my trousers, rubbing it until Ronnie smiled and said, "Gonna start a fire with that!"

"Can you do it?" I asked.

And that's how it began. For whatever reason, Ronnie hadn't made himself come yet, and although I never asked, the Crowd's assumptions were correct, and the two of us explored the various ways of kick starting the flames with our mouths and hands. I would imagine Emily's mouth; I would imagine Emily if she had a penis.

But in the back of my head, where I assumed Jesus stayed when he came to visit, a scenario I had developed as a kid unspooled: I could feel the flames I fanned and put out upon Ronnie's skin lick at my heels, singeing what I imagined were my ankle-wings—wings waiting to soar me into the bosom of God the Father and the Holy Mother like a Greek god. I had already promised myself to Jesus. Surely, if intercourse was to be staved off until the sacrament of Holy Matrimony, then licking your best buddy's balls for the sheer thrill of illicit contact, waiting until he performed the same to you, was tantamount to murdering your mother— especially if your calling was Holy Orders.

Ronnie and I would lock ourselves in his room (always his room—I think Ronnie thought twice about giving head in plain sight of my holy card collection, festooned along the walls and on the back of the door) and performed our mortal sins for the duration of a single side of one of Ronnie's precious Who albums, the phonograph arm starting the platter over, as we took enough of a breather in between (about five minutes) to start fresh. But Jesus wouldn't let me go. I heard His voice somewhere in the murk of Ronnie's hitched breathing and Pete Townshend's windmill stutters: Emily, Emily, Emily.

And then there was the Crowd to consider: Big Mike dropping in one day to borrow a Hüsker Dü album, Ronnie barely pulling up his shorts in time, careful not to show his profile for fear his boner would betray him. An increased amount of faggot jokes circled the Crowd's social gatherings. No longer was I sought out for spiritual advice in matters of the heart; now it was: is eating Kim out a sin?; if my mother smells Candy on my fingers, will she recognize it?*; and other questions I had little to no experience in dealing with.*

I started to come around to Ronnie's house less and less. My head would toss back and forth in the pillow crevice, and morning would approach without me so much as closing my eyes. His voice. His voice. This was the Cool Elvis: "Freedom is only precious," the Cool Crucified Elvis whispered to me as I lay in bed, my hard-on throbbing against my stomach, willing myself not to attack my own penis—"Freedom is only precious if it is practiced rather than kept and maintained," Cool Elvis' voice tickling my ear. And, one morning, when I finally caved in (I was no more successful at quitting my penis as a teenager than I am at stopping smoking as an adult), I found myself in Ronnie's bedroom, sweating, a summer fever marching through my body like a victory dance. Ronnie pulled his shorts down and spread his legs. I was not surprised to see my shorts were already on the floor nor was I surprised to see the head of my cock directing air traffic. "Here, just put it here," Ronnie said, and I lay on top of him, pushing my penis under his balls, so it rubbed against his bottom. I came in a shout and left Ronnie's room, my shorts and underwear in my hand, crying the Lord's Prayer until I reached my house, the fever enveloping my body like a hug from Aunt Grady.

Dappled: Johnny Galoshes shielding my eyes and I hear Him scream my name.

My mother, momentarily moved to abandon her hibernation, knocked on my door offering soup and crackers, and I lied to her until I heard her descend the stairs. I was sure of my own death. I wrote a will on the last page of my Bible. Jesus would not stand for empty covenants—priests-to-be do not indulge in the wares of the flesh. God had answered my prayers once—the same God who had ignored my love for Winifred Waxman— and had given me a glimpse of His power. And mine. With the stroke of a pen, Emily had been erased. When I grew hard after falling asleep for a little bit, I squeezed my balls until my eyes felt like they were stained on the ceiling.

And then: NOTHING. I awoke again in the middle of the night, cured, my aches distant echoes. Jesus sat serenely in the back of my head, perusing a news magazine, tisk-tisking *the horrors people played upon each other. I had a hard-on, but suddenly my penis and I were on the same team. I played with it, cleaning up with a sweat sock. No, I would not, could not, dare not go back to Ronnie. I knew my powers came from Him; I knew He had tied Emily's fate to my lust. And as much as I found myself in a struggle at times, my sneakers flapping pavement dirt as I made my way to his house, I swore never to return to Ronnie, although I thought I could make him come to me if my resolve ever failed. In denying myself, I thought I had saved Ronnie. But God—Jesus—hell, call Him whatever you like—wanted a sacrifice; prove your love was His demand too. The cost was heavy. Thirty bags of silver heavy. It would soon be Ronnie's turn to save me.*

Oh, I masturbated like crazy, trying to piss Jesus off, and imagined my brief, first, and only encounter with the opposite sex—Tammy? Denise?—the Blow Job Blonde—as she explored the joys of oral sex in the aftermath of last year's party. I conjured every girl I ever wanted— except Emily. But what girl, in the waking world, could compete with my all consuming obsession with God?

So the self-gratification continued unabated. Oh, I couldn't stop. Would I be branded, I thought, would I be forsaken? Still: NOTHING. And that's when I first fermented my Almighty Thesis for an Ambivalent God. That's when the belief system seemed less important than my faith. I didn't consider myself gay. I didn't consider myself straight. I was SEX. I was all the nasty dreams made flesh, damp with acrid scents, and as long as I tempered this realization with some restraint, as long as I thanked the Lord for each and every orgasm and held each shudder precious, then surely the Jesus who supposedly changed water into wine for an orgy of writhing wedding guests would understand. And if He did or not mattered little. I felt IT. I inhaled an IS. I sensed the Hand leading me from my struggles for Good to the relative calm of Good Enough. My heart focused and I renewed my promise. Not so much to Jesus, but to myself and to the Hand. I had been raised Roman Catholic, so a Roman Catholic priest I would become, but I was sure that if I had been raised Muslim or Jewish, the path would be the same—just with a different uniform. Why get caught up in iconography?

My task would be to save others, to light as many candles as I could against the encroaching dark of ignorance that lurked within each and every soul. Fuck Lucifer. Screw Satan. But I could feel the beer-breath of the Crowd at my collar; schoolyard scuffles were now sidelong glances and snickers into the back of the hand; invitations to even casual gatherings never reached my mother's phone line. I had promised myself to God (or at least to relative goodness) and I knew the True Enemy to be within—I thought Good Enough would satiate the Crowd—I knew Good Enough would be more than enough for most parishioners, enough to keep them from strangling their wives, or diddling their daughters, or drowning their neighbors' cats.

A belief system requires little but helplessness and ordained ignorance. I had killed—I had been a god. Jesus: what's in a name? If my faith could kill, it could also save.

Jesus moved out of the back of my head after my realization and didn't bother to leave a forwarding address. I assumed He'd become a roomie of Johnny Galoshes. He did, however, leave a mess and years later, I'm still cleaning it up; the vestiges of organized hoo-ha are not easily overthrown. It's another struggle, not all that different from the Penis Wars of old: True Faith—my faith —requires a persistent effort, a little dirt removed from the prison wall, bent spoon by bent spoon, until the utensil becomes the object of affection, becomes the very definition of Holy.

Jenny is my bent spoon—if I save Jenny, I am absolved from What Happened Next. And despite the efforts of the Lucifer within, of the fallen angels banished and huddled inside my bowels, despite my attempt (and abject failure) to compose the murder of Mrs. Winter, to strangle her with the shackles of her own superstition, a good night's sleep and a healthy sheet stain can buttress a soul, can dissolve Lucifer into just so many gas pains. My own heart was defeated by Jenny's ramparts— without faith and prayer, I can write Mrs. Winter into the ground all the live long day—but like the actor hidden behind the werewolf's makeup, the best parts are usually the hidden ones—and I keep my faith hidden. The angels I've swallowed swell my stomach; I know I've devoured the lion. And as I scribble in my journal, medical books surround my body; my bed is awash in words that float over my head until I wrestle them into understanding.

And it is through that understanding, it is through the freedom practiced by Cool Elvis: the idea that there's little to lose so don't fucking hedge anything—*that I will save Jenny from a life sheltered. My sacrifice? I quit smoking—as much to focus my thinking as to make a good faith offering. And even as I sniff my fingers, the last vapors of Lucifer's gastric-hell assault my nostrils. Enough writing; time to study, time to prepare the battleground. Faith and prayer, redemption and retribution…*

"Oh Lord, won't you buy me a color TV…"

The Judas Moment 1

Recorded here is but one of the Acts of an Apostle, during a Time Shortly Prior to What Happened Next and the Subsequent Seminary Stay and Taking of the Holy Vows, presented, for the Sake of Clarity, in the Form of a Brief Play.

This is the Crowing of the Cock.

This is the Handing Over of the Thirty Pieces of Silver:

HUMPER

Am I doing something wrong?

DONALD THE FAIR

No, it's not you. Maybe I should have a drink.

HUMPER

Would you like me better if I was a boy?

DONALD THE FAIR

I'm sorry?

HUMPER

I think I would like to be a boy. I would like to have a dick. It's not complicated equipment. You just tug on it.

DONALD THE FAIR

Right. I should go.

HUMPER

The Crowd knows. I know. I think I know.

DONALD THE FAIR

They know?

HUMPER

Who's Johnny Galoshes?

DONALD THE FAIR

How do they know? Galoshes? No, I don't know him.

HUMPER

Wasn't that Tammy sucking you off at the party last year?

DONALD THE FAIR

I passed out. I don't know.

HUMPER

Yes, you do. I watched.

DONALD THE FAIR

Why are you asking if you watched? I was trashed. I don't remember.
I don't know. Maybe.

HUMPER

Makes 'em feel dirty, Donnie. They trusted you because you're going
to be a priest and all—then you go and do this—this thing...

DONALD THE FAIR

...with Tammy?

HUMPER

Shit, no. You just said it happened because you were drunk. Looked
to me like you were having the same problem then as here. Least you
finished with Tammy.

DONALD THE FAIR

Right.

HUMPER

I mean they *really* trusted you, looked up to you. I did too. I told you
things. But now, maybe, you're getting off on those things. Maybe
those things are making you excited in a way that I can't, but a slut
like Tammy can when you're fucked up. You sure you don't know
Johnny Galoshes?

DONALD THE FAIR

Never heard of him. You've got the wrong man, lady.

HUMPER

Hmm. Is that—what do you call it?—the True Bible Truth?

DONALD THE FAIR

Please—drop it. The Crowd knows what, Deb?

HUMPER

You must like girls a little bit, right? I mean you asked out Her Holiness Emily, before she—

DONALD THE FAIR

Emily.

HUMPER

I was there too, Donnie. You asked her to your prom. Last year. At the same party as the Tammy Incident.

DONALD THE FAIR

I skipped the prom.

HUMPER

If you asked Emily out, you must like girls, right? If you can come for Tammy, you must get off on girls too, right?

DONALD THE FAIR

Emily Who Smelled Like Flowers.

HUMPER

Does this feel good when I put it in my mouth?

DONALD THE FAIR

Is she dead?

HUMPER

Your penis is a "she," Donnie?

DONALD THE FAIR

Emily.

HUMPER

No, she's still walking on water.

DONALD THE FAIR

She's not dead?

HUMPER

Nothing? What if I use my teeth a little? Move my tongue around a bit?

DONALD THE FAIR

Maybe my mind's on my studies.

HUMPER

My shirt's off, and you haven't even looked at me. Not touched me. Nothing.

DONALD THE FAIR

Maybe I'm abstaining.

HUMPER

Kiss me at least.

DONALD THE FAIR

Okay.

HUMPER

Close your eyes.

DONALD THE FAIR

Then I can't see.

HUMPER

Do you have to see to know I'm kissing you?

DONALD THE FAIR

So, the Crowd—they're not happy with me?

HUMPER

I told them about Tammy sucking you off, but everyone knows you were fucked up.

DONALD THE FAIR

But I asked Emily to my prom.

HUMPER

And you also ramble on and on about someone else every time you drink.

DONALD THE FAIR

Ouch.

HUMPER

Sorry. Shouldn't talk with my mouth full.

DONALD THE FAIR

Who?

HUMPER

Me. I said I shouldn't talk with my mouth full.

DONALD THE FAIR

No, no. Who do I ramble on about?

HUMPER

Donnie, you know. Jesus, what the hell am I doing wrong here?

DONALD THE FAIR

I don't know what you're talking about?

HUMPER

Your friend. Ronnie. I'm talking about Ronnie.

DONALD THE FAIR

Ronnie? I haven't seen him in—I haven't seen Ronnie since we walked to the mall that day. Remember, Big Mike was pissed that we were singing along to Elvis on Craig's boom box?

HUMPER

Big Mike.

DONALD THE FAIR

Shit, sorry.

HUMPER

He doesn't know I'm here.

DONALD THE FAIR

You know, maybe I should just—

HUMPER

What are you doing?

DONALD THE FAIR

Pulling my pants up, Deb. I can't do this. You're Big Mike's girlfriend. It's not right.

HUMPER

Look, no, sit down, Donnie. What Mike doesn't know, blah, blah, blah. I mean, I love him and all, don't get me wrong. But, it's like…

DONALD THE FAIR

Yes?

HUMPER

…like he's John the Baptist.

DONALD THE FAIR

Jesus Christ.

HUMPER

I'm just trying to use terms, you know, you're familiar with.

DONALD THE FAIR

Right.

HUMPER

What did Emily have that I don't?

DONALD THE FAIR

Emily is…was…

HUMPER

Don't tense up on me…get it? *"Past, present future tense…say it so it makes some sense."*

DONALD THE FAIR

Emily…I don't know…Emily is—

HUMPER

Dead?

DONALD THE FAIR

Dead.

HUMPER

I was just trying to help fill in the blanks.

DONALD THE FAIR

Dead.

HUMPER

They know, that's all I'm saying. I don't know how, but the Crowd knows. You were the geek, and now you're closer to God. Impending Holy Orders and all that. See, they trusted you. When all else was going dark, you brought some light. You simplified things by showing them that sometimes the roughest path, the path less tread upon, if you pardon the cliché, is actually the path of least resistance. But then they find out you're, well, maybe not fully gay, but at least half-gay.

DONALD THE FAIR

Half-gay?

HUMPER

What do you call it?

DONALD THE FAIR

I'm not gay.

HUMPER

What are you doing with Ronnie?

DONALD THE FAIR

I haven't seen Ronnie since that time we drank in the Bowl, up on the bleachers.

HUMPER

Look.

DONALD THE FAIR

Yeah?

HUMPER

This. Where did you get this bruise?

DONALD THE FAIR

Fell.

HUMPER

I know they pushed you in school.

DONALD THE FAIR

They were just messing about. No biggie.

HUMPER

You have a little crown of bruises here.

DONALD THE FAIR

Monkey business.

HUMPER

The Crowd's not happy. They feel like they believed in you, they unburdened themselves to you, and then, when it counts most: end of the school year, graduation, prom, etc., you turn out to be a faggot.

DONALD THE FAIR

Listen, Deb, the last time I saw Ronnie was in the hallway in school. I swear.

HUMPER

Is it worth it, Donnie? All of this: is it worth it? We all thought you wanted to be a priest. We all thought you were going to enter the seminary.

DONALD THE FAIR

I am!

HUMPER

With all this on your soul? With your own Crowd backing you against a wall? A virgin—with girls?

DONALD THE FAIR

Deb!

HUMPER

See, you can get hard.

DONALD THE FAIR

Stop, stop.

HUMPER

They're going to turn against you. They trusted you with their dirty little secrets. They confessed their sins, threw out the bath water, whatever.

DONALD THE FAIR

Shit.

HUMPER

Feels good? See, you can do this sober.

DONALD THE FAIR

But I haven't changed, Deb. I'm still the same person I always was.

HUMPER

You don't even know you change, Donnie. You should have seen yourself at that party. Yeah, you had enough beers to confront Ol' Emily Who Was Full of Shit, but then your funny *bons mots* became little stink bombs, and your breath was curdled like milk. You changed. I watched you. Big Mike was busy punching pencils through beer cans in the kitchen. I was watching you. I saw you change.

DONALD THE FAIR
So this is to set me straight. So to speak.

HUMPER
Call it whatever you like, Donnie. I wanted to be here with you. I want to help you because the guys, they're not real happy right now, and who knows what's going to happen next.

DONALD THE FAIR
Like a mercy fuck.

HUMPER
Donnie, if I had to choose between Big Mike and you, say the word, and I shall be healed. I'm yours.

DONALD THE FAIR
Okay, then. Mercy.

HUMPER
Am I squeezing too hard? You're drooping.

DONALD THE FAIR
They were just messing around in school. Horseplay.

HUMPER
Donnie, you were the donkey. You were the ass. No horseplay. I'm telling you. Trust me.

DONALD THE FAIR
I don't understand.

HUMPER
Remember in grade school, when you hit puberty? Like seventh or eighth grade. Remember? And you started growing peach fuzz on your upper lip and scraggly sideburns.

DONALD THE FAIR

Yeah?

HUMPER

And the Crowd started calling you Wolf Man and Lon Chaney Jr. and shit like that?

DONALD THE FAIR

Yeah?

HUMPER

And then they stopped. Do you know why they stopped?

DONALD THE FAIR

No.

HUMPER

Because it started happening to them. You just discovered it first. Until they felt their bodies changing, you were a freak. Same thing is happening now, except they're experiencing sex, or something like it, with just girls.

DONALD THE FAIR

What are you saying?

HUMPER

I'm offering you the world, Donnie. I'm offering you dominion over everything. Worship me and all this is yours. Trust me when I say you won't be disappointed.

DONALD THE FAIR

Matthew 4:9. The Morning Star in his fairest form..

HUMPER

That's sweet. Who is Johnny Galoshes?

DONALD THE FAIR

I don't know him, I tell you.

HUMPER

Donnie, if your eye offends thee, pluck it out.

DONALD THE FAIR

Deb?

HUMPER

They'll do it for you. The boys want so much to be saved from all this. It's too much for them.

DONALD THE FAIR

What are you saying?

HUMPER

Is this doing anything for you? You've completely flat lined here.

DONALD THE FAIR

Give him up?

HUMPER

Yeah. Sometimes people just get led astray. Maybe that's what happened to you. Ronnie was drifting away from everyone anyway. Just bring him to us.

DONALD THE FAIR

Big Mike is drifting.

HUMPER

Yeah, but just to another crowd, his future frat crowd. Big Mike's just slipping away to another drinking level. This is different. Nothing?

DONALD THE FAIR

I feel like my insides are in pieces, Deb. I feel like my bones are floating away toward the ceiling, seeking—I don't know what— seeking the stars, maybe. And it's so dark, Deb, so dark I can't see my hand in front of my face.

HUMPER

It's always darkest before the...do not go gentle into that good...I never drink— wine.

DONALD THE FAIR

Deb, I can show you where we meet sometimes. I can bring the Crowd to where Ronnie's parents or whoever won't be around.

HUMPER

Do this and everyone will like you again, Donnie. You'll be back in. You can enter the seminary intact.

DONALD THE FAIR

Is that your alarm clock?

HUMPER

Yeah, I stick it under my pillow. It goes off three times before I can even get my ass out of bed, but the bell is so loud, I get pissed off each time, so I stick it under there.

DONALD THE FAIR

Sounds like a bag of coins.

HUMPER

You're not concentrating.

DONALD THE FAIR

Try your mouth again.

HUMPER

You'll bring him to us?

DONALD THE FAIR

I'll bring him to you. Deb, watch your teeth.

HUMPER

You'll be remembered forever for this.

DONALD THE FAIR

I should go.

HUMPER

And not only that, but you'll have me, Donnie—at least before you take up the collar. Big Mike's going away to college. Between me and keggers, you know the choice.

DONALD THE FAIR
He likes his beer.

HUMPER
We were each other's second choices anyway.

DONALD THE FAIR
His first was beer.

HUMPER
Mine was—

DONALD THE FAIR
Ouch, Deb! Your ring.

HUMPER
Bring him to us, and everything will be cool, Donnie, including you.

DONALD THE FAIR
Is that the sun coming up?

HUMPER
What are you, a vampire?

DONALD THE FAIR
No. A werewolf.

HUMPER
Raise the bar, Captain.

DONALD THE FAIR
I should go.

HUMPER
Pretty good wages for one little kiss.

DONALD THE FAIR
Have you seen my socks?

HUMPER

No money shot? Get a little something for your trouble, Donnie.

DONALD THE FAIR

Deb, come on, let me go. You're going to choke me.

HUMPER

My noose hold!

DONALD THE FAIR

Let me go, Deb.

HUMPER

I thought this was what you wanted.

DONALD THE FAIR

I appreciate it. I do, Deb. But I have to go.

HUMPER

Get out, hurry, they're waiting.

The Book of Winter 5

The priest wanted a cigarette, and watching Mrs. Winter pull on a Merit made the muscles in his calves twitch. He leaned on his pile of books.

"It's rare," said the priest.

"This condition?" said Mrs. Winter.

"Yes."

"And this is what you believe, considering your years of medical training, is 'wrong' with my Jenny?"

The priest blushed.

"If nothing else, Joyce, it couldn't hurt to take her to a specialist."

When Mrs. Winter laughed, the smoke exited her nose like two jet streams.

"Father—we don't have health insurance. Hell, Fred don't bring home what he used to."

"Maybe the Church could help, Joyce. There's plenty of wonderful programs."

Again, the twin afterburners.

The priest glanced around at Mrs. Winter's house of piles. The donkey chair was in the corner, but a tower of yellowed laundry was piled high upon it, and a few magazines and torn envelopes were perched on top of the laundry. The house was quiet—no Gloria bellowing from beneath an ashtray on the couch, no television blaring. If Jenny was home, she must be standing absolutely still. Nothing this morning disturbed the layers of dust demarcating newer objects from possessions that had long ago settled.

"I saw Him again, you know."

Mrs. Winter's eyes crinkled like a laugh.

The priest's mouth was sucked dry of saliva. He would kill for a cigarette. He would suck off Christ himself for a cigarette.

The priest cleared his Sahara throat.

"At the parade?"

Mrs. Winter squeezed her eyes shut and looked down at her ashtray, little chuckles expelling like Merit smoke.

"No, no, no, Father. Nothing like that. This was when Gloria had the food poisoning and was at Friends Hospital."

"Joyce, Friends Hospital is a psychiatric facility."

Mrs. Winter waved her stubby hand at him.

"Food poisoning can do some strange things to people, Father."

The priest chose to ignore her explanation and carefully sipped at his coffee, mentally prepared for another peanut butter onslaught from the heavens.

"But, there I was visiting Miss Gloria, and she wasn't doing too well. They had her on all kinds of medication, and my Gloria wasn't saying much, just lying there and drooling. She wouldn't go to the therapies, but I understood that. What good was that going to do against food poisoning? But I went everyday to visit, and finally, this one time, Gloria's sitting up in bed, and she wants out. I tell her I can't help her, that it's up to Dr. Scavager. She's cursing and screaming and clawing at herself. The nurse has to come in with some other people and give her a big shot to calm her down. Probably vegetable oil, that's what I thought. That's what my father always gave to me and my brothers to lower us a notch. And they strapped Gloria's arms and feet down. It was all so confusing, Father. I asked the one nurse why the straps, and she says withdrawal symptoms, and I say to myself, 'For food poisoning?' The nurse says to me that maybe I should leave and let Gloria get her rest, so I lean forward to give her a kiss, and Gloria spits in my face. Well, I can tell you, I was mighty upset. Gloria's screaming still, and the nurse is guiding me out, and Gloria's thrashing against her straps. I'm asking the nurse to undo the buckles; the straps are chafing her skin and that's why Gloria's screaming so, but the nurse just leads me out of the room, and, bang, like that, I'm in the elevator heading down to the lobby, and I can hear Gloria's screaming in the back of my head, like a radio turned down too low to make out the singer, but just loud enough to hear the tippy-tops of the drums and brushes. Nice, God, nice, I'm thinking."

Mrs. Winter lit another Merit and picked up an onion from a basket at the end of the table.

"Jenny's waiting on me in the lobby and even though it's two floors down, I know she could hear her mother screaming in the back of her head too. I just brush it off and out of my skull, and then it's gone from Jenny's as well. Just like that."

The priest nodded. Mrs. Winter began peeling the onion.

"So we have to cross the grounds to get to catch the bus, and I figure, since it's nice out and kind of a short cut, we should just cut through the near side instead of minding the path. And I'm so angry with God. The trees were all bloomed that time of year, and it was like you could hear the prayers of the leaves as they sprouted from the trees. Now, Gloria's gone from my head, but I'm railing in there—I'm telling God, really yelling now, that he needs to let Gloria leave so she can go back to the couch and the television—she can't be comfortable in that hospital bed, all tied up in those leather straps. And I guess I'm crying a little—Gloria's my daughter, after all. I'm holding Jenny's hand, and I'm crying, but I'm trying not to let it show. I'm tying it up in the bundle where I've kept all the bad stuff since I was a little one. Do you know what I mean, Father?"

The priest glanced up from the onion.

"Yes, Joyce. God helps us all with—"

"Do you have a sad bundle, Father?"

"Joyce?"

"Do you have a special place where you hide all your sorrows? Where you hide all your secrets, Father?"

Mrs. Winter peeled another layer from the onion, and the priest could feel his eyes water. He didn't know if this was from the onion or not.

"I think we all have a place inside where we bury things that are unpleasant."

Mrs. Winter smiled and nodded her head.

"Bury. That's a good word, Father."

"Joyce, we should be talking about Jenny."

Mrs. Winter pulled a large knife from beneath a pile of newspapers and began dicing the onion.

"And there He was, just sitting beneath an apple tree. He must have just finished an apple or two 'cause there were a few cores lying around Him. The squirrels were just nibbling at them, not paying any attention to us at all. He's just sitting there, talking to the squirrels in a low voice, like a soft little wave –like an undertow, slowly pulling you in. There He was."

"Jesus?"

Mrs. Winter looked up at the priest. Her hands continued to manipulate the knife.

"Of course, Father. Haven't you been listening?"

"Jesus."

"Now, I didn't recognize Him right off. I was too awash in my pain. I see Him, just having a sit beneath that old apple tree, speaking with the squirrels. But something tugs at the corners of my eyes—I know this man. So I say to Him, 'Don't I know you?' and He answers back, not turning His head from the little squirrels, 'You used to.' Then He looks at Jenny, and she runs to Him, and He hugs her tight. The squirrels stayed put; they didn't run away. I'm just standing there, my mouth probably all hanging open, and the man with the soft looking beard slowly lifts His head so His eyes meet mine, and we're both swimming in it a little, or maybe it's just me, trying to look through all that water. 'I think Jennifer here needs to go home. I believe she wants some peanut butter, Joyce.' Jesus held Jenny's chin in His hand. 'What's so good about simple old peanut butter, Jennifer? Can you tell me?' And Jenny says back to Him, clear as the outdoors, 'It makes everything stick together in my stomach. It helps my bones.' And Jesus laughs. 'See Joyce? It makes everything stick together. Take our Jennifer home.' So I do. We catch the 57 bus, and we eat peanut butter sitting on the front stoop, Jenny sitting a step below, between my legs, as I pulled apple blossoms out of her tangle of hair."

The priest clutched at his little pile of books: his Bible, the medical books he borrowed from the library, the little catechism he brought for Jenny. Empty talismans, he thought, fingering the little bottle of holy water in his trouser pocket. Empty against real belief no matter how delusional, no matter how fucked up. The priest counted in his head the number of shops on the way back to the rectory that sold cigarettes.

"Will you be staying for dinner, Father? The kids call this my kamikaze coleslaw 'cause I use onions in there. I do love my onions so."

The ceiling creaked, and the priest could hear padded feet moving quickly overhead.

"Is Jenny…?"

The priest could smell it—it overtook even the ingredients of the kamikaze coleslaw. He looked down at his coffee cup, and it was filled with it—huge chunks of peanut butter floating in the mud colored coffee. The smell made the air thick, and when he looked up, Mrs. Winter was staring at him with a fistful of onions in one hand and the knife in the other. A trickle of blood oozed between the fingers squeezing the onions.

"I do believe I cut myself. I love you."

The priest left the house, the books still on the table, and stopped at every convenience store on his way to the rectory, buying packs of cigarettes, smoking two, and crushing the rest under his Florsheims, until by the time he reached his room, he had smoked twelve of them and could no longer smell peanut butter on the back of his hands.

March 9, 4:47 a.m.

"God will give you the strength, as much as you lack, because it is necessary—it is necessary for me to be killed and for you to betray me. We two must save the world. Help me."

Judas bowed his head. After a moment he asked, "If you had to betray your master, would you do it?"

Jesus reflected for a long time. Finally he said, "No, I do not think I would be able to. That is why God pitied me and gave me the easier task: to be crucified."

Nikos Kazantzakis, *The Last Temptation of Christ*

Exegesis:

My fingers are red like I've been lying in the snow, like I've been making snow angels all morning, like I've been chopping my fingers up in the onions. It's my fault, I know. I am the cause. I am the endgame. And I feel NOTHING. Numb. I can find no comfort. If I don't save Jenny soon, the stain of What Happened Next will become a birthmark. The faith I wear so proudly upon my sloped shoulders is slipping off, becoming lost...

I think I can hear Ronnie's voice when I'm taking a shower.

I think I can smell Ronnie's hair from the other side of an empty confessional.

I will fashion a crown of thorns.

I will sleep on a bare floor.

Am I chosen or am I atoning?

I will embark on a hunger strike.

I will say His name until my true nature is revealed.

Am I damned or am I the one who damns?

And I'm remembering my buried treasure, my big bronze cough drop tin, the one I used to collect and hide my TREASURES in: the initial ring my parents bought for me after my Confirmation; the pearl rosary that belonged to my grandmother; my scapular; a picture of a girl, taken from behind, with short dark hair, wearing clean white underwear, the edges of which crept up enough to reveal her bottom to me, that I had torn from one of my mother's catalogs; the list of books I had read, the list I thought separated me from the animals tossing various balls upon various fields at school, balls I could barely throw or catch or bounce or kick. It was one of those damn books, it was Treasure Island, that slid the idea under my nine year old radar, and before I thought about the consequences, I was wearing an eye patch fashioned from construction paper held together with a rubber band, burying my pirate treasure, my cough drop tin, out behind the holly tree in the backyard near where my father had buried the guinea pigs and rabbits. The plan was that I would dig the tin out in fourteen years (the number of the Stations of the Cross), at which time I had calculated my objects of affection would have gained in value and I would be rich, rich enough to sit up front in church, where my father said all the rich people sat to be seen.

But it was like cigarettes or vodka or, well, you know—the need gnawed at the back of my neck, the backs of my legs, the tips of my fingers, the sheen on my lips. I couldn't wait fourteen years; I couldn't wait fourteen days. I needed my objects of affection. All the prayers in the world couldn't stop me from grabbing my little shovel early one Saturday spring morning, before my parents arose, trudging out past Mother's little carefully cultivated vegetable garden to my own little bed of despair. Suddenly, the small area between the rusted back fence and the curve of the holly tree (holy tree?) seemed to have grown into an acre at least. I no longer had a clue where I had buried my treasure chest. So I dug. I dug and pulled at dirt and roots all morning, ditching the plastic sand shovel for the sound my fingernails made hitting the hard ground. And while digging, the sun was dappled in my eyes, and I saw how far away the Crowd was, felt the wind tunnel separating me from the beliefs of my parents. By the time my mother found me, I was covered in brown dirt, little pieces of animal bones encircling me, babbling about pirate treasure, Kamikaze Ball, Johnny Galoshes.

And I am there again: now even my faith appears to be lost, and I am surrounded by bones. My fingers are red like I've been lying in the snow. I am beyond guilty, and I am surrounded by bones. Bones I know.

The Judas Moment 2

Recorded here is Yet Again a Specific Act of an Apostle, presented, for reasons of heightening, somewhat, the Dramatic Tension of our Morality Tale, as a Flashback occurring during the Ritual of Communion, in which our Priest, calling upon a Deity whose True Name he has long ago forgotten, transforms Wafers and Wine into the Body and Blood of an Executed Savior.

This is the Betrayal in Gethsemane.

This is What Happened Next:

Sung: *Dying you destroyed our death, rising you restored our life.*

The Priest: *Lord, you are holy indeed, the fountain of all holiness.*

> And there I was, not twenty-four hours later, fully aroused, pounding away at Ronnie's ass like it was made of clay, and I was God fashioning Eve from a stray rib.

The Priest: *Let your Spirit come upon these gifts to make them holy…*

> While Ronnie slept, snoring the kettle drums of the drunkenly satiated, I knelt for reasons other than oral satisfaction and asked God to help me, begged God to rescue me from my wayward, queer desires and needs. Still on my knees, I wrote a letter to God, a mash note, if truth be told, swearing fidelity in all matters, and asking for this sin to be removed from my plate, for my plate was surely full. And when I awoke in my own bed, pillow between my legs, I wasn't sure it hadn't happened.

The Priest: *…so that they may become for us the body and blood of our Lord Jesus Christ.*

> I left Ronnie a note inside a copy of the *Elvis is Back* album, from which I had removed the original vinyl,

replacing it with the *Roustabout* soundtrack. *"Meet me in Gethsemane,"* the note read, for it was in the underbrush surrounding the outside of McDonald's where we used to meet if Ronnie's parents were home. *"Meet me in Gethsemane, seven o'clock,"* the note read, deliberately using code known only to Ronnie and myself so that, in case of a dire situation, no connection could be made between Ronnie's walk several blocks to McDonalds's and What Would Happen Next. As I waited behind the Drive-Thru sign, the smell of burnt meat making my eyes water and my throat catch, I combed my hair in the sign's greasy reflection, the full moon an unblinking eye above me, the stars all scattered. My stomach grumbled, for it was empty. I longed for it to be filled.

The Priest: *Before He was given up to death, a death He freely accepted...*

I could hear them rustling in the bushes. I could hear the way my lies traveled from throat to ear and back again, still worthy of inspection hours after confession, my lies were fed and expanded until they were bloated enough so that not one of the disciples hiding behind the row of cluttered berry bushes could ever imagine me with a cock in my mouth, let alone enjoying it. After ensconcing the disciples, after making sure Ritchie stayed awake (the war tonic of choice had been copious amounts of Budweiser in cans), I trod to where I now stood, the moon staring through my hiding place, picking the blood red berries from the bottoms of my sneakers, their trails like snails' blood whispering on the black tar of our neighborhood McDonald's. I could hear Big Mike pissing his Budweiser in the bushes.

The Priest: *...He took bread and gave you thanks. He broke the bread, gave it to His disciples, and said: Take this, all of you, and eat it: this is my body, which will be given up for you.*

Behind the blaring yellow sign, I pulled at the hair on the side of my face. My father had once offered to teach me to shave, but I knew this night would be my True Bible

Truth rite of passage, more so than pubic hair or masturbation or the deepening of my voice, for, although I managed to jerk off several times a day, this was to be my Bar Mitzvah. If I passed, I would be a man. Men do not suck dick. That was what Big Mike had said. All the disciples had laughed. "If Ronnie wants to suck dick, then maybe removing a few teeth might help," Big Mike had said. Ronnie was Big Mike's best friend. But this was how these things went. Someone in the berry bushes farted, and someone else hushed a warning, and the footfalls of my friend, my lover, my confidant, could be heard on Castor Avenue.

The Priest: *When supper was ended, He took the cup. Again, He gave you thanks and praise, gave the cup to His disciples, and said: Take this, all of you, and drink from it…*

And there was Johnny Galoshes, in all his cowboy-booted splendor, Fonzie cool, Elvis cool, Jerry Lee's pompadour raging a few inches in the air, his confident boots smacking the throbbing drum beat of a man who believes he is about to get laid. When the boot falls angled at the corner, past the medical supply store, cutting through the Synagogue driveway to hit the McDonald's blacktop, I could see Johnny was Ronnie and that Ronnie had always been Johnny—I had used and abandoned them both— and like Iscariot before me, I knew my fate, I had always known my fate. Ronnie's sister had told him, right in front of me: "You're gonna get your ass kicked someday," but we couldn't understand how she would know of our illicit liaisons, of our stubborn and awkward gropes; we allowed her words to grow and fester unheeded, and yet, here they were: her words seconds away from flowering in full bloom, like the way the sink filled with my father's blood when he had cut himself shaving.

The Priest: *…this is the cup of my blood…*

I heard them: *werewolf, werewolf, werewolf,* and before Big

Mike shushed them, I realized that it was I who effected the miracle of changing my skin—a miracle I would sustain later upon taking my vows and swearing my fidelity to God. I stepped out from behind the sign, and Ronnie smiled, his teeth white and scary in the moonlight, in the glow of sickly McDonald's yellow, in the smell of the sacrifice of hundreds upon thousands of cows. "Donnie," Ronnie's skull said to me, and his Dockers—no cowboy boots—crested the slight hill I stood upon, the Drive-Thru sign on my right, the berry bushes on my left. "You want me to come to you, is that it?" Ronnie said and laughed, a genuine expression of solidarity and carefree good humor. "I'm not kneeling down in those berries, Donnie," Ronnie said, and the smile didn't leave his face, not even when Big Mike struck his hand out and smashed a fistful of berries into Ronnie's jaw. *Werewolf, werewolf, werewolf,* they cried. *Werewolf, werewolf, werewolf,* they chanted, and upon Ronnie's painted visage, the smile turned itself into a question mark as I stepped back behind the sign.

The Priest: ...*the blood of the new and everlasting covenant.*

I didn't need to kiss his cheek; the berries left a mark like my mother used to leave on my face when she and my father embarked on an evening out together, light years before the ritual of Thursday Nights Out. Only the blood-red berry kiss didn't come with explicit admonishments and behavior-rattling encouragements on how to spend one's evening. This kiss smeared like a beetle does after it is trod upon and dragged the length of a school playground. *Werewolf, werewolf, werewolf.* They picked Ronnie up and kicked his balls and pummeled his jaw line and broke his nose, and I swear I saw two of his teeth sitting near a dirt-encrusted bag of french fries, one of the teeth appearing to sink into a spot of grease as if gorging itself. *Werewolf, werewolf, werewolf.* My mother never left the house anymore; her kisses came only with the stale breath of an expired star, fallen far from the sky, like the way Ronnie's teeth were expelled from his mouth.

Ronnie's smile was permanent now, more a grin, really, and he never took his eyes off me, not if he could help it, and I tried to stay hidden behind the Drive-Thru sign, but the moon was full, and my true nature was revealed among the scattered stars of the sky like blood on the white remains of shaving cream, like blood staining the tips of Dockers bought by parents wanting their son to be in fashion. *Werewolf, werewolf, werewolf.* An old Styrofoam container was squashed onto Ronnie's head as he fell near the berry bushes. Big Mike pulled out his penis and pissed into the Styrofoam. Ronnie kept looking at me, marking me like I imagined God had marked Cain: KNOW THIS MAN FOR HE HATH KILLED A BROTHER. *Werewolf, werewolf, werewolf.* The pack looked hungry for more, they looked sorry, they looked sad, someone tried to help Ronnie from the ground and someone else pushed his hands away. Some started at me, but stepped aside, bewildered, for they knew now that what was previously only whispered was in fact True Bible Truth. Some wiped their hands on their jeans. Someone, Big Mike maybe, tried to stifle a cry that sounded like an animal giving up the ghost, and its cornet-like blare heralded the retreat of the disciples. Ronnie moaned, and a bubble of crimson emerged from the place where his teeth should have been and popped audibly. I walked backwards for a few steps, crossed myself, and, turning, ran to Humper's house.

The Priest: *It will be shed for you and for all so that sins may be forgiven. Do this in memory of me.*

Humper was crying in the dark and everything felt a little bit like that scene in *West Side Story* after Bernardo and Riff were killed, but Ronnie was alive. Ronnie didn't die. This wasn't the story of Ronnie's death, but of a friendship extinguished, and Humper found herself naked and wet, and my trembling body entered hers, and despite Big Mike's boasts and brags, I could tell she was a virgin because she was so scared—I was too—but I did it again and again, pulling out on her stomach, until I was empty, until every bit of poison had seeped from my body. When I crawled from the dark, Humper was weeping again, and when I found myself home, I stood in the bathroom and stripped my clothes off, alternately reveling in the loss of my virginity, and drowning in my double cross, wondering if Ronnie was still lying in his own spit and blood in the McDonald's Drive-Thru lane, the smell of burnt cow heavy in his nostrils, the grease scent tickling the little ball in the back of his throat. As I peeled off my underwear, I mistook the crimson on my fingertips for Ronnie's blood, until a rapid inspection of my genitalia revealed that it too was covered in red and sticky to the touch. My cries woke my mother, who rushed into the bathroom, and I was revealed in all my naked, blood covered glory. My mother knelt before me, and heedless of embarrassment or other more classical psychological manifestations, manipulated my penis and testicles, and washed them down with a warm Scooby Doo washcloth. My mother turned away as if to look for my father, and I imagined him shaking his head as if to indicate that, no, not every teenage boy suffers from genital bleeding. But my father was in the Holy Land of South Jersey. My mother asked me her name, and at first I wasn't sure who she meant, but after a moment I said "Deb," and my mother nodded, not affiliating "Deb" with my childhood friend "Humper," and it was my turn to shake—not from fear, but from the fact that I had nearly uttered Ronnie's name instead. I was not afraid of the blood anymore. God had brought this blood to me, much in the way I had brought the blood to Ronnie. "She was menstruating, Donald," my mother was saying, but I didn't hear her. I was praying. I was praying for Ronnie. And I was thanking God. I was thanking God for taking this cup away from me. And I was promising I would make it all right someday. I knew, even then, the cost of being saved.

The Priest: *Let us proclaim the mystery of faith: Dying you destroyed our death, rising you restored our life. Lord Jesus, come in glory.*

The Book of Winter 6

The fire started in the left bedroom. Someone tried to pour some candle wax from a coffee saucer. The candle fell into the trashcan and that someone panicked and ran out of the house, leaving her mother and daughter asleep in the next room. No one else was home at the Winter house. The flames ate their way out of the left bedroom, licked their way through the square hallway, and split into two: one line going down the wooden banister to the first floor, the other flames remaining behind to burn the flesh away from Mrs. Winter and Jenny until only their bones remained.

I love you.

This the priest learned days later from the firemen who fought their way into the left bedroom from the back alley window. The priest came to the firehouse to say a prayer for their companion, a Catholic fireman, whose confession the priest had heard on the spot at the fire zone—the man had wanted forgiveness for cheating on his wife, had wanted the ability to stop her suffering so she could begin her life again. The fireman had made a quick act of contrition, the whole process taking no more than forty-five seconds, and then rushed into the burning building. He never came out, although the priest sat on the curb long past dawn, awaiting his return. The fire engines and the police cars and the ambulance that carried away no survivors were long gone.

I love you.

That night, the priest fought his way through a bottle of vodka and called the police station twice to surrender. The first time they sent a squad car but found his babbling to be just that and departed after a cautionary word to Father Sailor, who escorted the besotted priest to his bed. The second time, they didn't even send a squad car. The priest vomited in his sleep and escaped death only by rolling off the bed when he heard himself scream, "I love you" in a dream.

March 13, 3:39 a.m.

"Yea, mine own familiar friend,
in whom I trusted, which did eat of my bread,
hath lifted up his heel against me."
Psalms 41:9

Exegesis:

Judas is the most fascinating character in the entire Bible, for he alone, although appearing to have free will, seems to have been used and then apparently abandoned. He makes Job look like a piker. And, oh, how Judas saved the day! But there was to be no redemption for Judas despite his diligence. Judas' vocation was betrayer, and he suffered much for being the Chosen One. It's all in the Old Testament, if you ask the True Believers. His treachery of Jesus was predicted— but was it predestined?

For years I struggled to understand Judas' position. If Judas didn't do it, would someone else have stepped up? Was it a matter of anyone or was Judas the most logical choice? Was God's omniscience such that He knew Judas would choose this path, or was the matter out of the poor apostle's hands? Did Judas hang himself out of remorse for speeding along the death of the Son of Man, or was he distraught at the treatment of his best friend at the hands of the Romans?

I think the latter—I believe the latter. It's the only explanation that makes sense. He didn't betray Jesus for the money, although that's what he took—he betrayed Him, I think, as a way of stopping the madness that was spiraling beyond the sect's control. Judas most likely thought he was doing the right thing and in doing so, hastened the death of his friend, his teacher. Did Judas believe himself to be filled with the lion, or did the lion devour him? It takes more than a little pride to believe in the power to save.

So, yes, he was guilty. Guilty of love. And pride. And so am I. No, I didn't start the fire, but Joyce's burnout daughter was my match. My prayers were answered. I removed Joyce from the picture and rescued Jenny—sort of. Jenny is with the angels now—despite the ignorant Catholic myth of dying unbaptized— and I am sure her suffering is over. And maybe God used me like He used Judas. I gave the Crowd Ronnie in order to save my own skin. And in trying to redeem myself for Ronnie, in trying to save Jenny, I betrayed her too, and gave Jenny back to God. You cannot reverse what has been ordained—even if you started the bleeding yourself.

The wood of the Cross of Jesus is born from the seedlings of Judas' Hanging Tree. It could be no other way. The Cross is a symbol of weight—the weight of knowing God, the weight of feeling his Hand guiding yours. Judas knew this weight, and in the end, he swung for his knowledge, he swayed in the arid wind for playing the part assigned to him. Can something that is spoiled be redeemed?

So I am Judas again, only too frightened to face Him to hang myself. God allowed me to play my part, and I needed very little coaxing. In trying to save Jenny from ignorance, I betrayed her with my own. You could say Jenny died for our sins of nescience and our transgressions in the name of Good Enough. For mine and Mrs. Winter's. For Emily's. For Ronnie's. For Gloria's and for the wanton fireman's.

Only now does my faith come crawling back. It has to: the angels have abandoned my stomach for the disparateness of the stars. Elvis has left the building. And last night, as the owls called to their own echoes in the city night, I knelt among the ashes where Penn Street met Saul Street and begged for forgiveness.

STOP THE TAPE, ARCHANGEL.

Yes, sir. Should I open the gate?

LET HIM BURN FOR A WHILE, ARCHANGEL.
LET HIM BURN. JUST FOR A WHILE.

-end-

Limbo:

Wake Up and Breathe!

This is Limbo.

"Each night in dreams I see your face.
Memories and time cannot erase.
Then I awake and find you're gone.
Then I'm blue and all alone.
So far away from you, so sweet and warm,
Just out of reach of my two empty arms."
Solomon Burke, "Just Out of Reach (Of My Two Empty Arms)"

"I need someone to pull the trigger
'cause there's a hole in my heart getting bigger,
and everything I'll ever be I've been."
Matthew Sweet, "Someone to Pull the Trigger"

"I'm not dead yet!
I'm not dead yet!
Are
you
hungry?"
Lola and the Shivers, "Two Vultures"

1.

"Jean, Jean, you're young and alive;
Come out of your half-dreamed dream
And run, if you will, to the top of the hill;
Open your arms, bonnie Jean."
      Oliver, "Jean"

"WAKE UP AND BREATHE!"

"Wake up and breathe," is what I think she says, but I can barely hear her voice, just the rasps of the traps the cigarettes set the evening before.

"WAKE UP AND BREATHE!"

I am thirty-one years old, and I am lying in bed next to a woman I barely know, a jack-in-the-box of dyed black hair, a woman whose lips sucked me off not a few hours before, after the last drop of gin bounced off my tongue. I am thirty-one years old, and every second of my existence reeks through my bones, rattled as they are in the throes of yet another hangover. I am thirty-one years old, and I have loved—no, no, delete—I *am in love* with two women, neither of whom inhabit the expanse of skin and hair and stale smoke that snores next to me.

My alarm clock is one of those with little number slates, and I can *feel* each click against my teeth, each little passage of time a gun to my head. *Pull the trigger, you bastard, just pull the goddamn trigger.* Then, just when I believe I've passed it, just when I think the warm flow of air in my nostrils signifies the wisps of sleep: CLICK CLICK FUCKING CLICK.

I almost bought a digital clock twice, but each time I felt as if I was losing an old adversary. Click-Clock has been through the whole journey. How could I surrender the battle even at this late, desperate date? But there, behind the fuck dreams, the dead mom dreams, dreams melting events just passed into the trials of the way-past, dreams of apparent whimsy laced with a hint of dread, beyond all the bad '70s songs, lies a pillow of a man between two women. All the CLICKS in the world can't wake me up enough to change that fact.

You know I've loved two women; you know I love them still...

A small diagonal portion of me knew that I needed to find an anchor in a woman I could not project onto—just into. But that didn't quite work out now, did it? Tonight my seed bounced off her stomach, young enough to be smooth, large enough to contain a world of valleys and hills and deadly ripples. This is not a Love Song, this is the Stomach Blues, and oh, boy, have I got them. I'm trapped actually. Never mind the fact that I set the trap and left the bait. I'm here and my loves are far and farther.

"WAKE UP AND BREATHE!"

So Lucille lies next to me. Lucy, to her friends. Lucky Lucille if we happen to be in a bar, playing one of those poker machines. Licky Lucille if she's feeling frisky—I always have to try not to laugh at that one, but I'm usually breathing too hard to rally a good hoot. Lucy Lucille: a cat's name, but instead, my Lucille is a big, friendly dog—not too bright, eager to please. Lucille likes to think of herself as a Tall Glass of Water or a Wake Up Call—a Reality-Check-Your-Hat-and-Coat Girl, she told me once after many swallows of whiskey. Alas, my Lucille is forever peeing on the rug, getting attention, trying to make a sullen, pouty point, leaving a stench even twenty dogs couldn't beat.

She smokes too much, so her night breathing is the sound of dice rattling in a cup. She drinks too much, so her breath frequently has that pungent stench of the recently dead. She fucks too much too—or I should say, she *fucked* too much—not exactly a tight fit, but I'm not really complaining. Lucille wears too much perfume, splashed in every conceivable crevice, but to me, she smells of fresh earth. I can practically see the dirt beneath my fingernails after an attempt at intercourse.

"WAKE UP AND BREATHE!"

The soundtrack in my head reflects—no scratch that—*is* the little tan radio my mom always had playing in the kitchen. And there they are all—stuck in my head like so many needles pricking my brain: the Carpenters, Oliver, Tony Orlando and Dawn, Olivia Newton-John, Gary fucking Wright stage-whispering "Dream Weaver," and more, much *much* more. Their inane choruses resound between my ears until I can no longer think of love without recalling Karen Carpenter or possibly watch a rainfall without hearing Johnny Nash. I often think the reason I can't sleep is because my pre-installed radio turns its own volume up. I often think the reason I stop breathing is to try and kill the pantheon of '70s one-hit-wonders resurrecting their careers right behind my bloodshot eyeballs.

And on the rare occasion when the radio is turned down, it's the Disney records my mother bought for me at Woolworth's, spinning endlessly on my Fisher Price. The '70s were a bitch, man, and they've never left.

I turn my head to watch another hour dive, to witness another measure of time take its own life and plunge from the serrated edge of Click-Clock. My hands naturally stray to the center of my body—I think maybe if I can get it up, I can rouse Lucille and lose myself in her folds of flesh again, but I stop when I notice the only sound is Click-Clock's studious, taunting patterns. No husky intakes of air, no noisy tunnels of wind—no snoring from the other side of the world. *She'd been snoring, right?* I reach across the middle ground and touch not something warm and pliable, but cold and unyielding—AND THEN—like the part in the movie where the music stops and the camera closes in on our hero in his or her Moment of Clarification— IT ALL COMES FLOODING BACK—blood into penis, air into lungs, sun into previously, carefully shaded eyes:

I killed someone last night.

Or tried to.

Or am trying to.

Conjugate and divide.

I check my hands rapidly, take an inventory of my body's extremities, and PUSH my brain against my skull, my memory scratching against the dirt in my head, excavating, shifting grains— nothing. How long have I been asleep? I am so used to *not* sleeping, I barely comprehend a full night of uninterrupted rest. How would I know how long I've slept? Click-Clock is prone to tricks. In the past, I have experienced lifetimes, I have made passionate, noisy, messy love to my Angels for hours upon hours, only to awake and have Click-Clock mock me with an expanse of time no more than seven to ten minutes across. My penis is flaccid, but that doesn't mean a whole hell of a lot anymore—not when it comes to Lucy Lucille.

Is this blood on my hands or just shadows from the street lamp playing across the windowpane?

Did I kill someone last night?

In the back room of my head, behind the locked door with its peeling paint and ether smell, I can hear someone scream, I can *feel* someone's eyes roll upward and away. There's a Solomon Burke song—I think it's Solomon—fighting against the current of '70s corporate musical mediocrity, snaking its way through my ears into my head, and someone, someone with purple sockets for eyes and a girl's mouth, is emptying a set of lungs into the snap of fall air descending upon the dried out city streets. Lucille doesn't stir when I ease out of bed. Lucille, who spends each night deep in her dreams, her body wrestling across the sheets, ungraceful even asleep, her snores battle cries against the encroaching gloom of night and the machinations of Click-Clock, now, quite possibly, the mouth on the other end of the screams twisting just out of range in the back-back of my throbbing skull.

Out of bed—free from the blankets of fire and the sheets of blue ice—I pull my father's suitcase from the top cedar shelf in the closet, running my hands over its cracked façade, feeling the bumps of ancient rust on the gold buckles on top. The suitcase's skin is a map—my father's map—the breaks in the skin like Braille detailing each time he left my mother to dip his wick in the wax portals of just so many eager to please Ball Suckers and Tug Huggers, as my father rendered them in his cups. My father would have liked Lucille; here was a girl prone to sticking things in her mouth for extended periods of time. A Good-to-the-Last-Drop Girl. I wait to see if I can catch a boner from the Lucille Slide Show of Oral Deeds Past, but my body does not respond and the packing commences—just a few concert t-shirts, an extra pair of pants, some socks (none matching) and underwear (the holy variety). Lucille never stirs. Fuck.

I stand before the open window and count the stars dying silently before me. My God, I am bone-tired. Hypnophobia, sleep dread, the doctor called it. I can feel the *years* without sleep upon my skin; I can feel my skin stretch itself to cover the holes where sleep seeped out and loosed itself upon the blotchy skin of fuck-buddies (is that Lucille's true title?) and the pure Sky Castles of my Two Loves, my Angels. Tears drip from my chin and grace my toes before huddling naked like eyeballs out of their sockets upon the hardwood floor. Who did I kill last night? Wake up and breathe, indeed.

I am nobody if not the result of two women, my Angels, neither of whom lies cold and unnaturally silent in this bedroom. Am I Stone-Cold-Killer Boy? Am I like God before His stars, choosing that one and this one, marking them for expiration? Or am I just an old playing card flapping against the spokes in His wheel? I sit on the edge of the bed and pull on my sneakers—the left first, my playful little tug to my cuckolded mother who believed, quite firmly, that the right shoe or the right glove went first for the greater glory of God— and there, on the right tip of the left shoe, a splotch of red. Evidence.

I lay my head back on my pillow and my Theme Song echoes between the scraped bedposts:

You know I've loved two women, you know I love them still...

It's my religion—they are my saints.

I settle my head on the pillow and enumerate the ceaseless deaths of the stars.

2.

"What goes up must come down;
Spinnin' wheel got to go 'round;
Talkin' 'bout your troubles, it's a cryin' sin;
Ride a painted pony let the spinnin' wheel spin."
        Blood, Sweat, and Tears, "Spinning Wheel"

"Is there a boy you've met that you haven't sucked off?"
Alison chewed on the split ends of her uncombed hair.
"Go fuck yourself."
My knuckles flicked white as I gripped the sticky steering wheel.
"No, seriously, how many guys have come in your mouth? I mean, it's got to be a lot. You must have an obscene amount of semen clinging to your stomach walls."
Her body fought a shudder and then went still.
"Everyone except you. Everyone's cock except yours."
Her face was red; her eyes focused on the strands of hair.
I could visualize every time she had sucked someone off, replaying carnal events I had never seen *ad nauseam*, and Alison knew this. She also knew, that despite how verbally violent this was going to get, it was temporary. She could no sooner let me go than I could her. Oh, Alison liked to think of herself as a girl who refused to acknowledge her roots, but they were deep within this five year friendship—sometimes burrowed deeper than she liked, and Alison spent an inordinate amount of time trying to yank the roots from the firm earth, to little avail.
"You say shit like that to get to me. You're just looking for a reaction," I said.
Alison peered from between her curtain of damaged ends.
"Oh, like your blow job questions were just friendly banter? You're a broken record. Go fuck yourself."
I caught an organ swelling from the radio—Otis? No. Maybe some old Marvin number.
"I just don't understand. You criticize your cousin for going out and sleeping with two different guys at the same time, but yet you do

the same thing."

"What do you care? Damien? Why does this make a fucking difference to you?"

Solomon Burke. It was Solomon Burke. The reception was terrible, but I could tell ol' Solomon anywhere.

"Look, you don't need to get mad. I was just asking," I said. "But would it kill you to not curse, maybe expand your vocabulary a little?"

Alison's skin shone apple-red, and she fiercely chewed upon her hair.

"You're an obsessed little fuck. I don't even know why we're friends anymore. You're a broken record."

"You're repeating yourself."

"Fucker. Limp dick motherfucker."

Solomon fought to be heard beneath the static. I reached across for Alison's hand. She pulled away.

"Alison—"

"Yeah, you were just asking—you were doing it again. Trying to light a fire under my ass to see what would burn. Broken record fuck bag."

Solomon was there somewhere, beneath layers of fuzz—Solomon was there like the warm blanket somehow pushed away to the floor, like the star you see sputter out from the corner of your eye.

The light had been green for some time as the car moved toward the intersection.

"Why are you slowing down?"

"It's going to turn yellow," I said.

"A color you're familiar with."

"Why are you so goddamn mean? Alison?"

"Will you just fucking drive?"

The car shuddered ten feet from the light; my right foot was a numb chunk of flesh. I resisted clenching the muscle.

"I think my foot fell asleep."

"It's yellow! Go!"

Alison pulled more hair in front of her eyes, and her body gave a slight shiver.

Yellow turned red.

The boy rode a silver bicycle, his bottom just an inch of air away from the black banana seat, black tassels issuing from the grips of his chopper-style handlebars, a playing card, the Joker, held firm in the back wheel by a weathered clothespin. The boy, who had what appeared to be a newspaper delivery bag slung over his left shoulder, never flinched nor acknowledged the end of his life when the golden thirteen-year-old Volvo my grandmother had bought for me tore through both him and his blur of a silver bicycle.

My numb right foot thundered on the brake and Alison's nose smacked on the dashboard, a little squirt of red diagonally gracing the glove compartment.

"Jesus-fucking-pussy-ass-Christ!" she yelled.

I pushed open my door, and its squeak met Alison's exhortations, both rising toward the sky like blind offerings to an ambivalent god.

"You should always wear your seatbelt," I murmured. Alison never wore her seatbelt.

But my words drifted away on the night air. One of the paperboy's white sneakers sat near the car, and my dead foot splashed in a puddle near where the boy's head should be. Over Alison's continued wails and curses, I wondered when it had started to rain, pausing to try and shake some of the boy's blood from my shoes. I thought I could hear Solomon Burke on the radio still, trapped in some programmer's idea of hell, between the endless cursing and the sound of a wheel slowly stroking the Joker card as its rotation slowed down time like a bad dream.

3.

"Livin' alone,
I think of all the friends I've known,
But when I dial the telephone:
Nobody's home.

All by myself;
Don't wanna be all by myself anymore;
All by myself;
Don't wanna live all by myself anymore."
    Eric Carmen, "All By Myself"

    Attack and retreat, attack and retreat—anyone who spent any significant amount of time with Alison knew the routine. She took each man into her life, into her mouth, between her big lips, between her legs, in her ass, and raised him into a god; his words were revered, his sneeze adored, his penis rubbed raw. But the traps were set: little prickly pears awaiting a bare leg—Alison continually drew blood as if to remind herself, in some perverted way, of her suitor's humanity. Eventually, unless the suitor was significantly self-centered—and none were as far as I knew—he would crawl torn and bloodied from Alison's stained mattress, and Alison would once again loose herself upon the world.

    For the rest of us, the contingent that didn't sleep with her, the traps were set and hidden and reset on an endless basis. The few satellites in Alison's twisted orbit were forced to step lightly or find ourselves chewed upon and criticized for every stray breath. To be friends with Alison was to live within the narrow confines of a stuck groove on a 45 record. One learned when and how to tape the penny to the turntable arm and jump the chasm or get bruised trying.

    I wore my bruises with a mixture of pride and self-pity. Alison was the only friend left in whom I could honestly confide, the only piece of familiar driftwood in the Wake of Katrina with whom I could attempt to bury the horror of the Blue Face and the Unfogged Mirror. And despite, or maybe because of, Alison's continual challenges—her leg was forever stretched out, jumping a little, just *waiting* for someone to trip—I was consumed by her very smell, drawn into her large, judging eyes, lost within the perfume she wore that drifted from her neck like the last hanging bough from a long dead tree.

Not that Alison wasn't a true friend and not that she got off on cruelty; rather, Alison waged a struggle against herself for control: her body would tense itself so that touching her was like caressing steel; torrents of profanity and sexual acting out were her body's only releases. The bear traps set amid the florescence of friendship were there not so much to bring everyone else down as to give Alison a reason to rise above. Far from verbally introspective, Alison tempered her wants and needs through her painting and could only achieve the proper perspective from a great height, where her very soul seemed in danger of dashing upon the jagged rocks below. But Alison didn't use her art to merely ascend—quite the opposite. Alison's artistic expression was a constant, unyielding series of attempts to ground herself in a world where she believed she didn't quite belong.

Alison dressed as if she just stepped out of a Fitzgerald short story: her grandmother's clothes sustained a continual reinvention—not in order to fit in, but to establish herself in some indelible way, a presence not easily forgotten—thus enabling her not to forget herself. Alison was constantly vigilant. Alison's grandmother was a little woman who long ago accepted her fate—a husband more present in his absence than when he shared their wedding bed; Alison's grandmother never failed to set a plate for him despite his abdication—going out for a gallon of milk—decades before. But rather than cloak herself in loss and longing and self-pity, Alison's grandmother obscured herself beneath the vestiges of a dotty old lady, allowing her wit and keen observations of others to surface only when they could be used to an extreme comic effect. The opposite of Alison, her grandmother tried to violently force herself inward, as if paying penance for an undying love, only to find herself unable to allow her unique world view to remain buried for long. Alison wore not just her dresses and shoes—despite their polar approaches, Alison adorned herself in her grandmother's restless re-imagining of what she thought true love should be.

My friendship with Alison began shortly after Katrina moved out. And at first, that's all it was: a friendship, albeit one with an underlying sexual tension—at least on my part. I assumed, even then, that most of Alison's platonic friendships subsisted on some diet or other of unrequited lust and edge-of-your-seat longing—the kind of longing that manifested itself in early morning boners and encircling soul-song sexual scenarios played out in the winking of yet another superfluous sunrise. It wasn't as if Alison had no clue; our acquaintanceship lurched into friendship after I asked her for a date. Her quick response and the date's subsequent derailment—I couldn't find the restaurant I'd picked for two hours; Alison noticed that my fly had unzipped itself during the long drive; and when we finally reached the restaurant, it was closed—sealed our friendship. Alison treated the disaster as good theater, refusing to allow me to stop at a gas station to ask for directions home.

Alison had brought a few cassettes for the ride, and after crossing the same train tracks for the third time, after Alison asked me, peering into my lap, if I was airing myself out, after listening to a homemade Leo Sayer compilation tape, his Broadway melodies forever tattooed on my brain (so much so, that for years I masturbated over Alison to Leo's tremulous mewling), I could feel something inside me loosen. Part of me was beyond disgust—after Katrina, I ceased dating, if not diddling altogether—but another small slice of my wounded heart could sense a genuine comrade in Alison just below the surface of sexual tension. Alison was an artist, a painter, and my own artistic temperament, my writing, had been gasping in a stranglehold in the Wake of Katrina. Although Alison and I circled each other with absolute caution in the aftermath of this non-date (my attempt at a good-night kiss was only successful alone at home with my shorts around my ankles), the lines of communication remained and soon a day would not be complete without one checking in on the other, sharing tales of heartache or artistic constipation over a glass or two or three of red wine.

And in direct opposition to her seemingly uncontrollable urge to mine every vein of cruelty in order to level her playing field, Alison could suddenly excavate a startling measure of kindness, and in those few moments, the skies would open, the rain would taste like butter melting on a warm piece of rosemary bread, and all would be forgiven. In between the sudden bursts of tenderness and the everyday explorations of verbal torture, more than anything, Alison was *fun*. It would be nothing for her to trespass on a local farm to do little more than sit upon a bundle of hay with her sketchbook, alternately chewing on the long brown hair that descended upon her eyes and singing snatches of old soul songs between the full red lips that seemed to stretch themselves across her jaw like railroad tracks to the wilderness heaven of her wet mouth and darting tongue. Except: her mouth was far from uncharted territory—it was a land many, many men had conquered or been admitted to without forethought. All of these observations (okay, judgments) skipped through my unwavering eyes as I sat below Alison in the shade of another haystack, memorizing every tightening of the jaw, every shudder that ran through her body, watching her try to control whatever lurked just beneath the surface study of restrained artistic objectivity.

"You have a girl's mouth," she said.

"*Who made me? God made me.*"

"How can you believe in God? It's not logical."

"God brought me to you."

"Your dick brought you to me. There is no God. There are just predators and stool pigeons."

"Come again?"

Tapping her colored pencil against her bare thigh—her flapper dress was hiked up almost to her waist—a smile creepy-crawled the ceaseless length of her lips.

"Which are you, Damien? Which are you?"

It was during one of those stolen afternoons this past fall, traipsing across an unending expanse of arching yellow grass that stretched far into a large shadow always just a few yards out of reach, that Alison told me of the Death of Sebastian. Sebastian was the latest in Alison's long line of Supermen—a tool belt with a smile and an empty wallet and, according to Alison, a ten-inch penis. The mere fact that it was me who trespassed with her rather than Sebastian, whom I'd imagined trespassed Alison on a nightly basis, should have been a clue, and with eyes brimming with mirrored water, Alison detailed his dismissal—she wanted someone to play with more than she desired someone to transgress her smooth stomach and spread her muscular legs.

My heart nearly betrayed itself through my eyes. I had found a love in the aftermath of Katrina, and she marched in front of me, her hawk-like profile scanning the fields, exploring the far shadow with drowning eyes, her mouth never ceasing—oh, how I loved the Death of Sebastian, how I imagined the arrows piercing his side—but martyrdom was not for Sebastian—this Sebastian was murdered by his lack of imagination or, perhaps, my own strenuous yearning and praying. Maybe God wasn't so ambivalent after all! And lost within my victory dance, I failed to notice how we had penetrated the shadow, failed to see the unused barn, steel wires laced across its façade, blocking all but the highest windows. When Alison sucked in the late afternoon air and swore in a whisper, her breath drifted into my nostrils, tainted not with the smell of other men's excesses, but with the welcoming scent of a clear wood in spring.

"Jesus fucking Christ," Alison whispered.

Sitting in the uppermost single window, centered beneath the triangular side of the barn roof, the old man's knees were like two globes, his legs disappearing in the dark reach of shadow that had somehow grown thick like muddy water and had crawled its way to the roof. In a slow turn to the left, the old man revealed a long, curved rifle. The barn dissipated and in its place stood a not so abandoned asylum, buried within the false shadows of desertion. Alison grabbed my arm—not for safety, but to loosen my grip on her elbow. Free, I stepped back into the mud as the old man raised his curved shotgun into the air—and spread his wings, landing on an unused telephone pole a few feet away. I was already running in full retreat when I heard Alison's voice—not next to me but far behind.

"Two vultures," Alison said.

I tripped, my right foot caught in a muddy hole.

"Two vultures are staring at me," Alison said.

I pushed myself from the ground, my chest expanding, descending, and turned to watch as the second bird of prey—the old man's right knee—raised its curved beak into the air like the Winchester rifle of an Indian hunter from some old black and—decidedly *purple*—Western.

By the time I brushed myself off and swore the vestiges of fear from my trembling hands, Alison was sitting cross-legged amid the mud and tall yellow grass, sketching the great birds as they huddled within the shadow of the barn. I sat behind her, letting her long brown hair, drifting in the slightest of breezes, secretly caress my face, allaying the beating of my heart with the absolute certainty that all the tests had been passed and Alison was mine.

That evening, the night before Alison's birthday, we met up with her cousin and her cousin's new boyfriend at a bar in a little offshoot of a town fabled for its antiques. As I stood in the restaurant bathroom, furiously wiping mud from my shoes, the cousin's boyfriend slapped my back.

"She's a fine one, that," he said.

My leg was balanced on the edge of the sink like some perverted ballerina.

"I'm sorry?"

"Alison, my friend. A fine one," the cousin's boyfriend said.

I knew I was home. I had traversed and failed within the spook house confines of Katrina, and now my reward sat sipping Bloody Marys at a bar height table within the blackest corner of a dark, dark bar—it was something out of a novel. And as the evening progressed and the cousin disappeared with the boyfriend, Alison and I shared the laughter of the recently released. The old men glued to their bar stools swapped Alison's sketchbook back and forth, their slurred critical commentaries coming closer to the mark than any classroom of peers. When Alison left to pee, one hoary old man—whose face I couldn't help but paste to the twisted phantom shotgun wielder high atop the vulture's asylum—tossed the sketchbook on our little round table, missing the collection of empty cocktail glasses by an inch or two.

"Hey, be careful."

The old man pushed himself from his stool and approached the table; his cronies whispered exclamations of humor and encouragement. The man's hair, tousled with random curls like points of punctuation, was as white as the stubble gathered in crop circles on his wrinkled chin. His hands were bunches of constricted muscles, his breath like the bottom of a bottle of gin, his profile a scarecrow attempting to right itself against a strong wind.

"You almost knocked the glasses over, that's all."

The man's crippled hand gripped my shoulder with significantly more pressure than should have been possible. I winced and pulled myself away, squirreling Alison's sketchbook under my chair.

"Raise the bar, Captain," the old man breathed into my eyes.

When I opened my lids, the old man was gone and Alison stood before me, an alcohol grin stamped across her face. Alison didn't drink often, and the liquor lit her face up: an angel atop a Christmas tree. I handed Alison her sketchbook and let my fingers brush hers. Normally, if I even touched her by accident, her body would tense up and she would wiggle away as if I were a leper. At the bar, she leaned into my minute caress.

"It's like a movie—with the vultures and everything."

"Kiss me like in the movies," I said. I had drunk more than my share.

Alison swayed on her feet.

"Two vultures—nature uncontrollable."

"Then lose control with me." I was the King of the Romantic One-Liners.

"My cousin is screwing that boy in the ladies' room. I was standing guard for awhile, but I could hear her making humping noises, and I left."

"Classy. Kiss me like in the movies"

"I want to sketch you."

"I want to kiss you."

I placed my arms around her waist. Alison reached for her pencil.

"It was like we stumbled into their world—the vultures'—right in the middle of ours," Alison said.

"You can sketch me, but you have to movie kiss me first."

Alison leaned into me; I yearned to feel her nipples pressing against my chest.

"Like this?" Alison asked.

With her lips pressed to mine, I lost myself. No tongue; it wasn't necessary. This kiss promised both true love and gratuitous lust, flower petals tickling bare stomachs and wet, desperate smells unearthed amid dirty sheets and fingernail scratches.

When I finally let go, her eyes were open wide, studying my face. Her fingers, stained with pencil smudges, grabbed at the crotch of my trousers.

"Wow, you *do* have girls' lips."

I nodded my head and leaned toward her face.

"I could never love you, you know," she said.

Her fingers traced the outline of my penis.

"I've loved before. They all say they love me, but I've loved before. I could never love you."

Alison squeezed gently.

"I could have loved Patrick, but he didn't let me. And I loved Viggo. I think I loved Sebastian. I grew to love him. I could never love you."

My breath came in clumps as Alison ran her palm over the front of my trousers.

"Are you getting hard?"

And the darkness surrounding the vultures caught up to me, and when it started to drift away, we were in my car, the clothes she'd torn off her own body tossed upon the dashboard, so wet, she'd soaked through her underwear. Alison's stuttered breathing was an alcohol-laden blanket, and the darkness crept back—a farm cat stalking a field mouse—overtaking me, devouring me.

"I want to watch you play with yourself," Alison said, her wide eyes focused on mine. She never blinked. My fingers were melting inside her like a sand castle on the beach; I wondered where all the waves were emanating from. I was lost in her undertow.

But Alison refused to touch me. She wanted to watch.

Her game, her move, who cared?

I finished noiselessly.

Alison dressed herself.

Before she opened the car door, she used my shirt to clean the bar gunk from her sketchbook.

"Don't ever touch my sketchbook again," she said, as I used a sock to wipe myself down. Alison threw my shirt into the front seat, backed fully out of the car, rose to her full height in the fake yellow of the street lamp, and slammed the door shut.

Oh, the sky became so black, I couldn't see my hands in front of my face, just fleeting traces of a slippery rainbow dying behind my squeezed eyelids, reflected in the trapped tears and mashed eyelashes.

And there we were in a circle—squeezed into the corner of a Thai restaurant the following evening, watching her divorced parents interact with each other and their new spouses, Alison's grandmother perched atop a phone book like a child and a queen, an empty chair, filled with Alison's luggage—sketchbook, pocket book, pencil case, used tissues—ominously separating Alison from me. I hadn't seen her since my solo performance in the back of my car the night before—she had fled, stating, "I'm not watching you clean up." I had no idea how I found my way home, and my hangover dragged its way through my bones until it was time to drive into the city for Alison's birthday dinner, hastily wrapped presents shoved into my backpack. Waiters and busboys circled our tense table like—well, like vultures.

"*What* a DUMP!" exclaimed Alison's grandmother.

"Mother," said Alison's father. His new wife squinted her eyes and refolded her napkin upon her lap for the hundredth time. Alison and I exchanged a laugh with our eyes, mine lingering upon her cheekbones, darting from her breasts to her neck, my palms sweaty, my heart a hijacked train screaming for release from a dark, dark tunnel.

When the boy entered the restaurant, I ignored him, and ignored the way Alison stared at his six foot, three inch frame, pretended she wasn't painting targets upon the muscles pushing their way out of his too tight turtleneck. He smiled and walked toward our table.

"This is Bryan with a Y," said Alison, as the boy took the seat between Alison and I, placing her belongings underneath the chair.

"Hello Bryan with a Y," Alison's grandmother said, "this place is a DUMP."

This time everyone laughed, and her grandmother's eyes twinkled beneath the craftily fashioned mask of old age. Their laughter sucked all the air from the room, and as I immersed myself in a gin and tonic, the bitterness of the lime invading my mouth, tingling my teeth, Alison lifted her hand in slow motion, tracing blurs in the fried, smothering air, and caressed Bryan's cheek. The rest of the table ignored the gesture—all except Alison's grandmother, whose eyes flitted from her granddaughter's to mine to Bryan's. Alison leaned into Bryan's face and, with a little dart of tongue only I could see, pressed her skull to his. Everyone except me studied their menus with intense concentration, and as the last wisps of oxygen snapped out of the room like a cap gun going off in a closed closet, Alison's grandmother picked up a piece of complimentary fried noodle, charred black at the edges.

"This place is a DUMP! *What* a DUMP!"

The room went suddenly slack, and I spent the rest of the evening hiding in its folds, willing my stomach not to empty itself upon my plate, irrigating its trenches with copious amounts of alcoholic beverages. The after dinner banter stretched itself thin, as the two parental couples sniffed at each other and warily kept the conversation to fake *oohs* and *aahs* as they judged each other's birthday gifts. Alison held the new boy's hand, even when she opened her presents. Discarded wrapping paper littered the table, and when I stood up, tottering on two gin-soaked legs, pieces of brightly colored birthday clowns adhered to my forearm. Everyone took that as a cue and, after arguing over which parental unit would foot the bill, collected themselves, moving into separate corners. I tore the tape from my arm and stared at the little hairs clinging to the adhesive.

Alison's grandmother stood next to me, her head swiveling this way and that, soaking in the sheer *dumpiness* of the situation. Her little hand rubbed my arm, red from the tape attack.

"Sometimes," Alison's grandmother stage-whispered to me, "sometimes, things aren't as they seem."

Alison's grandmother pulled her four foot one frame ramrod straight and looked at Alison's father.

"David, take me home." She peered myopically at her son's new wife. "You—sit in the back."

It took me another minute to realize that Alison's grandmother had most likely prevented me from witnessing Alison's lusty goodbye to Bryan with a Y.

Alison was outside the restaurant, shivering despite the fall heat, her cheeks chafed from Bryan's stubble. I offered her a ride home.

And then we spoke of blow jobs.

And then Alison's mouth cursed its way into my heart. Pierced.

And then I realized I could kill. Didn't mention that before.

And then Solomon Burke burst his soul upon my dashboard.

And then I smashed the boy on the bicycle, I think.

4.

"There's got to be a morning after;
We're moving closer to the shore;
I know we'll be there by tomorrow,
And we'll escape the darkness—
We won't be searchin' anymore."
     Maureen McGovern, "The Morning After"

"WAKE UP AND BREATHE!"

Gasping, I emerge from a brief darkness, my penis throbbing against the bulk of Lucille. If she is inclined to rescue me from my stuttered sleep for a round of thrusting and parrying, Lucille doesn't betray her desire. Quite the opposite—it's like dry humping an iceberg. I pull my underwear over my tumescence and knock my father's suitcase from the bottom of the bed.

Lucille doesn't stir.

Is this another dream? My skin is a spotty rubber band fastened around a dusty, cracking book cover. But what, pray tell, what's *inside*?

"Lucille?"

Click-Clock does a flip—and TA-DA, another stale minute has passed.

I count the cracks on the ceiling—last night there were seventy-two tributaries emanating from three distinct fissures in the aged paint. My hand down my underwear, I absently rub my penis and count backwards from seventy-two and then forward again until I am so close, so near to exploding, I squeeze the head and feel the liquids within me fight against the undertow that suck them back toward my swollen balls. Even my eyes seem to fill with the fluids of fantasy. I am awash in Alison's sticky sea of surrender; I am smothered between Katrina's modulating muscles of fear.

My fingers caress the great hump of Lucille's shoulder; my lips explore the expanse of her bare back. It's like falling face-first into the driveway in the morning after a great frost. I place my hand over her mouth, looking for some sign. I pinch her nose.

I am trying to hump a dead person.

If I close my eyes (and I can do that), I am in one of Fitzgerald's boats, *"borne back ceaselessly into the past"*:

"*What* a DUMP!"

"I'm sorry?"

"*What* a DUMP," Lucille repeated as she walked into my little two bedroom apartment. Her lips were apart, a laugh poised on the precipice.

"Well, it's, um, it's home."

Lucille reached over with her large paws and squeezed my face. Her mouth formed baby words as she launched little kisses across the puffs of my cheeks. Her stomach pushed into mine.

"Aw, it's okay. I was kidding, kiddo. No blood, no ambulance."

Lucille's breath was stale with Marlboro Lights, and as I moved away to mix a few cocktails, Lucille landed with a plop on the cracked black surface of the couch.

"Light on the cubes, alright?"

Yeah, light on the cubes—hey, easy on the couch too, while we're at it.

Katrina was away—far away. Alison was immersed in another man-boy. And this was date number five with Lucy Lucille.

The first date had been a blind date—set up by a friend of a friend of someone I barely knew—and I had been half in the bag, my gentle sideswiping burps (so as not to offend this thrice removed friend) tasting like gin afterbirth, when I agreed to meet Lucy-Lucille-She's-So-Sweet-You'll-Just-Adore-Her-She-Used-To-Be-So-Heavy at one of those theme restaurants, the kind Alison called an In-Between, the kind Katrina called an expensive night out.

I was put off by her size. Lucille wasn't fat. In the parlance of my mother's generation, Lucille was big boned. Lucille was obsessed with the TRUTH. Her ex-husband had parlayed his rise in the corporate world into a rise in his sexual fortunes, and Lucille detailed vivid sleepless nights, surrounded by the smell of another woman's vagina rising from her husband's contented face, framed like an angel's by his pillow. Lucille said she felt like a lesbian just kissing her husband goodnight.

But within three dates—chaste sofa sitting, cocktail sipping dates—I found myself struggling up a hill entirely of my own construction. While true that I found Lucille less than visually appealing—not that she wasn't attractive, but she was far from the skinny Angels with whom I lost all sense of self—I became enamored with the laugh that wasn't released until absolutely necessary and the internal chains that held in reserve the messy, oversized contents of Lucille's central ingredients, for she swallowed incessantly: liquids, smoke, drunken men's floppy dicks.

The last bothered me little, to my surprise. I had spent most of my twenties engulfed in the twin streams of Katrina and Alison while many of my peers had subsided into the arms of holy matrimony. My twenties were lost—my sexual proclivities were submerged within the stew of obsession, returning only in barely controlled, scalding desire, often as not extinguished within my right palm. When I wanted to relive an errant hand job from my high school days, I used my left. This was the extent of my sexual upbringing. Lucille having experienced multiple partners and seemingly innumerable after-hours gropes in the dim light of the dreaded last call bothered me little. The obvious concern for disease was tempered by my sheer lack of self, worn as I was from the endless devotion at my Two Altars of Unrequited Passion and a disturbing trend toward a marked aptitude for not sleeping.

The night I gave myself to her, after wrestling with a condom—I could barely remember how to put one on—I wept like a child in the bathroom while Lucille disturbed the gods with the snores of a drugged animal. And although I hadn't finished, or perhaps in spite of that, I knew I had crossed a river whose bridge, charred and smoking, was forever gone. I had joined the ordinary. I had faked an orgasm—silent, gripping moans and hard shoulder bites—the whole enchilada. Hell, I was beginning to define ordinary.

I wondered: if two people died fucking, would anybody mistake their screams for anything but those of completion?

I'm slipping away.

Slip slidin' away.

Back to present:

"Lucille, you awake?"

The neighbors' dog moans in his sleep and Click-Clock mocks the silence of the room like a child giggling during Mass. Usually Lucille's snores rattled the shot glasses, meticulously arranged, in the tiny kitchen cupboard—the downside to sleeping with Lucille is that while sleep proved elusive nights I slept alone, with Lucille I might as well be napping upon an industrial lawnmower. But now—nothing— not a peep. The temperature of the bed seems to drop until my penis responds in kind, and as I climb out, I am surprised to find my father's suitcase sitting open on the floor near the foot of the bed. Yes, yes—packing—I am leaving—*a fugitive!*—escaping—a dead woman beneath the blankets, a mangled boy on a bicycle chasing after me in my oh-so brief dream states.

A dead woman?

Obstructive sleep apnea is defined as the cessation of breathing during sleep for roughly ten seconds at a time, sometimes as often as thirty, or even fifty times a night, according to the various books littering my crowded room. God's way of fucking with me. Whoops—you stopped breathing while you were asleep—so sorry. Please resume the position. Or turn over. Or pinch your pillow. Or perhaps you'd prefer to fight sleep by reading frightening articles about apnea-induced RISP (recurrent isolated sleep paralysis) and REM atonia. Or you could count the cracks above your head. Or try to stick it in the woman's crack next to you. Or fantasize about someone else's crack (whether or not you're inside the woman taking up space in your bed). Or count sheep. Or imagine shearing them. Or visualize killing them with your bare hands.

A dead woman?

Frequently accompanying sleep paralysis are hallucinations involving a sensed presence, someone the books refer to as the Intruder. But he is not a stranger to me; I see him every time I look in the mirror—and that only makes him more terrifying.

I pack my father's suitcase and wonder if this is how *he* felt all those times he painted the night sky with the trails of his departure. I pack my father's suitcase and find the rusted clasps as cold as the thing that was Lucille—the Lucille obstinately *not* snoring. I pack my father's suitcase and shiver as my bare toes touch the hardboard floor. I pack my father's suitcase and imagine my mother unpacking it upon every whiskey-soaked return—my father: a radio station you are *just* unable to dial in to the right frequency, its song a distant spark on an alien shore, a promise in the dark, a hand slipping away across the icy sheets of a shattered marriage bed. I pack my father's suitcase until I realize that it is already packed.

WAKE UP AND BREATHE!

Was I sleeping? My head hovers above the pillow, my right hand still grasping my father's suitcase by my ragged fingernails—like my mother trying to hold onto my father's shirttails as he slipped into someone more comfortable.

A dead woman?
You know I've loved two women, you know I love them still;
Love those little girls so damn much, and my time is mine to kill...

If I squint with my left eye and cast my right to the heavens, the cracks on the ceiling paint the worry lines on Katrina's gentle skin, tiny tributaries awaking as a great river tears itself asunder.

5.

"You got no money and you got no home;
Spinnin' wheel all alone;
Talkin' 'bout your troubles and you never learn;
Ride a painted pony let the spinnin' wheel turn."
      Blood, Sweat, and Tears, "Spinning Wheel"

The door chain prevented my grand entrance, so I knocked on the spare bedroom window of my apartment—*my* apartment, goddamn it; I *let* her live there!—until the glass cracked and Katrina's face appeared on the other side, split into several distinct pieces.

And then the *other* girl—the one with the spider tattoo on her left cheek—raised her considerable mug, framing Katrina's, overtaking Katrina's and subsuming it within its shadow.

"It's the rapist," the woman with the spider tattoo said. Her voice squished its way through the bloody crack.

"Damien, go away," Katrina said.

Katrina. My Kat. My First Love.

"This is *my* apartment," I countered weakly.

My neat little apartment.

Blood dripped from my knuckles and stained my sneakers.

"Kat, this place is a DUMP. Let's go," the Spider-Lady said.

Kat. The fat fuck had called my First Love Kat.

"Damien, just go away for a little bit. Go to the bar. We'll leave and you come home and take a shower," Kat said. "You need some sleep."

"I think that's just what you need—some sleep—hah!" I countered, unsure the second the words left my mouth if my comeback meant anything—or everything.

In that moment, if a cracked pane of glass had not been separating me from my First Love and the ball of fat eating her out, I could have killed. I had little doubt.

And I as drove from the bar, two hours later, after last call's bitter resurrection, Tom Waits distilling the blues, fragmenting them until my brain fractured along the lines of the road home, I screamed my alternate responses into the *whoosh* of the night air, its cold fingers all thumbs upon the 2 A.M. version of me.

"Oh yeah, is that what you were doing? Sleeping? Hah!"

Fuck it.

"Is that so? Is this what you call Kat Knapping? Hah!"

The sleep of the dead.

"Yeah? And what were you doing? Licking the proverbial sheep?"

Fuck it. I want to die.

My foot found the gas pedal giving and lenient in the crisp late winter evening—hungry in fact, and I fed its need for speed—I pressed the pedal to the metal—I gunned it—tramps like me and Tom, baby we were born to run.

He must have been starting his paper route early. Or else his parents emphasized pedaling in the dark as a wholesome form of exercise. His head hit the hood of the car and flicked back disturbingly on his neck before collapsing below my sight line. I could *feel* the car settle upon his bicycle frame before I backed up a little.

"Yeah? You even know what sleep is, bitch?"

I crept out the passenger door and stood behind the car, listening for the cries of a police siren, the squeals from worn tire treads, the screams of a startled neighbor. The boy moaned once, but the wind carried it away like the ephemeral whispers of a nightmare upon the first light of day.

Then: nothing—dead silence. I giggled. *Dead* silence.

"Oh and what were you doing? Spinning webs with Spider-Woman?"

Dead silence, except for me that is.

"Wake up and breathe, Kat! Smell the coffee!"

There was a flower shop on the far right corner, and the street lamp reflected the colors from the window arrangements to the rear bumper of my car. I bent down to smell the flowers. I bent down to breathe them in, for nothing else on this street, for nothing else in this dead-end night seemed as concrete as the bursting reds and greens and yellows swimming upon the dust encrusted chrome, crashing in little waves as the bumper hummed along to the idle motor.

And as I bent down lower, my nose pressed against the back of the car, the sputtering exhaust invading my nostrils, overtaking the sting of the gin waves that fought for a moment of exhaled glory, I could see the bicycle's rear wheel spinning, the Joker card between the spokes, and a small white sneaker sitting alone in the shadow of my Volvo.

So I crawled. I crawled to the boy under my front wheels, keeping an eye out for his paper bag—sure that the headline would detail the drunken collision, anxious to see if the newspaper was folded in half horizontally or if it opened like a magazine. I didn't want my photograph creased along the fold.

The paperboy was in a frozen pirouette upon the twisted frame of a silver bicycle with a black banana seat. As I crawled on my hands and knees to his head, the gin, now thoroughly mixed with the thick flavor of exhaust, threatened to violently evacuate. His blood was added to the claret stain on my sneakers.

"This is sleep? You will sleep with the fishes!"

I cradled his head in my lap and took off my sneakers.

"Wake up and breathe, Kat! Coffee's burning, baby!"

I placed my sneakers next to the dead boy's curiously bent legs— they looked like an orgy: limbs strewn this way and that, muscles taut, ready for the plunge, the excruciating release of the first of many little deaths.

"You call this sleep? You always sleep with your head between a spider's legs?"

With my right foot, its sock withered down so my toes appeared to be five inches long and drooping, I grasped the boy's abandoned sneaker, and the rear bicycle wheel spun it final cycle: Click-Clock Click-Clock. Tom Waits rasped something over the murmuring motor: *"...and the dream that I was chasing, and a battle with the booze, and an open invitation to the blues..."*

"Wake up and breathe!"

Awkwardly, I squeezed my floppy sock into the paperboy's sneaker, the back of my foot collapsing the back, obliterating the endorsement of some sports figure or other.

"Wake up and breathe!"

I caressed the dead boy's hair.

"Wake up and breathe!" I whispered into his crimson ear.

The boy's sneaker slipped violently from my foot.

"You don't know what sleep is," I sighed into the tiny hole on the side of his head.

And as the wind kicked in and the Joker began another lazy spin, I laid down next to the dead paperboy, cradling his sneaker, wondering if the Spider-Lady had made my Kat moan like the departing soul of the dead boy in my arms.

6.

"Well, I keep on thinkin' 'bout you,
Sister Golden Hair surprise,
And I just can't live without you,
Can't you see it in my eyes?
I've been one poor correspondent,
And I've been too, too hard to find,
But it doesn't mean you ain't been on my mind."
America, "Sister Golden Hair"

She appeared indistinct and merged with the waves of motion surrounding her exterior antennas—the ones that captured every slant of mood and turn of phrase. Her voice was like a newborn stream in a thunderstorm: its gentle southern cadences ebbed and flowed, found undiscovered passages over long discarded leaf-strewn pathways—then suddenly soaked into the mud, subsumed into the fauna, forgotten, or perhaps bubbling under the surface. When Katrina whispered to me across the narrow valley of pillowcases, I could feel the very blood in my veins pull toward her too skinny body and lose itself in her persuasive undertow.

Katrina wasn't from here; she had moved from the South with her family. We had met in the office of a therapist—exchanging glances over stale magazines until one day, after my session was done, I waited down in the parking lot, pretending to have car trouble, my head peering under the hood so as to not to startle her. She wore a tattered smiley face t-shirt; her arms were decorated with a river of red scars.

"You don't know anything about cars, do you?" Katrina asked.

"Why do you say that?"

"I think you just disconnected your windshield wiper fluid hose."

I called her Kat. She called me the Punnett Square—some mathematical theory for something or other. Our friendship blossomed with sex edging just along a back alley like some gangster in a movie from the '30s. We weren't platonic; occasionally, after far too many mixed drinks, our mouths would be entangled and our limbs would find themselves tossed aside in pursuit of something far more bitter.

Kat spoke little; she allowed her musical voice entry into conversation only when she felt her opinions were warranted. Unless she was drunk. Then, awash in the back sting of tequila or the bitter seas of vodka, Kat's voice would tumble out past her tongue and mount whichever absurdities her brain would conjure forward. She also liked to strip down to her underwear while we drank, huddled around my tiny kitchen table. I would steal sidelong glances of thigh and ankle and ass. I was a goner, I knew. I stood in the shower and prayed to God—any god who happened to be listening—to let Kat be the one, rubbing myself to completion with a skinny bar of soap.

"I don't know," Kat said.

"Couldn't tell you," Kat stated.

"Wouldn't *you* like to know?" Kat queried.

It was one such evening, floating, it seemed, upon the cracked fake-wood tabletop, exchanging tall tales over shots of tequila and an endless stream of cheap cigarettes, when I decided to ask her to marry me. Down on one wobbly knee, my hands clasped over her warm thighs, I proposed, and Kat accepted, lifting me up with her hot hands, tapping a measure of salt in the cleft of my left shoulder blade—for the right shoulder was for God—proceeding with her tequila shot from the starting point of my skin.

Kat pulled me into the bedroom and peeled off her clothes while I struggled to free myself of mine. We had never had intercourse. Just oral and other deviations—and only when absolutely inebriated. When I entered her on our engagement night, her breath caught, and she clawed at my back.

"Are you close?"

"I can hold out."

"Finish quick," Kat said. "Please."

I did as instructed, and we smoked like movie stars after sex, shooting blurry little tunnels towards my cracked ceiling. I asked why the hurry.

"I don't know," Kat said.

"Couldn't tell you," Kat stated.

"Wouldn't *you* like to know?" Kat asked.

I blew it off, but it was weeks before I was allowed reentry between her legs, and when I was finally there, going slow as to burn every thrust and moan into my besotted skull, Kat screamed and dug her ragged nails into my back and tears leaked from her too blue eyes, tracing the early wrinkles of her too pure face.

I retreated to the floor, shaking as much from Kat's continued writhing as from the drafts invading the bedroom.

"There's blood on the sheets," Kat intoned.

"There are stains on your penis," Kat offered.

"I am filled with blood," Kat stated flatly.

We didn't bother with sex too often after that. A few blow jobs, maybe, but that's all. Even those often ended with Kat tearing her mouth away, her teeth dragging along the head, enough to leave scarlet tracks along the purple ridge, and me finishing myself to whatever drum beat emitted from the stereo. It got so I couldn't tell who was singing: Billie Holiday? Tom Waits? Solomon Burke? I came to the sounds of a radio station not quite dialed to an exact frequency.

"I can't come during sex," Kat said.

"There's so much fucking blood," Kat informed me.

"Crazy," was my response.

Kat stared over my head. That's me: always sensitive to the needs of others.

"Blood crazy," I amended, as if that explained everything.

But I was convinced I could save her—speaking of "crazy."

I decided to stop seeing the therapist. There was nothing he could tell me I didn't already know.

"You need some sleep, my man," the therapist said when informed of my intention to terminate.

The therapist was corpulent to the extreme—his dress shirt could only be called tucked in because the very ends of the cloth were jammed into his pants; beneath the billowing canopy and strained buttons, a hairy mass of flesh was squeezed above an overly strained chaffed leather belt. Dr. Wackerman was in dire need of an undershirt.

"I need strange fruit," I said in return. "*Here is a strange and bitter crop.*"

"I'm sorry, my man?" the therapist asked.

"I don't know," I volleyed.

"Couldn't tell you," I declared.

"Wouldn't *you* like to know?" I finished.

The therapist—I couldn't quite get past the indefinite article; I could never consider this barrel of laundry *my* therapist—rubbed the edge of his palm in a violent motion under his nose until little flakes drifted upon his desk, the volume or degree of his rubbing modulating in direct response to my responses.

"My man, let me ask you this. Can I ask you this?" the therapist asked.

I perused the various framed diplomas and what-have-you slanting from the cramped walls, the paint peeling just like on my ceiling. One could lose oneself within those cracks, I thought.

"Shoot."

"Okay, my man, okay. If I were to ask you if you preferred to have sexual relations with Eve or Steve, what would you say?"

What a DUMP was the only answer bouncing around my brain. Kat was filling my head: Kat asleep on the couch, missing the end of a movie—Kat's neck muscles as she achieved orgasm lying in the bathtub, her feet planted on either side of the spout, the water splashing down on her red private area—Kat inhaling her cigarette smoke like she was swallowing the finest champagne.

"I don't know," my mouth stated.

"Couldn't tell you," my lips flapped.

"Wouldn't *you* like to know?" my teeth clacked.

The therapist rattled his papers and attacked his nose. He must be upset, I thought, as he squeezed an envelope into thirds and then released it like an exhausted accordion.

"I think you need a hug, my man," the therapist said.

He sighed and pushed his bulk from the chair, its seat sticking to his over-abundant ass cushion, the chair lifting a few inches from the floor before smacking back down, its wheels drifting it a few feet away in safety.

"What do you say, my man?" the therapist asked.

"*A-womp-bop-a-lula-a-womp-bam-boom,*" I replied, pushing my hands against his advancing stomach, my hands *soaking* themselves in his gut like a glass slowly filling up with soapy water in a stopped-up kitchen sink.

I was out of there like Vladimir.

At home, I relived myself of excess sperm, wiping it up with a dirty sweat sock. When I opened the kitchen cabinet and reached for a can of soup, my hands rested on an empty gallon bottle of cheap gin.

"Curious," I whispered to myself.

Underneath the sink, next to the Draino and my collection of detergents—courtesy of my mother—sat a drained plastic bottle of the world's most inexpensive vodka.

The phone rang as I pulled an extremely light bottle of whiskey from behind the washer and dryer.

"My man!" the ancient answering machine said.

There was an empty six-pack behind the winter coats in the hall closet. Domestic.

"We need to talk, my man," the machine continued.

I squeezed my muscles tight so as not to, you know, *lose it*.

Behind the television, enmeshed in the tangle of wires and extensions: a small but impressive collection of airplane bottles: red wine—white wine—schnapps—vermouth.

"You *did* try to off yourself, my man," the machine declaimed.

And I was back there: back in the bathtub, my mother calling up from the living room, something about making sure I scrubbed the tub when I was finished, and me grinning into the faucet, admiring my Joker grin, twisting my head back and forth as if I was having a fit. I submerged another textbook—*Algebra II*. I always hated mathematics; it never added up to me.

"And make sure it's clean," my mother's voice drifting from the first floor—my mother: the one person in this world, I believed, who loved unconditionally. So she liked to clean. After the mess that was my father packed his final suitcase—worn from too many packings and unpackings, worn from watching my father fuck drunk fat women from its place on a motel closet's top shelf—my mother was forever cleaning.

Cleanliness is next to godliness, she would always say.

"I'm not dirty," I would say.

But I was. Magazines—Sears catalogs—neighbors sunbathing—the inside of a fur lined winter glove—the rush of blood to the head (*that* head) as I swung back and forth on the monkey bars.

I was dirty.

Focus:

There was a half-empty bottle of cooking sherry shoved between the record albums underneath the stereo.

I squeezed my muscles tight so as not to swear at the good Lord above.

"My man, we need to confront our issues," my answering machine said. The possessive pronoun.

"Justine. You have to get over Justine, my man," the little silver machine stated with much emotion.

Did I not pay him before I left his office of peeling paint and askew university merits of distinction? I checked to see if the initial ring my mother gave me was still on my left hand and not buried in the abyss that was the therapist's stomach.

Justine: like she stepped out of some over-hyped but much adored post-modern excuse for a novel, her clothes carelessly worn with care, her hair coiffed just enough to be perfectly disheveled. Justine: chaste kisses behind the grade school convent. Justine: letting me push my fingers under her skirt. Justine: kneeling next to me before a little statue of the Baby Jesus wearing a dress, swearing our love before an understanding God. Justine: trying to jerk off my eager purple penis, squeezing it so hard, I passed out on her unmade bed. Justine: dumping me at a concert, during the best song of the night no less (*"...if you twist and turn away...if you tear yourself in two again..."*), leaving me to ride the subway home alone, rubbing tears away from my face so the boogie man I'd always imagined as a kid haunting the night cars, his flannel flapping enough to reveal the shotgun at his side, wouldn't pick me out of the crowd: *die, crybaby, die!* Justine was no Angel—pure puppy love, a curtailed kitten crush. The '80s were fucking cruel.

A barely touched bottle of rum lay tucked into the slippers my mother bought me last Christmas—"To keep your feet clean," she had said. I pushed all the half-finished bottles, the empty bottles, the bottles with a little liquid still painting the bottom of the glass, into the dishwasher I'd never really used before, pouring all of the concentrated powder detergent over them before slamming the door shut.

And that was just the first lot.

Another thirty-one bottles were laid out near the stereo like chessmen awaiting a match.

"My man, this suicidal ideation, it's no good. You have to let it go," the clean shiny box my mother bought at the Five and Dime said.

A rattle of keys and there was Kat, fresh from her part-time job at an art supply shop.

"Hey, that pretty girl with the big lips was in again today. Do you think she's—?" Kat said as she closed the door behind her. She stopped short of walking into the gathering of empty bottles.

Like something out of a Tennessee Williams play, the southern heroine grasped at her chest, as her eyes sought an escape she could never quite make on her own.

All my girls were from the best novels, the greatest plays, the most moving sonnets.

"You were fucking snooping, Damien," Kat said. Her voice was flat like bad club soda. Her voice was thin like old tonic water.

"My man, letting go is the only way. And sometimes the only way to let go is to grab at something or someone near you for support," the machine cackled.

I thought: doesn't this tape ever run out?

My Kat: Hemingway would shoot an elephant for her, Faulkner would carry her dead body in a wagon hundreds of miles to properly inter it into the hard, hard ground, Hawthorne would make her an exquisite sin, Fitzgerald an exotic drink topped with a purple umbrella.

"Is that Dr. Wacker on the machine?" Kat asked.

"It might be," I mused. "It certainly sounds like Wackerjob."

We stood facing each other like gunfighters.

"Why is the Wackman talking into the machine?"

"I think he needs a hug," I said.

My mother would run inspection after each chore was completed, running her detector-finger across tub grime, through bookshelf dust, over dinner dish stains. My mother was very into cleaning. She loved me more than anything, she would tell me, but she loved me *even more* when I was clean.

I was a dirty bird.

"You're drinking a lot, Kat."

"You wanna talk about it?" she asked.

"No. Yes. Well, maybe you should speak with Wackhead about it."

"About you snooping or me drinking?"

"Both, I guess. Wack-A-Doodle would like both."

"My man," the answering machine sighed.

"Wackoff likes to call people 'my man'," said Kat. "Even me."

"When are you drinking all this?"

"Here and there," Kat said.

"My man," the answering machine moaned.

"This stuff doesn't mix well with your meds. You could, you know, die. Kill yourself."

"I'm sorry?"

"You know, overdose from alcohol poisoning. Kill yourself."

"Not today, Dami, I'm tired today."

"My—" and then the answering machine clicked.

"Think he finished?" Kat asked.

"I'm sorry I snooped. I wasn't looking for anything. I just found one and then another and then I couldn't stop."

"Either could I," Kat said, pushing an errant dirty blonde hair from her cloudy blue eyes.

"Where's your southern accent?" I asked. "I don't hear it today. You've been east too long."

"I don't know. Maybe I left it at work or in Wackmouth's office yesterday."

I approached her and could smell cigarettes smoked in a closed car—I could smell the heat from her skin rising from beneath her sweatshirt.

"Kat, I'm sorry."

"I know."

"I love you."

"I know."

I pressed my body against hers, my boner throbbing in time to Billie Holiday's orchestra snaking out of the stereo.

"Damien," she said like she wanted to push me away, but she didn't. She couldn't.

"Kat."

Her hands ran down to my bottom and squeezed, her teeth scraped past my neck.

"We can't."

"Kat," I said, digging deeper against her waist.

"I can't. I want to sometimes, but I can't," she said.

The phone rang once. Stopped.

"Last time, I swear," I begged.

She surrendered. "Dami," she whispered as I ran my hand between her legs.

The phone rang again.

"Your mother's signal," Kat said.

"Damien?" the answering machine queried.

"How much room is left on the goddamn machine?" I asked.

Kat was unzipping my trousers. "It's a miracle, really," she said. "It holds a whole hell of a lot."

"There! There's your southern accent."

Kat was on her knees.

"Are you cleaning, Damien? Running the vacuum?" my mother's voice, trapped inside the answering machine, asked.

"Fuck," I said.

"I know how it is," the machine chuckled. "Always cleaning."

"You're so hard, Dami," Kat said from her position the floor; alcohol fumes drifted from her mouth and invaded my nostrils.

"You're drunk," I said.

"Got to stay clean," the answering machine ghost intoned.

"Mouthwash," Kat replied.

"Make sure you bang the dust out of that doormat, Damien," the answering machine instructed.

"There are vultures on the roof, waiting for me to die," Kat said.

"My mother will vacuum their feathers, not to worry."

My mother sneezed into her phone.

"I'm dirty," I told Kat.

"I know. So am I," Kat said. "Filthy."

"Do you ever hug Dr. Wack?"

"Bang it out good," the answering machine said patiently.

How did everyone know they could just rattle on?

"Once in a while. He smells like old socks up close."

"Does he get a hard-on?"

"If you have to, after you bang it, hang it over the railing," the answering machine ghost detailed.

Kat had to take my penis out of her mouth to answer.

"Sorry about that," I said.

"Oh, no matter. A hard-on? I don't think so. I assume his miniscule member is lost in his folds."

"Bang it and hang it," the answering machine cackled.

"Watch your teeth," I said in a rough intake of breath.

"Oh, that's rich. Bang it and hang it. Oooh. I should be careful. I'm being taped, right?" the answering machine sputtered.

"Sorry," Kat said. A string of drool hung suspended like a bridge between my love's mouth and my rigid body.

"Bang it and hang it! I should write to *Reader's Digest* about that!" the answering machine crowed.

"You're losing it," Kat said.

"You're drooping," she remarked.

"Bang it and hang it," the answering machine intoned.

"I can't take it," I said in between gasps.

I pulled my trousers up, kissed Kat's forehead, and broke into a jog toward the answering machine.

"Bang bang bang. Hang hang hang," the answering machine rhymed.

When I reached the kitchen floor, my left foot caught the first puddle of suds, and I surfed, limbs strewn, into the hallway, banging my head on the little washing machine.

"*Bang all the live long day!*" the answering machine sang.

"What the…Kat?" I asked.

Behind me, a wall of soapsuds nearly four feet high obscured the kitchen sink and half the refrigerator. The dishwasher churned like the chuckles sputtering from the little silver box attached to the little black phone.

There were spots of suds on those too.

"*I've been banging on the railroad—all the live long day,*" the answering machine bellowed off key.

I laid a few towels atop the mountain of soap bubbles and watched them slowly sink.

Kat was gone. The front door was closed and locked, and she had thoughtfully turned the Billie Holiday record to the other side.

When I reached for the phone, to ask my mother how to handle my Wall of Suds, she clicked off as soon as I picked up.

I squeezed my muscles tight so as not to kill.

When the Wall of Suds had subsided to a sticky swamp, and after finishing what liquor Kat had left, I went behind my building, tossing the bottles onto the roof, trying to calibrate the jingle of crashed glass into a neo-classical composition or some punk declaration—anything but the '70s, anything to keep the vultures quiet. When several porch lights blinked awake and querulous, muffled voices rose above the din of shattered whiskey bottles, smashed fifths of gin, totaled gallons of Russian vodka, I hid beneath the front of a parked pickup, lying as still as an accident victim, gripping my penis like I was gripping a fractured leg, staring at my reflection in the back of the bumper.

I waited for Kat.

Sneaking back to my apartment, ensconced beneath the blankets, staring at the cracks on the ceiling, I drifted into a thin ice dreamland, where Justine jerked me off nonstop, where Kat stood in front of the turntable, reflecting her wedding band in the shiny vinyl, where my mother announced my kitchen floor was now suds-free.

I waited for Kat.

When she returned, I was tugging at myself like I was pulling in an ocean liner. Kat stumbled into the apartment at half past two in the morning, and I could hear her unsteady footsteps cross the sticky kitchen. Kat leaned her drunken body against the hallway wall. She steadied herself against the washer. She puked her liquor into the bathroom sink.

Kat.

I listened to her climb into the little bed my father bought for me, the one we had set up in the spare room to give Kat some space when she needed it. I counted her breaths through the walls until they steadied into a low roar, until a thin cloud covered my brain and the pretty girl with the big lips and the colored pencils who frequented the art supply store allowed me to lick her legs, until the vultures who lived on the roof tossed back the booze bottles, until my father returned for his suitcase.

"WAKE UP AND BREATHE!"

When I awoke, it was a quarter to six and not a sound leaked through the walls. In my sleep I had shed my underwear, and my penis raised the blankets like a circus tent. I crept out of bed, pulled off my t-shirt, and quietly turned the knob on the spare room door. Kat lay still beneath twisted waves of sheets and blankets and pajamas. The left strap on her pajama top hugged her shoulder, and the outline of her small breasts was visible. I leaned down and licked her shoulders, tracing her name with my saliva.

"Is everything clean?" my mother had asked.

Kat's skin was ice cold. My penis throbbed like a heartbeat. Kat's breath was tortured, less a mixture of cheap cigarettes and cheaper booze than of rotting animal parts floating in the bottom of sewers. A little dot of semen appeared on the tip of my foreskin. I wiped it with my finger. Kat's breath smelled like dead field mice, too long in the heat. I stuck my stained finger in my mouth.

When I pulled at the knot of bed coverings, Kat's hands were laced together into one large first, pressed tight against her stomach.

"Kat?"

I let my fingers slide up her thigh.

"Kat?"

I climbed on top of my love and placed my waist just above her mouth.

"Kat?"

My thrusting caused her head to shift to the left, her dirty blonde curls on the right side crushed from sleep, and a thin line of blue vomit leaked from her mouth.

I jumped from the bed and knocked into the nightstand. An empty bottle of antidepressants rolled to the floor along with a makeup mirror and an empty airplane bottle of Southern Comfort.

"Kat? Kat?"

I flipped on the light. Kat's face was blue—the blue of a pretty dress—the blue of a secondhand dress found at the bottom of a thrift store pile, now ironed neatly, hung just so, ready for the dance, prepared for the banquet, looking for all the world like a brand new purchase.

That was Kat's face.

That was her skin, her pallor.

Her skin matched her eyes.

I took the mirror from the floor and held it against her blue lips.

"WAKE UP AND BREATHE!"

And waited.

"*...boats against the current...*"

When Justine dumped me, I swallowed seven sleeping pills on an empty stomach, drowning my algebra and chemistry textbooks in the bathtub while I waited to die. All for puppy love! She wasn't even an Angel; I know that now. You don't just love an Angel—you want to be them! Unaware then of the distinction between puppies and Angels, I was rushed to the emergency room. My mother was crushed; she cleaned ever more vigorously. My father never came to the hospital.

"*...borne back ceaselessly...*"

Kat's eyes were two lumps of skin, and when I pulled the left lid up, she was looking for God. When I let go, the lid flapped shut with a CRACK.

A BANG.

A FUCKING REALLY LOUD SMACK TO THE SKULL.

I listened for the neighbors. I listened for the vultures.

"WAKE UP AND BREATHE!"

And I waited.

"*...boats...*"

When some girl I slept with in college turned around and blew one of my best pals, I inhaled copious amounts of mint liqueur after swallowing fifty-three caplets of extra-strength something or other. My mother cleaned every ceiling in the house, using just a stepladder and a tiny sponge. My father didn't come to the hospital, but he sent the bloated woman he was fucking to my room with a card that would not have been out of place in the room of a five-year-old.

"...borne back..."

I returned the spaghetti strap to Kat's shoulders, I covered her up in the blankets and sheets, I ran to the other room, our room, and found some of her stuffed animals and placed them around her head.

I squeezed my muscles tight so as not to join her.

"WAKE UP AND BREATHE!"

And I waited.

"...ceaselessly..."

When they finally locked me in a clean little hospital for carving into my wrists, interrupting my already spotty college career, my father visited. He had his suitcase with him. I remember thinking that was odd. My father leaned into my face; he wanted to know why I didn't like Bubbles. I flicked his cigarette ash from the side table and noticed the steel wool scratches in the wood. My mother had visited earlier and had cleaned the common room.

"Bubbles?"

"Bubbles."

"That's her name?"

"You know damn well that's her name."

"Which one is she?"

"Don't you fucking—"

"The one whose nips meet her navel?"

My father smacked me in the mouth, and I smiled and swallowed the blood.

As he was leaving, I shouted to him:

"You left your suitcase! You left your suitcase! You left your suitcase! You left your suitcase! You left your suitcase! You left your suitcase! You left your suitcase!"

A male nurse plunged his hands into my back and someone else pulled the emergency signal—the one they used to let the rest of the facility know they had a basket case coming unwoven.

"...into the past..."

But, oh, such sentimental journeys into bygone times were poor form when someone in the present couldn't wake up and breathe.

And I couldn't wait any longer for Kat to breathe. I could hear the vultures on the roof. My muscles were compressed into little balls. I dragged the phone into the hall and let the mechanical voice know my First Love had come undone.

When the ambulance arrived, I confessed, I pulled out my limp penis for the cops and showed them the stretch marks, I swore I would never do it again. I told them about the suitcase. I offered to show them the vultures' roost.

And they ignored me and used a resurrection spell.

They locked my Kat away.

Dr. Wackhead left dissertations on the answering machine.

My mother came and cleaned the apartment.

I locked the spare room. It smelled of dead skin. Food for vultures.

And I squeezed and squeezed and squeezed.

"Wake up and breathe!"

Kat came home on a Thursday. Her skin looked stretched. She was quiet. But she smiled and hugged me and told me I saved her life. I was going to turn my penis in for its crimes and beg for her mercy, but I kept my mouth shut. Especially after I grew hard while she was hugging me.

"I felt that," Kat said.

"We need to talk, Dami," Kat told me.

Dinner turned into dessert turned into a bottle of wine turned into several bottles of wine.

"I don't understand," I told Kat.

"Girls," she said.

"You mean…"

"Girls. I like girls."

"But what about, you know, us? Marriage. House on a lake. Two point five kids. What about us?"

"I'm sorry. It's who I am."

"Because he abused you?"

"That's too fucking easy, Dami. My stepfather has nothing to do with this. I think I've always known."

"When were you going to tell me?"

"I think about girls all the time. I pretend you're a girl sometimes."

"Who? Who do you think about?"

"The girl at the thrift store."

"I think she's gay, Kat."

"That's the point. And, um, the girl with the big lips. The one who draws."

"She's not gay."

"How do you know? And what if she isn't? Does it matter?"

Kat moved her stuff into the spare room—it was no longer just a place she used to get away from it all, from me—and began to go to the bars.

The next day at work, I hid in the toilet, perched upon the porcelain, and cried until my eyes were raw little eggs just ready to hatch. I cursed God out. I revoked my prayers.

The first few girlfriends Kat brought home were polite but awkward. Nobody you would want to have a threesome with, that's for damn sure. But they were nice. We rented movies. We broke bread. I went to bed with a headset so I wouldn't hear any moans through the walls. I searched the apartment for hidden bottles of alcohol, and when I found none, I bought a few and hid them about, hoping for a backsliding miracle.

Hey, God, if you're listening, I prayed, fuck you very much, but in case you have a change of heart, you're the best, man.

Kat's stepfather arrived on a Thursday night with an old dresser that belonged to her mother. The family was moving back south. When he hugged her goodbye, his hand crept down to her ass and squeezed.

"Your stepfather should meet my father," I said after he left.

"He smelled like sweat."

"Mine does too."

"Bastards. Both."

"Vultures," I said.

"Plastic. Rubber soul," Kat said. "Not real."

"Wanna do a shot?" she asked.

"*Every half hour until the sun…*"

"*…breaks free of the moon,*" Kat finished. She was grinning, and when she hugged me, she didn't mention my hard-on.

Two hours and four shots apiece later, Kat rested her feet, clad in soft little socks, upon my lap.

"You're my savior, you know that?"

I blushed and kept my mouth shut. Kat swallowed some cigarette smoke.

"I am alive because of you."

Her toes wiggled in my crotch.

"You deserve more than this. Get out and date. Or just get out and fuck. Who cares? It's your turn to feel good, Dami," Kat said.

"You know who I want."

"The girl with the big lips?" Kat smiled and swallowed more smoke.

"No. You."

Kat pressed her toes against the bulge in my trousers.

"You're 'wild at heart and weird on top,' you know that?" Kat asked.

"*Treat me like a fool / Treat me mean and cruel / But love me.*"

Kat poured herself two quick shots.

"I must be fucked-up," Kat said as she dug her toes into my trousers, and when I lifted her out of the chair, pulled her pants down, and laid her on the floor, Kat covered her eyes with her hand.

"You saved my life."

"Save mine," I said, but it sounded like a movie cliché—it sounded fake, plastic, not real. Rubber soul.

When I entered Kat, she gasped and dug her nails into my back.

"Quick," she said.

"Are you okay?" I asked.

"I don't know," she replied.

"Couldn't tell you," she opined.

"Wouldn't *you* like to know?" she questioned as I pulled out on her stomach.

The next morning Kat wouldn't look at me. She must have left my bed in the night, for I woke early, and she was gone, just traces of her shampoo and sweat on the pillow, a little stain on the sheet. She was brushing her teeth when I left my room a half-hour later.

"Hey," I said.

Kat spit into the sink. Her eyes looked at me: puzzled, questioning, probing.

"I'm the gentleman caller who ravaged you last night, darling," I said in my best imitation of Kat's southern twang.

Kat spit into the sink again.

"You have blood on your face," she said.

As Kat skirted around me, I peered into the bathroom mirror at the twin streaks of blood on my forehead. I heard the front door slam shut.

Kat spent the day away from the house, and when she returned to pick up a change of clothes, I peeked out of the living room window at the car idling in the driveway.

Spider-Woman.

"You coming back tonight?" I asked.

"I don't know." Kat gritted her teeth.

"Will I see you tomorrow, then?"

"Couldn't tell you." Kat sniffed at a pair of corduroys and stuffed them into the washer. A good sign, I thought.

"Who's the chick with the tattoo?"

Kat stopped in her tracks and retrieved a bottle of Wild Turkey from beneath a sofa cushion.

"Wouldn't *you* like to know?"

But she returned. After I left to go the movies by myself, to drown myself in fake butter and somebody else's fantasies, Kat returned.

Kat was in the bedroom fingering the Spider-Monster.

Kat was in the spare room eating out an arachnid.

Kat was spreading her legs extra-wide for an extra-large insect.

The shadow painting of limbs and breasts and tossed hair—at first I thought it was Dr. Wack-On-You, his huggy bear outline against the spare room window. He looked like he had a shotgun.

Then: a moan. Then another. *Was the shotgun a dildo?*

Then I broke the window. *Two vultures are staring at me.*

Then the Spider-Bitch called me a rapist. *Wake up and breathe, mister.*

Then I went to the bar. *First came the vodka, then came the gin, then came the whiskey by its chinny-chin-chin.*

Then: Alison.

Then/now: the dead woman. Lucy Lucille.

And, somewhere, sometime, I think I killed a boy on a bicycle with my Volvo.

I do remember this: the next day, I tossed the answering machine into the trash, next to the shards of broken glass from the empty spare room window.

Kat was gone.

7.

"Knock three times on the ceiling if you want me;
Twice on the pipe if the answer is no.
Oh my sweetness—
Means you'll meet me in the hallway;
Twice on the pipe means you ain't gonna show."
    Tony Orlando and Dawn, "Knock Three Times"

"WAKE UP AND BREATHE!"

And as the dream flows down my drain into my bloodstream, the dead boy on the bicycle drifts away too, and I am back in the ceiling cracks, back with Click-Clock, lying next to the Carcass of Lucille.

"Wake up and breathe."

That's what I was trying to do with Lucille—escape the suffocating thread stuck in the back of my mouth from the Twin Blankets of my Two Loves.

Alison is on the answering machine, although I don't remember buying a new one.

Alison is telling me to surrender, but FUCK HER—she doesn't know the meaning of surrender, and I will never lay down my arms to her again.

I have come for her. That is surrender enough.

Betrayal comes in many forms—the smell of pussy on Lucille's husband's face—eating out the Spider-Woman in my apartment—Alison's sexual games—even the dead boy on the bicycle in my dreams. Would I have left him in the waking world? Would I have abandoned his lithe, twisted body, his scattered sneakers, the Joker in his rear wheel?

Wake up and breathe—it's all about killing the lie. It's all about obliterating Kat and Alison and the Blob Father and Dr. Wack-My-Head, even my mother.

On the floor, next to the bed, is my father's suitcase. A few items of clothing have been squeezed in its yawning, cracked mouth in obvious haste. I peer out the window, and the sun is nowhere in sight—what else is new, I think, as I quietly pull open a drawer to retrieve some socks.

Murder is a serious charge—there: my understatement. Do I turn myself in? Do I escape before dawn's early light and the rockets' red glare? For a moment, I consider calling Alison. Granted, I would wake up whomever she is sleeping next to, but Alison knows how to freeze a moment, at least on paper with colored pens and paints. Perhaps, I think, Alison will know how I should handle this.

I play Alison on the answering machine again: "Surrender."

Surrender?

But Alison never mentioned the boy on the bicycle in any of her messages.

Alison.

Kat.

Lucille.

Lucille regarded Alison with a wary eye. If I spoke of Alison with any enthusiasm, Lucille shut down, escaped into her squirrel cheeks and rum and Coke. If I ranted about Alison, those rants eventually led to my litany of Guys Alison Fucked, and Lucille would down her cocktail and crack the ice with her large yellow teeth.

Alison was supposed to be my savior. Why else would God have sent her to me? Katrina broke me, and Alison was the glue. Only to Alison, I was kindergarten paste—another toy spurting its mess into the empty air.

Subsequently—except for last night, or is it still last night?—I couldn't get it up for Lucille. Not an inch. Not a semi. Lucille could suck on it for forever and a day, but the minute I prepared for entry: NADA. A wilted flower. While my father humped his fish-white stomach ball against Bubbles' bubble—while Alison sucked and sucked and sucked until I imagined her already full lips were swollen as a result—while Kat plunged into Spider-Innards—I performed oral on the mass of flesh that was—past tense—Lucille, whacking off in the bathroom afterwards like a kid in grade school—like a kid in high school—like I do every night:

Kat Alison Kat Alison Kat Alison.

I can feel something stir below my waistline, a tingle, and, as always, I follow Alison instructions to the letter: I surrender, my face to the pillow, dry humping the bed with a limp noodle.

8.

"You're no good, you're no good,
You're no good—baby, you're no good;
I'm gonna say it again:
You're no good, you're no good,
You're no good—baby, you're no good."
    Linda Ronstadt, "You're No Good"

WAKE UP AND BREATHE!

I sit on the bed and sort my socks. So many are come-crusted. I want to take only clean socks with me. When I leave, I want all the dirt and come to remain behind. I can only take one suitcase—I have to make a movie-exit here. No time to call the landlord. No time to call my mom. Once I am on the road—THE ROAD—I can waste all the quarters I want. And if they catch me, well, there's always visiting day.

My father's suitcase is faded yellow, and the outside material is bumpy—its paths lead to nowhere in particular—just like me.

I rest my head upon the pillow—just a catnap.

Hey Mr. Sandman, bring me a freakin' dream, would ya?

And he comes out of the front door, my mother's vociferous exertions following quickly behind, his whiskey-vapors painting the front porch in waves of cheap Hawaiian guitars. When he bounds from the porch, my father knocks past me (what did *I* do?), and I fall from the silver bicycle where I have been sitting, my right foot twisted just enough in the pedal to go numb. Newspapers spill out of my bag.

Wake. Gasp.

I rest my head upon the pillow—just a quick forty winks maybe.

And that's when it occurs to me—on the cusp of shut-eye, seconds away from being in the arms of Morpheus.

That's when it occurs to me to kill my father.

9.

"Look out, look out!
Pink elephants on parade,
Here they come:
Hippety hoppety;
They're here and there,
Pink elephants ev'rywhere.

Look out, look out!
They're walking around the bed
On their head;
Clippety cloppety;
Arrayed in braid,
Pink elephants on parade."
  From the soundtrack to the film *Dumbo*

WAKE UP AND BREATHE!
This is how I knew to kill my father:
It comes to me in a dream, although I don't sleep. Ever. I swear.
The two vultures are perched at the foot of the bed on the wood frame, pruning themselves occasionally, spreading their wings for effect. Their purple is like a bruise, a bruise that breathes—the color expanding, contracting like the tide. They are squeezing their muscles; they are holding it all inside.
"No, we're not. We're just imitating you."
"I'm sorry?"
The larger of the two vultures, the one with a little orange stain on the left side of his (his?) beak caws and ruffles some feathers.
" '*I'm sorry? 'I'm sorry?*' " he mocks with a mincing tone. "You're right: you're sorry—a sorry ass motherfucker."
The other vulture is slightly smaller with a dark purple patch on its (its?) stomach.
"His."
"I'm sorry?"
"Christ," says Orange Beak, "would you stop saying that."

"His," repeats Purple Tummy, "we're of the 'his' variety."

"I apologize."

"Jesus," says Orange Beak.

"How you gonna do him?" asks Purple Tummy.

"Who?"

"Your father, of course," replies Orange Beak.

The ceiling above the two vultures is a swirl of dying stars, twisting into a whirlpool that devours all colors, that dissolves all pigments.

"Stop with the ceiling," says Purple Tummy.

"You really should be paying attention," says Orange Beak.

"Take an interest," says Purple Tummy.

"And clean, for God's sake," interjects Orange Beak.

"Listen to your mother," finishes Purple Tummy.

"You know my mother?"

The two vultures roll their eyes. Orange Beak yawns. Loudly.

"What, exactly, if you please, did your maker do to you?" asks Purple Tummy.

"Your father," clarifies Orange Beak, giving a sideways glance to his partner.

"The Man Who Donated Sperm to Your Making," Orange Beak elucidates.

"Did he beat you?"

"Suck you off?"

"Make you suck him off?"

"Hmmm. Nasty business, that."

"Spit or swallow. See, Hamlet was wrong. *That* is the question!"

"Yummy yummy yummy, I got come in my tummy!"

The birds shudder with amusement, and two purple feathers float down upon the blanket.

"You, my friend, cannot carry a tune," says Purple Tummy.

"No, but I can carry a carcass," says Orange Beak.

"This is like a bad Disney movie," I say.

"A Disney movie on acid," says Purple Tummy.

"A Disney movie you watch completely naked, jerking off to the clever turn of a well drawn ankle," adds Orange Beak.

"We're always naked!" exclaims Purple Tummy.

The two vultures quiver with pleasure and squeeze their muscles tight.

"Well," says Orange Beak, "did you play with Daddy's peeper?"

"Did he sit on your face and fart for hours at a time?" asks Purple Tummy.

"Oooh, hate that!"

"Ditto."

"Nasty business, this."

"What with the farting and the Shakespeare and what not."

The whirlpool painted on the ceiling spins in lazy, concentric circles, and I wonder how long I have been asleep. I let my left hand steal over to Lucille to feel her cold, cold skin.

"Enough of this, already, Dami."

"Dami, Dami, Dami. You got to pay attention."

The ceiling is gone, and the whirlpool is a red angry bruise, pulsing on the offbeat, swallowing the bedroom whole. Should I check Lucille for signs of livor mortis? I think I read about that in a book once.

"You saw it on the television, perhaps," opines Purple Tummy.

"He could have read it in a book. He does read you know."

Ignoring Orange Beak: "Dami, what did Father-Daddy-Suck do to you?"

"PUSH YOU OFF YOUR FUCKING BIKE, DID HE?"

"Or maybe—maybe he reached under the covers, sweetie."

I can't take my eyes off the whirlpool. Any second now I'll be inside. Just another half a heartbeat, and I'll be sucked off, sucked into, swallowed whole by my ceiling.

"He didn't love me back," I say.

The two vultures tremble and shake. Purple Tummy dances on one foot and whistles "The Mexican Hat Dance."

"Capital crime," says Orange Beak.

"Gotta die," says Purple Tummy.

"Wasn't Mommy's love enough?" asks Orange Beak.

"Not when someone who is supposed to love you doesn't," Purple Tummy answers for me.

"Hence the two women."

"Hence."

"Quite."

The whirlpool is now a red cloud, and Lucille and I are two dead stars, biding our time until our light reaches some far off destination and we extinguish ourselves.

"Kill kill."

"I'm sorry," I say.

"There he goes."

"Annoying as all get out."

"Who did I kill?"

"My turn: I'm sorry?" asks Orange Beak.

"Did I kill the boy on the bicycle?"

"Who the fuck is the boy on the bicycle?" asks Purple Tummy.

"The important thing here, Dami," says Orange Beak, "is to know how you're gonna do him."

"You might need some help. He's a big guy."

"Fat."

"Juicy."

"A sausage waiting for the squeeze."

I am lost in the red. I am swallowed. I am one with the ceiling cloud.

"I'm going to kill my father?" I ask.

"Good boy!" says Orange Beak; his beak is dripping crimson.

"I'm going to bring Alison and Kat," I say.

"For help," says Purple Tummy.

"For aid," says Orange Beak.

"For support."

"For the occasional wet dream impetus."

Purple Tummy's tummy drips on the blankets; it's like a melted crayon.

"He. Didn't. Love. You."

"It's all about the Freud."

"Hell of a guy," says one of the two vultures, blood and saliva sliding from his beak to his crooked claws.

"The Two Women: your Knights of the Round Table."

"Yes, you must be careful and use your Rage for Right."

"That's why your winkie won't work."

"No direction."

"Reach skyward!"

"Raise the bar, Captain!"

The two vultures cackle and spread their wings until they form a blanket, and I crawl inside. I crawl inside, and I know I have to kill my father.

10.

"First I was afraid,
I was petrified;
Kept thinking I could never live
Without you by my side;
But I spent so many nights
Thinking how you did me wrong,
I grew strong."
    Gloria Gaynor, "I Will Survive"

WAKE UP AND BREATHE!
Road Trip, Baby!
When you're planning to kill your father, always, always, make sure you bring his suitcase. I used to imagine it came with a set of wings, pre-packed, at the ready whenever the jones hit him. My mother made sure to always have a change of underwear, a pair of socks, and a stock of deodorant set aside, but my father packed his own suitcase. My father was a salesman, see, and sometimes he had to travel, and sometimes he had to *travel*. Ramble on.

When you're planning to kill your father, motive isn't as important as you'd think, although in actuality, it's everything. You just tell yourself it isn't. Here's a list of things you *don't* think of when you're revving the engine: you don't think of the time your father left you alone on New Year's Eve to go out on a date rather than baby-sit you as planned—you had the flu, you see—and your mother was "celebrating" the new year's first inhalation by spending time with *her* sick mother. You should never think of this night, or the way the *hoo-ha* at midnight sounded like a thousand vulture wings flapping in lazy unison. Oh, yeah, you shouldn't obsess over the time he pushed you from a moving car after he asked you what you thought of him settling down with a woman called Bubbles. Honesty is the innocent man's folly. If you think said Bubbles deserves to be popped with a condescension-detecting divining rod (can't you just *see* your father, my father, some overweight father figure sitting in a night lounge, the plastic coverings on the booths replete with holes, some chubby double-bagger perched on this father's knee, this father telling said percher that he wanted to pop her bubbles, and this woman's laughter—smelling like the back of an old one dollar bill, her skin greasy from too much make-up, too many Two Sisters cocktails— barely reaching the ceiling, her laughter dying just seconds away from somebody's father's eager, chubby tongue), you should always keep it to yourself. Especially when the car is moving. Specifically if it's tearing down the Boulevard. Never think of him prying the phone away from your ear when you called for help that time you said you didn't care for Bubbles' cooking (the hot dog hadn't been quite thawed, and you choked and spit it out in your glass of flat Fresca), never recall the way the phone smacked against your head, or your mother's voice at the far end of the universe, repeating "hello." Never recall threatening letters, nor the syllables his fat fucking tongue used to form words like *dickweed, fuckhead, shitbrains,* and *spermwaste.* And never, never, *never* recall the rough scrape of his whiskers against your cheek, or the way he used to tuck you in with a father-kiss, or the times he would take you fishing—for those—those are the memories that hurt the worst.

You could strangle him with the cracked leather belt that kept his socks from mingling with his Skivvies inside the suitcase. A quick snap across his flabby neck would do the trick. You could sneak up behind him and smite him upon the skull with a large object. A suitcase perhaps. You could lure him into a subway tunnel or upon the elevated platform, and when the train comes *whooshing* along and the smell of decades of ruin and the promise of decades more rises into your nostrils, threatening to scorch layers of skin, you could *push push push* into the *whoosh whoosh whoosh.* You could stuff half-frozen hot dogs into his throat until he turns into the blues. You could force him to sit under a little tan radio and listen to Olivia Newton-John detail the vagaries of her love life while you patiently peel the skin from his sagging jowls. You could spit in his eye. You could hack one on his face. You could pull out his eyeball with your pinky finger and feed it to the vultures.

Road Trip, Baby!

11.

"Chick-a-boom chick-a-boom, don't ya jes' love it?;
Chick-a-boom chick-a-boom, don't ya jes' love it?;
Chick-a-boom chick-a-boom, don't ya jes' love it?;
Chick-a-boom chick-a-boom-boom-boom."
　　　　Daddy Dew Drop, "Chick-a-Boom"

WAKE UP AND BREATHE!
"Are you awake?"
I touch Lucille, and her skin feels like a slab of extremely cold pudding.
I am so fucked.
Things I remember about the last twenty-four hours with Lucille:
- sloppy head,
- a screaming face,
- a boy on a bicycle,
- a playing card,
- fucking like an animal.

One of these things will lead me to jail. One of these things will lead me to jail.
If I didn't kill the boy on the bicycle, who did I kill?

12.

"I'm lookin' for a place to go so I can be all alone
From thoughts and memories;
So that when the music plays, I don't go back to the days
When love was you and me.

Oh, oh *moja droga, ja cię kocham*
Means that I love you so;
Moja droga, ja cię kocham,
More than you'll ever know;
Kocham ciebie całym sercem,
Love you with all my heart;
Return to me and always be
My melody of love."
      Bobby Vinton, "My Melody of Love"

    WAKE UP AND BREATHE!
    Kat moved away with the Spider-Woman. I wrote letters. I didn't have her phone number, but I left messages on an imaginary answering machine. I masturbated with her face in the front of my mind. I walked the streets of the downtown neighborhood where I thought the Spider-Woman kept her web.
    (Click-Clock shows One, Click-Clock presents One-Thirty.)
    Then, three years later, a random postcard from out of state, a crooked smiley face near the signature, a tentative phone call, a drunken meeting wherein Kat kept me at bay only by smacking me in the balls.
    (Click-Clock rings Two; Click-Clock ring-a-dings Two-Thirty.)
    Another year, another try, Kat's arms carved like a totem pole, reminders of whatever mysteries of her past she had succeeded in burying even deeper. There she was: a miracle of modern science, propped up and happy with antidepressants and antipsychotics and a cocktail of mood elevators, the scum of her life successfully scraped from the top of the glass and hidden beneath enough pharmaceuticals to choke a horse.

Of course I tried to sleep with her, and of course, she retreated from me.

That all fades away when I pick her up for the Road Trip.

13.

"Guess mine is not the first heart broken;
My eyes are not the first to cry;
I'm not the first to know there's
Just no getting over you.

You know I'm just a fool who's willing
To sit around and wait for you;
But baby can't you see there's nothing left for me to do;
I'm hopelessly devoted to you."
     Olivia Newton-John, "Hopelessly Devoted to You"

WAKE UP AND BREATHE!

I saw Alison at the movies. Frequently. I would sit two rows behind her and duck behind my popcorn. I would watch her squeeze her muscles shut tight until I realized I was squeezing mine and, quite possibly, she was sitting absolutely still. I saw Alison at the gas station, and I could make out the shadow of a masculine figure sitting in the passenger seat, patiently ticking away the minutes until he received his next blow job. I saw Alison at the foot of my bed, pulling her clothes off in a haste usually reserved for books my mother called Bodice-Rippers. I would finish in my fist and shake my startled sperm at the space where Alison had been.

(Click-Clock shoves Three-Forty-Five into my face, and I knock it to the floor with a trembling fist; Lucille doesn't budge; Lucille doesn't blink.)

I wrote Alison poems. I composed songs for Alison. I argued with her in my head: *how could you let me touch you, but leave me to masturbate in the back of my car? How could you suck so many, but refuse mine when my love was so fucking real?* I would tear at my own skin when I came with Alison in my head. How could she be so deaf to the beating of my central organ, how could she be so blind to the dull fires fighting for air beneath the teardrops stored behind my eyes? How would she interpret my need to sleep whenever Thoughts of Alison pervaded my everyday activities?

But all that melts away when I pick her up for the Road Trip.

14.

"Country roads, take me home,
To the place I belong."
    John Denver, "Take Me Home, Country Roads"

My father's suitcase is packed, stuffed to the gills with potential weapons and a couple of changes of socks. I ignore the vultures at the end of the bed. I ignore the Carcass of Lucille. I ignore the Joker playing card on the nightstand.

And when I lean back and lay my head upon my sweaty pillow, I am on a set of railroad tracks, steel fingers stretching away to the left beyond a little hill of trees, strewn with trash, little mementos of discarded living. I am walking along the rails, carrying my father's suitcase, which is somehow cleaner, newer, heavier. The air is heavy too with impending rain, the kind of rain that doesn't so much clean the dirty streets as burrow deep within dirty souls, the kind of rain that can never be outrun.

If these rails are still in use, I am unaware. I know of an emptiness in my chest that no amount of exhaustion from walking will fill. I am aware of the distinct pinprick of having loved without having been loved in return. Like an eager tongue flicking a tender tooth, my imagination constantly pokes at the source of the ache. My muscles are beyond fatigue. My face doesn't remember words like *laugh* or *smile*. I would take my own life except I'm too bone-weary.

And as the tracks take a turn and emerge upon a little street, I see the boarding house upon the crest of a hill on the left, a box of bricks and self-discarded souls sitting amid crab grass poking through cracked concrete. I drag my father's suitcase to the peeling paint of the front door, its flakes of green littering my tired sneakers, and as I raise my hand to ring the bell, I see my father's hairy knuckles coming swiftly toward me to cover my eyes and knock me off my silver bicycle.

15.

"O-o-h child,
Things are gonna get easier;
O-o-h child,
Things'll get brighter."
    The Five Stairsteps, "O-o-h Child"

WAKE UP AND BREATHE!
My mother knew I wrote little stories in my dream journal when I was a kid. She had bought the journal for me when my nightmares had increased to the point where, even as a child, I would try and force myself to stay awake, counting the hoots of the owls or imagining the pretty girl who sat behind me in Math buck naked in my bathtub—anything to stay awake.

My mother preferred life to be as neat as her house. My father was dirty. He smoked. He nibbled on raw hamburger. He spat great gobs of greasy grimy gopher guts—hackers, he called them—lugers. Nothing about my father was neat. He knew how to fish; he knew how to tie knots: fishing lines, boat lines, tent lines. He could hook anything and reel it in, my mother said. But tents had dirt floors; fish had slimy entrails—dirty. My father would later go on to use his reel talent with female barflies—cocktails and his suitcase as bait—a businessman on the go (despite the fact that he "borrowed" most of his bar money from Mother and lived just down the road from the bar strip).

"Write me a story," my mother would ask, but I could not. My stories were filled to the brim with straying Catholic schoolgirls, muttering prayers to their patron saints while pulling down their pleated skirts; my writings were chock full of revenge stories, stories of a palmed fishing hook tearing into the jowls of a fat man sitting on a log watching a bob or tying a lure; in these stories, the price for wantonness, the price for turning my mother from a neat freak into a sparkling, shining example of obsessive cleanliness, was a Swiss Army knife in the belly or the point of a fishing rod in the eye. I could no more write my mother a story than I could coerce the girl in Arithmetic to show me her breasts.

When Father left for good, when neither he nor the suitcase returned after the money ran out or after catching some itchy red rash on his stray peter, Mother sliced her days into Cleaning Chunks: ten minutes dusting the dining room breakfront, a half an hour on the bathtub. Sometimes she would catnap between these little chunks; sometimes, after school, I would too: falling asleep on the living room couch, the television rattling its tubes just behind syncopated little snores, my school books on my lap obscuring my After-School Boner.

Boners were dirty but not discussed—not until Mother found my blanket besotted with stains, stains that revealed the aftermath of Early Morning Boners (not to mention Bedtime Boners and Middle of the Night Boners and General Anytime Boners). My blanket was dirty. Thus began Blanket Checks; my mother couldn't abide her son sleeping in such a dirty setting. So in this way were boners discussed—not as a natural phenomena of puberty, but as Makers of Messes. Mother instructed me to use tissues if I found myself in the position to Make a Mess, but I couldn't bear her knowing how often my body forced itself to Make a Mess, and I began to soil my socks until they littered my bedroom like little chess men: white sweat socks, black dress socks.

It would be years before my Twin Loves broke my boner, I thought, before my boner could no longer respond to anything except rapid tugs on What-Might-Have-Been or Things-That-Happened-Once-And-Never-Again.

So, as I warm the car and plot my route, as I trace Lines of Kat on a map and draw battle plans for the Rescue of Alison from her Bed of Sperm, I know I am merely following my mother's hallowed instructions: it is time to make things clean. I am going to erase the dark blob of a man who sucked out sleep from my eyes. I am going to bury my creator and punch a hole in the sky.

But more than anything—more than my love of Kat, more than my lust for Alison, more than vengeance—I want sleep, glorious sleep, motherfucking sleep.

16.

"Gonna keep on dancin' to the rock and roll
On Saturday night, Saturday night;
Dancin' to the rhythm in our heart and soul
On Saturday Night, Saturday night;
I-I-I-I, I just can't wait;
I-I-I-I, I got a date."
       Bay City Rollers, "Saturday Night"

WAKE UP AND BREATHE!

That's Alison. She's sitting in the passenger seat of the car where I placed her, kicking and screaming, after quietly lifting her off her bed and away from whatever lump was currently sawing away post-orgasm.

"Are you going to rape me?" Alison asks.

"*I don't know how to love Him; I don't know how to move Him,*" I sing in reply.

"Bryan asked me if I thought you would rape me."

"*Should I bring Him down, should I scream and shout, should I speak of love, let my feelings out?*" I sing, squeezing my muscles tight so as not to explode all over Alison.

"Stop doing that," Alison says.

"Doing what?"

"Clenching yourself in a bunch like that."

"That's you, Alison, not me."

Alison places her bare, dirty feet on the glove compartment.

"Let's just kill him and get it over with, okay? I've had enough of your shit for one lifetime."

Alison and I follow the red lines I had carved into the crumbly street map.

Hang him from a shower rod. Force him to swallow bleach cleanser. Trip him in the bathtub.

"Cut off his cock and stuff it in his mouth," adds Alison.

"Thank you," I say.

"Fuck off," says Alison.

Kat is extracted from between the meaty thighs of an out-of-state replacement arachnid.

"I thought you were picking me up first," says Kat as she slides next to Alison.

"*You kissed me and stopped me from shaking—and I need you today, oh Mandy*," I sing in reply.

Kat places her hand over Alison's face for a moment, then leans back. Kat is wearing cut-off dungaree shorts, and her legs are carved with a roadmap of slices and scabs.

"The girl with the big lips," says Kat.

"Your stepfather fuck you, is that it?" asks Alison, looking at Kat's arms and legs.

Stick his head in the oven. Roll over him with my car. Put him on a bicycle and run him down.

"Everyone did," Kat says. "Everyone fucked me."

"I let them. Except him," says Alison, gesturing to me.

Shove a pencil into his nostril. Kick his face in until he's unrecognizable. Beat his dick with his own suitcase.

"Place a pillow over his face," suggests Alison.

"Or, or—pee on his head," adds Kat.

I hit the brakes, and Alison and I turn toward Kat.

"Someone did that to me when I was little. Tied me to the banister and peed on me," says Kat.

Alison kicks my leg.

"Drive. We'll pee on him when we're done," she says. "Not a problem."

"Are you going to fuck him first?" I ask.

"You're going to fuck his father?" asks Kat.

"I'm tired of fucking," says Alison.

"I was tired of getting fucked," says Kat.

"I'm just tired," I say.

"Road trip!" say Kat and Alison in unison.

And so our car eats up a dream expanse of tar and yellow dashes. We are following his scent, we are following his trail of weak sperm and hair sprayed cocktail waitresses and some bitch named Bubbles.

Drown him in a swimming pool. Place his fingers in the toaster. Push him down a long flight of stairs.

"Pee on him while he holds the toaster," offers Alison.

"Slice his toes until he bleeds his guts out," is Kat's two cents, "then pee on him."

The road seizes our car and drags us ever onward, the trees and the stars and the squished road kill just so much ephemera of the hunt.

"Is this a dream?" asks Kat.

"We've been driving for hours," says Alison.

"If it's a dream, it feels pretty real," says Kat.

Alison's feet play along the glove compartment latch, and when she succeeds in opening it, an avalanche of empty airplane booze bottles spills to the floor.

"Binge drinking!" exclaims Kat.

"Hiding booze, Dami?" asks Alison.

I squeeze my muscles so as to save my blood lust for my father.

You know I've loved two women; you know I love them still;

Love those little girls so damn much, and my time is mine to kill...

17.

"Look for the bare necessities,
The simple bare necessities;
Forget about your worries and your strife;
I mean the bare necessities,
Old Mother Nature's recipes
That brings the bare necessities of life."
       From the soundtrack to the film *The Jungle Book*

WAKE UP AND BREATHE!
That was Lucille months ago. She was awake because I couldn't fuck her and her insides were still on fire; I had spilled my insides in the bathroom a few hours before. Funny part? I thought I was faking sleep.
"You're going to choke to death some night," said Lucille.
"Did I wake you," I asked. "I apologize."
Lucille leaned her body into mine.
"You wanna stay awake?"
"Sure," I said as I nuzzled her breasts with my chin.
Lucille's hands played over my middle.
"Anything?" she asked.
"I'm trying," I said.
"Talk dirty. Do you want to talk dirty?"
"I guess so."
"You first," said Lucille.
"I want to…play with your big boobs."
Lucille stopped rubbing my penis.
"That's it? That's the best you could do?"
"That wasn't good?"
"You're a writer, for God's sake!"
"Exactly. I'm not a talker, Lucille. I could *write* it for you."
Lucille rolled over, and I could see a large pimple on her back.
"You don't think I'm pretty do you, Dami? You never say it."
"Say what?"
"I'm not skinny like Alison."

"I think you're attractive."

"Or tragic like Kat."

It was my time to roll away, although the act was largely symbolic—Lucille wouldn't be able to tell if I had rolled away. It was a small bed, and along with big boobs, Lucille had a sizable bottom; there really was nowhere left for me to roll to.

"Don't talk about Kat."

"Attractive?"

"I would prefer if we didn't talk about Kat."

"A lamp is attractive, for fuck's sake."

"What's wrong with attractive?"

"Oh, like Kat is some holy figure. You let Alison run down Kat."

"Maybe I should leave."

"It's your bed, Dami."

"I know. Maybe I should leave it. I've been here forever," I said, and my eyes sought out the place, behind the closed closet door where my father's suitcase lay in waiting for my trembling fingers and oh-so bloodshot eyes.

18.

"In a little while from now,
If I'm not feeling any less sour,
I promised myself, to treat myself,
And visit a nearby tower.
And climbing to the top,
Will throw myself off,
In an effort to make clear to whoever,
What it's like when you're shattered."
      Gilbert O'Sullivan, "Alone Again (Naturally)"

Lucy Lucille.

The suitcase sits packed on the floor. I'm not in the car with Alison and Kat. I'm not enumerating methods of patricide. I'm not holding a conference with two Freudian vultures.

Murder.

This is bordering on the ridiculous.

"Lucille? Wake up and breathe, Lucille."

I shove at her shoulders with both hands. I stick my tongue in her ear. I squeeze shut her nose. I flick a finger on the side of her head.

Nothing.

Okay, so what if Lucille is dead? Why haven't I called the police? Why haven't I called my mother?

Lucille's neck is purple, but in the dark, I can't distinguish a hickey from strangulation marks, and there is no way I am turning on the light.

I dial Alison's number and a man answers, so I hang up.

So, the boy on the bicycle was a dream? He's alive, throwing newspapers on people's lawns, living for another collection day?

So, my father is breathing peacefully, nowhere near his final moment, no Volvo of Death speeding toward his sprawling fat, three assassins tucked in and honing their anger?

When I pull the sheet down, there are bruises all along Lucille's inner thigh. My penis is adhered to the inside of my underwear as if stuck there with glue.

When Click-Clock's alarm sounds, and some DJ blares out his fake corporate smile all over the end of Al Green's "Let Stay Together," reminding me that substantive music and thus reality remain frustratingly out of reach, I pull the sheet over Lucille's face and sit on my father's suitcase, jerking off to pass the time. (How is it I can come alone, but not with Lucille?—ah, it's better not to look too close, my friend.) I am careful to clean up with a bath towel—I wouldn't want to Make a Mess—and I wait for the sun to overtake the sky so I can call my mother and ask her to help me with the body.

19.

"Such a feelin's comin' over me.
There is wonder in most everything I see;
Not a cloud in the sky,
Got the sun in my eyes,
And I won't be surprised if it's a dream.

Everything I want the world to be
Is now coming true especially for me,
And the reason is clear:
It's because you are here;
You're the nearest thing to heaven that I've seen."
          The Carpenters, "Top of the World"

WAKE UP AND—
Yeah, I know the drill.

I spent weeks after Kat left living among her belongings; she had left almost everything. I knew the inventory like the back of my hand, like the inside of her thigh. I knew where I could hide my empty booze bottles should it come to needing a hiding place. When Kat stopped loving me, all I had left were objects of affection, and those I cultivated like fine seedlings; I tended to their needs, I counted the collection of old hand mirrors, I enumerated the tubes of lip balm, I placed in order the years of therapeutic artistic endeavors piled about her room like so many discarded playing cards, I spoke at length with the stuffed animals perched upon the end of her bed.

I slept between her covers. I covered myself in her sleep smells.

When Alison left…Alison never really left. My phone never stops ringing; my answering machine never stops filling up with Alison's takes on various world events: the discovery of a stray cat, the departure of yet another lover, the realization of a line or two of poetry—Alison feels the need to announce her mental journeys and eventual destinations. She plays on the fact that I want her. Alison never completely discards the people she's fooled around with: she uses them like puzzle pieces in her own bit of myth building, and in that way, I recognize my father, the cocky, newly coroneted checker king, swinging to and fro without regard for the safety of the other pieces.

But she never mentions the boy on the bicycle.

Despite knowing that I would just buy another one soon enough—so fearful am I that Alison's messages will stop—I tear the phone line from the wall and heave yet another answering machine into the trash, enjoying the *ching* as it shatters an empty bottle of gin.

I squeeze my muscles shut.

I carve my father's initials in my arm.

20.

"I wish I were an Oscar Mayer wiener;
That is what I'd truly like to be;
'Cause if I were an Oscar Mayer wiener,
Everyone would be in love with me."
> Oscar Mayer hot dog commercial

WAKE UP—

Just stop.

It was a family gathering, and Lucille was too big and too obvious—not that the obviousness was her fault; on the contrary, I felt my family would see through the thickness of her thighs and the bulk of her back to what she represented: NOT Alison—NOT Kat. The fact that Lucille was a big girl—big boned was how my aunts would have put it, not unkindly—was possibly not necessarily her fault either. We can't help the way our genes are arranged—some things are just stacked against you that way—like my big lips, some weird amalgamation of my mother's tender, puffed, wrinkled distributor of good-night kisses ("good night, sleep tight…") and my father's Camel cigarette receptacles. Lucille was cursed with constantly traveling through life like a roadblock—always in the way, filling a passage, soaking in outside stimuli and dulling them, never allowing them to reach the center of her. Lucille, in the past, had attracted a not inconsiderable collection of rogues and barflies.

My mother looked as if she wanted to clean Lucille—my mother circled her like a vulture, pushing hors d'oeuvres, giving Lucille a wide berth, but unable to prevent herself from assisting Lucille in the liberation of a piece of a lint from her smart suit jacket or a tiny fuzz ball from her conservatively panty hosed knee.

Lucille, for her part, didn't want to be there. Not that she didn't feel strongly about our relationship, but an afternoon and evening spent with my family implied something larger looming in the next frame, and Lucille had become convinced that I would erase the next chapter; Lucille didn't feel mythologized. To compound this fear, Lucille's failed marriage made her suspicious of men in general; her reaction was more earthy than Kat's or Alison's—Lucille didn't need to push men out of her life nor did she need to consume them (except literally); Lucille simply used them as necessary—the dessert topping at the end of a long night of bar hopping—and didn't believe or feel the need to have any of them stick.

In Lucille's spongy mind, behind her large forehead and perpetually wet brown eyes, I was sticking.

All in all, with the exception of Alison's name coming up several times, thanks in part to my twin aunts who saw in Alison a too skinny girl in need of food (prepared by them, of course) and a future with a sensitive husband—namely me—the dinner went off without a hitch. Kat's name rarely came up at family gatherings; years of support during Kat's twilight struggles against the demons of her history had left my family gasping for its collective breath. When Kat split the scene with the Spider-Woman in tow, my family, in particular my mother, who saw such behavior as dirty, branded her a Judas and washed their hands of her dirt.

Despite being big boned, Lucille didn't eat much; being big boned was purely the result of DNA and not of any particular dietary conviction. Lucille smiled her way through dinner, offering conversation when necessary, responding in kind when spoken to, passing to the left as was my aunts' wont. Lucille was perched between wanting to give a good impression because of the way she felt about me and merely being polite because I had forced her into this gathering of blood relatives.

"Eat. Eat," said Aunt Madge.

"You can always walk it off afterwards, sweetie," said Aunt Theresa.

"Where? To your house, Theresa? Maybe you two can jog together," said Aunt Madge as she sucked on another Merit, my mother dodging Aunt Theresa's opulent hand gestures to reconfigure the position of the astray in relative proximity to Madge's equally wandering hand. Madge's voice was like glass traveling through a blender; Theresa's was only slightly smoother through a concentrated effort honed through years of service to local parish boards and spaghetti dinner fundraisers.

"No, I'm okay. I'm good. Thank you," said Lucille.

"You're full?" asked Aunt Madge.

"You don't like the deviled eggs, doll?" asked Aunt Theresa.

"What do you mean she doesn't like your deviled eggs, Theresa?"

Aunt Madge opined, "She ate two of them."

"Liked them a bit better than those little brown sandwiches of yours. Cutting the crusts off was a bad idea," said Aunt Theresa.

"No, they were fine," said Lucille.

"Your deviled eggs give me gas something fierce," said Aunt Madge.

"How do you know you didn't arrive with the gas, Madge? You're quite often tooting away when I pick you up."

"Now, now, ladies," said my mother, who regarded any talk involving bodily functions as possibly dirty, although even discussions involving the brushing of one's teeth were cause for alarm. To my mother, fulfilling a need was, without warning, a path to dirtying the soul—especially cigarettes, but she dared not challenge the aunts.

"The problem," said Aunt Theresa, igniting her own Merit, ignoring my mother and the way she darted to and fro with the ashtray, "the problem is that most folks don't know how to be polite when they *don't* like something."

"How so?" asked Lucille.

"Take my sister's open-faced sandwich wedges," said Aunt Theresa, waving her Merit like incense in church. "If you didn't like them, if they repulsed you the way they repulse me, all squishy center without proper fencing—you need the crusts dear," Aunt Theresa said, her eyes catching Aunt Madge's in a well-practiced side swipe, "—then you are left with the decision to spit or swallow."

"I beg your pardon?" asked Lucille.

My mother looked at the meticulously vacuumed rug as if she wished it could swallow her whole; she picked a half-inch thread from the side of the love seat.

Aunt Madge managed her own sidelong glance, sweeping her Merit so it came dangerously close to Aunt Theresa's hooknose; Theresa never budged.

"What my vulgar sister means is that to spit or to swallow is the question—Hamlet was wrong; that is the question!—the question every young lady must face when confronted with such gaseous poison as Theresa's deviled eggs. If you were at home, well, you might just spit the foul concoction into the sink like so much garbage..."

"Nobody," Aunt Theresa said between puffs, "forced five deviled eggs down your throat, Madge. Your gas, while a matter worthy of encyclopedic detailing to you, merely disgusts the remainder of our niece's company."

"…but in mixed company, well, you can't just spit the poisoned eggs into a napkin, can you? But still, the choice is there: spit or swallow."

"If one were to judge you merely on your dress size, Madge, one would have to agree that your choice invariably involves the latter," said Aunt Theresa.

"Don't kill the chef," my mother laughed nervously.

I remembered Lucille squeezing my hand, and my aunts exchanging a glance amid the forest of Merit smoke. I was on my fourth gin and tonic. It wasn't even dark out yet.

Afterwards, on the drive home, I thanked Lucille for putting up with the unholy trio, and she placed her hand in my lap.

"Is this okay," she asked. "Can I do this?"

And the truth of the matter was this: I didn't know if it was okay, I didn't know if I was marking time with Lucille, but it sure felt like it—I could feel the seconds Click-Clocking away while my mind wore the Twin Stones of Kat and Alison smooth. I couldn't even finish when I jerked off without one or the other dancing in my head.

Lucille's hand was interfering with my driving. I pulled over and pulled it out.

"Put it in your mouth," I begged.

Lucille stared at me and lowered her head, and the world squeezed it muscles slightly, the streetlamps becoming like little stars, like little shattered bottles of alcohol fertilizing the bottom of the trashcan. I could see the little hairs on Kat's back and behind, I could feel the ridges like tree rings deep inside her, I could taste the revulsion in my mouth at the knowledge that those ridges were man-made and not natural; I could feel Alison's eager nipples between my teeth, I could hear her strenuous instructions involving the placement of my hands and mouth. I could feel the weight of my father's suitcase, and I realized with a start (that Lucille took for an involuntary muscular reaction to her oral activities) that I could feel its weight even as it sat upon the top shelf of my bedroom closet. I realized with a moan (that Lucille took for an auditory affirmation of what she considered to be her estimable skills) that that weight was *all* I could feel—its weight bore down on my shoulders and brain like an avalanche of empty, sudsy bottles of booze, like a runaway flight of multicolored vultures.

I came without fanfare—all sensation, the whole writhing eyes-squeezed-muscles-taut-teeth-grinding variety, subsumed into my shaking toes, overshadowed by the slow drip of fluids leaking from my brain.

I felt nothing.

"I can't feel anything," I said.

Nothing was all I felt.

My penis was as numb as my right foot.

Lucille exploded.

Lucille had the reaction usually reserved for the recipient of the orgasm.

Lucille went bat shit.

"What the fuck is wrong with you?" asked Lucille, as she spat my sperm back into my lap. "I can't believe this. What am I doing wrong? You came, didn't you?"

Lucille's jowls were shaking; her eyes were submerging themselves into pools of mascara and salt water. I hoped Lucille wouldn't ask me to eat her out. I wasn't in the mood.

"You want me to be somebody else," said Lucille.

I started the car; I turned the key.

No, Lucille, I thought, *I want to be somebody else.*

Anybody else.

Nobody would be mighty fine too, okey-dokey with me.

21.

"I've just closed my eyes again,
Climbed aboard the dream weaver train;
Driver take away my worries of today
And leave tomorrow behind."
      Gary Wright, "Dream Weaver"

Spit or swallow.

"Is that why you're gay?" Alison asks Kat.

"Is that why you fuck so many guys?" Kat asks Alison.

"Maybe we should talk about something else, ladies," I say.

"Patronizing fuck," says Alison.

"Ahh, leave him be. It takes a lot to pull this sort of thing off: kidnapping, murder—plus he's not the best driver," says Kat.

"A nightmare on wheels," Alison concurs.

"Am I dreaming?" I ask.

"Isn't everyone?" asks Kat.

Alison leans her body against Kat and purrs. Kat places her hand in Alison's lap.

22.

"When I was young
I'd listen to the radio
Waitin' for my favorite songs;
When they played I'd sing along;
It made me smile.

Those were such happy times
And not so long ago,
How I wondered where they'd gone;
But they're back again,
Just like a long lost friend:
All the songs I loved so well."
        The Carpenters, "Yesterday Once More"

A woman with a New Orleans accent answers the green door that sits among the bricks of the boarding house. Her name is Mrs. DeLuge, although there isn't a Mr. DeLuge, hasn't been for years, wink-wink, and how-long-you-gonna-be-needing-this-here-room?

A couple of days, I tell her.

Maybe a couple of weeks, I tell Mrs. DeLuge.

Whatcha-got-in-the-bag? she asks, eyeing my father's suitcase. Mrs. DeLuge speaks in a wind: all her words are crushed against the ones released before it. Her breath smells like she's been eating dead things and smoking ten packs a day.

Nothing, I tell her.

Everything, I think to myself.

Well-breakfast-is-at-6:30-Monday-through-Friday.   It's-over-by-seven-so-if-you-want some eggs-and-toast-you-best-be-there-at-6:30. Comes-with-the-room.

How much is the room? I ask Mrs. DeLuge.

I think I need to lie down for a little while, I tell my landlady.

Bathroom's-in-the-hall, she says. There's-a-corner-room-on-the-second-floor. You-gotta-share-the-bathroom. You-gotta-a-problem-with-sharing?

No, ma'am, I say.

A burly barrel of a man rolls down the hall. He has a neatly trimmed beard and boots with little torn windows so I can see his toes.

This-here's-Malachi.

Malachi shakes my hand, but his eyes never leave my suitcase.

What you got in there? he asks.

Bit of everything, I reply.

Whole lot of nothing, I say.

Malachi grunts—his breath reeks of scrambled eggs—and pushes past us in the hall.

I'll-show-you-'round, the landlady says. Now-do-be-careful-if-you-go-down-the-basement-for-anything, not-that-you-would. The-basement-stairs-is-where-the-late-Mr.-DeLuge-had-his-unfortunate-accident. Billy, he-keeps-his-spank-mags-down-there; I-don't-know-why-and-don't-you-go-touching-them, hear? Billy's-very-particular-about-who-he-lets-beat-it-to-his-mags. Anyways, Tom (Mr.-Tommy-to-you) told-me-he-would-fix-that-unfortunate-loose-step, but-hell, he-don't-get-outta-bed-until-after-twelve-or-one-and-then-he's-gotta-drink-a few-beers-just-to-equilibrate-himself, so-don't-go-giving-him-a-hammer. You-got-a-hammer-in-there? Mrs. DeLuge asks, her eyes caressing my suitcase. Looks-heavy, it-do.

No, no hammer, I say, shaking my head.

No-matter, here's-the-common-room.

A man in overalls calls out: nothing common in here, Swannie.

The room is tiny, and a black and white television is receiving signals on a wobbly tray. Huddled around a tall ashtray are three men. Another man is sprawled on the tiny torn couch in just his boxer shorts. I can see his thick patch of unruly pubic hair. The smell is of Marlboros and the faint whispers of cheap soap from yesterday's showers.

What's in the case, friend? asks the man in the overalls.

He-ain't-talking, Tom.

The hell he ain't. He looks like he can talk.

I-don't-mean-he-can't. I-mean-he-won't.

The curtains are a faded yellow and frayed at the bottoms. A man in a t-shirt that barely covers his protruding hairy belly sucks on a cigarette, gently touching the one tucked behind his ear.

What the fuck, Swan?

He-ain't-talking. I-don't-know what-he's-got-in-there.

Not much, I mutter to myself, covering my nose with my sleeve.

The whole fucking world, I think to myself, and wouldn't *you* like to know.

Not the friendly type, says the third man who's ninety if he's a day. He's wearing a black shirt and a priest's collar stained with black fingerprints. The Lord says suffer the little children unto me, says the old man.

That's how you got in trouble in the first place, says Mr. Tommy, and when he burps, the room fills with whisky vapors.

All the residents share a laugh, and the priest nods his head in time, his cigarette long with ash. Mr. Tommy leans over and flicks the priest's ash with two fingers. Most of it lands on the rug.

If-he-wants-to-keep-the-bag-to-himself, let-him. Maybe-it's-all-he's-got, says Mrs. DeLuge.

Maybe, Swannie. Maybe it's all *we* got, says Mr. Tommy.

The room erupts with laughter again, and the priest nods off into the stains of his collar.

Wants a room, I guess? asks the man in the t-shirt.

That's-the-way-it-looks, responds Mrs. DeLuge.

And we don't know what's in the suitcase?

Not-a-clue. Not-a-clue, do-we-mister?

No, ma'am, I say.

Yes, ma'am, I reply.

Must be import, says the man in the t-shirt.

Im-por-tant, corrects Mr. Tommy.

Either-way, says Mrs. DeLuge, we-ain't-getting-a-peek.

Give us each day our daily bread, says the priest in his sleep.

Gonna give him a room, Swannie?

Got-to, Tom, Mrs. DeLuge says. We-need-the-rent.

How much is the rent? I ask.

Is it much? I venture.

Tom, where's-Billy? asks Mrs. DeLuge.

Beatin' off, I suspect. Why?

Was-going-to-ask-him-to-run-this-mister's-bag-into-his-room. Billy's-gotta-earn-his-stay-somehow. I-ain't-running-a-flophouse.

More laughter. More exhaled smoke. The filter of the priest's cigarette starts to burn his carefully creased black pants.

Oh, Christ, be-a-hon-and-put-the-Father-out, would-you-Tom?

Sure as shit, Swannie, says Mr. Tommy as he smacks the filter from the old priest's hand. Want me to carry his bag?

I can carry it, I say.

The burden is mine, I tell them.

The priest rises from his seat.

Thou shall not commit murder, says the old priest.

Is this a dream, I ask?

This-smell-like-a-dream? Mrs. DeLuge asks, and I can smell the death of a thousand eggs scrambled; I am awash in the scent of ancient sweat socks and teeth barely brushed. My mother would have a field day.

I'm not sure anymore, I tell Mrs. DeLuge, but she's already leading me down the hall, and she has my father's suitcase in her right hand. I pull on her arm and remove the suitcase with a polite smile.

I have to carry it all the way, I say by way of explanation.

It belonged to my father.

23.

"When I need you
I just close my eyes and I'm with you,
And all that I so want to give you,
It's only a heartbeat away.

When I need love,
I hold out my hands and I touch love;
I never knew there was so much love,
Keeping me warm night and day."
                Leo Sayer, "When I Need You"

Zing zing zing went my heartstrings. Ding ding ding went the bell.

That's not AM fodder from the '70s. Real music is seeping through.

My mother answers with her afternoon voice despite the fact that it's barely dawn.

"Mom?"

"Damien?"

"I think Lucille is dead," I say.

I can hear my mother sit up in bed.

"Which one is Lucille, dear? Is she the little Irish girl who dirtied up my bathroom?"

"No, Mom, that was Iris. Mom, that was in grade school."

My mother sighs into the receiver: "Thank God. I could never take that mess of a girl."

"Mom, it's Lucille. We were just at your house with the aunts."

"The vultures?"

I pull the phone away from my ear and stare into the receiver.

"No, the aunts."

My mother hums briefly into the phone: "She didn't eat much, that one. Doesn't strike me as the swallowing type."

"Mom!"

Now I can hear the kitchen sink running.

"Sorry. I'm going to do the dishes, so you'll have to speak up."

"There were dirty dishes in the sink overnight?"

My mother laughs: "Don't be silly, Dami. Sometimes you can see the spots you missed better in the early morning light. You woke me up, remember? Something about the heavy girl. You know your friend Alison—she needs to eat."

I cover my eyes with my hand.

"Mom, I need you to stop washing the dishes for a second. I need to tell you something."

The water turns off, and I can practically hear my mother straighten her frame and lean against the refrigerator, careful not to smudge the surface.

"Yes?"

"I think Lucille is dead."

"You'll meet other girls."

"Mom, I think she's dead here. In my bed."

"You're sleeping with her?"

"Not now. Now, she's dead."

"You brought her to your apartment dead? To sleep with her? Dami, Dami, we need to get you some—"

"Mom!"

"Yes?"

"Lucille sleeps here sometimes."

"Doesn't she have her own bed?"

"Mom!"

"Yes?"

"Lucille does, in fact, have her own bed, but sometimes she sleeps over, and tonight she slept over, and I think she's dead. I think she's dead right now. In my bed. Right now."

"Well, why would she go and do such a thing?"

"Mom. Mom. I think I killed her."

"Don't be silly, Dami. You were too busy committing a mortal sin with her to kill her."

I run my hand across my father's suitcase and study a stain on the one side. Mother didn't always live for cleaning—not that she was ever dirty. Mother has a cause and dust is the opposition; Mother developed a reason to live, and I have none.

"I'm not judging the way you live your life, Dami," says my mother, "but it seems to me that if you lived a clean life, you wouldn't have heavy girls die in your bed at all hours of the night."

"Mom, did you hear me? I said I think I killed her. I don't think she *just died*. I think I killed her—during sex."

My mother exhales a long sigh into the phone, and I can hear her rattling the silverware into their resting place inside a drawer.

"I thought you killed the boy on the bicycle."

"What?"

"This is starting to be a habit."

"The boy on the bicycle is *really* dead?"

"I'll be over soon anyway. Just do your poor mother a favor, Dami, okay? Just straighten up a bit before I get there, okay? I'll help dust those curtains, but just pick up those socks at least. Do it for me, Dami, okay? Just do it for your mom, alright?"

24.

"Did you find the directing sign on the
Straight and narrow highway?
Would you mind a reflecting sign?
Just let it shine within your mind
And show you the colors that are real."
    Blood, Sweat, and Tears, "Spinning Wheel"

Post Blow Job: we were not far from my apartment when the rain started. The radio had been calling for rain the past four days— slippery driving conditions, low visibility, the works. My ancient Volvo was motoring along nicely though. Lucille wasn't talking to me, but we were making good time, despite the rain.

When we crossed the railroad tracks, near the old brick boarding house, the radio reception started to fade and sputter. Lucille stared out the window, presumably counting the raindrops collecting on the glass or perhaps humming along to a song on the sputtering sizzle of the car radio's piss-poor reception. It was hard to tell. Occasionally, I saw her hand sneak to her little black purse for a cigarette, but I don't allow her to smoke in my car. Occasionally, my mother asks me to accompany her on an errand, which means I drive, and if my mother were to smell even the hint of enclosed smoke…

"You got a cigarette?" I asked Lucille.

Lucille just stared at the side of my head as my finger caressed the radio dial.

"Damn rains," I said, nodding toward the radio.

"Switch it over to AM," said Lucille, and I smiled to myself; I didn't think Lucille was the kind of girl who ever switched it over to AM. But I didn't—I liked the bluesy song on the radio—was it Solomon Burke? The singer was buried beneath layers of crunchy clamor and stormy static.

"Here," said Lucille after rummaging through her purse. She held out a cigarette for me. She had one dangling from her mouth.

"I was just kidding."

Lucille rolled down the window and deposited both cigarettes into the rain.

"I hate smoking. I was just seeing if I would. I'm tired," I said, turning my head slightly to Lucille. "I didn't sleep well last night."

"Just take me back to your place, and I'll leave in the morning. You'll sleep better."

I ignored Lucille and continued to fiddle with the radio as I stopped at the light. I couldn't quite make out the song; maybe it was a Delta blues guy: Robert Johnson? Son House? Muddy Waters? It was too fuzzy to tell.

The red light was giving off circular waves, and the rain was syncopating itself against my windshield. The whole world was awash in diagonal slashes of red; the whole damn world was submerged beneath a red sea, and Lucille and I were stragglers, just *this far* from the Promised Land, dawdling just enough for the Red Sea to come crashing down upon our heads in retribution for sins not yet committed, for acts of passion ignited without forethought, for moments of severe tenderness denied for seconds of agonizing, neck-twisting pleasure.

The radio was all hiss and haunted voices—words faded in and out of the mix: a phrase, the turn of a syllable like a woman's delicate turn of a leg. It was a blues—it was the sound of someone dying, someone shrinking underneath the weight of *all this shit*. You could hear the world crack if you listened close enough; you could hear all the angels of heaven fold beneath their wings and surrender before the whip-crack of pain, before the wake-up call of whatever crawls just under the skin, before their heads exploded beneath an orchestra of hate, a symphony of lies, a cacophony of broken bassoons, screaming violins, shattered cellos, and the no-longer-distant thunder of the kettle drum.

"Billie Holiday!"

Lucille turned toward me, then looked away.

"Fucking music means more to you than I do."

I ignored her and released the brake just a bit so the car lurched forward a little across the line—any slight movement might help the reception, any inch of forward motion might spring free the singer from her pain and plight.

"This is a long red light," I said to myself.

"*Everything* means more to you than me: Alison, your mother, this music."

Billie slipped out of the fog for an instant and then dissipated in the struggle of competing frequencies. I swore it was Billie. I would bet my girlfriend on it.

I *tapped-tapped-tapped* on the brake, and the caged singer released a note or two before being swallowed—but these notes were clearer. There was no mistaking the pain—"You Don't Know What Love Is"—*Lady in Satin*—it was Lady Day.

"*You don't know how lost I feel,*" sang Billie, as I eased the car up.

A boy on a bicycle appeared on the left street corner, a newspaper bag slung across his chest, its thick, once-white cloth now dark with rain, erasing the newsprint stains and fingerprint smudges. His bicycle was silver with a black banana seat and black tassels and a Joker card held between the spokes of the rear wheel with a worn clothespin.

"You can hear the whole world in her voice—you can hear surrender and you can hear addiction: you can taste its nagging pull, you can practically touch it as it pulses along her nerves, begging for something, *anything*, to dull the emotions overtaking her brain, storming her blood until it threatens to tear apart even her skin in search of escape."

I spoke to myself; Lucille just stared at the side of my face.

My foot tapped along the brake, edging, edging, just enough to free Billie. *Someone* needed to be free.

"It's just a song, Dami," Lucille said. "And an old one at that."

My fingers played along the radio dial as if feeling blind along an old piano, looking for the grounding of middle C.

The boy on the silver bicycle looked both ways and adjusted his bag beneath the eternity of the red traffic light.

In the back of my head, I wondered briefly if the silver bicycle would improve the reception before the song returned to the air or was subsumed by the static. I wondered briefly what kind of mother would allow the boy to deliver papers on a bicycle—in the dark—in this downpour.

"*...until you loved a love you had to lose...*" sang Billie.

The song seemed to exist on a continuum, an endless cycle of abuse.

Another wave of feedback drowned out Billie, and I jerked the car forward by releasing the brake gently, then slamming it to the floor. Again. Again.

Lucille bumped her head on the glove compartment.

"Are you fucking out of your mind?"

Slow. Slow.

Billie was pulled down in the undertow; Billie was sucked under a blanket of volcanic ash, vultures circling just above her stoic head, her eyes circulating within their sockets, celebrating another loss to the chemicals that soaked her bloodstream and entrapped the part of her brain that remembered laughter, that remembered the touch of someone who loved you back, that remembered the paint-stained leaves of fall reaching up to greet God in heaven before falling with a grace note to the hardscrabble dirt floor, littered with sacrifices.

"...for a love that cannot live but never dies..."
Slower. Slower.

I wanted to revel in it—I wanted to remember all of it
Slowest. Slowest.

Then: Billie was there, and Lucille was screaming, holding her head, and I released the brake, and SLAMMED it back down—then GUNNED it and SLAMMED it—and the boy on the silver bicycle was under my wheels, and his front tire exploded from the pressure, and Lucille was still screaming, and I could see the red sneaking from behind her fingers, from her forehead, and as I released and SLAMMED the brake down one final time, something crunched like a candy bar, and the twisted silver frame of the bicycle went *snap, crackle, pop,* and for one brief, excruciating moment, the Click-Clock of the Joker card against the spinning rear wheel filled every orifice, and Billie was gone.

Dead Fucking Stop.

Lucille pushed her car door open, jumped out, then jumped back in, the door shutting with a quiet click, her face a silly-putty mask.

"I need some sleep," I said. "I really do. I think I just killed a boy with my car. You better drive."

Click-Clock-Click went the Joker. Ring Ding Ding went the bell.

Lucille reached over toward my face and tried to claw out my eyes, but I thought I was asleep and my eyes were no longer my concern.

25.

"Oh Mama, I'm in fear for my life
From the long arm of the law;
Lawman has put an end to my running,
And I'm so far from my home;
Oh Mama, I can hear you a-crying;
You're so scared and all alone;
Hangman is coming down from the gallows,
And I don't have very long."
     Styx, "Renegade"

You know I've loved two women, you know I love them still,
Love those little girls so damn much, and my time is mine to kill;
You know I love two women—I said: love and never hate,
Yet still I see no angels, I see no angels at the gate…
Motherfucking Road Trip.

It costs just about all I have for this Road Trip, although I am not sure we're going to ever leave the state. Days melt into stiff nights upon stained motel sheets and thin once-gold blankets festooned with worn, hard nibblets on either end. Kat and Alison sleep on the opposite bed, and although I know Kat would have liked to, Alison gives up nothing more than lengthy cuddling sessions and an arm or leg thrown over Kat's body in her sleep. Alison has sworn off sex. She claims she never had that much as it was, but now she wants none. Alison claims LOVE has left the room, and she doubts even its brief presence. Kat, despite her hunger for Alison, spends her mornings smoothing lotion over her scarred arms—she claims now to only carve with her pen, and every motel receipt, every cheap restaurant napkin is filled to the edges with scribbled words and half-forgotten phrases barely captured. Alison fills in the Os and the Qs with red ink.

I lie in the opposite bed and jerk off under the blankets.

Motherfucking Road Trip.

But, here we are, and here he is.

Didn't take much to string him up like a sunny out of the pond I used to fish when I was a kid. He was like a sand crab trapped in the undertow at Beach Haven, where annually my parents loosed me into a world that wasn't just outside our front door. In a way, this Road Trip is like those last final trips to Beach Haven—before I was too old to vacation with my parents, before my parents ceased to be a plural object of affection.

The car (or at least the front seat) is packed tightly, if still comfortably, and Kat, Alison, and I sing along to all the bad, great '70s songs issuing from the radio like Morse code, *tap-tap-tapping* along the brain, sending coded messages of a saccharine love that exists outside of the barren woods inhabited by my mother and me.

Maybe that's where we should take him: Beach Haven.

"It's *your* dream," says Kat, her right leg drooped over Alison's left, her scars fading from her arms so quickly, leaving them smooth runways for angels, she says—Kat's arms look like the ones you imagine Venus had before her fall.

"Whatever it is," says Alison, "I wish you would get it over with." Alison is tired, and her eyes are two dimming stars reflecting off the windshield. "This," Alison says, gesturing to the car, to Kat, to me, "is taking way too damn long. I need to go home. I want to paint."

I don't know how I know this, but I tell Alison anyway: "Your paints are beneath the seat. Next to some of Kat's stuffed animals."

"It's *your* dream," Kat repeats.

And so it is. Maybe.

We duck down in our seats, safe for the time being in the car, and watch the Fallen Father Figure leave his hovel from across the street, and we follow him to a corner bar, wherein he inhales:

- 6 ½ beers (the cheapest domestic stuff)
- ¾ of a basket of peanuts and cereal mix (sprinkled with a gentle brush of cigarette ash)
- 14 cigarettes (even Kat, who smokes her way through our dream—my dream—stops and squishes her pack beneath her bare feet)
- 2 greasy slices of pizza ("Boardwalk pizza," identifies Alison with a shudder)
- 2 shots of cheap whiskey (okay, we actually assign the whiskey the adjective of cheap, but we figure it isn't top shelf from the looks of the establishment)

I send Kat and Alison into the Velvet Lounge. Around the preassigned time (about 12:45 A.M.), they leave the bar, escorting a vertically challenged man, one part alcohol, one part sperm donator, one hundred percent asshole. Here he is, and he is ours.

He doesn't recognize me behind the wheel; he merely whines about being in the backseat alone, he moans about driving so far from his home and would someone give him some cab fare. Once, I swear, he complains about all the vulture feathers strewn about the back of the car, but I don't ask him to repeat himself. I squeeze my muscles and dig a fingernail into my arm.

"Cheap motel?" asks Alison, and truth be told, I figure she knows best when it comes to the execution of filthy affairs.

"I haven't slept with as many people as you think, Dami," says Alison.

"Behind the shed or near the edge of the woods?" ventures Kat, and I knew for Kat, this was but an opportunity to enact revenge upon her sexual predator, her parental assailant.

"I'm over it, Dami," says Kat. "Therapy. Years of fucking therapy. Talked it out. Feel good."

"Looking good," says Alison.

Kat squeezes Alison's hand, but I could swear it was Alison's boob.

"Beach Haven," I say, "we're going to Beach Haven."

Beach Haven: images of my uncle's house: the sand beneath my feet, sand even in the upstairs bathroom, the old writing desk where my uncle wrote his historical essays and "plumbed the truth," he would say, his pink nose bobbing up and down in the crevice of a book, the rooms hidden within other rooms, rooms you could only reach by entering through the previous room's closet door, the white pebbles in the front yard, the peeling white shower stalls outside where you tried to wash away the sand before entering the house, the shower doors beginning some inches from the ground, so you could always scare a cousin by pushing in the plastic spider you won at the penny arcade or the sand crab you captured from the undertow. And the undertow: the yearly warnings like commandments from God, those commands eventually transforming into ritual, all of us, my mother, my father, and me, repeating out loud: "Mind the undertow, now." And the actual *tug*: the gravitational, hypnotic pull of the ocean at your feet—the sweet sense of surrender lingering just beneath the surface of salt-caked hair and half-yanked-off bathing shorts emblazoned with the Green Lantern or the hammer of Marvel's

Thor—that last terrible second, pulling yourself from Poseidon the arch villain's sleepy but insistently strong come-ons. Exhausting.

I am reminded of tossing a Captain Marvel action figure in the stony front yard after an afternoon spent teasing the ocean, my skin toasty from the sun, my stomach growling from the smell of corn on the cob drowning in the kitchen, my insides eager for another night prowling the penny arcade or spent playing cards on the sandy floor with my cousins. Higher and higher went Captain Marvel (*Shazam!*), until I began banking him off the sloped side of the roof, watching him bounce off the gritty tiles, slide down to the rain gutter, and spill over, ass over teacups as my father used to say, to the rocky front yard until, finally, one of his arms snapped off. I picked him up, examined his dusty cape, the torn lightning bolt on his chest, secreting him behind the soap dish in the outside shower. The next morning, I sneaked out while my parents prepared lunch for the beach, my mother neatly jamming peanut butter and jelly between slices of bread, my father feigning good health as he struggled beneath an inevitable hangover, both of my parents' eyes puffy: my father's from drink at one or all of the local bars, my mother's from lack of sleep, from a night spent tidying, for it was her method of keeping her mind away from what she called the Idle Impulses: homicidal, suicidal. On the beach, I walked out until I could no longer see my knees, until the ocean recognized my scent and ordered its undertow to tickle my feet and fuck with my head. I stood stock still, my ankles quivering, until at the last possible moment, my feet numb from strain, I tossed Captain Marvel as far as my skinny little arm could, running back to the house with my first short story dancing in my head, and later that night, staying up way past my assigned bedtime to scribble in a cribbed notebook (not at my uncle's desk, but tucked neatly between the sheets, the flashlight shadows painting between the lines), and my father, fresh from the bar, suddenly squeaking my door open, a brand new, still sealed Captain Marvel action figure in his hand, his other hand stealing under the sheets until I no longer remembered a single idea for my short story.

"Repeat!" cries Alison. "Always telling the same old stories."

Kat nudges her with an elbow. "It's touching."

"So, we're tossing him in the ocean?" asks Alison.

"Or are we tearing his arm off like Captain Marvel?" asks Kat.

"You have no idea why we're here, do you?" I ask, my fingers gripping the steering wheel, my fingernails digging soft moons into my palm.

"I don't know," says Kat.

"Couldn't tell you," Kat says.

"Wouldn't *you* like to know?" Kat finishes.

"Two vultures are staring at me," Alison adds. And although I cannot see the vultures, I smell their musky breath and hear the Click-Clock of their beaks striking bone.

Beach Haven: my father is so much liquid and nicotine and high caloric food product that moving him into the house is easy: we pour him into the living room, and as I tie him to a chair, Alison and Kat explore the house, discover the rooms you can only reach by going through other rooms, my secret rooms. I can hear Kat in the crawl space; I can hear Alison peeing in the second floor bathroom.

"Nice dream," Kat says with a grin.

"Have to hand it to you, Dami, you paint a nice picture," says Alison with a hint of admiration beneath the usual surface of sarcasm.

I slap my father across the face, like in the movies, to bring him around.

"Don't talk," I say.

"Yeah," Kat says, lighting a cigarette with a match scratched across my father's shoe. "It's his dream."

"Is this going to take long? How long do patricides usually take?" Alison asks.

My father's baggy eyes go wide, but there's not a hint of recognition until I kneel down before him, between his knees—his eyes go global, the blood rushes to his saggy unshaven face, and something not unlike fear overtakes his brief waltz of pleasure. Then: pain, for as I stand up and tug on the electrical tape and rope binding him to the chair, they tighten in his crotch until little tears appear in the corners of his eyes like vultures circling road kill.

I slap his face again to ensure his attention.

I tear open my shirt, just like in the movies.

I lick my lips.

"For crimes against my heart…" I begin.

"Oh, brother," says Alison, collapsing in a dusty cloud on the sofa.

"…I sentence you to *forever*," I continue.

"It's a good start," says Kat, "leave him be."

Alison shrugs, and Kat winks at me.

That was the length of my speech however—pared down from the essay I'd scribbled on the front of a playing card before we left for Beach Haven. *Forever*—that's where my demon belonged—in the same hell implied by my purgatorial sleep apnea—a *forever* designed to repeat, to turn on itself, until the everyday reality of the cracks on the ceiling merges perfectly with the phantom vulture feathers of lost thought and forgotten nightmares.

He placed his hand under the sheets.

"That's it," asks Alison. "All the way to New Jersey for a ten word speech."

"Shhh—the best part is coming," says Kat.

"If anyone is coming, I'm leaving the room," says Alison.

"No, silly, don't you get it? *Dami gets to kill the man who killed love.* That's why he needs us. Sure, Dami loves us, and yeah, sure, his love is real or as real as this sort of thing gets, but he *clings* to us because *he has to*! And now, he gets to stab the source, get to the heart of it, so to speak. Let Daddy suck on *that*—for all time."

Alison sits on the edge of the sofa, her feet tapping expectantly.

"Is that how you're going to do it? Stab him?" asks Alison.

My father's eyes swallow his face. He is boring me—all this eyeballing and milking of tears.

"I haven't thought about it. I was working on the speech."

"Christ," says Alison.

"Well, let's keep our heads about us, shall we," says Kat. "Your choices are myriad. Pick one, the one that best signifies what you want to say, the method that most represents *you*. You only get to do this once."

"What? Murder?" asks Alison.

"Oh, no, no, no," exclaims Kat. "That may have happened a couple of times already. The boy on the bicycle?"

"Or the fat chick!" cries Alison.

"Big boned," corrects Kat. "She was just big boned."

"Ah-ha!" Alison exclaims. "The past tense."

"Well, is she or isn't she?" Kat asks me, her chest purple in the rising of the sun just visible through the dust-coated yellow curtains.

"I bet he doesn't even know if he killed her. He thinks *this* is a dream," says Alison, the orange morning light dappling across her face.

"Stab him," offers Kat.

"Choke him," Alison shrugs.

"Got a gun?" asks Kat.

"Shove a rag down his throat," suggests Alison.

"But dip it in gasoline first!" Kat cries.

"Snap his neck."

"Choke him with your dick."

"Shove a pencil in his ear."

"His eye."

"His fat belly."

"His rear end!"

"Carve him."

"Slice and dice him."

"Drink his blood."

"Paint the walls with it."

"Dance in it!"

"Fuck in it!"

"KILL!" they cry in unison, in perfect harmony, and I do, and when I am done, I carry his head to the ocean, careful to mind the undertow, and toss it high above the cracks in the ceiling (if I am dreaming), not far from the watchful eyes of the carrion birds (if I am not).

Back at the house, I mop up the blood and wrap the remains in plastic trash bags—double bagged so they won't rip in the garbage man's hands. There aren't enough trash bags, however, and I am thankful for the old man's crusty suitcase.

When I start the car, I am alone. The front seat is cold. Kat and Alison are gone. There is no sign of the two vultures. As I pull out of the driveway, I stop when I notice the caked blood beneath my fingernails. My mother would be upset at the mess, so I use my teeth to pull the cuticles out until I can remove the offending nails. Mother would be so proud.

26.

"Awww—freak out!"
    Chic, "Le Freak"

"Fuck me," Lucille said, once we got home, and in her voice, no trace of longing or desire lingered; Lucille was trying to erase the boy on the bicycle.

We were in my bedroom, and the cracks on the ceiling must have yawned wide from Lucille's point of view, on the bottom, for when I pierced her, she seemed to be swallowed up into something bigger than either of us—not an object of lust, nor a tender lover—I was finally too erect for either of those.

"Fuck me," said Lucille, and I plunged into her middle with a shout. The bedposts lifted an inch off the wood floors and bounced back, Click-Clock rattled on the nightstand, my father's suitcase, for some reason no longer tucked inside the closet, but leaning against the bed, slipped with a thud to the floor, and Lucille's flesh shuddered in waves around my body. I was no longer a writer; I was no longer witnessing—I was the main event, the triggerman.

Between gasps of stale smoker's breath, Lucille said, "You killed the boy on the bicycle."

Higher and higher went my hips and backside—Lucille, the walls, Click-Clock were all ensconced in long blurs.

"You think you're in love with Alison," said Lucille.

I plunged my shaking hands behind Lucille's fleshy back; I dug my nails into her gelatinous portions.

"Because Kat never loved you the way you wanted her to," Lucille offered, her head bouncing off the mattress, her forehead occasionally colliding with mine in mid air. I sunk my teeth into her shoulder blade.

"Admit it, Dami," Lucille demanded.

I tried to scissor my legs to trap hers, but I was on top and positioning was crucial.

Above me, above the violent machinations of a body strapped to a numb, erect penis, the sky that masqueraded as my ceiling, the ceiling that hid itself within a river of cracks, split open, and the purple-bruise of early morning mixed with the screaming red and orange of the dying of the day, until my entire history could be glimpsed between squints, just under the glare of the birth cycle of the sun. And there I was born anew, without baggage, without love, without dipping a digit into the undertow of heartbreak. I wondered, in my newfound naked brilliance, that if a man was a sum of his experiences, then what was sum zero—what was the starting point. When was I ruined?

I raised my fists to the ceiling, and Click-Clock went silent, and my fists were two balls of crimson fury against the panorama unfolding between the cracks.

I punched Click-Clock. I killed time. The Joker card grinned from beneath the shards.

And when I lowered my hands and pulled apart my sticky fingers, Lucille's head seemed to be facing the wall in an extremely uncomfortable position, and my semen was spread across the expanse of her stomach.

"Fuck me," I said to myself, and I squeezed my balls with my trembling hands to see if I was asleep.

27.

"I wait in the darkness of my lonely room,
Filled with sadness, filled with gloom,
Hoping soon that you'll walk
Back through that door
And love me like you did before."
        Freda Payne, "Band of Gold"

And I list:

Kat's full name is Katrina, but she resembles a cat only in cliché—in the way a cat's owner will fuss over its independent nature, all the while spooning food from a can. Kat fought against this; Kat did not want to be spoon-fed.

Alison walks like a cat—her back undulates—she walks with her shoulder blades in the lead. Alison too is trapped by her own nature—Alison cannot resist the pull of someone rubbing her. Not that just anyone could rub Alison; Alison chooses her victims with care.

Kat swallows smoke like it is liquid. Her throat closes upon its tendrils, and for one moment, all the elements are hers to capture and play with as she likes.

Alison likes to curse. It gives her power—a girl who curses like a truck driver can still be shocking.

Kat can lose herself in a room of two or three. Kat has perfected the fine art of blending in.

Alison cannot resist her own mouth—it's always revealing what's beneath the magician's cloak or under the bed before any suspense can sink in.

Kat buys her clothes at the Salvation Army. Only her underwear is purchased new.

Alison dresses in her grandmother's cast-off silk chiffon flapper dresses.

Kat loves other women.

Alison has loved many, many men.

This is Kat's List: Kat is soft and her face is round and her eyes are distant and blue, a thunderstorm in the making. Kat's back is strong like a man's back. Her voice is a downy singsong thing you have to hunt and explore for. When Kat hugs you, there is no one else in her world, and you wonder if she will ever let go.

And this is Alison's List: Alison is all sharp angles; it is hard to find a grip. Alison is loud. Alison's brain works quicker than everyone else's because she thinks she has to outsmart everyone. She is the most talented person I know, and she does the least with it.

Kat suffered under the hands of her stepfather. To her stepfather, Kat was a punching bag and a fuck bag. Kat learned to hate the penis. Kat learned to hate herself. Kat learned that cutting herself focused her self-hatred, which in turn made it easier to bury, even deeper, her stepfather's extracurricular activities. Kat entered the world like a bruise, tender to the touch.

Alison only knows freedom. Her parents raised her in an atmosphere where she was allowed to grow and explore all her artistic needs without rules. Alison learned to hate rules. Men made rules, and Alison made sure that as soon as rules were set, she was gone. She shook only from trying to control what she considered uncontrollable: herself.

Kat's abuse became my abuse.

Alison's lack of control is now my lack of control.

Kat couldn't love me because I am a man, despite anything else she might feel. I have a penis.

Alison doesn't love me because I already love her. There would be rules, rings, vows. Alison knows this. There is nothing for her to conquer.

Kat is like a cat in that she needs to be loved but pretends not to.

Alison is like a cat in that she pretends to be independent but still needs to be fed.

I love them both, and they both scorned me.

Rejected me.

Abandoned me.

This is my list.

28.

"I don't know how to love him;
What to do, how to move him;
I've been changed, yes, really changed;
In these past few days when I've seen myself,
I seem like someone else."
    Yvonne Elliman, "I Don't Know How to Love Him"

WAKE UP AND BREATHE!
My father's suitcase is heavy as I pull it up the stairs of the boarding house.
Whatchoogot? A body in there?
I don't know.
Couldn't tell you.
Wouldn't they *like to know?*
In my rented room, on the bed, my father's suitcase next to me, I can feel the blood making its way to my penis, and my hand instinctively, softly brushes my crotch until my eyes fill up and the room is underwater.
I hear the men laugh bawdy laughs downstairs, and their cigarette smoke sneaks its way up the stairs to my lonely room.
Underwater, my room is awash in drifting shades of brown: the brown of old wood, the brown of streaked windows, the brown of shit-stained sheets, the brown of a cheap bureau, the brown of an unswept hardwood floor.
It's amazing how much brown looks like dried blood when your eyes are filled with tears.
I miss them: my vultures, my Angels, Kat and Alison. I miss the way their beaks picked at what my father left behind, at what my mother could never clean away.
I kick my shoes off to sleep away my pain, and I push at my father's suitcase with my stocking feet, but it won't budge.
My father's suitcase is full.

29.

"Someone is waiting just for you;
Spinnin' wheel, spinnin' true;
Drop all your troubles by the riverside,
Catch a painted pony on the spinning wheel ride."
    Blood, Sweat, and Tears, "Spinning Wheel"

WAKE UP AND BREATHE!

The cracks on the ceiling are just cracks, or rather, just one long crack with many tributaries. My alarm clock is broken and lies on the floor in pieces.

I turn to look at Lucille—I remember that my mother is on her way over to help me clean up the body—and for a brief second I picture Kat lying there, her eyes shut tight, her sleep scent so much like my own that we drift into one being, Kat lying on top of me and me fighting sleep so I could smell her all night long. For half a heartbeat it is Alison—Alison Who Smells Like Trees—Alison who sleeps naked with a glass of water by her bed, ever ready for any experience to take her away from the drudgeries of having to express her freedom day in and day out.

Outside the sky is pink as the sun pries open another day.

I know now of loss. I know now the sound of leaves leaping from the branch.

When I turn, Lucille is gone—just stray hairs on a pillow next to a folded up sheet of paper, the sheets molded into the shape of her body.

I didn't kill Lucille.

I smell the sheets and pull away. They smell of night sweat and too many cigarettes and cheap bottles of beer.

I didn't kill Lucille?

Lucille's note is just a scribbled line on a torn spiral notebook page.

What was my mother talking about then? The boy on the bicycle? I killed the boy on the bicycle?

I look for the Joker card, but it's gone—just like Lucy Lucille.

Lucille's note is short and succinct and spelled wrong ("feel" is spelled "fell"), and it is then I realize what is obvious: Lucille didn't stand a chance.

"Can you fell *this,"* her note read, *"can you?"*

I could not.

30.

"I can see clearly now, the rain is gone;
I can see all obstacles in my way;
Gone are the dark clouds that had me blind;
It's gonna be a bright (bright), bright (bright)
Sunshiny day."

      Johnny Nash, "I Can See Clearly Now"

So, let's talk of loose ends and guilty rushes that wake you up at two in the morning.

Ollie-ollie-oxen-free!

Who's dead?

The boy on the bicycle?

Lucille?

My father?

Well, Lucille *may* have escaped the cracks in the ceiling, leaving just a note. She was just an innocent bystander anyway—an innocent caught between two rushing cars.

The boy on the bicycle seems likely, but the Joker card spinning around his rear wheel seems a distant tale from another time—some cautionary exposé meant to educate rather than illuminate.

My father? For all intents and purposes, my father was born dead; he could never be his own man. And despite having spent a considerable amount of time sucking on the bloodlust and picturing his brains sliding off the bumpy yellow skin of his suitcase, my father is condemned to the Joker's fate: an endless turning at desire's behest.

So, let's talk of love and lust and jerking off so much over someone, you mistake the smell of your own skin for theirs. Let's talk of praying—nay, *begging*—God to make Kat fall in love with you. Let's talk of turning a back on Him—yea, *spitefully*—when Alison makes sure you're the only person not to sleep with her.

Let's talk of love.

Let's talk of my mother.

She's the key here. She loves me, unconditionally. But, for

whatever reason, she isn't enough, and the Joker turns and stops, and I can't tell if he's smiling, the bastard.

What it all comes down to is this: I feel nothing, and in feeling nothing so sincerely, with such a hope for nothing more than simply what I cannot have, what has been denied to me, I have carved out my existence—have I become my own god, or merely a spoke on His carnival wheel?— willfully disdaining sleep, woefully mixing reality with what is surely not, doling out death and carnage and such intense sex that it could only be referred to as *fucking*, and even that seems too common a word. Spin wheel, spin.

Let's talk of God. Let's talk of the universe.

The universe is my father's old yellow cracked suitcase.

And I am the Joker card, no better than my father, turned by another's wheel, spinning endlessly.

And God is laughing, the son of a bitch is laughing.

31.

" I see no need to take me home,
I'm old enough to face the dawn.

Just call me angel of the morning, angel;
Just touch my cheek before you leave me, baby;
Just call me angel of the morning, angel;
Then slowly turn away from me."
        Juice Newton, "Angel of the Morning"

WAKE UP AND BREATHE, GODDAMN IT!
Mother is at the end of my bed. It's obvious she's been here for a while.

"Where's that old suitcase," she asks.

Sitting up in bed: "Why?"

"Never mind—the funeral is in an hour and a half, so get yourself ready," my mother says, looking Click-Clock, back from the dead, straight in the face.

"What about—?"

My mother shakes her head and the tight frosted curls on top sway ever so slightly. I can see her roots.

"We'll talk about all that *after* the funeral. I'm bringing you straight back here."

At the funeral, I look for Alison.

At the funeral, I look for Kat.

All I see is Bubbles.

And I realize whose funeral I am attending and why my mother and I are tucked away in the back of the church like those worshippers who limit their time of worship to Easter or Vespers or when a favorite aunt dies.

I am driving my mother's car (where is my car anyway?), and on the way back home, with the clouds in the sky like marshmallows and the whole world like a children's cartoon, at a rather long traffic light, the red holding out against a backdrop of fuzzy Christmas mornings and the warm smell of the parental bed, a boy on a silver bicycle crosses by the front of the car, a Joker card flapping in the rear wheel, a newspaper bag flung over his left shoulder.

The car radio is not in tune, and as the boy on the bicycle crosses the windshield, black tassels streaming from the handlebars, Mother reaches toward the knobs and the '70s come pouring out and there is my father teaching me how to fish, there is my father kissing me goodnight, there is my father talking loud but saying nothing, pontificating on some book he never read, some film he didn't understand.

And before I realize it, before I can close my canyon mouth, the boy on the bicycle is gone. I think maybe he zoomed down a side street, his ball cap bouncing in time to a Carpenters song or something by John Denver, but I think I know he was never there.

My mother is speaking:

"Now, the police are coming over to talk to you at 3:00. You better rest up. Oh, Dami, it's almost over—I feel like I haven't taken a breath since I asked your father to leave all those years ago. He was a dirty man—everything he touched became dirty."

My mother blushes and then mentally pushes it away.

"That poor girl—that dancer—stripper—whatever. She was— well, just a good thing for her she wasn't there when whoever did what they did to your father."

We're still in her car, and my fingers are feeling the sides of my trousers for the outline of Lucille's note.

"He couldn't love, Dami," my mother says, "He didn't know how."

When we arrive at my apartment, my father's voice is on the answering machine.

He is asking for something back, but I don't listen—I look for Lucille's note, and tucked just under the rusty bottom of my father's suitcase, there it sits.

"Can you feel *this?"* the note asks. *"Can you?"* Her spelling is perfect.

I unleash the Holy Trinity. In my head, I pitch Billie and Solomon and Tom Waits against the bubblegum '70s.

"Can you feel *this?"* the note asks. *"Can you?"*

I didn't kill the boy on the bicycle then? He wasn't lying somewhere, his ball cap filling up with blood, his newspapers undelivered? No—the Joker card is no longer on the nightstand.

And somewhere, just behind the songs of the '70s, behind the music I made myself like to tie together any vestiges of commonality with my father, the questions are asked again: *why two women?—isn't your mother enough?*

Answer: *not when someone who is supposed to love you doesn't.*

And as I wait for the police to arrive—and I think I know now why they are coming—I laugh my father's laugh and imitate his voice, just like I do when I call myself to say "I love you, pal," and "Good night, sleep tight, don't let the bed bugs bite, sweet dreams, son," into my answering machine, which, like Click-Clock, never seems to stay disposed of when I throw it away.

And as I wait for the police to arrive and my mother scrubs away at some sinister stain near the front door, my head submerges into my pillow, and there's my room in the boarding house dream: it's nighttime, and as I pull back the shit brown curtains to peer at the yellow brick buildings across the way, my eye catches a pair of wings—two pairs of wings.

I place my father's heavy suitcase, its contents sloshing about, on the rented room's lone shelf, high above the tottering child's desk, and as I lay my head back down upon the stiff feathers of my rented pillow, the streetlamp makes a spotlight on the rusted buckles, illuminating the endless roads hibernating between the bumps. My father's suitcase and everything in it—my nothing—my nothing is something.

I awake. I am back in my bedroom again.

"I knew this would happen to him. I told him back then: if you keep hanging out at those kinds of bars, those dank, smelly bars, you're gonna run into a mess of trouble. Thank God they found those boys."

I am sitting on the floor now, my head resting against the mattress. I open one eye.

"I didn't kill him?"

My mother laughs a sweet, gentle laugh and tosses a tissue toward the wastebasket She misses, and the tissue rolls into the corner. I force myself not to crawl into the corner after it.

"Of course not! You're a neat freak. Murder is rarely neat. Dirty business, as they say, Dami."

I squeeze my muscles tight, I shut my eyes, and when I open them, I stare at the large purple blotches on the inside of my arms, blotches so purple, they look like the color of some exotic animal's stomach, they look like the color you imagine hides beneath every little sin you leave behind, dirty and throbbing. I try and rub away the bruises, and my fingers traverse the length of my left arm all the way to my armpit, tracing the tributaries of scars and abandoned motorways.

"He wasn't a good man," my mother is saying, "he didn't even know who he really was. You don't define yourself by what you think you are, Dami. Rather, everything that you do rolls up into one big ball, into one twisted ball of rubber bands, until you can't remember when you started raveling it, until you can't possibly extract even one rubber band without the whole ball coming undone. That was your father, and I'm afraid that's your inheritance, Dami. The mad don't unravel; they entangle. They entangle until the knots become their very reason for existence."

My mother's voice hitches, and I know she is trying not to cry, but I am, and I don't have the slightest clue why.

"But the police—"

My mother's voice raises itself in anger and just as swiftly sinks into the weary pattern of forced cheerfulness I should recognize from years of avoiding its recriminations and veiled accusations.

"Dami, if you drive a car into a telephone pole, wrap it around a utility pole—you were going 85 miles an hour, for God's sake—the police are going to want to talk to *somebody* about it. Suicide is far from a solitary act. Jesus, just look at your face. At least when you were in the hospital, I could keep my eyes on you. Remember when you were you were ten, and your father pushed you off your bicycle? That silver bike? You loved that bike. Had little playing cards or baseball cards in the spokes. I could always keep my ears on you at least—just listened for the cards in the spokes. Your father had packed his suitcase—again!—and you had crawled up the stairs and hidden it from him. Don't you remember?"

"I don't know."

"He knew it was you; I had given up by then. He was pissed. I didn't know where he was going, didn't care. Didn't know what he was carrying in that damn suitcase. Even when he was here, it was like gold. He kept it hidden and locked away. Could have been a body in there for all I knew. That's you in a nutshell. You're too much like him, I'm afraid: everything that makes you *you* is locked away in some worn suitcase that long ago lost its key. Do you know what I mean, Dami? I shouldn't ask, but do you know why you do that? Squeeze everything tight?"

"I couldn't tell you."

My mother snorts, and I can tell she is finally crying, but I won't open my eyes. There is too much light in the room, and I can smell the scent of too much sleep, of rooms closed off too long, of soiled clothes and damp sheets.

"Silly question, I know. I tried to help you. I tried to steer you away from his path. I was afraid just you being near him would bring you down to his level. If the police hadn't found those two boys, they would have been wanted for murder. Murder, Dami! They were trying to help your father! They didn't beat him up and leave him in his car! He'd been in a bar fight, in *another* bar, then stopped at this taproom, had himself a few more drinks, and ran a dryer hose into his station wagon. Murdered himself! The boys found him at the end of the street and tried to get him out. Their fingerprints were all over everything. They panicked. Ran. I would have too. Took the dryer hose with them, Jesus Pete! It's a sorry end, let me tell you. And now there's you: not sleeping, having sex with God knows who, those, those barflies you hang around with, this—what did the doctors call it?—this suicidal ideation. You should have stayed in the hospital. That nurse, the heavyset one who smoked all the time: now she was nice. And the doctor, the one that looked like a bird—Dr. Scavager—and his intern. Remember, Dami? I should have known, given your father. I should have—I don't know—moved us away or gotten you help earlier."

My mother's face is covered in rivulets, each stream tracing my name on her sunken cheeks. My eyes are now open. I wonder if I can ever close them again.

"And *why?* That's what I want to know, Dami. *Why?* Who cares if your father didn't love you? Who cares if those two girls didn't love you? *I love you!* You are my world, Dami. Wake up and smell the coffee. Wake up and *breathe*, goddamn it! There's a whole world outside of this—this castle you've locked yourself in. Don't you love me? Don't you want to know what's outside of your bedroom door? *Wouldn't* you *like to know?*"

"Mom."

"Close your eyes."

I am thirty-one years old, and I pretend I am in a cartoon and that I have to force my eyelids open with toothpicks.

"I have to clean up before the police come, Mom."

"Don't be silly."

The toothpicks are now sheer plates of glass, and I can see *everything*.

"But you said—"

"Good night…" my mother says.

"…sleep tight," I reply.

"Don't let the bed bugs bite…" my mother says.

"…sweet dreams," I finish.

As my eyes close, they make a veil around the coveted dented corner and sweat stained plastic handle of my father's suitcase. Then, before I know it: total darkness.

And finally, with no concern of paralysis, *I fall asleep*.

And, without noticing, the radio in my head goes silent.

And before I realize it, the tortured mumble of prayers for the love of two women do not tickle the tip of my tongue but rather hang there like the bittersweet saltwater of my Beach Haven.

-end-

HELL:

The Gift Room

This is Hell.

"At night I could hear the blood in my veins,
black and whispering as the rain…"
Bruce Springsteen, "Streets of Philadelphia"

"He was not Septimus now."
Virginia Woolf, *Mrs. Dalloway*

"Foxes have holes, and every bird its nest,
I, only I, must wander wearily,
And bruise my feet, and drink wine salt with tears."
Oscar Wilde, "Easter Day"

"Only dead gods are dead forever."
José Saramago, *All the Names*

Cast of Characters:

Mervin Quayle: Our Father Who Art in Heaven
Isabella Quayle: The English War Wife and Holy Mother
Sissy-Love: The Devil
Cindy the First: Dead
Cindy the Lesser: The Actress
Little Lord Peter: Elvis
Celia: The Indeterminate Maid
Mrs. Plunkett: Thunder Thighs
Mournful: Our Brief Dog
Sherrie: Receiver of the Grope
Angie Mascalino: The Receptacle
Reginald Zaber: Pinky
Cindy the Lesser's Husband: Absent
Samantha the Undoer: The Achilles Heel
Young William Browne: The Supplicant
Miles Davis, Bo Diddley, Skip James: The Soundtrack
Me: The Curator

1. Father Died in the Gift Room

I'm telling it the way I remember:

Father died in the Gift Room. The accident had taken his car, but not his mind, and somehow the old man had found his way home. His head slumped to the left, the drool caught midway between his few remaining teeth (yellow and oddly slanted) and the white stalks of his chin (no longer shaven each morning at five), he appeared to be sleeping in the fire-glow dusk the sun had painted on the map wall through the dust motes and thin curtains. Peter's glove was on the side table, but the autographed baseball, as much a part of the glove as the stitching, the magic markered "LLP," the dangling piece of leather Peter was forever tucking in—gone. Father never found the ball. Cindy wanted to bury Father with the baseball and the glove, so the search was fierce, but muddied, as things seem to be in the after works of a loved one's death.

It was Cindy, of course, who pushed through the mail and the magazines and the letters with a hospital postmark and the endless bustle of advertisements cluttering the hallway to find Father in the Gift Room with Miles Davis raging in the background. It was Cindy, in her best role to date, the one of the sheepish but diligent caretaker, who found Father in the red high-backed chair, his trousers stained from urine, Peter's glove on the side table next to a glass of chocolate milk and a shot of God's Dew. Cindy the Lesser we called her, but Cindy took care of Father when there was no one else willing or able or, in my case, just willing.

"I called his name. Twice," Cindy the Lesser said. "He had started sleeping in that old chair, and I kept telling him to find another spot. He wet the chair twice a week, at least. Twice. Chair's not going to last, I told him. Nothing does, he told me."

I roomed in a place a half hour to the west, near the bank, and was in the Gift Room within twenty-four hours of Cindy's call. Cindy hadn't bothered to phone an ambulance or the police or whomever you call when you find someone dead in the house of your childhood. The servants long since dismissed, Cindy made brownies and cleaned the downstairs bathroom. When I didn't arrive that night (I had an appointment with a carefully hidden bottle that I could not bear to break, not even for the old man's final pee-stained curtain call—besides, one doesn't simply walk out of these places without some sort of notice), Cindy left Father where he was until someone else arrived to take charge. Cindy the Lesser was in charge of Father when he was alive; I made the arrangements for his remains. I was the curator.

2. What the Gift Room Meant

This is the way I saw it: my telescope, my microscope. I am the lens. I'm telling it the way I remember.

"The worst thing," my father said, "is to have a conservative mind."

Our house was in an isolated community—"off-town," the locals called it—in Anchor Hop, the small northwestern borough of Mondauk County. We children loved the name Anchor Hop; that was our family in two words. Stuck but ready to jump.

In a larger home, or in the home of one of my wealthier friends, the Gift Room would have been called a library—not to say that Father did not earn a more than decent salary or that our family did not read. The Gift Room was filled with books: volumes stacked and stuck together in such a bizarre way that one could literally become exhausted searching for a particular author. To me the haphazardness was intentional, as if hinting at some stairway to undiscovered worlds where embossed lettering and exquisite binding separated the worthy from the merely satisfactory—readers, in other words, from everyone else. Father bought the books, and I remember him reading them aloud in his red high-backed chair when I was very little, Sissy and I sitting on his lap or by his slippers, for we so adored made-up stories. (Sissy preferred to be read to; she'd memorize certain passages, abandoning the book before any pat ending could ruin the experience.) Cindy the Lesser, although she dearly loved fiction (but would never be much of a reader; she was more of a *character*), already in bed for she was always being looked after as if she were ill, although I do not recall Cindy suffering from even the sniffles. Peter, even at that age, had little time for books, sitting behind the study door, flipping baseball cards, keeping one eye on Father as if, at any point, the chair would empty itself. As Father aged and Mother reached the high point of hysteria, we would take turns reading to the old man, but this exercise would often irritate him, and his chide remarks and off-the-cuff comments (not to mention his slowly dissolving speech patterns) dwindled his reading circle to just me, which suited the situation best, as I was the only child who read for pleasure and also the only sibling to have spent very little time with Father, being the last and a bit of an afterthought.

"The Gift Room knows no boundaries," my father would say, "it knows no rules, only what we bring to it—only reflections."

No, the Gift Room, despite the vast collection and Mother's diligent dusting (perhaps the cleaning made her despise the volumes, for she never read one and regarded new acquisitions with a strong suspicion, opening the boxes with a pen knife blade, chewing the lips she would eventually bite through in her illness), was not for reading or even for resting (although Father did a fair amount of napping and hiding from Mother as her Dawn Moment neared): it was for the giving and receiving of gifts. It is my earliest memory: us children lined along the staircase Christmas morning, our toes twisted away from the icy wooden steps, our mouths already curling from night breath despite being children ("This is how we know we're dying," I remember Sissy saying once), our fists and eyelids opening and closing involuntarily, Mother rattling sabers in the kitchen. For many years, it was quite the same: Father would let Mother know it was time and, in age order (oldest to the youngest, I remember with a grimace), we would descend, first marveling at the gnawed remains of carrots left for the reindeer, the crumbs of hastily gobbled Christmas cookies left for Claus, their little red sparkles dotting Mother's usually meticulously scrubbed hardwood, all clues to the arrival of presents, and, finally—the march into the Gift Room. I don't recall when the Santa Myth was exposed, and although we all believed at a certain point (Peter denied this), it was Father who would sit in the red high-backed chair and hand each of us our gifts and then exchange plain cardboard boxes with our mother. It was there, in the Gift Room, that we learned the heart bursting handover of giving and the humility with which to receive.

"The worst thing," my father said, "is to have a conservative mind. Do you want to think? Truly? Do you want to feel? Not effortless! Do you want to taste everything, even if only once? Do you? There is only one question: how bad do you want it?"

In the Gift Room, you handed the recipient his or her present in the bold light of the gathered family. As children, these gifts were often handmade or found. Mother would not take us to buy anything for each other or Father until we were performing more solid chores, at which point we were assigned an allowance and a place on the hanging chore tablet behind the basement door. As we grew older, earning our keep through school, or later in our careers (Sissy tried med school and settled into a patch of psychiatric nursing, conceiving children who arrived into her womb but never exited in the established manner; Cindy the Lesser married, maintained an immaculate household for a frequently absent husband who traveled without pause, and prepared herself for the role of a lifetime; Little Lord Peter: a jack of all trades, the king of retail service; me, a writer who worked for a bank, as opposed to a banker who wrote in the early morning dust near a leaky window—my own positive little spin), the psychology of gift giving was torn asunder amid the laughter or sighs or gasps of the tribe; no one held back.

The state of your affairs, the status of your wallet or purse were on display for all to see, effectively wiping their influence out, leaving you a supplicant before your loved ones. The act of giving was stressed above all others, and how you gave revealed to our family who you were, where you were going, and what you might have done to get where you were. When Peter was sleeping with Cindy's flighty friend Fern, an immature little leaf of a thing (her name was perhaps the only perfect name ever) during a stay when her parents were abroad, Peter's gifts reflected his cockiness and his need to be seen as someone in control. When Sissy dropped out of medical school, claiming hers was life of passion not found between book covers, her gifts were offerings to the gods, some way of seeking forgiveness for having fallen, although not a one, not even Father, ever uttered a single word when she made her announcement; the same went for the following fall, when at St. Patrick's dinner, Sissy revealed her pregnancy and the man with whom the baby was created. If you had no gift, meaning you had no money (or lacked the imagination that seemed to teem down the stairs Christmas mornings as a child), it was there you went before the birthday girl or boy and said as much before kissing a cheek. If you over gave, it was noticed and received with the same smile as if you had shellacked and ribboned April's first acorn. If it was food, or clothes, or record albums, each was received as an indicator of the position of the giver to the recipient. This is how we knew one another in our family. This is how we saw each other's doomed faces; this is how we grew under one roof, knowing instinctively how to give and which knee to bend, learning stoically to receive without judgment, without remorse, without passion. This was Mother's carefully articulated world vision.

My father, in reference to heeded calls to passion, would invariably say, "It's only fitting for a warlord," and be done with it.

Significant others, particularly during college, were allowed into the Gift Room for holidays and birthdays. With the exception of Peter, no one lived at home long after formal education had ended, and Peter only did so in service to his by then dwindling baseball career—until he married. Sissy's "friend," the man who helped her twice achieve a level of pregnancy that made her seem almost buoyant, was the first outsider to enter the Gift Room. Perhaps Sissy forewarned him a little of the solemnity. He was bewildered and blundered into sentences and half phrases and puns that stopped just short of making any real sense. We ignored him, feeling a trifle violated, and when he tried to pass a joke during the giving of a gift, Sissy's already pale face fading, her eyes lost in the bubble of her stomach hold, Peter belched the better part of the alphabet to save our sister from further humiliation. Peter's parade of collegiate conquests (I barely remember their names, just slashes of red lipstick, fiercely chewed gum, jangling bracelets, and my own barely manageable lust toward my brother's companions) made the Gift Room the hopping scene, with one girl blurting out the contents of a box and another rejecting a present as being "too red for my complexion," this despite having a hickey on her neck resembling a miniature map of South America. When one chesty little number (gilled out in gin and tonics) laughed so hard at one of Peter's jokes that she wet the chair she was balanced upon, Father merely offered her a piece of chocolate on a tissue, asking gently if perhaps the young lady wouldn't care to take a pause and refresh.

The girls I invited rarely made such an impression; I barely dented one on them myself. I indulged in second-hand adultery, lying in wait until one of Peter's dangling dates looped her way to the first floor bathroom, the one with the door that never closed all the way despite being in an almost constant state of repair. Careful not to creak the floorboards, I would crouch by the telephone stand, watching their supple vanilla thighs as they perched on the porcelain. As my dates dwindled (or rather, ended abruptly after one or two meetings, a phenomenon that occurred all during my college years like some twisted personal eclipse, my shyness overtaking every aspect of my features that wasn't already obscured by an upturned collar or a pair of sunglasses), I satisfied myself somewhat by watching my brother's girlfriends pee. Upon re-entering the Gift Room a few moments after Peter's dates, I was careful not to be next in the giving line, for I was sure my family would see through my rapidly beating chest and sweaty palms, plunging their eyes and opinions into my horny little heart. One Christmas, after swallowing copious amounts of Father's Tullamore Dew, I cornered Sherrie, a sometime steady of Peter's, whom Peter said performed oral as if she were sucking the jewels from a king's crown, and asked her if she would like to meet before returning to her college after the Christmas holidays. Sherrie was drunk too; it was her normal state of affairs. Sherrie refused my overtures but allowed me to feel her left breast under her shirt. When I returned to the Gift Room, it was my turn to give, and I presented Sissy with a fountain pen and a hand-bound diary. My palms were slippery, and the gifts slid from my hands to the floor. As Sissy and I bent down together and I retrieved the pen from between her toes (Sissy was so large with child, she had abandoned shoes), her eyes refused to be caught by mine. "Passion will out," Sissy said. The Gift Room always showed the truth.

3. The Movie Star

The old man crossed the bank lobby like a crab and cornered William Browne before the customer service representative could walk around his desk to greet him. The old man's remaining teeth glowed yellow, clumped together in his lower jaw like skinny vultures waiting upon the expiration of the white-spotted, desert-cling tongue. His t-shirt was untucked, and the area around the collar flapped to the left like a duck wing half blown away by an errant boy's pellet gun. His face was unshaven, and his hair was pressed back to his brown spotted forehead as if held there by paste. The old man shuffled, favoring his left side, his right arm crooked, his fingers crooked too, short and gray, clenched around an envelope ripe from too many creasings, too much hand sweat and pocket lint, far too many rapid unfoldings. The man's voice was a halting pattern of suggestive phrases coagulating into a sentence only at the moment when any string of clarity appeared near impossible. William could not lift himself out of the chair.

"What does. One have to do, now. Here. To open. An account?"

"I can help you with that, sir. My name is—"

"Browne. That is. An Irish name. Am I. Not correct?"

"Yes, you are. My mother's side of the family was from—"

"Let me. Ask you. A question. If I may. May I?"

"Sir?"

"How did. I know your name. Since you have not. Introduced yourself. To me. Formally. Since I. Entered the branch?"

William paused and looked behind the old man to the rest of the platform. He could hear the others in the back room, huddled around a box of doughnuts, blowing into coffee. The branch had been open for a total of ten minutes. He was new, thus the last to dig through the doughnut box on Fridays.

"My nameplate, sir? You read my name from the desk plate?"

"Is that. A question, Young William?"

William once more eyed the back room door and the tellers with suspicion. His mother called him Young William. No one else here would know that.

"No, I guess it was conjecture, sir." William ran his hands through his hair. "But that is my name. I'm William Browne. And you are?"

The old man licked his chapped lips and unfolded the envelope.

"You don't. Recognize me? I was once. A matinee. Idol. A movie star."

"Sir?"

The old man painfully turned his head to the left.

"You don't. Recognize me. Now? Here. My profile. Ahhh."

The old man dismissed Young William with a toss of a claw.

"What do. Young people. Know today. From movie stars?"

William eyed the intercom. Perhaps it was time to bring his manager into this.

"I am. Just kidding. With you. I am a. Retired. Army pilot. Have you. Ever. Flown a plane. Young William?"

"No, I haven't. I don't really like to fly. I flew to Nashville once, but—"

The old man's face creased, and as he covered his face with his free hand, William could see the cords in his neck shiver.

"I need you. To help me. Call these. Creditors. So they can. Automatically. Take the money. From my account. Monthly. I am. Switching banks. Young William. I am not well. Can you save me?"

William's eyes caressed the back room and office doors a final time, and then he smiled his best customer service *oh-how-fucked-am-I* grin, careful to hide his nicotine stained teeth from the old man's rolling eyes, less a mental comparison be made, by either party, between Young William's decay and the old man's jutting bunches.

"Can I save you?"

The old man waved his claw in the air again. William could smell medicine, years and years of medicine.

"I am. Mervin. Not Marvin. Do you know. How many times. They get that. Dead wrong? I am. Mervin Quayle. Will you. Help me. Young William?"

William stuck his hand out and grasped the claw.

"Of course, Mr. Quayle. Whatever I can do."

"Young William."

"Mr. Quayle."

4. Our Mother, the English War Wife

My mother's name was Isabella.

"Sun's out, you're out," was Mother's favorite phrase. What that meant was that during the summer months, after morning chores and general horseplay, the children were to remain outside until the calls for lunch and dinner. We were stationed rather close to the house, either in our own expansive backyard or in the neighbors', playing in the wading pool, or acting out scenes from movies on the old stone back porch, the dogwood tree's outstretched arms tickling the tops of our heads as we took turns dying off the side of the stoop.

Mother was stern, but with a laugh, at least during the Younger Years, this according to Sissy. I was the last child, and Mother's laughter had either been used up during the previous childhoods of my siblings, or perhaps Mother had ceased to find her world amusing. Her gaze would float across the breakfast nook, never landing on anything, a little like a thirsty bird too parched to recognize a reflection for a puddle of standing water. Mother would ask little questions, and in those queries, reveal enough information to let you know she was paying attention somewhat to her brood's current events. Sissy said once, "One Cindy was enough. But he wanted boys." Being the second of two boys, the judgment meant little to me, but I feared I was as unwanted as Mother's egg breakfast, cooked and formally presented before her each morning, only to be sliced and arranged in a series of opposite angles by Mother's nervous, stuttering fork.

Mother was born in England, outside of London proper, and had met Father during the war. Father was stationed not far from her hometown and frequently made his way to the Cock and Bull Tavern for after duty dinner and alcohol. During one of Father and his army buddies' sojourns to their favorite bar ("You wouldn't understand half the jokes we made," my father used to say to us, winking, "but we knew the best and prettiest ladies preferred the Cock and Bull!"), Father made the impetuous decision to stop along the row leading to the tavern to tease the pups and kittens and monkey kept caged in the pet store. Mother was buying food for her flatmate's illegally kept ferret. Father caught site of the uniform ("I didn't know it was a nurse's uniform," Father would say to us, "but it was a damn good thing! Shame about the monkey.") and preceded to goad and tickle the animals, showing off, making up a song about stealing away my mother-to-be as he did it (*"Gotta get on that train, gotta get me on that plane!"*), his baritone voice, gilded from years of Catholic choir practice, merging with his easy smile, matinee star charm, and stilted sideburns. When the monkey bit off the tip of his ring finger, Father finished a verse with a flourish and watched as the blood sprayed the litter of kittens in the next cage. Mother, who was in fact a registered nurse, and despite being pretty, was *not* headed to the Cock and Bull (the tavern's reputation made it impossible for proper young ladies to patronize, but Mother gazed wistfully after the diminishing sounds of the juke or the band as its doors swallowed another soul to its rhythmic hell; at least that's what we told ourselves, as Mother arranged her eggs into geometric proofs at the breakfast nook), yanked the scarf from her carefully coiffed head and bound Father's finger, all the while making sure her eyes never left his, even as the color in his face slid away; "Down the drain," Father would tell us. As stunned shoppers and Father's army buddies stood stock still, their mouths all giant "O's", and Father's eyes wide as they could be, Mother popped open the latch on the monkey's cage with her free hand. Without breaking gaze with the man she would marry in less than 33 days, the man with whom she would conceive five children, Mother spoke directly to the shop owner standing askance in a dirty shit-covered apron, still holding the ferret food out toward my mother in a stained fish and chips bag.

"The monkey is choking on the finger. Perhaps you should help save the monkey."

The shop owner lowered the bag of ferret food and peered inside the cage. Father opened his mouth to introduce himself, and the monkey fell over on his side, my father's finger firmly lodged in his unfortunately narrow esophagus.

5. Sissy

As Mother disappeared into herself, Sissy prepared for a life of undressing.

"Don't be a boo-lee," my sister said to me the first time.

"A boo-lee?"

"A ghost who doesn't know he's a ghost," said my sister, as Skip James rattled bones from her Fisher Price turntable.

For Sissy, even as a child, the world was a sexual playground, for it was in the forbidden and scary tangle of genitalia, acrid smells, and undercover-lover gropes that Sissy could feel what the priests called the Flames of the Holy Ghost flowing through her bloodstream, invading her overactive brain, pulsing through her private area, and sometimes jetting out with a yelp in a splash of unexpected urine. Sissy was the firstborn, which gave her certain privileges and a heightened awareness regarding parental presence. In her later teenage years, Sissy kept a red handled switchblade pressed between her mattress and her bedspring. She said it kept her mind *aware* no matter what activities engaged her body.

"I'm going to be a doctor, so it's okay," Sissy said. Being almost five years my senior, I wanted to trust her implicitly.

"No boundaries," she would whisper into my eyes.

I lay stock still across the foot of her bed, the tassels from her coverlet tickling the underside of my bare thighs. The cold tip of the listening device brushed past my chest. It seems funny to me now: I don't remember Sissy ever being without her stethoscope; each year, she retired the current one, and adopted another.

"What if I can't get a hard-on?"

"Don't worry," my oldest sister grinned, brandishing the maid's feather duster, "you will."

"Cindy will hear us."

"Cindy doesn't hear anything but the First Cindy."

"Peter, then."

Sissy paused; her relationship with Peter was wrought with terror, like two blindfolded ice skaters with butcher knives thrust into their sweaty palms.

"Baseball practice. It's Thursday, isn't it?"

"What if I can't get hard, Sissy?"

"Daddy had a woodie and the sperm popped out," sang my sister.

Sissy laughed into the ceiling, and we both looked down at my erection; Sissy then took it into her hands.

"Who do you love?" whispered my sister.

6. Two Cindys

The First Cindy arrived one November and departed soon after.

"There was no rhyme or reason," Father told us, his black hair slicked back, his damaged legs crossed, his once lithe body unnaturally still in the red high-backed chair. This was years after, but Father didn't hide too much in the way of the First Cindy. Not like Mother.

"What hair she had was dirty blonde, like yours," he said, gesturing to me, "and she had those black-black eyes like Sissy-Love." And Sissy would brush her face, squinting, against Father's legs and squeeze his ankles; Father's legs were already in bad shape, and he allowed no one but Sissy to rub them.

"And she was going to be strong and fast like our Peter here," Father said, winking at my brother, the two of them members of some secret men's club. "You could see it.

"Yes, my second born was something else, but I guess the Lord had other plans," Father said, his wristwatch tapping out a drunken New Orleans funeral march along his thigh. "Nearly killed your mother, she did. Your mother wanted a son, but she got Cindy the First, and then she didn't have her either. I bet she would have loved Cindy the First as much as she loved Sissy, despite it all. Never got a chance to though."

It was Sissy, through her rather clandestine relationship with Celia the maid and Mrs. Plunkett the cook (which frequently scaled the ridiculous, as the three of them jockeyed for privileges and position within the house; "Mind yourself," Mrs. Plunkett would say as I trailed after the unholy trio), who uncovered the story of the Coming of Cindy the Lesser, for Sissy had been but a toddler when it happened.

Mother was in the guest room downstairs, resting and drinking liquids, where she had been in the weeks since the Calling of the First Cindy, and Celia and Father would wait on her hand and foot, wash her body, feed her, read to her. Only once, after the help had dressed Sissy for a May Procession she was too little to attend, was Sissy allowed to be received in the guest room. There, Mother's long dark hair was splayed out in brown strands across the three pillows propping up her head. Across from the bed, Jesus bared his sacred heart, his face a mixture of derring-do and despicable self-pity. The television glared silently, a James Cagney picture rattling inside its tubes, the electric chair waiting in the next scene. As the help watched from the doorway, Father lifted Sissy to the bed. Mother grasped Sissy's hand, stared hard into her eyes, and told her she was in deep need of cleaning. When Sissy tried to pull her hand away, Mother grasped tighter and then, abruptly, fell asleep, her knuckles rapping against the metal bedposts like bones falling.

"The question always is," Father would say, "how bad do you want it?"

Father was not much of a drinker then, but Celia told Sissy, years later, that he would have her prepare a Tullamore Dew and a glass of chocolate milk before he would go to read to Mother and instructed the maid to leave another shot for him when he was finished. Celia's shift was over during the nightly reading, but each morning, three empty glasses awaited her in the kitchen, and one spring dawn, the empty Tullamore bottle, more than halfway full the night before, sat upright in the sink. When Celia made her first check on Mother during her regular rounds on that overcast early morning, that's when she found her: Mother's nightgown hiked over her crooked breasts, Mother's lips and cheeks pouty and swollen, legs still spread apart, staring straight into Jesus' messy, oversized heart. Father emerged from the little side bathroom, the white of his whiskers matching the hair on his bare chest. Celia said Father's face was frozen into a jutting combination of "I-dare-you" and "Fuck-me-dear-Lord-it's done."

"Have Mrs. Plunkett make us some breakfast, why don't you, Celia. We'll be taking it in the dining room. Both of us."

Mother's eyes never left the sacred heart (Sissy said that Mother's heart never left the guest room), and nine months later, batting third: Cindy the Lesser.

7. All Pause for the Whiskey Saint

Mr. Quayle sat with his hands folded over his knee, his yellow knuckles dancing and bucking, a fine white stream dripping from the side of his mouth down to his unshaved chin. Two wooden airplane models were perched on either side of Young William's desk. The sunspots on the wall behind Mr. Quayle arranged themselves in lazy, pleasing patterns, and William, the phone hugging his ear, frequently found himself drawn into their intricacies during the conversation about the planes.

"And this one. Is called. The Buffalo. Do you know. Why?"

"No, sir."

"I'll tell. You why. This plane. The Buffalo. Was the only. Plane. Manufactured. Right here. In Warminster. In Mondauk County. Did you. Know that?"

"No, sir, I didn't. I forgot they used to build planes at the old base."

Mr. Quayle's left arm shot into the air, and the sun patterns behind him choked and sputtered in his shadow.

"Not the. Old base! *This* base!"

"Yes, sir. No, we need it direct debited from his…"

"*This* base! Doesn't. This generation. Know how. To read?"

"Mr. Quayle's Social Security number is…"

The old man slapped his palm on the desk.

"They built. The planes. Right here. Right here. Right here. Damn you all. Right here!"

Mr. Quayle stopped shouting; his hand continued to keep time on the desk. Young William gently replaced the receiver in its cradle. Once again, the platform was empty; a teller gestured from across the lobby at the office door, then shrugged when Young William simply smiled.

"Would you like a glass of water, sir? Sir?"

Mr. Quayle's hand rose up and gently landed on the desk, his fingers splayed spider-like in the early morning dust-up. William noticed for the first time that his customer was missing most of his ring finger on his left hand.

"My late English war wife. Always said. The planes kept. Me. One step away. From being. Wherever I was."

"Do you have anybody you can talk to, sir? Like a relative. Does somebody help take care of you?"

Mr. Quayle's arm *pooh-poohed* the air.

"I have hundreds. Of the planes. Not like. The Irish. Air Force. Young William."

"Sir? No, I guess not. Maybe you should talk to our branch manager."

"I am. Talking with. You! What did. Oscar. Wilde. Say about the Jews. And the Irish? Do you. Know your. Irish history. Young William?"

The sun patterns fell to the left, then dashed to the ceiling. A syrup-drip of green descended from Mr. Quayle's nose and hung above his lower lip. The old man seemed to be sliding down into the chair, as if his back were struggling against Novocain or some other numbing agent.

"Our manager's name is Quayle too. Perhaps you know him. He's a really good guy, and maybe he could help us wrap these billing issues up."

"I have a daughter! One left. And that is. Enough."

The old man leaned into one corner of the small chair, and his jaw worked itself over, a wheel spinning on an upturned bicycle in the early spring air.

"You were saying about the Buffalo, sir?"

8. Our Little Elvis

The joke in our family went like this: Peter wasn't born with a silver spoon in his mouth; he was the spoon! The arrival of a son stretched the latex cartoon atmosphere of our corner of Anchor Hop until you could barely recognize even the walls, Sissy said. I would not arrive for another year, at which point, the ascendancy of Peter to the throne was complete.

There he was: Peter Q., six feet, two inches at full adult height (significant, since Father and myself never ascended past five-ten), the usual myopic Q. stare replaced by laugh lines fully developed at age seven, arms made for throwing cylindrical objects, legs seemingly detached from the torso at top speed; he had our nose, that was all. Sissy said Peter's penis (or "Peter's peter," as she called it) was a full seven inches long when fully angered; at the time, I chose not to explore how Sissy came about this knowledge. I did, however, spend the length of a depressing holiday weekend stretching my own penis until I could barely pee from the pain.

Baseball was Peter's game, and the game embraced his endless contortions, his arching jumps to the left for the line drive, his gallop from one base to the next, a grin of determination riding atop his jutting chin and jack-o-lantern eyes. Really, I thought the grin a mixture of derring-do (just like Jesus!) with a wallop of pity for the other fools who had to work to achieve a fraction of his grace and stillness-in-motion. On the diamond, Little Lord Peter ruled supreme, a general marshalling invisible troops, as no one could hit or field or steal worth a damn in comparison to his lordship. Girls loved him. Women loved him. Men adored him. I worshipped him.

Peter was a sore loser; so often were his conquests, so little did the competition matter, that if Peter lost, his whole team lost, and so did we. There was no consoling him. Even when he was in his late teens and early twenties, when baseball games, now just played for fun post-accident, were followed by evenings of revelry and beer, Peter could not be lured up from his self-imposed basement dweller status after dropping a game.

"Basement dweller?"

Peter merely stared past me and repeated himself.

"Basement dweller. *Don't be cruel to a heart that's true.*"

"Are you sure? It was a close game."

"Basement dweller. Could you get me another beer please?"

As opposed to Sissy, who instead of rebelling against the grand plans of her education, reveled in their darker corners ("You want me to be a doctor, okay then, I will doctor only to penises," Sissy told me once by way of explanation, but I was too close to finishing to fully comprehend her implication), Little Lord Peter accepted his inherent royalty and tried desperately to fit under Father's crowning hand. Rebelling, although natural in every teenager, was absent from Peter. To outsiders (and what else would you call the litany of teammates and girlfriends and overly-friendly but ultimately lonely and childless coaches looking for something back after years of back slapping, blow jobs, and sleepless brandy nights, respectively?), Peter was a cocky insurgent in the classic rockabilly mode; he wore his leather jacket even in summer. My brother would stand in front of the bathroom mirror for hours it seemed, practicing his moves, swooping his hair, swiveling, while I banged a frantic Bo Diddley beat on the door for fear of wetting my corduroys. But our father bought him his beer. It was me who hid with Peter behind the shed, sipping whiskey from a cleaned-out margarine container. Our father subscribed him to Playboy, whose issues Peter kept neatly stacked on the back of the second floor toilet he shared (thank God!) with me. No, like Elvis, Peter was no rebel; despite his rugged exterior, eyes of ice, and extremities of gold (as far as parlaying playground rumpus into adult fulfillment), Peter struggled to fit the mold. His sensitivities to others (two sisters helped there), to art (this would be from me), and his growing addiction to the bottle left him with little wiggle room: he was the star in Father's firmament, and it was Peter's job to hold the sky together, so, at the least of it, our household would have some center toward which to drift, as our mother sucked herself into an undertow, as Sissy ravaged almost any boy she came in contact with, as Cindy the Lesser haunted Mother's shadow, and as I prayed each night to hear Sissy's hot breath in my ear (I would never hear her enter my room) and feel her warm palm on my crotch.

Sissy's main contribution to Little Lord Peter's education came in the form of "shower humping." If Sissy knew Peter was in the shower, she would undress, pick the lock with a bobby pin, and jump in; there she would proceed to hump Peter's leg, rubbing her pubic hair against his muscular thigh. Peter said she would call him a "wimp-out" and exit as quickly as she arrived the moment his boner popped up or if he reached for her breasts. I was beyond jealous; I couldn't sleep or eat or even jerk off. I knew Sissy was with other boys, but the idea of her with Peter obliterated all other thoughts, until all I could see behind my eyelids were her legs wrapped around his back, and all I could remember was the taste of my sister's nipples in my mouth. I planned extravagant methods of revenge upon my older brother, but Peter reassured me, every single time: he never touched Sissy. I should have believed in him; Peter had other fish to burn.

Sherrie was the long running gnat to Peter's flame. Neither as smart nor as pretty as Lisa, Peter's steady early in high school, Sherrie was what Sissy called a "stop-gap." "To fill the time," Sissy said, her chin in her hand, golden-brown wisps of hair falling into her eyes, shooting continual hot puffs of air to push them back. "He didn't know from Lisa until she left him, and then his wee heart went *kaplooey*. Too young. Hurt Father at first more than it hurt our Petey. Then Brother Peter exploded like a penis head. Next time won't be so pretty."

Sherrie was easy gravy, Peter said. There wasn't much she wouldn't do. And of course, that was exactly why Little Lord Peter sent her packing (much to my chagrin) not soon after meeting (and initially being put off by) Samantha the Undoer at some softball function or other. Sherrie liked to drink, and the more she drank, the more she wanted to ramble on somebody's shoulder, pour out her miserable little existence (born poor, mommy drinks, who's daddy?), so she could stoke the coals and see if she could set off a crying jag. (Peter called them, "The marry-me-marry-you-and-save-my-ass blues.") Peter avoided the scene as soon as Sherrie rediscovered the little dirt road to her secret dirty heart.

Sherrie: "My mother's boyfriend once held a gun to my head."

Me: "Really? Wow, that must have—"

Little Lord Peter: "Jesus. Is there any more beer? I'll go get some!"

And using the aforementioned boob-grope as my launching pad, during Sherrie's meltdowns I would pull her into a spare room or closet or shower stall or berry bush and hold her inebriated Marlboro-Man-smelling body close to mine, kneading her nipples through her shirt, sometimes caressing her ass or thigh, always inching for more intimate territory. But I never slept with Sherrie or even received a lousy hand job. Once she licked my ear and told me it tasted good, but then she passed out, and I had to crawl from the spare bedroom so no one would think I was feeling up my brother's girlfriend. Needless to say, I was aghast that Sherrie had been banished from our little world without so much as a passing word to me.

"Hell, Petey. I liked Sherrie. I thought you loved Sherrie."

Peter grinned and bared his fangs.

"*Caught in a trap, I can't walk out.* Meet me in the Gift Room in ten minutes."

"Maybe it's not too late though. I could call her for you, Petey."

"Fat chance. Just meet me in the Gift Room."

And he was off, a distant gallop passing through the second floor. From the dining room foyer, I could see Celia and Sissy emerge from the large linen closet nearest the balcony railing, trailing sweet smelling smoke, exchanging furtive looks in the fear that Peter's horse racing was one of Father's frequent booty raids.

In the Gift Room, I quickly immersed myself in the dilapidated bookcases. My plan that summer was to work my way through the alphabet, sampling an author from each letter if possible. To me the Gift Room held the entire world along its overstuffed walls, and little of Mother's "sun's out, you're out" dictum could prevent me from falling deep inside someone else's words for an entire morning and afternoon.

"You know, if you keep reading like that, you'll grow hair on your palms."

Peter stood directly behind me, pressing a white envelope into my hand.

"What's this?"

Peter's fangs glittered, then disappeared inside a laugh.

"What you need."

Inside, on those instant Polaroid photographs, Sherrie was inserting various digits into her storied (to me) orifices. In a series of pictures obviously taken in quick succession, it would appear the little gold ring Sherrie always wore, the one with the even littler fake diamond, was left behind.

"Let your fingers do the walking, it's a snap!"

"You took these?"

"No, Father did. What the fuck? Yes, I took them. Now they're yours, little brother."

"How could you ever give this up? I don't want to sound—"

"Samantha is prettier, Samantha is smarter. Hell, Samantha is smart, period. Samantha makes more money than God. Samantha tastes like a frozen chocolate éclair. Samantha is what I always wanted (Lisa who?), and she will be my bride. She will. I guaran-fuckin'-tee it. The question *always* is: how bad do you want it?"

9. Free-Fall at the Post Office

Mr. Quayle fell down and lay prone on the dirty blue mosaic tiles of the Warminster Post Office at exactly 12:17 P.M., according to his retirement watch, exactly two years after he discovered his eldest cold and half naked, three years after they found his first son swinging.

"Jesus Christ. Sir, you, this man just. Jesus, you okay, mister?"

"Someone call somebody."

"An ambulance. Somebody call an ambulance."

"Use my cell."

"Is that his bank deposit? Stick it in his pocket so no one will, you know."

Lines. He hated lines. Munching on his lower lip, he wondered what it would take to part this line like Moses. Wait any longer, he thought, and he'd wet his pants. Look at her hair. How could anyone live with that hairstyle? He resisted the urge to ram his yellow stubby fingers into her bee's nest. His eldest daughter had control. The bastard couldn't take that in the end. The loonies couldn't pry that from her stiff fingers or shake it loose from her drooping skull—"Drop dead from the neck down," as his own father used to say. The neck down. The lines. He hated lines.

"Mister, can you hear me? We called an ambulance."

"Can I help whoever's next?"

"I was next."

"Is he breathing?"

"Is there someone we should call for you, sir?"

"Two stamps please."

"Should we move him over a little?"

"Ask Carl."

"Nobody's touching him."

Carefully, he had placed both of their belongings in green burlap sacks. One for her, one for him. He had thrown them over his shoulder and then into the back of his sedan. He supposed the Tullamore Dew was about equal parts to his blood on a daily basis, for he never remembered unloading the car. There were days when he would amble about the house, holding the ball cap, looking for more: his eldest son's switchblade (which the boy's mother forbade him to have, but which he bought and helped his son hide under his mattress anyway—when his son gave it to his eldest daughter, well, he could have just about spit—but he knew his children and became convinced the contraband lay waiting for his *shaking crooked fingers!); his firstborn daughter's signed edition of that book she loved, the copy he had bought for her although the price was well over $200, the one she had carried under her arm for years like a Bible; the fucking Mike Schmidt autographed baseball—these things, all of them, were no longer in his house. Maybe his other son moved them, but there were days when he couldn't even remember his other's son's Christian name, and he felt a distant tug, for he thought he loved the last child as well as the two that were lost. Nothing alike, his other son and he. And then there was the other daughter. Just like her mother. Smelled like her too, in the morning.*

"There's a card in his pocket."

"What are you doing in his pocket?"

"Hiding his bank deposit. What the hell do you think I'm doing? Robbing this old guy in the freakin' post office?"

"The envelope has a phone number on it. William Browne's."

"Call it."

"Isn't the ambulance coming?"

"He's not carrying a wallet."

"Hello? Did I just call...I'm looking for William Browne. Is this a bank?"

He had called the other daughter, had asked her to stand in front of his chair like they all used to do when they were little. He had told her things: he had told her about the planes and his English war wife; he had spoken of authors to read and poems to memorize. He had pontificated on the state of the Army, on strippers and their primal need for the almighty dollar, on peanut butter and jelly eaten with a spoon, on the way your pee smells after you eat asparagus. After he had spoken at length, he stopped and rubbed his legs, for he had reached his point: one glass, red wine: the Red Wine Moan, and how when you knew it was time, you just fizzed a couple of blue sleepies in a bottle of red (St. Emilion's would do just fine, thank you oh-so much) and drifted off in a little open mouthed haze of starry-eyed rushes and just-before-dinner sparkles.

The last daughter had nodded her head in all the right places. But he couldn't be sure she understood. He knew that he was a thin tissue away from a wall of rage: he had given this daughter life *when her predecessor fucking died after exiting her mother's belly! He had resurrected her goddamn* name*! Lesser men would have keeled over from sheer strain. It started the slow-kill process in her mother. Ahh, let it go, old man. If she nodded, she nodded. Yes, sometimes when she changed his sheets after he soiled them, he would find himself tucked back into the same damp sheets. But from time to time even he forgot to flush. She was loyal. Red Wine Moan. Maybe that wouldn't be a big enough splash. Gotta go out with a bang:* Gotta get on that train. Gotta get me on that plane.

"The banker's coming over. It's the bank across the street."

"Ambulance is here."

"I think he's drunk."

"Make some room."

"Who's next?"

10. Gone Baby b/w I Want You

"She always said I was one step away from wherever I was."

I was The Last. The End of It All. A mistake. A late drop from a bottle of Tullamore.

"You were the Final Drip from the Batter," Little Lord Peter said.

"I'm sorry," said Cindy the Lesser.

"Stop thinking about it and concentrate; my arm hurts," said my sister Sissy.

This was during my adolescence, when questioning my existence was a luxury, and Mother was still alive (although you could only tell from the *husk-husk* of her heavy breathing; all other indications were that she was quite dead). This was during the beginning of Cindy the Lesser's extraordinary acting career, albeit one that only took the stage within our house on Landing Street. (Sissy said the street name was just about the only thing landed around here; Peter said, after watching me creep out of Sissy's room stark naked, that it should have been called Laid 'Em Street, and I couldn't think of a single argument there.) After months spent as Maria from *West Side Story* and a week or two as Ray Bolger's scarecrow (no costumes for Cindy the Lesser, not yet; she worked from within then, and *exuded* the persona), Cindy, whose life achievement award was granted for best supporting role in a crib death, who would never stoop to actually *being* (i.e. dressing as) someone else (or so we thought), initiated a startling two month run as Julie Andrews' character from *The Sound of Music*, which found her running from room to room, attempting to mold the Q. children into a stylized von Trapp ensemble.

During one of her mad rushes (*"Doe a deer, a female deer..."*), Julie/Cindy burst into my bedroom mid-ejaculation—her bursting, my ejaculating: mid-song, and my sperm arcing, landing all pearly white on Cindy's smock.

"Holy shit," said Cindy the Lesser, "what is it?"

"Daddy had a woodie and the sperm popped out." Sissy called it her Finishing Song.

"That's sperm? You spermed on me?"

"You didn't even fucking knock, Cindy," I said, as I eased my shorts up.

"Will I get pregnant?"

"Can you just leave now?"

I held my bedroom door open for her, but instead of leaving, she leaned against the rock'n'roll posters and concert ticket stubs.

"Is this what happens when Mournful moans at the ceiling? Is this being Mournful?"

Blushing, I handed Cindy a couple of tissues.

"Here. No, I don't know. I'm sorry, Cindy."

"No thank you. I'm going to save it in a baggie and freeze it."

I shut my bedroom door.

"You can't do that. What if someone sees it and wants to know what it is?"

"Mayonnaise. I'll tell them I froze some condiments."

Coming from Cindy, my family wouldn't even have blinked; although rarely ill, Cindy was often the recipient of the best medical care Father's money could buy, as if there *had* to be an explanation for our lost sister. But something more happened that day than was immediately apparent. The movie roles ended for a time, and religious figures, saints and the like, emerged to lead the wary and the stray into the gates of heaven, although how much Cindy the Lesser believed in the dogma was not as important as the gravity she brought to these sacred roles. Cindy was an actress, or so my family believed, and it mattered little (except to me, who blamed my errant and surprised sperm) that her current subject matter was less topical than universal. Most disturbing was her growing reliance on props and sparse costumes. Cindy spent the better part of three months honing the role of the little girl to whom Our Lady of Fatima appeared, dutifully sewing herself a little purple hood. Some of the subtleties were lost on my family, I'm afraid, and Sissy took to calling Cindy: Fatima, or Fat Little Pig on the Farm, or just plain Fattie. (Cindy, while not fat, was evidently well fed and under-exercised, but to be fair, her roles were demanding and all consuming, and a proper diet was not always Cindy's number one goal.) Cindy swallowed Sissy's words and commenced an intense exercise routine that involved obsessively walking our brief dog.

Oh, and how brief this dog was, our cocker spaniel, Morning, a fuzzy little blonde fellow. Following the death of several backyard squirrels, Sissy changed his name to Mourning (the puppy would burrow beneath the dogwood leaves and await the squirrels' industrious frivolity—after the dismembering, the dog would hang his head and mope about Landing Street, somehow unaware that squirrels came by the dozen), but after witnessing his nocturnal song, we called the pooch Mournful. The dog slept in my room, directly below my parents'. Mournful would wait until I was asleep, then curl above my head on the pillow. He would have been a good guard dog, for as soon as the ceiling shook and Father could be heard stage whispering what sounded like landing commands, Mournful would bound from the bed and howl at the ceiling, reaching a fever pitch just as Father and Mother reached theirs. Sex was stressful to my dog: his balls were in a jar somewhere, and perhaps he felt he was warning Father of a similar fate. Some nights, it was so bad, all the children would gather on my bed and try to shush Mournful—all except Sissy that is; she tickled his golden stomach and sunburst sides to help increase the volume. It was so disturbing, Mournful's Serenade, Sissy and I tiptoed our unholy dances around his perky ears, and I wouldn't even dare masturbate in my own room at night for fear of Mournful breaking into song. Sissy claimed Father bought Mournful for me because our mother didn't love me like she loved Peter for being the first boy, or fear me like she feared Cindy the Lesser, or adore me like the firstborn, Sissy-Love. But I was allergic to the dog (although Cindy received the allergy shots!), and one morning, the front door stood suspiciously ajar: Mournful was gone, "running with the pack," a cardinal sin to my father. *"Gotta get on that train, gotta get me on that plane,"* Father added, closing the door with a wink.

As for me, in between intermittent mashes with Sissy, I fantasized about Celia the maid, her indeterminate European accent, and what she would sound like when she came. Although significantly older and slightly washed out, as if she had spent the first part of her life as some sort of addict, and the second part trying to wean herself from whatever it was that had gotten her to this point, there was little hiding her once-pretty face. (And what was *once-pretty* to a teenager with his pants down?) I lurked about the laundry room in the desperate hope of finding Celia undressing to wash out a stain from her dress. I stripped for my morning bath in the hall or with my bedroom door open, my penis pointing skyward, awaiting Celia as she delivered fresh towels or collected dirty linens, to no avail. Often as not, Peter would find me standing in my doorway, posed naked, frozen in the act of removing my final sock. I even masturbated about Mrs. Plunkett and her large ham hock thighs.

By the time my initial high school appearance arrived, three things were self-evident: my mother's dalliance with hard reality was a thing of the past (she signed my last report card with apple cinnamon oatmeal); my masturbation had escalated to an alarming seven times a day, thus taking up valuable time most kids my age were filling up with school dances, dating, homework, sporting events, and the like (and having spent considerable homework time jerking off, school had become a time-killing place in between tugs on the old magic rope trick); and my hunger for Sissy, my big sister, had outgrown any containment and filled each and every spare moment, so much so, that I stole her underwear and slept with it on my face those nights when Sissy wouldn't waste time and fluids with me.

How telling, of course, that during Christmas of my sophomore year in high school, when Sissy presented me with a full set of girls' days of the week underwear ("It's a number thing," said Sissy), Father was too deep inside his Tullamore Dew, and Mother was too busy sewing the hem of her dress into the doily beneath the red glass lamp to see that I was in desperate need of rescuing. Cindy was saying the rosary, so only Peter, thrusting his Elvis lip forward, exchanged a furtive glance beneath raised eyebrows with me, as I tore the wrapping paper off to reveal my Christmas gifts.

Sissy, leaning into me: "They're dirty."

But not everything was wine and roses and musty scents.

Sissy grew weary of me, as the boys lined up for dates and gropes and long dull stares across the college campus. My little secret waltzes with Sissy (now performed more openly, as only the discreet Peter seemed to notice) were further and further between and often took the form of artistic masturbation: Sissy sometimes simply refused to touch me or allow me to explore her, so I would lie on her bed and make myself come while Sissy watched my face, her own flushed with some secret rumbling or other. When I finished, Sissy would leap off the bed (her stethoscope dangling above her bare chest, its cold steel brushing her nipples), open her door (we rarely bothered to lock it anymore), and return to whatever psych book she was currently consuming.

My own dates were also spaced further and further apart, owed in no doubt as much to my shyness and adverse introverted stance as to my loyalty to Sissy. My one sexual encounter outside of my sister-dances occurred with Angie Mascalino from Cindy's high school. See, boys rarely bothered with Cindy, and Cindy only bothered with saints and apparitions; her roles were too demanding for her to pay much attention to appearance—other than costumes. (Despite her religious fervor, her sea blue eyes and raven hair made her stand out in a crowd, thus Cindy often wore massive purple Easter bonnets to shade her face from the *mal occhio* of the secular world; the man Cindy would eventually marry won her heart when he told her he'd always wanted to be a priest—he only had one obstacle: he found abstinence too confining a concept.) Other girls avoided Cindy altogether; her streak of individuality meant little in a school of uniform green vests and skirts and pushed down knee socks, where the rebellion of the day was to "forget" to wear underwear. But Angie needed help with theology homework; Cindy was theology incarnate. Angie didn't wear underwear, and her thighs were a dark hued entranceway to heaven. It stood to reason that Cindy's brother (me, not Peter, although he would have been tripping himself in a rosary to crawl between Angie's legs) would make himself available during valuable after-school study time; I offered Ms. Mascalino a ride home to meet with my sister. Cindy, of course, was home with a temperature of 99°.

I must have either impressed Angie with my religious acumen or else an afternoon spent with the sickly Saint Cindy the Lesser filled her body with a need for fulfillment in a more earthly sense, for as soon as I started the engine, her hands were manipulating my penis through my trousers, and we ended up parked down the street from my parents' house, her head buried in my lap. As my previous experiences all involved Sissy, and because I had grown used to Sissy's quirks and preferences, when I climaxed, I did so without heed or warning. Angie yanked her head up, stared at me, and spit my excess toward the rolled-up passenger side window, where it splattered back on her green Catholic school vest.

"You came in my mouth!"

It ripped up from my toes, the laughter, and I forced it into a fake sneeze. But in a quick, keen state of precipitation, horror seized me as I pictured a mingling of parental units, hers and mine, discussing the issue of oral ejaculation.

"I'm sorry, Angie. I thought you wanted me to."

"Your whole family is sick, you know that?" Angie asked, as she unlocked the passenger side door and pushed at it with both her saddle shoes.

I had no idea.

The next day, the rains began and lasted for more than a week. Our backyard turned into a mud filled battleground, complete with dips and rivets, and the whole house smelled of damp breath and anxious feet. With all of us trapped inside and Mother busy that fall stuffing goldfish into squash (a hobby that lasted quite a few months; Little Lord Peter ended every night, just before he went to bed, collecting the various squash, meticulously placed throughout the house, and tossing them and their stiff inhabitants into the trash barrel), I pursued Sissy relentlessly; after my squeeze play with Angie, I didn't want to be with anyone else. I knew Sissy had moved to the dorms to help me defeat my sister-addiction, but she slept at home and invited me to her dorm room out of boredom far too often to accomplish either. But now Sissy ignored me, pretended she didn't know me (in the Biblical sense), and generally made the rains seems heavier, denser. After almost a week, I broke down in front of Peter, who, although he couldn't say anything to me, knew exactly why I was sobbing. My brother left me on his bed; he returned a few minutes later.

"After the rain."

I sucked snot into my throat and wiped my nose on Peter's pillowcase.

"What?"

Little Lord Peter caught my eyes in his and then picked up a ball glove.

"She said: 'After the rain.' "

Peter tossed a ball into the air.

"Peter?"

The ball landed in my crotch.

Peter, laughing, gesturing outside: "Want to practice sliding?"

"I'll get my glove."

"Race you."

And we were off, through the hall (strewn with discarded comic books, hockey pucks, and one bicycle wheel), around the staircase (the banister dotted with little yellow squashes, miniscule goldfish tombs), past the bathroom (someone had left the water running in the sink), to my bedroom, directly across the stairwell from Peter's (the girls' rooms and our parents' boudoir were on the next floor). I tore my room apart, albums and books flying, looking for my ball glove. Peter amused himself by going through what he called my museum: my collection of rock'n'roll tickets, and posters, and piles and piles of 45s I'd inherited as the youngest child and added upon from flea markets and garage sales.

"Why do you keep these?" Peter asked, his fingers shuffling through a stack of scratched platters I could not bear to be rid of. "You need more of the King," he added.

"You could lose your life inside a 45," I laughed, as my fingers grasped the ball glove underneath my bed.

"Look at Cindy in the backyard," Little Lord Peter said, his nose against the window, and that's when she started screaming.

Peter dropped the ball and glove, and his feet barely touched the steps as he descended the stairs. I didn't follow far; Peter was in charge. From my room, I watched out the window as if at a play. Cindy the Lesser stood in the middle of the backyard, beneath the dogwood tree just starting to lose its blooms, pointing, her normally sotto voce voice hoarse and guttural.

"I SAW HER. I SAW HER. I SAW HER."

Sissy was behind me, afternoon sleep still in her eyes, her fingers clasped around an engraved silver cigarette lighter, a gift from a hopeful suitor, her stethoscope dangling backwards. She flicked the lighter top open and shut absently. Her underwear was a slight purple, and her t-shirt was two sizes too small. I could make out the shadows of her nipples; I could smell her sleep scent.

"What the fuck?"

"I SAW HER. I SAW HER. I SAW HER."

Sissy and I crowded into the window, my arm circling her waist with no resistance.

"Open the fucking window," Sissy said to me. "She saw what?"

"Boo-lee?"

I opened the window with one arm, anxious to not lose my spot. Four damp, wrinkled dogwood blossoms floated into the bedroom. Maybe Sissy wanted to wait until after the rains since everyone was stuck inside the house.

"I SAW HER. I SAW HER. I SAW HER."

Peter was beside Cindy the Lesser in an instant, and she pointed violently, as Peter tried to put his arm around her and calm her down against his chest. Rain tore down on both of them, and Peter's pompadour fell flat against his head. Sissy pushed my hand off her waist.

Sissy, with her head out the window: "What is it?"

Peter, without looking up: "Cindy says she saw the Virgin Mary in that window."

Sissy, under her breath: "T'aint no virgins here, mister."

"In my window?" I asked.

Peter glanced up, annoyed.

"Yes, your window. She said the light reflected off the rain, and then the Virgin appeared, and then the Virgin was swallowed whole."

It was hard to yell over the rain, two stories down, but I didn't want to leave, not with Sissy in my room in her faded purple underwear.

"Probably just rookie here, lobbing sperm at his window," Sissy shouted down to Peter and a trembling Cindy.

My eyes widened, and I took a step back.

"What did you say?" Peter yelled.

"Nothing," I screamed back.

"Cindy's afraid for the Virgin. She thinks something bad might happen," Peter yelled up to us.

"Peter, bring her in. I'll make some tea," said Sissy, and she slammed down the window just as Mother's body, in that pretty red dress I always told her made her look like some exotic lounge singer, tore across my sight line and landed with a plop into the mud a few feet from Little Lord Peter and Cindy the Lesser and the dogwood tree. Mother loved that dogwood tree.

Plop.

Now, when this incident shifted down to a slow boil (as Father would say), and we were drying off by the ambulance under the eaves, Peter preparing to follow the driver to the hospital, Cindy staying with Father (we had called him at work, and the suddenly old man had ensconced himself in the red high-backed chair, easing a bottle of Tullamore Dew into his bloodstream), I jockeyed to remain behind with Sissy; just rubbing the towel past my crotch made every bone want for mending in the harsh light of Mother's first suicide.

It was Cindy, of course, who'd reached Mother first, tearing the blouse off her own back to wipe off our mother's face. Sissy was in the picture in an instant, a flash of muted sun skidding off the stethoscope, Little Lord Peter like a scarecrow, his sneakers now almost ankle deep in the mud, sinking, picking Mother up (not very wise if she had broken her back, I thought from my window), and running with her in the summer rain, looking for all the world like some cannibalistic footballer, his mouth open to the dripping sky, wordless yawps exiting into the mud and wind. Mother's initial ring, the one Father had bought her because he couldn't afford a wedding band "way-back-when," sparkled in my eyes as lightning struck the dead-dead sky.

I would rather be the devil than to be that woman's man…

The blues from Sissy's turntable crept into my head, then merged, as I watched from the window, into Sissy's Rain Song from when we were very little, and Mother seemed like a warm safe circus tent, overwhelmed with tantalizing scents:

Come down rain,
Come down rain,
And wash, wash away
Every bit, every little bit o' my pain.

Oh, what we knew even when we believed the Santa Myth!

Afterward, I followed Sissy to her bedroom. She didn't close the door on me but instead went about the business of making her bed and folding blouses as if I wasn't standing in the room, my dirty blonde hair plastered to my large forehead ("That's an eight-head," said Little Lord Peter when he was seven, and oh, how we laughed and how it filled the Gift Room).

A clearing of the throat.

"Peter told me what you said."

Sissy never looked up.

"I'm making all the beds. Strip 'em and make 'em. Celia showed me how to do it in four minutes flat."

I pulled my penis out of my trousers and advanced.

"The ridiculousness of the pink thing," was all my sister had to say on the subject.

I withdrew my penis.

"Peter said—"

Sissy looked in my eyes for the last time. Ever.

"Have you no common sense?" my sister asked.

I merely stared back into her black-black eyes.

"It'll never stop raining," Sissy said.

And then she looked away and spoke into a towel she had folded in and out of various square shapes.

"Go ask Mrs. Plunkett for a drink. Tell her I said. Go on."

And I left. Mrs. Plunkett fixed me a cocktail with crushed ice, and later that night, after Peter returned from the hospital, after Father had passed out in the red high-backed chair, I wandered through the house, not belonging to any particular nook, not feeling an affinity with any creak or knick-knack despite this being the house of my childhood. Somehow, I had overstepped; the thoughts in my head and the actuality of what was right in front of my nose every single fucking day never meshed. My memory was like a train that always left early, one that I would never catch. Years later, when I revealed this thought to Cindy, she told me that's when I started *really* being a writer.

And it was that night, wandering, that I found myself at a stranger's gate: Cindy the Lesser's bedroom door. It sat slightly ajar, a candle flicker visible between the frame and the wood. With one finger, I pushed it open and stared into my mother's face, smeared but visible, arranged meticulously across three pillows. Mother's eyes were shut, but her lips were pursed, as if for a kiss. The impression of Mother's face on Cindy's blouse was like a black and white photograph: stark, blunt, yet vivid in its contrasting shades.

"Like Veronica's veil. Isn't it beautiful?" asked Cindy the Lesser, and I left her room without closing the door and threw up in the girl's bathroom down the hall, masturbating into the sink after I cleaned up the vomit. Mother was a boo-lee.

And that was that.

Mother had jumped or fallen (depending upon your particular bent) from the girls' balcony. The mud had saved her. She suffered minor bruises, nothing broken (at least not bones). Mother's specialist, Dr. Scavager, confined her to Friends Hospital, a psychiatric facility, despite Father's best attempts to have the whole thing written off as a slip in the rain, but Mother's disconcerting habit of mixing the ordinary with something else (in this case, a stalk of celery was found in her underpants) overrode Father's fancy hairpiece lawyer.

However, Mother wasn't the only Q. family member to log valuable medical attention that season. But I didn't jump. Nor did I fall. But that autumn, my left eye slowly grew dark, my short term memory stretched itself thin across the loving details of my story, and, for the grand finale, full erections became a thing of the sticky past (not that I ever stopped playing with myself). As the multiple sclerosis played its tried hand along my frayed endings and shattered infrastructure, I wondered how I could tell the doctors that this was but a minor occurrence in my family's routine life-wheel. That I didn't feel whole after the onslaught of MS merely confirmed what my family already breathed in as Bible-truth: everything is there, but the kid has naught to offer. Wasted.

"You shouldn't have looked at the blouse," said Cindy the Lesser.

And behind my rapidly shrinking, formerly trivia-oriented mind, I could hear the *clump clump clump* of my first summer job supervisor, the stump end of his cane landing a few inches in front of him, his shoulder against the wall, his left eye cascading inward. There was no element of surprise with Mr. Kane; MS had taken that away as well. Then, I believed a man without surprise was a man without a destiny, for how could you take the world by the balls when your own were dragging along like little wheels for all to judge.

So began years of sexual self-abuse. Since I merely toyed with writing anymore (each page was a struggle to recall the previous one), toying with my sexual organ didn't seem such a big deal—hell, I rarely had an orgasm thanks to MS. I left college. I avoided dating. I only had to look at Cindy's pathetic union (she increasingly spent more and more time as Father's caretaker and less time with the phantom she wed; her husband resembled nothing if not an angry pear, slightly bruised on the one side, a pear better suited for a pastry than an after-dinner snack; one could see what attraction there was for Cindy: the pear could clearly stand up for himself, but his *inner self*, a paltry place inhabited by daytime talk shows and supermarket sweatpants-wearing checkout come-ons, was bereft of attention; the pear spent so much time on the road selling stain protection paraphernalia that Cindy was left with our increasingly bone-empty rattle of a patriarch) or Sissy's twisted little arrangement with the future father of the ghost babies to know that I wasn't missing much. Still, Peter's Samantha seemed a catch, and I flirted with her at every Gift Room gathering, rapidly winking so my drifting eye would seem less obvious. Sometimes she flirted back, but she always laughed, and her good white teeth and strong skin tone belied an upbringing well outside of what the Q. children accepted as normal.

"Perception is everything," Sissy told me once many autumns ago, after I had broken down, terrified of being caught, her smooth hand cupping my balls. I think she meant that if I acted like I was getting blow jobs from my sister, then it would be breakfast table news. By the time of Peter's engagement, I began to believe that perception was all I had left: fantasies, scripted vignettes, vigorously stroked playlets where I would be the recipient of mercy sex, my increasingly useless limbs suddenly filling with captured light, floating above my sex partner like a minor god descended from some ceiling painting in the Gift Room. Sissy Sissy Sissy. Others too, but mostly Sissy: Sissy as a child, fondling me even then; Sissy the teenager, engulfing herself in oral pleasure, her newest stethoscope dangling from her bobbing neck; Sissy as a college student, just before the whole thing went to hell, fucking me so hard, I would sit behind her dormitory after she threw me out, waiting for some divine intervention, so I could limp my way to the bus stop. Then: Sissy pregnant. My whole world tumbling down as her stomach blossomed. The switch from family medicine to psychiatric nursing had led her to this bent little man who apparently wielded a potent form of sperm.

I moved out and tried (unsuccessfully) to stay away from the family manse; I should have known better—I couldn't even move outside of Anchor Hop, and the door to my old bedroom yawned invitingly whenever I dared wander past its serrated maw.

Then, in the seventh month, the baby was gone. Like that, it vanished and no one spoke of it. No one tucked away objects of affection in remembrance, no memorial service was held. The baby vanished, like someone had popped the bubble that was Sissy, let the air out, and told her to get on with her life. The man remained, his sperm awaiting another chance to find purchase. I didn't believe in a god necessarily, but if I did, I could not fail to see how plainly the Lord had laid out the course for my return to Sissy's arms, my triumphant reentry between her legs. I called. I left messages. I hung outside her (their) apartment. I sent flowers. I read E. E. Cummings into her answering machine (figuring it would just go over the Sperminator's head). Nothing.

It was Peter, and his blunt reaction to being anything but number one, who helped bring an end to my seemingly interminable whack-off phase. Peter wanted me to say the blessing at his wedding reception (despite the fact that the Q. children, although ostensibly raised Roman Catholic, all practiced a rather benign form of distanced agnosticism); Peter wanted me to write the prayer and arrived unannounced (a no-no; my dedication to the craft of self-manipulation required distance) to coax jewels from my worn husk.

"What are you working on now?" asked Peter.

"Stuff. Things," I replied.

With his head in my fridge, looking for another beer (he swallowed the first before his jacket hit the floor), Peter said, "Can I see?"

"You don't read."

"Since the second grade, I swear."

"I haven't written anything in a while."

Peter blew something off the top of a can of beer.

"I thought you said you were working on stuff."

"In my head."

Peter collapsed on the sofa and finished the can in two swallows.

"Wow. In your head. Crowded up there, is it?"

"Cut it out. Look, I've been busy."

Peter surveyed my apartment, his head swiveling like one of those moving fans. As this was a surprise visit, I hadn't had the time to stuff the clothes into a hamper or hide the huge pile of dirty dishes under the sink. I had tucked the pornography behind the television as the doorbell rang.

"Mother ate another bloodroot today."

"Jesus Christ, Peter. Why doesn't Celia stop buying them? There are thousands of fucking plants out there."

Peter coughed.

"Sissy. Sissy orders the plants."

"Oh."

Peter launched himself off the sofa.

"Well, you know best, kid. I only get married once, right. See what you can do for me, dedication-wise, prayer-wise, you know."

"It's all about time, Petey."

"Well, maybe it's time you put down the penis and picked up the pen. I have to go. Thanks for the beer."

My brother left, and I masturbated until it hurt, until I finally achieved the mythical blindness, sitting there in my own dark, jism running down my hand. Write this, motherfucker, I thought.

But Little Lord Peter was right. This time, his insistence to be the best or nothing was true. What else did I have to lose since losing my sister-lover? I had reached bottom: nowhere else to go but up. It was the only true thought in my carefully wrought inner sanctum. I threw out the X-rated videos and magazines, as well as my shot glass collection and marijuana pipe. I started light exercises. I listened to the neurologist. I tried to eat healthier (goodbye chips and dip, hello natural hues). Most importantly, I learned to *remember* (more on this later). The MS had fucked with my physical appearance: my left eye strained to the right permanently, my gait was a shuffle, and my face was inflated from the medication. Occasional acne eruptions flared up the side of my bloated neck. Not a monster, but not someone you necessarily wanted to spend pillow time with. So I wrote. I wrote until my fingers were numb from typing. And one cold morning, changing my stained sheets (as my medical condition deteriorated, I began losing control of my bladder), under the mattress I found the instamatics of Sherrie and the fake diamond ring planted square in her middle. Suddenly I was in the Ford my father had when we were kids, all four of us crammed into the back seat, Mother up front in the passenger side, Father driving, his head tilted to keep the sun out of his eyes. I heard Mother tell him to make a turn, and Father asking: "What? Where?" and Mother mock-yelling at him to slow the hell down, and Mother's laughter like a pebble in the water, the four children now ripples in giggles, Father slowing down at the turn, the wrong turn, always, and then speeding up halfway through, all four little bodies crushed to one side of the car, Cindy behind Father (where she pretended to drive, fastidiously fashioning every gesture after his) thus squished the most, yelling out "Watch my bones, dammit, watch my bones!" and me thinking: fuck her bones, my sides hurt so much from being a ripple, distracted from snorting by Sissy's hand on my shorts, me hoping I didn't let a little pee out from laughing so hard, and then Sissy, traditionally, ending the scene with her famous last line: "See, this is why we're all so fucked up!"

I finished composing the wedding prayer, placed a copy of it, along with Sherrie's portfolio (I no longer needed it), in an envelope, and left to drop it off at Peter's apartment, taking the bus (I no longer had a car, my vision being a twisted distinguisher; thank you MS!), feeling the wind rush through the window, the sky weighty with pregnant clouds, and I wondered, not for the first time, if this was as good as it got.

Anchor Hop will never ensnare me, I thought. And prayed.

11. Mother Waves Goodbye

"She always said I was always one step away from wherever I was."

Father would tell us: it was ours—all of it—"...for the taking—no limits except those you set yourself—to remind you of where you came from, so you can forget and rush past it like a wave."

Mother would sit in the shadows and do Mother things: sew, knit, read a women's magazine—I don't recall Mother things. Mother came to Father fully independent: educated, a nurse in the war, a wealthy family, a sense of humor, and a sense of good. Good sense. And structure—Mother believed in structure. Chores were posted on a hanging list, and allowances were doled out based not only on whether the chore was completed, but also on how the task was carried out. Every bit his equal, and careful enough never to show it, Mother nevertheless took on the role of rival. She never gathered the children around her chair to pontificate or ponder aloud; rather, her quiet presence and immaculate education were spoon fed beneath piles of sugar or jelly, much like medicine trying to hide.

All this Sissy told me, and it's like I was there. It's like I knew this mother: benign yet tough, this mother ran a tight kitchen, as they say. My mother was less. Oh, I remember certain instances where she *seemed* like the person in Sissy's stories—sometimes she was *exactly* the mother that Sissy had, just left of center. But Sissy said the First Cindy and What Father Did knocked most of the Isabella out of Mother. Cindy the Lesser avoided Mother altogether. Mrs. Plunkett and Celia ran the kitchen now amid a haze of acrid smoke and Sissy's admonishments and encouragements. "She'd been knocked down a notch," Sissy said, not without a grin, as if that could ever happen to her. Privately I thought, if anyone ever needed a mom, it was Sissy, although I couldn't picture in my head, the stories Father would tell of the Birth of Sissy-Girl, the mother who bounced Sissy on her lap, sang her old war songs, or drew on her face with paints to make little Sissy giggle. When Father would turn to these tales, Sissy would simply stare at me until I lost the trails of the story and gained an erection.

The picnic was Samantha's idea. With the wedding looming, Samantha wanted to bring the two families together on a semi-regular basis, not just squeezed into the traditional wedding meet-and-greets. So there we all were: Samantha's family, robust, tan, doing sports-like things; and then the Q.'s (with the sole exception of Peter) pale, a little bewildered in the sun, a bunch of myopic nocturnal creatures. I sat in the shade and wrote in my journal (newly rededicated to the craft of writing as I was). Cindy the Lesser, in a full tunic, sat in a lotus position next to me and presumably counted her breaths. Sissy was with the man who would shortly make her pregnant for a second time (although no one ever spoke of the first; Peter even confided in me that he wondered if the significant other even knew she had been pregnant; the simple man merely smiled his way through any Q. family gatherings), and she was busy pushing his curly hair out of his eyes (the man had a receding hairline; his hair never reached his eyes), feeding him crackers, as if they had just met and not just lost a baby, her nipples hard and full beneath a worn, pink Rolling Stones t-shirt. (Sissy never listened to rock'n'roll music; she told me once, "Nothing could match what I already hear in my head.") Pure fantasyland. Pure Candy Land. Father brought along a folding chair and sat sipping Tullamore Dew in the heat, alternately offering Samantha's father advice on how to cook the meat and regaling whomever he trapped with Stories of the War. Mother was eating potato salad out of a Frisbee with her fingers, her face and hands splotchy with pimples grown red in the sun. A radio was playing the Hot Hits, and a rambling DJ competed with the steady swish of traffic from the nearby road. The picnic resembled nothing, I thought, as much as a misplaced pauper funeral, with various denizen strangers gathered round to pay respects out of boredom, or a sense of duty, or perhaps because the bastard owed them a buck or two.

And in my head, there we all were back in the Gift Room, before Peter's accident, before Mother really turned a corner, before Sissy ceased all undercover activities. Father would sit us in a loose circle: Cindy on his lap, Father wiping her nose; Sissy close enough so she could occasionally smooth his pant cuffs and rub his damaged legs; Peter, flexing for the girls; me, just outside, eager to join but knowing I didn't quite belong in the same way—this wasn't reading hour. Father would tell us our family history, the same way every time, and we would remind him if he forgot something, and he would thrill us by adding a little detail he may have left out in the last telling. I don't remember Mother during all this. Perhaps she was there, doing the things I remember her doing all the other times we gathered in the

Gift Room, or maybe my memory has her frozen in the act of finger painting with egg yolks or masturbating in the foyer with a stalk of celery. This was Father's time, I remembered.

And in my ever shrinking brain, in the ever present past, Father wove the family story, and told us to remember every word—and *then*, this singular time, instructed us to forget every single bit of it! "...like an anchor," Father said, his words seeming to fall in raindrop patterns of clipped syllables, two or three or four of them gathered together, occasionally garbling the thrust of the sentence, then righting themselves at the last moment: "History is...I can't remember a damn time when it didn't fascinate me so...the thing to be—an actor: true in interpretation, free from history (being fictional), and yet tied to a grand tradition, albeit one, due to its wanton nature, sure of the skies of freedom." And we became those jumbled words, each of us shedding a little more every year to inhabit the promise, to make flesh his word.

And now, at the picnic, Sissy's voice, a bell: "Look, there's Mother waving goodbye!"

Mother was standing near the clearing by the curb of the road, and she had turned, her bonnet hat cocked to one side and back, one pant leg rolled up to reveal her shin, her blouse flapping over her skinny torso and loose skin, waving slowly, her eyes squinting in the sun. Cindy waved to Mother; Father squinted back from his chair. Sissy was on her feet but didn't move, not even when I stood behind her and put my sweaty palm into hers. Peter was halfway to the road by the time it happened.

Mother waved goodbye and stepped into the traffic. Subsumed.

I felt Sissy's hand drop mine, and I wished we were back in the Gift Room.

Everyone else: melee, frozen. Not sure which.

Peter turning to Father, ice in my brother's too blue eyes: "It's only fitting for a warlord," my brother said, and Father, for the first time, smacking him across the face, breaking the nose already broken twice.

Mother was gone.

12. Mind Guerillas

Young William eased over the F-16 model and dug behind the monitor for his pen. Mr. Quayle was before him, brandishing a Japanese Zero and a German Dornier, his suspenders hung over a misshapen yellowed t-shirt.

"And out. They went. They were prepared. Their lives. Were geared. Toward this single. Purpose. It was hard. To fight. Against that sort. Of mentality. It's not that. Much different. Today. With the terrorists. That kind of. Determination. Requires a different. Sort of. Mindset. On our part. Don't you agree. Young William? Or are you. Thinking of. Re-upping. With the. Irish Air Force?"

Young William blushed. So it was going to be like this again today: cat and mouse, dog and cat, let's play the cliché, shall we? With at least two Quayle-hours lying ahead and two more plane models to admire and memorize for next week's quiz, not to mention that in all the branch, not a single pen was to be had, and the platform was, once again, oh-so mysteriously empty, William slid over a plane he could not identify on sight, but whose tail wing should have given it away, and loosed a Tums from his bag.

{*Now hum. Hum loud and drown out Abraham's shouts. Drown out the whittling of his knife. Shot time! Make it a double, barkeep! Oh, but he could hear their talk—could hear the old man's voice. It wouldn't be long before the door opened. Everyone would see soon. He didn't know how he felt about that.*}

"I think the terrorists were cowards. Killing innocent—"

Mr. Quayle spat on the edge of the desk, his clutch of yellow teeth like a beacon; William couldn't take his eyes off their long twisted peaks.

"They were. Soldiers. Foot soldiers. At best! And they used. Themselves. To deliver. The "bombs." Cowards? Young William? I think not. And that is. Our problem. How do you. Counter that. Type of thinking? What was. The name of. The man who led. The IRA. All those. Years ago. By using terrorist. Tactics?"

"Michael Collins?"

Mr. Quayle was shouting; the echoes banked off the branch's high ceiling.

"Asking me. Young William? Know your history! Yes! Michael Collins. He brought a. Different kind of. Fight to the British. When your sworn. Enemy is using. What is comfortable. Against you. Then circumstances. Require. Extraordinary. Measures. The terrorists. Used it against. Us. Watch my words. Young William."

{*Their voices carried through his door; they were discussing his case. Oh, how he had prayed for disease if only to distinguish himself in a house of extraordinary children. He inherited neither his English mother's beauty nor the old man's cunning, scheming brain. Just the lust—he had his father's lust.*}

The bank clerk coughed and looked toward the office door. At some point, he would have to hand off Mr. Quayle to his manager or, at least, the assistant manager. Mr. Quayle's visits resembled social calls with an irate tutor bent on humiliating his pupil so that he may be broken enough to learn.

"Have you heard from your son, sir?"

"I have. One daughter. Left. And that is—"

" 'And that is enough.' I know, sir. But at the hospital, when they took you to the hospital, they said your son was still alive and in the area." William cleared his throat. "We already spoke about this, sir."

"It was the bus. That clipped him. He was. Riding his bike. On Bustleton Avenue. And, wham! As sure as could be. The bus clipped him. He wasn't. Having his. Best season. It was his. Senior year. And the colleges. Were all out. Shortstop. Peter played shortstop. Any of the. Colleges would have. Taken him. Bad season or not. But Peter had his. Sights set on one. The best, I'm sure. Can't recall. Which one. One of the. Vagaries. Of getting old. No one asks. Old movie stars. For their autographs. Anymore."

The old man relinquished hold of one of the new plane models and wheezed into a shredded white ball that William could only assume was a tissue. William moved aside the Helldiver and pushed a box of tissues towards Mr. Quayle.

"Took himself. Out of the running. With that hit. No more. College baseball. Still played. The game. But not with that. Special need. Anymore. For fun! Pah!"

"Well, it is a game, sir."

Mr. Quayle rolled his eyes back into his head and spat a significant lungful onto the desk, having missed his spit of a tissue.

"He did manage. To marry up. But then. Samantha. Left him. Just like that."

Mr. Quayle sneezed on one of the planes.

"He was. Our little lord. And he had it all. Good paying job. Beautiful wife. Funny too. And she made. A lot of dough. Let me tell you. Advertising. Sell you anything. Those people. Can't see. The forest. For the trees. But they make you. Believe you can't. Either. And the next thing. You know. You're staring. At their lowest. Common. Denominator. Advertisements. In between. The canned laughter. Of stale sitcom jokes. That weren't funny. The first time. They wrote them. Back when. I could still get. An erection. Without pills."

Mr. Quayle's breathing was coming in staccato pulls and releases. Although Mr. Quayle's last free-fall had been in winter, the old man appeared ready for another shot at the big time. Young William stood up to call his manager, or an ambulance, or both.

"Sit the fuck down. Young William. And that was. The end of it. She left. And he drank. Classic tale. Of love really. Never told us why. Maybe he told his brother. Maybe he told the writer. Never told us. Stopped playing baseball. Yeah, in fact. All his Mike Schmidt. Memorabilia. Was gone. When they went into. His apartment. Afterwards. Don't know. If he sold it. Or if Samantha came. And took it. Or if the landlord. Helped herself. Peter liked that. Schmidt retired. Rather than. Burned out."

"His brother? Peter is…Peter passed away? I'm confused, sir."

Mr. Quayle hacked into his hand and wiped it on his trousers. He snapped his suspenders.

"The writer knows. It all. I'm sure! Peter's little brother. The writer. Peter looked. Up to him. Smarts. That's all he had. The writer. And where is he now? Ha! Never strong enough. To fight, that one. His oldest sister. Made him once. Fistfight. The kid around the corner. Just to stand up. For himself. Didn't want to see. Her brother picked on. All the time. 'Course, Peter had to. Step in! The writer. The reader then, I suppose. Didn't know how. To throw a punch! Probably still doesn't. Probably still sitting. Around somewhere. Waiting for something. To happen!"

"And that was the son the hospital called?"

{*Ghosts. They are just outside the door. He could hear them—talking like he wasn't even there. Hallway ghosts, flittering past his room, dragging him away from his museum duties, into the sordid, sticky past. "Open the door, and you'll see no one is there," they told him. Hah! They open their mouths like the devil spreads her legs. You know who.*}

Out of the corner of his eye, William could see the office door open and the branch manager's face squinting out of the darkness into the bright morning sun of the branch lobby, his dirty blonde hair catching glances off the chrome fixtures.

"My other daughter. Is her mother. Through and through. She takes care of me. When I let her."

The office door slammed shut, and a lady in the teller line jumped and exclaimed, "Merciful heavens," as if God or mercy or anything else, William thought, had anything to do with the skeleton melting down before him.

"Your other daughter? The one who takes care of you, sir? So you have two daughters and two sons?"

"I have one daughter. And that is enough. There is no one else left."

"I'm sorry, sir?"

"Did I show you. My planes?"

13. Fever Glass

This is the way I learned to remember: you need objects, like voodoo dolls, touchstones, memorabilia, memory stones—you need to cultivate them and curate them and let them grow until the memories root themselves inside your brain, let them grow until they can never be torn asunder.

We were never out when the sun was out. That is the truth. Father had raised us to be internal little creatures, scurrying from one book to another, our postures reflecting our lifestyle—although, like I've said, I was the only child who read for pleasure; everyone else had ulterior motives. Mother, despite being English (Father had pounded England's pregnant weather into our heads, as if it was a place where you wouldn't dare be caught out of doors), adored being outside. Among the children, Peter was the sole exception, and by the time Peter was born, Mother was an internal creature too, although her cocoon was largely self-made and definitely singularly inhabited.

The lack of any concrete mother-son relationship disturbed our Peter, who felt it was his natural right to be at least in competition with his eldest sister for the top spot. With Mother, he barely blipped on the maternal radar, raised more by Cindy and the smoking help: Celia and Mrs. Plunkett. Afterwards, when Peter was gone, Sissy said in a letter (her only solid communication to me in years it seemed; I smelled that letter until I had little paper cuts on my nose) that she blamed Mother for it all, but that was too easy. We had freedom. As children, freedom was given to us without hesitation, and we were told to make of it what we would. With little to lose, we staked our claims as both objects of affection and effectors of objects, warlords, after all.

Peter, like the rest of us, threw nothing away. It would not be peculiar to dig through a closet and discover Cindy the Lesser's Our Lady of Something habit (worn after Cindy began adopting the particular costume of that month's role model, as if merely *acting* was no longer sufficient), or a baseball (but *not* the autographed Mike Schmidt baseball) Peter hit over the backyard fence line when he was four. It was like we were preserving our strange little history in these objects of affection, storing them away until we had the need or the wherewithal to pull them out, examine them in some benign form of reflection (my family was not given to deep recourse over past actions; we heeded Father's earliest instructions and lived in the moment, right?), and then reinstate the objects so that they now echoed both their far history as well as their newer incarnations as inter-personal-cultural touchstones.

Regardless, Little Lord Peter kept a little something from each and every sexual conquest: an earring, a bracelet, once a vase with silk flowers, one time a dog collar and a stuffed and mounted mallard (posed in some sort of attack position, beak at the ready). These souvenirs were tucked in and around our Anchor Hop home. Even after Peter moved into his first apartment, and then later into the house he briefly shared with Samantha (both in town), they would occasionally pop up, murder victims bobbing free of their chains to grace a thrice-dragged river. Post-Samantha, I met Peter in several bars about town, and there always, clinging to his still quite impressive muscles, was an intoxicated beauty or two, all with centerfold type names (Bunny, Lola, Veronique), gloriously scrubbed incisors, and empty pocketbooks; I could only assume souvenir hunting was in full season.

Peter even kept the receipt for the rope. It wasn't carelessly tucked into his trousers, but rather neatly folded and placed in the top drawer of his nightstand. But don't let the carefully folded receipt fool you; like a good Q., the messy top drawer was a microcosm for the rest of his post-separation efficiency apartment and contained not a few objects of affection, tokens of carnal collisions.

One year, before Mother's balcony slip or her causal stroll into streaming traffic, but long after we had ceased believing the Santa Myth (and why would we perpetuate that fable when we were smothered in our own legends in Anchor Hop), at Sissy's behest, each of the Q. children gave a prized possession to another for Christmas. Peter gave his red switchblade to Sissy (Father practically had a hissy fit!); Cindy gave Peter his autographed Mike Schmidt baseball back (she had stolen it the year before in preparation for a new role; two weeks after the holidays, Sissy re-stole it); Sissy gave Cindy her dog-eared *Illusions*, the signed copy Father had bought for her (Sissy stole it from Cindy a month later and stashed it behind some unread Kennedy biographies Father collected for Mother); I was left out by accident.

But that Christmas was grand nonetheless in our own peculiar Q.

way. My gifts to each of my siblings (I found the rules too confining) were words: an essay on Patti Smith for Cindy (I thought she would empathize with the *"Jesus died for somebody's sins, but not mine"* atmosphere), a short story about the burning of the October leaves, splattered with Elvis references, for Peter (the fall season was as close as I could get to writing about baseball!), and a love ballad for Sissy. I could not, however, for love or money or Mournful orgasms, give Sissy her song. When my oldest sister found me, huddled behind Father's red high-backed chair at the midnight holiday crest, humming my "Love Song for Someone," she realized I had given without having received and sensed I was strenuously keeping an object of affection from her. She pulled me off the floor. Ensconced in her bedroom—all hospital corners and meticulous appointments—Sissy demanded what was hers. The turned down red and gold blanket and the revealed crisp white sheets were altar cloths covering the site of the coming sacrifice. I stood before my sister-love, engulfed in crimson, and read the lyrics in a halting voice, not unlike Father's in his twilight, sweat gathering on my upper lip like rain water on an upturned leaf, never falling, a bold reminder of the weight I imagined bore down on my near-Christian soul.

> *Oh, tonight,*
> *I'm so restless;*
> *Wish you were here;*
> *Can't get past it.*
> *Oh, how long*
> *Will I wait*
> *When I'm too close*
> *To be in focus?*

> *And when I say: 'Don't waste your time on me,'*
> *It means I fell for you again;*
> *And when I cry: 'Let me immerse myself in sleep,'*
> *Know I want you more than anything.*

> *Oh, I thought*
> *I saw you flying;*
> *Was it in a dream?*
> *Are you the same as everyone?*

So, spread your wings;
Let them ruin you;
Write their songs;
Here's one for you though you can't see me.

I'm consumed by all that you are;
I'm consumed by all that you are.

And when I say: 'Don't waste your time on me,'
It means I fell for you again;
And when I cry: 'Let me immerse myself in sleep,'
Know I want you more than anything.

Oh, tonight,
The band played something
'Bout what's been chasing me
My whole fucking life.
So knock on my door;
Take me on;
You say you can make me do anything
But you can never make me stop.

And when I say: 'Don't waste your time on me,'
It means I fell for you again;
And when I cry: 'Let me immerse myself in sleep,'
Know I want you more than anything.

I keep your photographs in a shoebox.
I keep your photographs in a shoebox.
I keep your photographs in a shoebox.
I keep your photographs in a shoebox.

"Give me your virginity," my sister said to me, and I folded into her, the leaf unburdened.

"Pull out and come on my stomach," Sissy said, and I cried when I came.

"Do this in memory of me," my sister-love instructed, her gentle laughs cascading off my trembling, suddenly adult body.

And like Peter's sexual memento drawer, each of us tried to hold onto our exchanged gifts or, in Sissy's case, stole them back. Sissy could never fully let go; neither could I. Sissy said we performed this Gift Ritual (her phrase) to remember that we were the only important objects of affection in Anchor Hop.

And so, here we all were, flung dozens of moons ahead, gathered for the holiday season, arrayed in the Gift Room, Father in his red high-backed chair, Mother's chair empty. Sissy had cleared off the knitting needles and was preparing to settle in, but Cindy the Lesser slowly raised the needles back to Mother's seat, effectively sealing it off as another museum piece in the Q. standard of living. Quite possibly, it was Cindy's only overt act of aggression, and Sissy took it in stride, seeing the action for what it was, and missing, like the rest of us, what it implied.

Little Lord Peter was drunk, as was Father, as was I, but they had several hours head start. Celia was off, but Mrs. Plunkett was cooking (was there a Mr. Plunkett?), although I don't recall ever sitting down to a meal. The day seemed to consist of the sound of ice cubes rattling like fresh bones in a fever glass. Sissy was cordial to me, but her eyes never met mine. Cindy waited on Father mutely and discreetly, pretending not to hover over the abruptly old man, as if to acknowledge her duties were to, in some way, disrespect our dead mother, who, in fact, had served no one but the demons within. All in all, still a typical Q. holiday dinner.

Then it was gift time, and we each played our roles for Father, who seemed quite impervious to all the pomp, shuttling back and forth in a drunken throes while enthroned in his red high-backed chair. Sissy's gifts were too big, as was the grin of the man who would shortly impregnate her a second time. What the fuck was his name? Cindy's gifts were split evenly between homemade items so intricate, our store-bought fleecings seemed like a light layer of snow on a school morning, and, as usual, little used knickknacks, mostly of the religious icon variety, to mount upon our dashboards—strange, considering that rarely did any of the Q. children drive, due simply to the fact that we were too busy living like adults as late teenagers to involve ourselves in driving classes, or proms, or ring dances for that matter; I dutifully stuck my saints, every year, on the back of the toilet. What I wanted was Cindy's blouse impression of Mother's face. It wasn't until after I discovered Cindy's penultimate role in Father's homegrown farce that I finally got what I wanted. Cindy mailed it to me after Sissy left us, but where I live, they have to open all the packages, and by the time it reached me, dear Mother's face was but a purple splotch on a ragged piece of cotton.

Father had reverted to the obsessed collector we all knew lurked within him; the planes he'd collected as a young man were back in abundance. It was about the only positive item on his agenda since Mother's exit, and although it was a one note melody, it was his, and we endured and displayed and dusted wooden model airplanes, festooned with decals signifying their position or affiliation with the various factions of World War II and beyond; Father gave us planes for Christmas. The gifts I gave were simple. I followed a rule: give them something they want, and barring any good ideas, give them something they have to hide or destroy after the holidays. Thus, Sissy went home one year with a little monk statue that played "Hava Nagila" when used as its intended incarnation (a back massager), and Mother spent the better part of a fall, following her birthday, moving a six foot, two inch, cigar wielding, wooden Apache from room to room, changing his role from hat bearer to underwear hanger to thing-that-props-open-the-cellar-door. My gifts this particular year, although slightly subdued in my newfound humility and rededication to the craft, followed the same train tracks.

When it was Peter's turn, he stood before Father (the old man momentarily stopped swaying), and addressing him (although he was speaking to us), made his announcement:

"I have no gifts."

Nothing more needed to be said. Little Lord Peter had been turned out, and we all knew that despite a decent job high up on the retail kill-chain, a large portion of his wages still supported the woman who, for all intents and purposes, carried his name in name-only.

"What did he say?" Father asked.

"Peter has no gifts," Cindy told him.

"Yes, he does. Best shortstop the Prep has seen since before my day!"

Sissy walked around me, careful not to let go of ol' what-his-name's hand. I noticed with a shudder that our mystery man wore a pinky ring. Combined with his pillow-over-the-face cologne (Peter said he smelled like a French whore, and to be honest, I figured Peter was the leading authority of late), Sissy's Pinky-Mate resembled nothing if not an extra from a Scorsese movie, albeit with a *Cuckoo's Nest* haircut.

"Peter has no gifts," Sissy said.

"Brother O'Brien told me the same thing," Father said, looking around for a sign of encouragement. " 'Your boy can play ball,' he told me."

Sissy dropped Pinky's fingers, took Peter by the hand, and led him out of the room.

"Peter has no gifts," I said, although the words were flat soda. The father I worshipped from afar was out to sea, and I did not recognize the man inhabiting the red high-backed chair.

Father's neck shaded into crimson, and he shook his fist at me.

"YES, HE DOES," Father said, pointing at Cindy, "ASK THE VIRGIN! SHE WATCHES HIM ALL THE FUCKING TIME!"

I could hear Sissy and Peter's footsteps as she led him upstairs. Pinky merely grinned the grin of the perpetually medicated, rocking back and forth on the footrest where Sissy had left him. I wondered where Cindy's husband was; Cindy looked a trifle nervous and pale to me, but maybe it was just her winter face, or maybe it was years of watching us, and the prospect of years of watching Father. Sissy and Peter's footsteps stopped on the third floor landing, and I could hear them navigating their way in the dark to...

Everyone was looking at me.

"Care for a cup of tea?" asked Cindy the Lesser, and her fingers shook as she dropped two sugar cubes into her mug.

14. The Sordid, Sticky Past

You never know when it's all going to catch up to you. It's like multiple sclerosis. They (meaning the scientific powers that be) have no idea how you contract it. You just do, and then slowly, on its own damn terms, it eats away at the sheaths that cover your nerves. I'm oversimplifying, but you get the picture, in full wavy watercolor. That's what happens, and that's what happened. In the Gift Room. Where else?

"I have nothing left to give."

That was Sissy, nervously flicking the silver lighter top (it was now of use after picking up smoking from Pinky); that was Sissy, standing before us in the same way, the year before, Peter had stood and told us that he had no gifts.

Peter was gone, and we were in the Gift Room for the holidays again. Another year, another shot of Dew. But the truth will soon out, I thought. Fuck passion.

Sissy's man was gone too, although not the same gone as our Peter. Pinky simply gave up and went back to the little psych ward in the little hospital of the little shit town he crawled out of before he captured our Sissy-Love. Peter, on the other hand, was literally a ghost. The difference was not subtle, but Sissy felt both losses and carried them much the way a saint would in one of Cindy's picture books, her fingers restless at her chest, as if at any moment, she would reveal her sacred torn heart.

My time was coming soon. Oh yes, soon-soon.

Peter hadn't been gone long. Not quite a year even.

Neither had Sissy's second baby.

This baby lasted a wee bit longer than the first Houdini, but as the time to emerge approached, this baby: Just. Fizzled. Out. And then Pinky left. And then Peter became a ghost. This is the order. Are you getting it all down? Do you need a time line to dissipate your confusion, darlings?

Little Lord Peter had decided to move; he said he would breathe easier out west. We could just picture our pale Q. skin roasting in the western sun!—not a concern for our tan Peter. He gave away all his important objects of affection: his two hundred dollar tennis racket, his baseball card collection, his bronzed eagle (I got this for some reason; Sissy said he was trying to make a point, but it was lost on me as is the eagle now), even his '68 GTO, a car he rarely drove, but which I think he bought merely to impress girls. A classic case, no? He wrote large checks, gifts. I got one of those too. "To help you get by while you're writing the Great American Novel, little brother," Peter said. We had a party immediately upon his announcement, although Peter wasn't leaving for two months. Peter took each of us out individually to lavish dinners at good restaurants, and not one of us thought to ask what happened—why was Little Lord Peter separated from Lady Samantha the Undoer? "*I'm left, you're right, she's gone,*" was the only thing Peter had to say on the subject.

If anyone could have asked, if anyone should have asked, it was Sissy. You would have thought they were attached at the hip (as my father would say). My brother and sister defined inseparable those last couple of weeks.

Then Second Baby gave up the ghost near as it could to the last possible second. Maybe Second Baby received some sort of transmission, some indication of how fucked up things were going to be on the Outside, and decided, "to hell with this," and allowed itself to return to dust. Maybe Sissy looked at Pinky, and looked at Peter, and beat her stomach until Second Baby was winded and tossed about the internal sea-sack. Maybe maybe maybe.

Pinky left her shortly thereafter. And then Peter had to be there for Sissy. Sissy didn't want to go back to her apartment right away, so she took up residence in the Q. family house for a little bit, until Peter was so much dust too anyway. Cindy waited on Sissy like a good little maid, like she did with Father, like she might have done with her traveling salesman husband, if he wasn't always traveling. ("Practicing being absent," Sissy used to snort). Peter was a good brother; he delayed his departure for the west and took care of all of Sissy's needs, which were many.

"Neurotics build castles in the sky; psychotics live in them. I am the caretaker," said Sissy. When I found her crying in the garden, out where Mother had jumped into the mud oh those ages upon ages ago, Sissy said, "Sympathy pains" and nodded toward her psych case folders. Still, she wouldn't look me in the eye, not even when I leaned her sob-wracked body against mine, eased my hand up her thigh, under her skirt, and stroked her between her legs. (Sissy never wore underwear.) She merely waited until she was wet, then using her left hand, slammed her fist into my balls and walked away. As I lay on the ground where Mother fell, I imagined I could see a dark stain on Sissy's skirt; if she had been that wet always, Second Baby could have slid right the hell out.

"I have nothing left to give," Sissy-Love declared in the Gift Room, but that wasn't *completely* true, now was it? We would see.

"She's so open, vulnerable now, she takes on whatever ails them," said Peter to me a couple of weeks before he became a ghost, as we strolled, sharing an after-dinner cigarette. "She always took on too much as far as her patients went, and now, on top of the baby, she's alone, so of course she *becomes* her patients. It's easier, more manageable. Sissy always brought her work home anyway."

Peter stopped walking and crushed the cigarette. I could smell liquor on his breath even though we just finished one of Mrs. Plunkett's lavish feasts.

"So to speak," I said.

Peter spit. "Maybe it was for the best, the baby. Who knows what the hell was wrong with Pinky."

Then, BOOM, a few more visits, a few more times to notice how my brother's breath reeked of alcohol *before* we went out, a few more times to say goodbye and stake claim to his prized possessions, and then Peter was gone. Real gone.

But first: The Squirrel Incident: I was visiting Father, but he didn't know I was there. He had started with the Tullamore Dew soon after breakfast and was sitting in the red high-backed chair, muttering a discourse to himself on the effect of wind resistance during free-fall. The one mirror in the Gift Room, our Snow White mirror, was covered with a black cloth like Jewish families do when someone passes. Cindy said he slept all the time; when I asked him, he snorted at me: "I'm practicing for dying," and I noticed how yellow his teeth had become. After a few dead minutes, I exited and made my way toward Sissy's old room. Sissy wasn't in—maybe she was with Peter, I thought. It was obvious she'd been sleeping there though. I poked around her clothes; I sniffed a few pairs of dirty underwear, but I couldn't smell her. I lay in her bed and stared at the old Cigar Indian, tucked into the far left corner. I *could* smell Sissy's shampoo on the pillow, and despite the fact that I knew I wouldn't be able to climax (thank you, oh thank you, MS), I pulled my penis out and began stroking it, my focus on the old Cigar Indian, my memory cruising up Sissy's full white thighs, my nostrils pulling every last vapor from her pillow, my one good eye going out of focus, the

Cigar Indian fading in and out, in and out, and then twisting its head to one side.

I stopped cold, my half-limp appendage drooping in my fist. The squirrel sat atop the Cigar Indian's head and stared at my half-naked body sprawled on my big sister's bed. I peeked behind me at the open window and back again to the squirrel. I eased off Sissy's bed, careful to smooth the coverlet, never taking my eyes off the squirrel. *Easy does it. One two three.* When I reached for the doorknob, the squirrel leapt from the Indian's carved noggin, heading for the bed perhaps, or the large makeup mirror that loomed above the desk. Of course, as the squirrel launched forward, I jerked back away from the door, and we collided in the middle of the room. I'm not sure who screamed louder.

Cindy and Celia were there within half a heartbeat (although not half of mine; all the air had gone out of my lungs, and my tongue had dried up).

"Close the door, close the door," I said, from my position on the floor. "Get down. He flies!"

"What are you...?" asked Cindy, as the squirrel jumped from wherever it was catching its breath to atop one of the bedposts. Celia screamed (even her scream seemed to have a come-hither, though indeterminate, European accent), and as she dropped to the floor next to me, I wondered if I could still get it up for Celia the maid.

Cindy was on the floor too.

"Why are your pants down?" Cindy asked.

I rolled onto my back (and noticed Celia stealing a glance at my privates), started pulling my trousers up—then stopped. I had an erection.

"Jesus Christ," I said, and stood up. Celia and Cindy stared at my hard-on from their positions on the floor.

"You were masturbating with the squirrel?" asked Cindy.

"No, I was—"

Maybe the squirrel thought it was food. Maybe he saw it as a weapon and figured to attack while I busy trying to explain my personal path to self-love to Cindy the Lesser. Regardless, the squirrel *seemed* to leap for my penis just as Father swung the bedroom door open and lurched into the room.

"Good God, man, where are your pants?" asked Father.

The door and rodent met in mid air, and the twice-unlucky squirrel hit the floor with a sound not unlike the one Mother made landing in the backyard all those years ago.

"Whose squirrel is this?" asked Father.

The squirrel's tiny little face was inches away from Celia's; our maid remained frozen on the floor, gasps of accented surprise escaping from her lungs. This was the Squirrel Kingdom's revenge for Mournful's backyard rampages, I was sure.

I pulled my pants up, and Cindy tore the sheet from Sissy's bed. We wrapped the squirrel in a hobo-sack (its little chest was going up and down, so he wasn't quite the goner I had first supposed) and paused to collect our breaths and wits enough to explain to our soused *patris* the origin of the squirrel. As Cindy eased the makeshift carryall off the ground, the squirrel regained consciousness and began a mad scramble to free itself, knocking Cindy back to the floor. Celia hid behind the Cigar Indian.

And here's why I bothered to tell this story: Father calmly picked up the sheet-sack, walked to the open window, and with a toss of his wrist, flung the sheet open, releasing the dazed squirrel into our backyard. I tell this story, for in that moment I loved him, for in that one tiny heroic effort, he was the Grand Old Man, high atop his red high-backed chair, ready to right the wrongs and lead the pack. A warlord. I never thought of him like that again.

"Damn monkey," my father said, holding his finger stump in the air, his mind thousands of miles away in a land less foreign than our own Anchor Hop had become.

And then, like I said, Peter was gone.

I called his place of employment after receiving a near-panicked phone call from Sissy; she hadn't heard from Peter in almost a week. I let Sissy go off, her words speeding by a million miles a minute, as I tried to jerk off with the phone balanced in such a way so that she wouldn't hear my breathing.

Finally: "Are you done? Find him." And Sissy hung up.

So I called, and Little Lord Peter Q. was "no longer employed with the firm," and no amount of high talking could dislodge any bit of information concerning why.

And there I was, not a week later, with Cindy (Sissy locked herself back in her old bedroom and took the phone off the hook), cleaning Peter's swinging bachelor pad, wondering where all the Mike Schmidt memorabilia went, wading through mountains, sheer mountains of empty booze bottles, cases of empty beer bottles. I positioned myself in Peter's bedroom (it was more like an alcove in this efficiency apartment), thinking it might be better if I took care of the top nightstand drawer rather than Cindy. Little Lord Peter's note had left me in charge, a dubious honor, and one that precluded that Peter was, in fact, "in charge" of our little tribe. Peter was a leader, no doubt, but as was becoming obvious to me as I read a photocopy of the note, Peter's cramped elementary school writing style made even more claustrophobic by Cindy's attempts to make sure both sides of his dispatch (a rambling soiled account of the fidelity he imagined in each family member, scribbled on two sides of a Christmas card) were on the same page—we were absolutely rudderless, a tub full of boo-lees awash in a sea of Tullamore Dew and smeared ink stains. And there I was, the Keeper of the Nightstand, mere days after getting dressed up to put my brother in the ground. As Cindy scrubbed the bathtub and cleaned the toilet of all signs of our Peter, I peered into the top drawer, and there amidst a couple of bracelets, one earring, and a single left red high-heeled shoe with thin tantalizing straps, was a stethoscope. I stuffed it into my backpack and left Peter's apartment, muttering to Cindy something about finding Peter's Mike Schmidt autographed baseball.

Back at my apartment, I cranked the stereo, Elvis Presley's Memphis sessions (which in a pique of Sissy-inspired scheming, I had nicked from Peter), and paced with the stethoscope. I wasn't angry with Peter; Lord knows, your penis can lead you down some strange and twisted alleys, but Sissy: welcoming Peter with open legs, as if he were just another in a series of so-called brilliant men who fucked her (without protection!—the Queen of Common Sense!), as if he were just another strutting peacock, kept like the rest, just long enough for Sissy to realize their flaws and force her mouth to lie about them. To put Peter in that company, in the same company as Pinky (who, admittedly, outlasted all of Sissy's previous bangs)—my stomach seized itself in recoil. Peter went to her for comfort; Peter went to her to give something of himself when Second Baby crawled into limbo. Passion will out, my ass. Fucking whore.

And as my taxi pushed through the rain toward Anchor Hop, it all made sense. Peter would be here were it not for Sissy's wetness, if not for what was apparently her life-creed: if you don't understand something, fuck it, and at least everyone will feel better. I would expose Sissy in the Gift Room and let judgment fall among its dust spiders and half-eaten book jackets.

My hands were sticky as I gripped the stethoscope. My fingers left little gummy marks on the banister, as I took the front stairs two at time like I did when we were children—racing through the house, the loser being forced to walk naked on the girls' balcony or drink Mrs. Plunkett's garlic ball soup cold. I paused on the second floor landing. I could hear muted laughter and muttering from below, like when we used to play hide-and-seek amid Mother's old clothes, losing ourselves in the two big L-shaped closets, my excitement escalating as my siblings failed to find me, my headphones in place blasting the blues, reveling in being alone and, for once, the center of attention, then so swiftly frightened without their hot breath and constant stream of opinions surrounding me like an extra blanket in winter, that I peed a little down my leg—Sissy discovering my hot face and helping me quietly soak up the pee with one of Mother's old floor length nightgowns. That was the first time she touched my penis. I was a goner right then and there.

On the third floor, I pushed Sissy's bedroom door open, and I knew she had moved out just from the way the bed was made. Cindy had made this bed, or maybe Celia. It had none of Sissy's hurried dishevelment (which proliferated despite Celia's attempts at training). Her silver lighter was on the floor, and then in my moist palm. As I turned to leave, something else seemed amiss. I looked out the window, down to the ground where Mother had landed, where Cindy had wiped her face, and Mother had given herself back in gratitude. The dogwood was dying. I turned toward the door and knew then that Sissy had taken the Cigar Indian with her. I reached between the mattress and the bedspring.

Fuck unveiling Sissy in the Gift Room.

Then, behind my eyes, Mother was there: like out of a pool in summer, Mother peeled her onion layers of darkness, shedding years of cocooning, to reach toward me, just after my diagnosis: "I would take this," my mother said to me. It was then I knew to collect and hoard, for as Anchor Hop swallowed itself whole, someone needed to be in charge before the past confused itself with the present. Peter was right.

Back down the stairs, and again, the muted laughter—was it laughter?—moaning, perhaps. I called for Celia. I called for Mrs. Plunkett. Maybe Father was in the Gift Room (there was the book I needed to steal, I reminded myself, the one hidden behind the unread Kennedy biographies), and as I turned from the bottom of the stairs, Mother quietly exited the guest bedroom, carefully shutting the door behind her. Mother was wearing the pretty red dress that made her look like an exotic lounge singer, and as I turned to tell her just that, to squeal on Sissy, to hold her and ask her why she never held me, I could see Mother had a severe case of blow job lips and that the left side of her neck was covered in bite marks.

Cindy stared at me with those calm, steady sea blue eyes, their color severely clashing with Mother's old dress which squeezed my sister into shapes that were not her own. Father bellowed from the bedroom.

"I think you should go," Cindy the Lesser said to me.

15. Bone Rattles

"I know. Nothing of you. Young William."

"It's not important. What do you want to know?"

"I found her, you know. After she hadn't. Come around. For a few days. I went to her. Apartment. And found her."

"Found whom, sir?"

{*Now hum:* gotta get on that train, gotta get me on that plane. *He had been tracking the hallway ghosts, and the trail, once warm, then cold, was red hot. He could smell them outside his very door. No boundaries indeed, Abraham. The firstborn is dead, sir, and here I lie, ears to the door. Whiskey vapors? He heard Nurse William ask his question. How could he not know whom?*}

In a gulp, followed by a spray of spittle William ignored out of respect, the old man said, "My firstborn!"

"Sir?"

Young William glanced at the time on his computer. Mr. Quayle was early for his appointment with the branch manager. William looked toward the closed office door and drew up his posture. For months now, he had been entertaining Mr. Quayle's stories, shielding himself in professionalism whenever the old man went off on a tangent, and listening; William had done more listening than was required by law, he thought. But, in a twisted fashion, he liked Mr. Quayle. He admired his sharp brain (at least for events that happened years before) and his way of bringing you into a conversation with compliments and gentle jibes. He had grown to like the way the old fellow called him Young William, as if he were some attentive neophyte prostrate at the feet of someone wiser. Perhaps he was; he was quite taken with Mr. Quayle in some odd way. When he made the appointment for Mr. Quayle with his branch manager, William was surprised at the fury spilling from the normally reticent supervisor.

"Beware of him, that's all I'm saying."

"Of Mr. Quayle?"

"Don't believe his stories."

"Do you know him?"

"And for God's sake, don't accept any gifts from him."

"And the planes?"

"Get rid of the goddamn planes. Take them home!"

{*Oh, how he used to pray for disease. Oh, and he won. The rest of the house was so astonishing, he could only stand out by falling down. Ha! Thanks, God, thank you for listening! His penis was a tissue, his left eye an empty come-on, his legs numb little twigs. Shhh! They'll hear! Father Abraham was among the hallway ghosts!*}

Tears crowded the wrinkles around Mr. Quayle's eyes. William reached for a tissue. Mr. Quayle waved him off, brandishing his own stained handkerchief.

"The man. She was dating. Or screwing. Or whatever. He was one. Of her day patients. Should have. Been a doctor, that girl. A therapist? Pah! Mind like a steel trap. She had more brains. Than Carter had pills. I can tell you. This man. This Reginald. This Reginald Zaber. What kind of name. Is that? Nutty as a loon. Fucked in the head. He *drove* her there. What with his. Medicines. And talking. To the television. Oh, you think. I don't know. But I know. Just sitting there. Smiling. Just sitting there. *Needing*. And Sissy. My independent. Liberated. At age. Seven Sissy. *Giving* it to him. Like she *had* to. Like it was a drug. She'd been better off. Shooting shit. In her arm. That much I know."

Mr. Quayle blew into his handkerchief. Young William stole a peek at the office door.

"So they found out. At the hospital. Found out. Their star child. Was humping. The poor fuck. Who put mustard. In his own hair! And they fired her. Just like that. No fraternizing. With the patients, I guess. Best part of all. Young William, best part? He had left her. Not a week before! Not a week. Or two. After she lost. The second baby! Bastard. Fuck him to hell!"

Snot shot out of Mr. Quayle's nose, and he made no attempt to cease the steady stream of tears crisscrossing his wrinkles.

"Peter was history. Not too much afterward. Right after he. Lost *his* job! It's all about. The job you do, see? Without that. You are nothing. My children. Knew that. You think I'm blind. I don't see. What's in front. Of my goddamn face? And there she was. I go over, see. 'Cause I don't hear from her. My English war wife. She always said. I was always one step. Away from wherever. I was. Not his time, pal. No way. José."

William ignored the escaped sliver of light blinking from beneath the office door.

"And there she was. Her clothes. On the floor. Her back against. The headboard. Green shit from her mouth. All slid down. Her pale,

pale cheeks. Oh my Sissy-Girl! Her breasts. Exposed. And her stomach. Distended. From the pills. They said. And the green vomit. On her hands. On her throat. On her chest. My Sissy-Love! My Sissy-Girl! My firstborn!"

Then: silence, broken only by the bone rattles of the old man's breath. William paid no attention to the sliver of light under the office door as it extinguished itself.

"I found her," Mr. Quayle repeated to himself.

William struggled with the appropriate reply. The old man buried his chin in his chest.

"How is, um, how is Cindy?"

Mr. Quayle looked up, his eyes sharp.

"Who?"

"Cindy," said Young William. "Sir," he added.

"Her mother. Through and through."

"And her brother. The other one, not—"

"Wasted potential. Look that up. In the dictionary. And there you'll find. A picture. Of my last son. Ha! Peter's *wittle* brother. The reader." Mr. Quayle spit into the handkerchief for emphasis.

For one brief twist of air, William wished for this kind of life—not the tragedies, of course, but the *full-on* passage: war, sex, marriage, children. William envied Mr. Quayle his very full life.

"Well, I think our manager should be out soon."

Mr. Quayle banged his fist on the desk.

"Can't handle me?"

"No, it's not that, it's just, well, I thought bringing my manager into this might be to your advantage, sir, and he—"

"Chicken shit. Can't do nothing. On your own. Is that it?"

"Well, no, sir. But—"

"Did you call. Social Security. For me? Are they going. To direct deposit. Into this bank?"

"That will start next month, sir, for now—"

"Chicken shit bastard. Lazy is what you are."

Mr. Quayle spit on the desk.

"There. That's for you. You little piece of—"

Mr. Quayle clutched at his chest.

"Sir?"

"Get the fuck. Outta my way," said Mr. Quayle.

The old man pushed his chair back and stumbled away, lurching to and fro, until he stood center ring in the bank's marble lobby

Pointing toward the office door, Mr. Quayle's shouts echoed in the dome ceiling: "I know. You're in there! I can smell you!"

And then Mr. Quayle reeled toward the large glass doors, paused a moment before hitting them like an over-anxious bird, and let himself out into the early spring afternoon. A warm rush of air caromed through the bank (it smelled like an old train), and William could feel himself crying.

16. Hey Bo Diddley

This part of the story requires a Bo Diddley beat.

My mother couldn't sleep for the ghosts.

I remembered creepy-crawling to her room, staring at her with my one good eye:

"Mother?"

"Yes, son?"

"I want to kill you."

But I didn't.

Oh, how rock'n'roll.

Her dead baby. Her husband: torn from the pages of a boy's adventure novel, a dead child not part of the plotline. And me: the littlest ghost of them all! A ghost that breathes!

Mother sleeps rather soundly now, I expect.

I walk forty-seven miles of barbed wire;
I use a cobra snake for a necktie...

This part of the story requires a Bo Diddley beat.

As I scribble this, the lesions on my brain keep time. Short term memory loss, my ass. I wonder: could I be lost between the measures? Would I mind?

Loud. Thunder drums pulsing like blood congregating at my temples.

Yeah, yeah, that's it. Go go go. Shave and a haircut. Go, baby!

Then:

Come down rain,
Come down rain,
And wash, wash away
Every bit, every little bit o' my pain.

Sissy's Rain Song clashes on the offbeat. A real battle royal.

Like Mrs. Plunkett always said, so true in Anchor Hop: mind yourself!

I got a brand new house on the roadside,
Made from rattlesnake hide...

There are ten objects of affection.

Actually, there are twelve.

And if there are twelve, there have to be thirteen. I'll explain this later.

Now then: there are ten objects of affection, and they are arranged on the bureau top, arranged over a lace doily crafty with dirt.

This should be a love story but it's not.

This should be a noir but it's not.

This should ring a bell but it doesn't.

Peeled.

I approached Sissy's apartment in the dark. No scratch that. I approached Sissy's apartment *like the dark*. Better. *Clump clump clump*.

Sissy never locked her door. I felt like the narrator in "The Tell-Tale Heart." Her Christmas tree was still up, all brittle bristles and dashed promises. I could have sat there and listened forever. It had taken me a year to get this far. I listened for her breathing; I listened for wracked sobs.

We could call this section: What Happened to Sissy.

Peeled like an onion.

So Samantha found the Polaroids. That's the story in a nutshell. She was looking for presents; it was close to her birthday. There was no acceptable amount of explaining from Little Lord Peter. He never called on me as a witness, and maybe, as Sissy said, this was just an excuse for Samantha the Undoer to leave. Sissy saw her as a social climber, and, at the time, Peter had been on top. Yeah, maybe his post-baseball retail upper management career had turned into a stagnant-waste-o'-time, but HE HAD WON! Love, exciting and new. The real deal. It was his.

We could call this strand of the story: What Happened to Peter.

Watch my bones, dammit.

We already know what happened to the First Cindy.

We turn our eyes away from what happened to Cindy the Lesser.

"Her mother, through and through," *patris* said more than once.

The color of my eyes. I've forgotten the color of my eyes.

What Happened to Sissy Part II:
"Who's there?" she called.
Damn. I'd been trying to measure my breathing with hers while she slept..
"Is that you?" she asked.
Ah, the second-person personal pronoun.
I had no name, see. Not anymore. I was a writer, and I couldn't even give myself a fucking name, one I could keep and remember.
Then Sissy-Love said my Christian nom de plume, and my heart, or what was left of it, shifted ever so slightly. A wounded-animal noise escaped past my gritted teeth.
"Don't just sit there. Come in," my sister said, and truth be told, I wasn't sitting; I was crouched like a jungle cat over expired pine needles. This brought me back to my senses a little.
"Who do you love?" I asked, bringing myself to full height (*clump clump clump*), my left hand jammed deep into my trouser pocket.
My mother's name was Isabella,
My mother's name was Isabella,
The beautiful one.
My left hand, for Mother said the right hand was for God, touched the red handle of one of the ten objects of affection.

I got a brand new chimney made on top;
Made out of human skull…

What Happened to Peter Part II:
It was only fitting for a warlord.
Peter didn't jam the receipt for the rope in his trouser pocket; he folded it neatly for his memento drawer. And then he left a long letter that made little sense when read between globes of liquid fucking pouring out your eyeballs, for He-Who-Was-Left-Behind so missed his brother, that he wept like Jesus before the scourge.

Now come on, take a little walk with me, Arlene,
And tell me, who do you love?

There are ten objects of affection:
1   The autographed Ping-Pong paddle.
2   The Cigar Indian.
3   Mournful.
4   Mother's ring.
5   Things That Sissy Gave Me.
6   Peter's autographed baseball.
7   The book I stole from the Gift Room, the one missing a page.
8   Cindy's blouse impression of Mother.
9   The red switchblade (Sissy's).
10   This journal.

Who do you love?
Who do you love?
Who do you love?
Who do you *love?*

I wrote a story once where the mother called the son "Pickle." My mother's name was Isabella, and that means beautiful one, and she never called me "Pickle." A pickle could be an object of affection. One could learn to love a pickle.

Tombstone hand and a graveyard mind,
Just twenty-two and I don't mind dyin'...

What Happened to Peter Part III:
My father had to identify his body, which they pulled off the dogwood tree, and in those moments I least expect it: in the shower, trying to masturbate a limp penis, putting words to a terribly blank page, dusting the ten objects of affection: Peter is THERE, his eyes bulged out, his face a crayon color, drool glued to his chin. My brother, the baseball-legend-to-be, swinging from Mother's dogwood like some forgotten Christmas ornament. Number one with a bullet.

Who do you love?
Who do you love?
Who do you love?
Who do you *love?*

What Happened to Sissy Part III:

Bo Diddley wailed in my head, crushing Sissy's Rain Song like a bug ("Hey, Bo!"), and I pulled what was hidden out of my pocket and cleaned it with my tongue.

I rode a lion to town, use a rattlesnake whip;
Take it easy, Arlene, don't you give me no lip…

I said there were actually twelve objects of affection, and before the killing floor gets too slippery, I should explain, no?

Mournful was gone, and then there was the stuffed Mournful. Sissy said Mother gave him to me, but I don't remember. I just remember waking up, and the stuffed animal was stuck between my arms. I was a teenager. Sissy said I should never ask Mother about it, because Mother didn't want the other children to be jealous of Mournful. I don't know if I believed her then or if I believe her now, but I wanted to. Perception is nine-tenths of the law.

So two (the live and smelly and drooly and apparently sexually frustrated Mournful, and the stuffed shadow) rolled into one.

For sure, Sissy gave me two objects, which I also mashed together on my list, on my soiled doily: the silver lighter, engraved with her name (okay, she didn't actually *give* it to me as much as *left* it for me to find), which I carried with me every day until the name wore off from being in my pocket (I had to hold it up to the light to even make out where it was), and the slim black rubber bracelet, like a vacuum cleaner belt, the twin to the one Sissy always wore, bought at the Five and Dime. "Together, we'll always be together," Sissy had said. Sissy had no fucking idea.

Who do you love?
Who do you love?
Who do you love?
Who do you *love?*

I'm telling it the way I remember.

Everyone on my unit signed the Ping-Pong paddle after I won that tournament. Most of those people are gone. I will never be gone from here. That's what the doctors say anyway. I'd ask Father, but I'm planning to kill him, so I don't. I'd ask the Cigar Indian (he's seen so much after all), but he's not real, and this type of situation demands clarity.

Night was dark, but the sky was blue;
Down the alley the ice-wagon flew...

Thirteen. There are actually thirteen objects of affection. It's a number thing. If there are twelve, there have to be thirteen. It's a number thing.

Hit a bump, and somebody screamed;
You should have heard just what I seen...

What Happened after the Dogwood Tree:
He was buried in his leather jacket. Samantha tried to arrange the funeral. Their divorce was one day shy of going into effect, which gave her POWER. She shed not even crocodile tears, and when I passed by my brother's coffin, strewn with baseballs (but not *the* baseball), gloves, pennants (I couldn't look at him, although I wished Cindy the Lesser would have wiped his face down like she'd wiped Mother's), I approached Samantha, grabbed her head in both my hands, and jammed my tongue down her throat. Peter would have liked that. "Who do you love?" I asked her.

Dressed up to put my brother in the ground, I tore a page from the book I stole from the Gift Room, the one by Richard Bach. It read: *"The bond that links your true family is not one of blood, but of respect and joy in each other's life. Rarely do members of one family grow up under the same roof."*

I should have placed it in Peter's coffin during the wake. Instead, I knelt in the cemetery dirt three days later, and with my hands, dug into the ground, and buried the page next to my brother.

Who do you love, indeed?

I'm not dead; it just feels like I am.
I'm no boo-lee.

Father visits sometimes with presents, and he's old now. He likes the open air instead of the hospital's air conditioning, the industrialized blow of fake air, so he's always opening the window in my room, and the breeze blows my little slips of paper around: there, on the floor, between the red high-backed chair and the wall is the piece of paper with "Mother's ring" scribbled on it. Oh, and fluttering down from the soiled doily to the dead-blue rug is the slip that reads "red switchblade" tucked into the one that reads "Cindy's blouse impression of Mother." My objects of affection float to the floor like dead dogwood leaves. It's almost time for lunch, then midday meds—antidepressants, antipsychotics—yummies. I'd jerk off with Sissy in my head, but I can't finish. Isn't that funny? Between the MS and the damn meds, I'm just another daughter. My father has no sons!

Who do you love?
Who do you love?
Who do you love?
Who do you love?

What Really Happened to Sissy-Love:
It was like the most majestic music in the world, and it poured out of Sissy's apartment: Miles Davis' *Sketches of Spain*. It was red and sad and like the death of a king and the soundtrack to my whole life, except now Bo Diddley was bashing it to bits back deep inside my head.
Could the First Baby have been mine?
Let's not play that game, mister.
I pushed Sissy-Love on the bed, my pants around my ankles, my flaccid member flapping against my balls. In my left hand was Sissy's red switchblade. In my head, Bo was preparing for another battle of the bands. Sissy just looked up at the paint peels on the ceiling through the sheer canopy, her too black eyes counting the cracks with complete passivity, her worn little fingers, Mother's ring perched on her left hand, caressing my limp penis. I removed the ring from her finger.
The room was dark-dark, and Miles Davis swelled, competing (and losing) against old Bo, and then I saw her prescriptions, some mind altering substances no doubt, some psychobabble treats, on the nightstand, and I pressed Sissy's own red switchblade, Peter's Christmas gift to his sister, against her neck. The Cigar Indian watched from the corner.
My mother's name was Isabella,
My mother's name was Isabella,
The beautiful one.
Let's switch to the present tense. Quick, before I deteriorate. For kicks and giggles. For the *immediacy.*

"Take them," I say, gesturing with my eyes toward the nightstand, and my sister, my love, does as she is told, and dry swallows each one, feeding herself with her right hand, her left hand stroking me.

"*Take a little walk with me,*" I sing along to Bo in my head.

Miles is extinguished.

"Spit in my mouth," Sissy says, "for I am so dry."

And I do as my sister tells me, for I love her more than anyone alive or dead.

"I want the baseball," I say.

"It's yours," says she.

The requisite death scene transpires, and soon my love is gone-gone—drop dead from the neck down and more. I buckle my pants and turn up Bo Diddley.

I got a graveyard mind, after all. Suicide or murder, let the coppers decide. I hoist the Cigar Indian and haul ass.

"Who do you love?"

I know, and now, so do you.

Arlene took me by my hand;
She said 'Ooo-wee, Bo, you know I understand…

Present tense, baby:

"Thirteen," says my father.

It is visiting day.

"Thirteen," says my father.

I step closer to the mirror, the one in the little bathroom.

"Thirteen," says my father.

I remove the black covering.

"Thirteen," says my father.

I inch closer, my stomach pressing against the basin.

"Thirteen," says my father.

I look into the glass, my one good eye searching for purchase along its oh-so slippery surface.

"THIRTEEN," says my father.

A green eye. Mine. A one-eyed boo-lee.

"Thirteen," I whisper and write it down on a little slip of paper so I always remember.

17. Father Forgets to Wave

"Remember this. The worst thing. To have is. A conservative mind," said Mr. Quayle, his bruised hands opening and closing to a hidden random beat.

Young William nodded his head.

"I want the planes back," Mr. Quayle snapped.

"Sir?"

"The goddamn planes. I want them back."

"I'll…sure. Not a problem, sir."

Mr. Quayle scratched his forehead, and a flake of skin floated down upon William's desk.

"Is he ever. Going to come out?"

"Sir?"

"Your manager. Is he ever. Going to come out. And face the music?"

William shifted uncomfortably. His manager had been locking himself in his office almost all day for the past two weeks now. His newly installed curtains were drawn before most of the employees arrived. He imagined that very little light penetrated the office but sometimes it seemed as if the gloom within seeped out like tendrils of a virus yet unnamed. It used to be that the *tap tap tap* of his supervisor's cane ruined any element of surprise as he made the rounds. Now his manager rarely ventured forth to pee, let alone meet with a customer, not even the ones he had an appointment with— especially Mr. Quayle.

"I don't know. I'll follow up with the assistant manager."

{*The disease ate at him; it gnawed upon his memory. Yesterday never happened; yet, he remembered how his sister smelled after she awoke, he remembered the way his mother clung to chairs and sofas and walls, terrified she might slip out of her nightmare house, her knuckles white, determined to pay for her frivolous dismissal of a promising nursing career by living among the strangers she gave birth to, giving them structure, and the intruder, the foreign body she welcomed between her legs.*}

Mr. Quayle dismissed William with a wave of his claw. The fingernails were chewed and as yellow as his teeth.

"Think about dying. Do you. Young William?"

"I try not to, sir."

"Haven't made a will. Some wish list. Of girls you wished. You banged. Books you should. Have read? You do like girls. Young William?"

"Yes, sir. To liking girls, sir. No, I haven't made a will."

Mr. Quayle cackled and pushed his hunched frame out of the chair.

"Just the list. Of girls, right?"

"Sure thing, sir." William grinned at the old man in spite of feeling uncomfortable. An odor from Mr. Quayle wafted over as the older gentleman pushed the chair out of his way and stared out the window.

"I have made my death bed speech,
and the walls still shake with
declarations from my as yet not-dead tongue.
Arrangements have been made—
I am to draw the curtains nigh
just after the midnight show."

William stood up and sat down. His mouth opened, then closed. Being with Mr. Quayle was like being thrust into the middle of a violent story, finding your character careening helplessly toward a brick wall.

"Do you know. Who wrote that. Young William?"

"No, I'm sorry, I don't"

"Guess, goddamn it. Use the head. God gave you!"

"Um, Cummings? Shelley? Sylvia Plath? Eliot? Rimbaud?"

"Ahh, you're just. Pissing. In the dark. You're just. Spitting. Out your poor. American. University. Education."

William could feel a blush initiate a hostile takeover. He hoped this wasn't going to turn out badly, but he was prepared to not take Mr. Quayle's shit again, despite any affection he felt.

"Do you know. Who wrote that?"

William cleared his throat.

"No, Mr. Quayle, I do not."

Mr. Quayle released a brief snort and shimmied his way toward the lobby. When he reached the tall glass doors, despite being visibly exhausted, the old man slammed the heavy slab open before one of the tellers could run around to help. Mr. Quayle turned, his laughter booming in the lobby like gunshots. An elderly woman in the tellers' line dropped her pen with a jolt.

Mr. Quayle spit in the general direction of the office door before exiting. The startled old woman whimpered "Dear lord!" and someone else shushed her.

{*He could leave it all: tending the objects of affection, endlessly refining the journal-task before him—how easy would it be to throw open the door and walk into the sun? How easy would it be to toss off the sheet the hallway ghosts had thrown over him and walk into the Gift Room one final time? He had given everything to his father's rendering; he had given everything to* want *and to* desire. *He needed to see what remained in the Gift Room. He needed to see if anything was left, or if he was to stand naked before his family and expose* everything. *He used to believe a man without surprise was a man without a* destiny. *If he could just open the door, if he could just extinguish every part of his father that flowed through his veins. He could hear the hallway ghosts call his* name.}

William sat at his desk for a moment or two and decided he did not, in fact, have a conservative mind, and although the bank job was sufficient for now, it was not his end-all goal. He pushed himself away from the desk and strode across the lobby to his manager's closed door. He could see his reflection in the brass nameplate: Mr. M. Quayle. Bo Diddley was playing quietly on the radio piped in above the lobby. No boundaries, William thought.

Then, honking.

"William, it's Mr. Quayle," said the pretty young teller with the large eyes and Irish last name. William made a mental note to ask her out for coffee and pie before he quit.

Mr. Quayle sat in his sedan near the exit of the drive-thru lane, facing the busy road ahead at a perfect right angle. William pushed himself through the tall glass doors and hung his head out into the spring heat.

"I did! I wrote that, Young William!"

Mr. Quayle revved his engine.

"I wrote that, Young William. Me! Tell your Mr. Quayle! Breathe, Young William!"

{*The Gift Room was a heavenly maze, intoxicating—no better yet, it was a funhouse mirror, reflecting what you wanted to see rather than what really was, the truth always one step away from wherever you stood. There could be no boundaries; there could be no rules. It was all so fitting for a warlord. His father had a passing acquaintance with the truth; not so for his last son. The Gift Room stood empty now, the last son knew—like multiple sclerosis squeezing the nerves shut, its door seized in the act of seizing. All that remained were boo-lees. Graveyard mind, remember?*}

Mr. Quayle gunned the engine, his head tilted to keep the sun out of his eyes.

He tore into the traffic.

The crash was like a wave.

The office door opened just a crack and then slammed shut.

-end-

"This is something you should have
published when you're dead.
And when everyone else around you is dead."
Margaux

About the Author:

Things to know and memorize; points of possible interest:

1   *I See No Angels* is Michael's second book. This is the second
    edition, or revised edition.
2   *Deep Autumn* was the first.
3   The author's full name is Michael-Patrick Timothy
    Harrington.
4   Michael was raised Roman Catholic, which was a mouthful.
5   Michael has nothing against religion, per se, just against
    absolute doctrines of faith. They give him the *shivers*.
6   Michael believes rock'n'roll may be the only true religion—
    just with worse clothes and better wine.
7   Seven is Michael's favorite number. He doesn't have a clue
    why, nor does he believe it has any special significance.
8   The author lives in Ambler, Pennsylvania. He really likes the
    town.
9   Michael's dog, the black Labrador retriever Raven, aka
    Helium Raven Teardrop, aka Boo, passed away in 2011, but
    he was around to celebrate (with many cookies) this book's
    original release in 2004. He is survived by his stuffed monkey,
    his basketball, and the devastated author.
10 Michael was raised in large part by very strong women: his
    mom (hi Ma!), his sister Kathie, and his grandmother Ro-Ro.
    Ro-Ro taught him many things, including, but not limited to:
    blackjack, poker, how to watch movies, and how to live your
    life so that someday people will write a book about you.

Contact the author at:
michael@michaelpatrickharrington.com
or
www.michaelpatrickharrington.com

www.ingramcontent.com/pod-product-compliance
Lightning Source LLC
Chambersburg PA
CBHW060303260626
47160CB00007B/2486